UNHINGED

AMULET BOOKS
LONDON

A NOVEL BY

A. G. HOWARD

The Library of Congress has catalogued the hardcover edition of this book as follows:

Howard, A. G. (Anita G.)
Unhinged : a novel / by A. G. Howard.
pages cm
Sequel to: Splintered.
Summary: Life gets complicated once again for teenaged Alyssa when her mother returns home from an asylum and the mysterious Morpheus tempts Alyssa with another dangerous quest in the dark, challenging Wonderland.
ISBN 978-1-4197-0971-5 (hardback)
[1. Supernatural—Fiction. 2. Characters in literature—Fiction.
3. Mothers and daughters—Fiction. 4. Mental illness—Fiction.] I. Title.
PZ7.H83222Un 2014
[Fic]—dc23
2013026395

ISBN for this edition: 978-1-4197-1047-6

Text copyright © 2014 A. G. Howard
Title page illustrations copyright © 2014 Nathália Suellen
Book design by Maria T. Middleton

Amulet Books are available at special discounts when purchased in quantity for premiums and promotions as well as fundraising or educational use. Special editions can also be created to specification. For details, contact specialsales@abramsbooks.com or the address below.

THE ART OF BOOKS SINCE 1949
The Market Building
72-82 Rosebery Avenue
London, UK EC1R 4RW
www.abramsbooks.co.uk

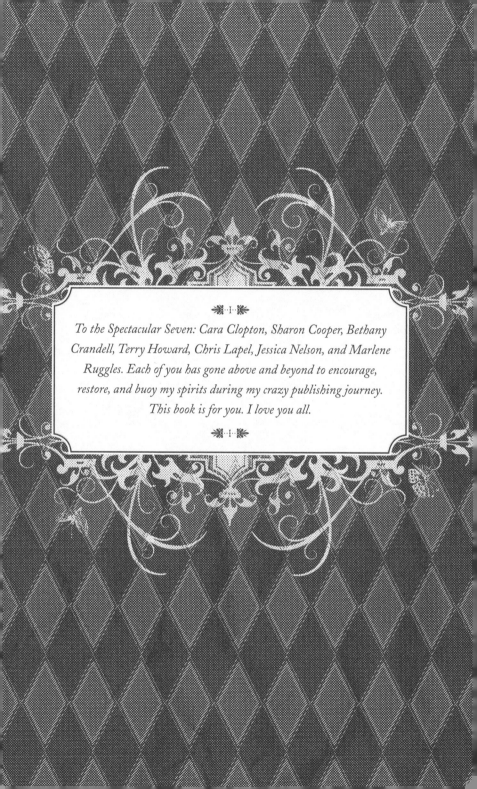

To the Spectacular Seven: Cara Clopton, Sharon Cooper, Bethany Crandell, Terry Howard, Chris Lapel, Jessica Nelson, and Marlene Ruggles. Each of you has gone above and beyond to encourage, restore, and buoy my spirits during my crazy publishing journey. This book is for you. I love you all.

BLOOD & GLASS

My art teacher says that a real artist bleeds for her craft, but he never told us that blood can *become* your medium, can take on a life of its own and shape your art in vile and gruesome ways.

I shove my hair over my shoulder, puncture my forefinger with the sterilized safety pin I had tucked in my pocket, then position the final glass gem on my mosaic and wait.

As I press the translucent bead into the wet white plaster, I shudder at the seeping sensation. It's like a leech at the tip of my finger where I touch the glass, sucking and siphoning my blood to the underside of the gem, forming a pool of deep, velvet red. But it doesn't stop there.

The blood dances . . . moves from gem to gem, coloring the back of each with a line of crimson—forming a picture. Breath locks in my lungs and I wait for the lines to connect . . . wondering what the end result will be this time. Hoping it won't be *her* again.

The last bell of the day rings, and I scramble to cover my mosaic with a drop cloth, terrified someone might see the transformation taking place.

It's yet another reminder that the Wonderland fairy tale is real, that my being a descendant of Alice Liddell means I'm different from everyone else. No matter how much distance I try to put between us, I'm connected forever to a strange and eerie sect of magical creatures called netherlings.

My classmates gather their backpacks and books and leave the art room, giving each other fist bumps and high fives while talking about their plans for Memorial Day weekend. I suck my finger, although there's no blood leaking from it anymore. Hips leaning against the table, I look outside. It's cloudy, and mist specks the windows.

My 1975 Gremlin, Gizmo, had a flat tire this morning. Since my mom doesn't drive, Dad dropped me on his way to work. I told him I'd find a ride home.

My cell phone vibrates in my backpack on the floor. I push aside the fishnet gloves folded on top, lift out the phone, and open a text from my boyfriend: *Sk8er grl . . . waiting in east parking lot. Can't wait 2c you. Tell Mason hi 4 me.*

My throat catches. Jeb and I have been together for almost a year and were best friends for six years before that, but for the past month we've only been in contact through texts and spotty phone calls. I'm eager to see him again face-to-face, but I'm also oddly nervous. I worry things will be different now that he's living a life I'm not a part of yet.

Glancing up at Mr. Mason, who's talking to some student in the hall about art supplies, I text my answer: *K. Can't wait 2c you 2. Give me 5 . . . finishing something.*

I drop the phone into my bag and lift the cloth to peek at my project. My heart falls into my feet. Not even the familiar scents of paint, chalk dust, and plaster can comfort me when I see the scene taking shape: a Red Queen on a murderous rampage in a bleak and crumbling Wonderland.

Just like in my most recent dreams . . .

I smooth the cloth back into place, unwilling to acknowledge what the imagery might mean. It's easier to hide from it.

"Alyssa." Mr. Mason comes to stand by the table. His tie-dyed Converse shoes stand out like melted rainbows against the white linoleum floor. "I've been meaning to ask . . . are you planning to accept the scholarship to Middleton College?"

I nod in spite of my bout of nerves. *If Dad lets me move to London with Jeb.*

"Good." Mr. Mason's wide smile showcases the gap between his front teeth. "Someone with your talent should take advantage of every opportunity. Now, let's see this latest piece."

Before I can stop him, he tugs off the drop cloth and squints, the pockets beneath his eyes magnified by his pink-tinged glasses. I sigh, relieved that the transformation is complete. "Rapturous color and movement, as always." He leans across it, rubbing his goatee. "Disturbing, like the others."

His final observation sends my stomach tumbling.

A year ago, when I used bug corpses and dried flowers in my

mosaics, my pieces retained an air of optimism and beauty, despite the morbidity of the materials. Now, with my change in medium, everything I create is gloomy and violent. I can't seem to capture lightness or hope anymore. In fact, I've stopped trying to fight it. I just let the blood have its way.

I wish I could stop making the mosaics altogether. But it's a compulsion I can't deny . . . and something tells me there's a reason for that. A reason that keeps me from destroying all six of them—from busting their plaster backgrounds into a thousand pieces.

"Do I need to buy more red marbled gems?" Mr. Mason asks. "I've no idea where I got them to begin with. I checked online the other day and can't seem to find the supplier."

He doesn't realize the mosaic tiles were clear when I started, that I've been using only clear gems for the past few weeks, and that the scenes he thinks I'm meticulously crafting by matching colored lines in the glass are actually forming themselves.

"It's okay," I answer him. "They're from my own personal supply."
Literally.

Mr. Mason studies me for a second. "All right. But I'm running out of room in my cabinet. Maybe you could take this one home."

I shudder at the thought. Having any of them in my house would only invite more nightmares. Not to mention how it would affect Mom. She's already spent enough of her life imprisoned by her Wonderland phobias.

I'll have to figure out something before the end of school. Mr. Mason won't be willing to keep them all summer, especially since I'm a senior. But today I have other things on my mind.

"Can you fit just one more?" I ask. "Jeb's picking me up on his bike. I'll get them next week."

Mr. Mason nods and carries it over to his desk.

I crouch to arrange the stuff in my backpack, rubbing sweaty palms over my striped leggings. The hem brushing my knees feels foreign. My skirt is longer than what I'm used to without the petticoats underneath to fluff it out. In the months since Mom's been home from the asylum, we've had a lot of arguments about my clothes and makeup. She says my skirts are too short and she wishes I would wear jeans and "dress like regular girls." She thinks I look too wild. I've told her that's why I wear tights and leggings, for modesty. But she never listens. It's like she's trying to make up for the eleven years she was away by being overly invested in everything about me.

She won this morning, but only because I woke up late and was in a rush. It's not easy to get up for school when you've been fighting sleep all night, avoiding dreams.

I lift my backpack to my shoulders and tip my chin good-bye to Mr. Mason. My Mary Jane platforms clomp along the deserted tiles of the hall. Stray work sheets and notebook papers are scattered like stepping-stones in a pond. Several lockers hang open, as if the students couldn't waste the extra half second it would've taken to shut them before leaving for the weekend.

A hundred different colognes, perfumes, and body odors still linger, interspersed with the faded yeasty scent of rolls from the cafeteria's lunch menu. *Smells like teen spirit.* I shake my head, grinning.

Speaking of spirit, Pleasance High's student council has been working around the clock to tape up prom reminders around every corner of the school. This year, the dance is the Friday before our Saturday graduation ceremony—one week from today.

ALL PRINCES AND PRINCESSES ARE CORDIALLY INVITED TO

THE PLEASANCE HIGH FAIRY-TALE MASQUERADE PROM, MAY 25TH. NO FROGS ALLOWED.

I smirk at the last line. My best pal, Jenara, wrote it with bold green marker at the end of each announcement. It took her entire sixth period on Tuesday to do it and cost her three days of detention. But it was totally worth it to see the look on Taelor Tremont's face. Taelor is my boyfriend's ex, the school's star tennis player, and the student council's social chairperson. She's also the one who ratted out my Liddell family secret in fifth grade. Our relationship is strained, to say the least.

I run my palm across one of the banners that escaped half its tape and drapes like a long white tongue from the wall. It reminds me of my experience with the bandersnatch's snaky tongues last summer. I cringe and rub the vivid streak of red in my blond hair between my forefinger and thumb. It's one of my permanent souvenirs, just like the nodules behind my shoulder blades where wings lie dormant inside me. No matter how I try to distance myself from the Wonderland memories, they're always present, refusing to leave.

Just like a certain *someone* refuses to leave.

My throat constricts at the thought of black wings, bottomless tattooed eyes, and a cockney accent. He already has my nights. I won't let him take my days, too.

Shoving the doors open, I step into the parking lot and get hit by a rush of chill, damp air. A fine mist coats my face. A few cars remain and students cluster in small groups to talk—some hunched inside hoodies and others seemingly oblivious to the unseasonably cool weather. We've had a lot of rain this month. The meteorologists calculated the accumulation somewhere between four and six inches, breaking a century's worth of spring records in Pleasance, Texas.

My ears automatically tune in to the bugs and plants in the soggy football field a few yards away. Their whispers often blend together in crackles and hums like radio static. But if I try, I can make out distinct messages meant just for me:

Hello, Alyssa.

Nice day for a stroll in the rain . . .

The breeze is just right for flying.

There was a time I hated hearing their fuzzy, buzzy greetings so much I would trap them and smother them. Now the white noise is comforting. The bugs and flowers have become my sidekicks . . . charming reminders of a secret part of me.

A part of me even my boyfriend is unaware of.

I see him across the parking lot. He leans against his souped-up vintage Honda CT70, chatting with Corbin, the starting quarterback and Jenara's new main squeeze. Jeb's sister and Corbin make an odd match. Jenara has pink hair and the fashion sense of a princess gone punk rocker—the antithesis of a typical Texas jock's girlfriend. But Corbin's mother is an interior designer who's known for her eccentric style, so he's accustomed to offbeat artistic personalities. At the beginning of the year the two of them were lab partners in biology. They clicked, and now they're inseparable.

Jeb glances in my direction. He straightens as he sees me, his body language as loud as a shout. Even at this distance, the heat of his mossy-green eyes warms my skin under my lacy shirt and plaid corset.

He gestures good-bye to Corbin, who shoves a strand of reddish blond hair from his eyes and waves in my direction before joining a group of football players and cheerleaders.

Jeb shrugs out of his jacket on his way over, revealing muscular arms. His black combat boots clomp across the shimmery asphalt, and his olive skin glistens in the mist. He's wearing a navy T-shirt with his worn jeans. A picture of My Chemical Romance is airbrushed in white with a red slash streaked diagonally across their faces. It reminds me of my blood art, and I shiver.

"Are you cold?" he asks, wrapping his jacket around me, the leather still warm from his body. For that fleeting second, I can almost taste his cologne: a mix between chocolate and musk.

"I'm just happy you're home," I answer, palms flat against his chest, enjoying his strength and solidity.

"Me, too." He looks down at me, caressing me with his gaze but holding back. He cut his hair while he was gone. Wind ruffles the dark, collar-length strands. It's still long enough at the crown and top to be wavy and is a mess from being under his helmet. It's unkempt and wild, just the way I like it.

I want to leap into his arms for a hug or, even better, kiss his soft lips. The ache to make up for lost time winds tight around me until I'm a top ready to spin, but my shyness is even stronger. I glance over his shoulder to where four junior girls gathered around a silver PT Cruiser watch our every move. I recognize them from art class.

Jeb follows my line of sight and lifts my hand to kiss each knuckle, the scrape of his labret igniting a tingle that races all the way to the tips of my toes. "Let's get out of here."

"You read my mind."

He smirks. The butterflies in my belly clash at the appearance of his dimples.

We walk hand in hand to his bike as the parking lot starts to clear. "So . . . looks like your mom won this morning." He gestures to my skirt, and I roll my eyes.

Grinning, he helps me with my helmet, smooths my hair across my lower back, and separates the red strand from the blond ones. Wrapping it around his finger, he asks, "Were you working on a mosaic when I texted?"

I nod and buckle the helmet's strap under my chin, not wanting the conversation to go this direction. Not sure how to tell him what's been happening during my art sessions while he's been gone.

He cups my elbow as I climb into place on the back of the seat, leaving a space for him in front. "When do I get to see this new series of yours, huh?"

"When it's done," I mumble. What I really mean is, when I'm ready to let him watch me make one.

He has no memory of our trip to Wonderland, but he's noticed the changes in me, including the key I wear around my neck and never take off, and the nodules along my shoulder blades that I attribute to a Liddell family oddity.

An understatement.

For a year, I've been trying to figure out the best way to tell him the truth without him thinking I'm crazy. If anything can convince him we took a wild ride into Lewis Carroll's imagination, then stepped backward in time to return as if we'd never left, it's my blood-and-magic artwork. I just have to be brave enough to show him.

"When it's done," he says, repeating my cryptic answer. "Okay, then." He gives his head a shake before tugging his helmet on. "Artists. So high maintenance."

"Pot . . . kettle. While we're on the subject, have you heard from your newest number one fan?"

Jeb's gothic fairy art has been getting a lot of attention since he's been going to art expos. He's sold several pieces, the highest going for three thousand bucks. Recently he was contacted by a collector in Tuscany who saw his artwork online.

Jeb digs in his pocket and hands me a phone number. "These are her digits. I'm supposed to schedule a meeting so she can choose one of my pieces."

Ivy Raven. I read the name silently. "Sounds fake, right?" I ask, straightening my backpack straps under his jacket. I almost wish she was made up. But I know better. According to some Web searching I've done, Ivy is a totally legit beautiful twenty-six-year-old heiress. A sophisticated, rich goddess . . . like all the women Jeb's around lately. I hand the paper back, trying to stanch the insecurity that threatens to burn a hole in my heart.

"Doesn't matter how fake she sounds," Jeb says, "as long as the money is real. There's a sweet flat in London I've been looking at. If I can sell her a piece, I'll add it to what I've already saved and have enough to cover it."

We still have to convince Dad to let me go. I refuse to voice my concern aloud. Jeb's already feeling guilty about the tension between him and Dad. Sure, it was a mistake for Jeb to take me to get a tattoo behind my parents' backs. But he didn't do it to make them mad. He did it against his better judgment because I pressured him. Because I was trying to be rebellious and worldly, like the people he hangs out with now.

Jeb got a tattoo at the same time, on his inner right wrist—his painting hand. It's the Latin words *Vivat Musa*, which roughly translates to "Long live the muse." Mine is a miniature set of wings on my inner left ankle, camouflaging my netherling birthmark. I had the artist ink in the words *Alis Volat Propriis*, Latin for "She flies with her own wings." It's a reminder I control my darker side and not the other way around.

Jeb tucks the heiress's number into his jeans pocket, seeming a thousand miles away.

"I bet she's hoping you're Team Cougar," I say, half joking in an effort to bring him back to the present.

Making eye contact, Jeb works his arms into the sleeves of a flannel shirt he had flung across his Honda's handlebars. "She's only in her twenties. Not exactly cougar material."

"Oh, thanks. There's a comfort."

His familiar teasing smile offers reassurance. "If it'll make you feel better, you can go with me when I meet her."

"Deal," I say.

He climbs onto his motorcycle in front of me, and I no longer care if anyone sees us. I snuggle as close as possible, wrapping my arms and knees tightly around him, face nuzzled into the nape of his neck just beneath his helmet's edge. His soft hair tickles my nose.

I've missed that tickle.

He slides on his shades and tilts his head so I can hear him as he starts the motor. "Let's find somewhere to be alone for a while, before I take you home to get ready for our date."

My blood thrums in anticipation. "What'd you have in mind?"

"A roll down memory lane," he answers. And before I can even ask what that means, we're on our way.

Tunnel Vision

I'm glad Gizmo's tire is out of commission, because there's nothing like riding with Jeb on his bike.

Swaying back and forth, our movements synchronize with the curves of the streets. The slick gravel makes him cautious, and he weaves slowly around traffic so he can brake without skidding through intersections. But as soon as we reach the older side of town, where only one or two cars share the road and traffic lights are fewer and farther between, he gives the throttle some gas and we pick up speed.

The rain picks up, too. Jeb's jacket shields my shirt and corset. Stray droplets lick my face. Pressing my left cheek to his back and tightening my arms around him, I shut my eyes to indulge in pure sensation: the roll of his muscles as he eases into turns, the scent of the drenched asphalt, and the sound of the motorcycle muffled by my helmet.

My hair whips around us as the wind presses in from every direction. It's the closest I can come to flying in the human realm. The buds behind my shoulder blades itch as if wanting to sprout wings at the thought.

"You awake back there?" Jeb asks, and I notice we're slowing down.

I open my eyes and prop my chin on his shoulder, letting his head and neck shield one side of me from the soft drizzle. His "roll down memory lane" comment makes sense as I recognize the movie theater, a frequent destination of ours during my sixth-grade year.

I haven't seen it since it was condemned three years ago. The windows are boarded up and trash nestles at the corners and foundation as if taking refuge from the weather. The Texas winds have knocked the oval orange and blue neon sign from off its perch above the entrance; it's hunched on its side like a shattered Easter egg. The letters no longer say EAST END THEATER. The only word still legible is END, which feels both poetic and sad.

This isn't our destination. Jeb, Jenara, and I used to have our parents drop us at the movies, but the theater doubled as a decoy for kids who wanted to sneak a few hours free from adult supervision. We would gather at the giant storm drainage pipe on the other side of the lot, where a concrete incline dipped into a cement valley. Stretching some twenty yards, it formed an ideal bowl for skateboarding.

No one ever worried about flooding. The pipe was made to drain the excess from the lake on the other side—a lake that had been gradually shrinking for decades.

Since it was as dry as a desert inside, the tunnel served as a hideaway for make-out and graffiti sessions. Jenara and I didn't spend much time there. Jeb made sure of that. He said we were too innocent to witness what was going on in the depths.

But that's where he's taking me today.

Jeb cruises through the littered parking lot and across an empty field, then takes the incline on his bike. As we descend the concrete's drop, I tighten my legs around him and let go of his waist, stretching my arms high in the air. My wing buds tickle, and I whoop and holler as if we were on a roller coaster. Jeb's laughter joins my giddy outburst. Too soon we're at the bottom, and I hold on to him again, the wheels skimming through puddles on our zigzag race toward the drainage pipe.

We stop at the entrance. The tunnel is as abandoned as the movie theater. Teens quit coming here when Underland—Pleasance's ultraviolet, underground skate park and activity center owned by Taelor Tremont's family—became the popular hangout on the west side of town. The rain's coming down harder now, and Jeb balances the bike so I can climb off. I slip on the wet cement.

He catches me with one arm around my waist and, without a word between us, pulls me in for a kiss. I hold both sides of his jaw, relearning how his muscles work under my fingertips, reacquainting myself with how the rigid planes of his hard body fit so perfectly against my softer curves.

Raindrops glide over our skin and seep into the seam between our lips. I forget we're still wearing our helmets, and the cold wetness of my leggings, and even the heaviness of my soggy shoes. He's finally here with me, his body pressed flush to mine, and those white-hot points of contact are the only things I know.

When we finally break apart, we're soaked, flushed, and out of breath.

"I've been dying to do that," he says, voice husky and green gaze penetrating. "Every time I heard your voice on the phone, all I could think about was touching you."

His heartbeat races against mine, and his words twine my stomach into a knot of pleasure. I lick my lips, unspoken assurance that I've been thinking of the same thing.

Together we lead his Honda into the tunnel and prop it against a curved wall. Then we take off our helmets and shake out our hair. I peel off Jeb's jacket and my backpack.

I don't remember the tunnel being this dark. The overcast sky doesn't help. I take a cautious step farther in, only to be bombarded with the worrisome whispers of spiders, crickets, and whatever other insects congregate in the darkness.

Wait . . . don't step on us . . . tell your friend to put his big feet away.

I pause, unnerved. "You brought a flashlight, right?" I ask.

Jeb comes up from behind and wraps his arms around my waist. "I'll do better than a flashlight," he whispers against me, leaving a warm imprint just behind my ear.

There's a click, and a string of lights flickers to life on the tunnel's wall, pinned in place somehow, like a vine. The lights don't give off much of a glow, but I can see that none of the skateboards are still lying around. Skaters used to leave their old wheels so everyone would have something to use when they came from the theater. We lived by a code back then. It was rare for a board to get stolen, because we all wanted the freedom to last forever.

We were so naïve to think anything in the human realm lasts forever.

Fluorescent graffiti glows on the walls—some curse words but mostly poetic ones, like *love, death, anarchy, peace*, and pictures of broken hearts, stars, and faces.

Black lights. I'm reminded of both Underland's and Wonderland's neon landscapes.

One mural stands out from the others—an ultraviolet outline of a fairy in oranges, pinks, blues, and whites. Her wings splay behind her, jeweled and bright. She looks like me. Even after all these months, I still do a double take when I see Jeb's renditions: exactly as I looked in Wonderland, complete with butterfly wings and eye patches—black curvy markings imprinted on the skin like overblown eyelashes. He sees inside my soul without even knowing it.

"What did you do?" I ask him, making my way toward the graffiti while trying to avoid squishing any bugs.

He takes my arm to steady me. "A few cans of spray paint, a hammer, some nails, and a battery-operated strand of black lights."

He flicks on a camper's lantern, which illuminates a thick quilt spread out under a picnic basket. The bugs' whispers fade in response to the light.

"But how did you have time?" I ask, sitting down to dig in the basket. There's a bottle of expensive mineral water as well as cheese, crackers, and strawberries.

"I had a lot of time to kill before school let out," Jeb answers as he selects a playlist on his iPad and props it on the backpack. A gritty, soulful ballad resonates from a miniature speaker.

I try to ignore that his answer makes me feel like an immature schoolgirl and pull some white roses out of the basket. These have been Jeb's flower of choice for me ever since the day we came clean about our feelings, the morning after I returned from my trip through the rabbit hole. The morning after prom last year.

I hold them to my nose, trying to blot out the memory of another set of white roses in Wonderland that ended up red with his blood.

"I wanted to make this special for you." He drags off his damp flannel shirt and sits down on the other side of the basket, an expectant look on his face.

His words echo in my head: *Make this special for you.*

The flowers slip from my fingers, scolding me for bruising their petals when they scatter on the ground.

"Oh," I murmur to Jeb, disregarding their whispers. "So . . . this is it."

He half grins, casting a shadow where his left incisor slants slightly across his front tooth. "It?"

He takes a strawberry out of the basket. Lantern light reflects off the cigarette-size scars on his forearms. I mentally follow them to a path of matching scars under his T-shirt: reminders of a violent childhood.

"Hmm. *It.*" Jeb tosses the berry, leans his head back, and catches the fruit in his mouth. Chewing, he studies me as if waiting for a punch line. The teasing tilt of his head makes the stubble on his chin look like velvet, though it's not soft like velvet. It's rough against bare skin.

Heat pools low in my abdomen. I avert my gaze, trying not to notice all those sexy things I obsessed about while we were apart.

We've discussed taking the next step in our relationship via texts and phone calls and on occasion in person. Since his schedule is so hectic, we've marked prom night on both our calendars.

Maybe he's decided he'd rather not wait. Which means I have

to tell him *I'm* not ready today. Even worse, I have to tell him why.

I'm totally unprepared, scared out of my head, and not for the usual reasons. My lungs shrink, aggravated by the dank air of the tunnel . . . the paint, stone, and dust. I cough.

"Skater girl." All the teasing is gone from his voice. He says my nickname so low and soft, it's almost swallowed by the background music and the rain pattering outside.

"Yeah?" My hands tremble. I curl my fingers into my palms, nails scraping my scars. Scars that Jeb still thinks were caused by a car accident when I was a kid, when a windshield supposedly shattered and gouged my hands. Just one of the many secrets I'm keeping.

I can't give him what he wants, not all of me. Not until I tell him who I really am. *What* I am. It was bad enough when I only had a week left till prom. I'm not prepared to pour out my soul today after being away from him for so long.

"Hey, take it easy." Jeb works my hands free from their prison of fingers and presses my palm to his collarbone. "I brought you here to give you this." He drags my hand down to his chest, where a hard knot the size of a dime presses back from under his shirt. That's when I notice the shimmer of a delicate chain around his neck.

He lifts off the necklace and holds it over the lantern. It's a heart-shaped locket with a keyhole embedded in its middle.

"I found it in a little antique market in London. Your mom gave you that key you wear all the time, right?"

I squirm, itching to correct the half-truth—that it's not exactly the same key she had saved for me, although it opens the same weird and wild world.

"Well . . ." He leans across the basket to place the necklace over my head. It falls in line atop my key. He drags my hair free, smoothing the strands to cover both chains. "I thought this could be symbolic. It's made of the same kind of metal, looks vintage like the key. Together, they prove what I've always known. Even when we used to come here as kids."

"And what's that?" I watch him, intrigued by how the tunnel's opening tints one side of his smooth complexion with bluish light.

"That only you have the key to open my heart."

The words startle me. I look down before he can see the emotion in my eyes.

He huffs. "That was cheesy . . . maybe I sucked in too many paint fumes while I was working on the mural."

"No." I balance on my knees and drape my arms over his shoulders. "It was sincere. And so swee—"

He puts a finger on my lips. "It's a promise. That I'm committed. To you alone. I want to make that clear, before prom, before London. Before anything else happens between us."

I know he means what he's saying, but it's not entirely true. He's also committed to his career. He wants his mom and Jenara to have nice things; he wants to help with college expenses for his sister's fashion career, and to take care of me in London.

Then there's the underlying reason that he's so committed to his art. The one reason he never talks about.

I have no right to be jealous of his determination to make something of himself—to prove himself a better man than the example he was given. I just wish he could find a balance and be satisfied. Instead, it feels like each sale and each new contact whets his appetite for more, almost like an addiction.

"I've missed you," I say, drawing him into a hug that crushes the basket between us.

"I missed you, too," he says against my ear before pushing us apart. A concerned frown meets my gaze. "Don't you know that?"

"I didn't hear from you for almost a week."

He lifts his eyebrows, obviously chagrined. "I'm sorry. I couldn't get cell phone service."

"There's landlines and e-mail," I snap, sounding more irritable than I intend to.

Jeb taps the basket between us with the toe of his boot. "You're right. It just got crazy that last week. It's when the final auction took place. And the schmoozing."

Schmoozing = partying with the elite. I stare at him, hard.

He rubs his thumb along my lower lip, as if trying to reshape my scowl to a smile. "Hey, don't look at me like that. I wasn't drunk or drugged out or cheating. It's all business."

My chest tightens. "I know. It's just, sometimes I worry."

I worry that he'll start to crave things I haven't even experienced yet. When he was sixteen, he lost his virginity to a nineteen-year-old waitress at a restaurant where he bused tables.

Last year, when he dated Taelor, they never hooked up; his evolving feelings for me kept him from crossing that line. But it's bad enough knowing he was with an "older woman" before me, that she was just a sampling of the temptations that surround him on a daily basis now.

"Worry about what?" Jeb prompts.

I shake my head. "I'm just being stupid."

"No. Tell me."

Tension escapes my lungs on a gust. "Your life is so different from mine now. I don't want to get left behind. You felt so far away this time. Worlds away."

"I wasn't," he says. "You were in my dreams every night."

His sweet sentiment reminds me of my own dreams and the life I'm hiding from him. I am such a hypocrite.

"Only one more week of school." He plays with the tips of my hair. "Then we'll be on our way to London, and you can go with me on all of my trips. It's time to get your art out there, too."

"But my dad . . ."

"I've figured out how to fix things." Jeb shoves the basket from between us.

"What? How?"

"Seriously, Al." Jeb grins. "You want to talk about your dad when we can be doing this?" He stands, dragging me up with him. His arms enfold me. I snuggle into him, and we dance to a ballad on the iPad, in sync at last. I forget everything but our bodies swaying. Our conversation settles into its own familiar rhythm. We laugh and tease, catching up on the little moments from the past few weeks.

It starts to feel like it used to, the two of us melting into one another while outside distractions fade.

When another song clicks on, a sultry and rhythmic number, my fingers slink along his spine in time with it, finding their way under his T-shirt's hem. I drag my nails lightly over the toned ridges of his back and kiss his neck.

He moans, and I smile in the dimness, sensing the change in him. A change I control. He eases us down to the quilt, guiding me to my back. A tiny part of me wants to finish talking about things that feel unfinished. But even more, I want him like this, intent on nothing but me, his weight closing in, comforting and demanding at once.

Elbows propped next to my ears, he holds my head while kissing me, so gentle and thorough, I can taste the strawberry he ate a minute ago.

I'm breathless, dizzy . . . floating so high I barely notice his phone buzzing with a text.

He tenses and rolls off to slip the phone from his jeans pocket. "Sorry," he mumbles and swipes to read the text.

I groan, missing his warmth and weight.

After reading silently, he turns to me. "That was the reporter from *Picturesque Noir*. He said they have a two-page spread available if I can move up my photo shoot at the gallery to this afternoon. After that they want to take me out to dinner for the interview." As if catching the disappointment in my eyes, Jeb adds, "I'm sorry, Al. But a two-page spread . . . that's a big deal. The rest of the weekend I'm yours, from morning to night every day, okay?"

I start to point out that I haven't seen him for a month and today was supposed to be all about us, but I bite back my tirade. "Sure."

"You're the best." He gives me a peck on the cheek. "Do you mind gathering up the stuff? I have to call Mr. Piero so he can set up my work in the display room."

I offer a curt nod, and he heads to the front of the tunnel to call his boss at the art studio where he restores old paintings when he's not out showing his own work. Darkness spreads between us—sad, shadowy shapes outside the lantern's reach that look as dejected as I feel.

I sit up and gather the basket and Jeb's iPad, so busy trying to hear his conversation—something about which showroom has the best lighting for the photographer—I barely notice how the bugs' murmurs have escalated until they unite as one:

You should've heeded him. He warned you in your dreams . . . now all your doubts will be washed away.

Drip . . . drip . . . drip.

I scramble to stand as a drizzling erupts from the dark end of the tunnel behind me. The sound lifts the tiny hairs on the back of my neck.

Drip . . . drip . . . drip.

I debate calling Jeb back to investigate, but a vivid blue tip of a wing painted on the wall catches my eye. It's just outside the ring of light. Strange that I didn't notice it earlier.

I inch toward the fluorescent drawings and, with a few quick yanks, drag down Jeb's light strand. The cord coils to the ground, then trails behind me as I start to move closer to the mysterious winged image, tugging the battery pack with a scraping clunk.

Drip . . . drip . . . drip.

I peer into the pitch-blackness at the tunnel's far end but am more interested in the graffiti now. With the cord wrapped around my fingers, I move my makeshift mitten of lights across the winged portrait to illuminate it, piece by piece, like a puzzle.

I know that face and the jewel-tipped eyes. I know that wild blue hair and those lips that taste of silk, licorice, and danger.

Eagerness and dread tangle inside my chest. The same convoluted effect he always has on me.

"Morpheus," I whisper.

The bugs whisper back in unison:

He's here . . . he rides the rain . . .

Their words work like a spike through my spine, nailing me in place.

"Run!" Jeb's shout from the front of the tunnel shakes me out of my mental haze. His boots slosh toward me through water I hadn't noticed gathering at my feet.

"Flood!" Jeb yells, stumbling into the darkness between us.

I panic and take a step toward him, only to have the strand of light come to life in my hand like a wiggling, snaky vine. It wraps around my wrists, twining them together, and then my ankles. I struggle against the cord but am tied up before I can even scream.

A gushing wave sweeps in from the dark end of the tunnel and knocks me off balance. I land flat on my stomach. Cold, dirty water sloughs into my face. I cough, trying to keep my nose above the current, but the light strand holds me paralyzed.

"Al!" Jeb's terrified shout is the last thing I hear before the water swirls around my trussed-up limbs and whisks me away.

DROWNING IN WONDERLAND

The string of lights around my ankles and wrists drags me against the current, farther into the tunnel, where the water is black. It's like being submerged in cold ink. I fight to get my head above water but can't. The chill leaves me numb, desperate to breathe.

Jeb finds me. Gripping my underarms, he draws me out enough that I get one swallow of air, but another surge of water tumbles him toward the pipe's opening and the vinyl cord jerks me in the opposite direction. I can tell by his distant shouts that he can't follow. I'm glad he's caught in the current. He'll be safer once the rush of water deposits him outside.

Things I learned in Wonderland a year ago . . . powers I practice alone in my room so Mom won't catch me and freak out . . . come back, as forceful as the cord dragging me underneath the gushing waves.

I relax my muscles and concentrate on the strand of lights, envisioning them alive. In my mind, the electricity that pulses through their wires becomes plasma and nutrients. They respond like living creatures. Their lights brighten enough for me to see underwater as the wires animate. Problem is, I haven't been consistent with my magical exercises, so even though I'm giving the strand life, I have no control. It's as if the lights have minds of their own.

Or maybe they're under someone else's influence.

Convulsing against the need to inhale, I force my eyes to stay open under the water. The cold makes them ache. I'm shuttled into the deep end of the tunnel, as if riding an aquatic chariot harnessed to electric eels. The cord hauls me toward a door—small and ancient—embedded in the concrete wall. It's covered with moss and out of place here in the human realm, but I've seen it before. I have the key to open it around my neck.

It doesn't make any sense that it would be here, so far from the rabbit hole in London, which is the only entrance into Wonderland from this world.

I jerk against my binds. I'm not sleeping, so this can't be a dream. I don't want to go inside that door while I'm awake. I'm still trying to get over the last time.

My lungs draw tight inside me, ravenous, until I have no choice. Going inside is my only way out, my only way to breathe and live. Straining against the bindings on my wrists, I bend my elbows to reach for my chest. With both hands, I snag the key on my necklace, shoving Jeb's heart locket out of the way. The current pounds my head against the concrete wall. Pain shoots from my temple to my neck.

I sweep my bound legs like a mermaid's tail in order to reposition myself in front of the door. I thrust the key into the keyhole. With a twist of my wrists, the latch gives and water funnels out. At first I'm too big to breach the opening, but then either the doorway grows or I shrink, because somehow, I fit perfectly.

I ride the waves through the door, lifting my face to gulp air. A hillock stops me, hard enough to knock the air from my lungs. I'm left coughing in the mud, my throat and lungs sore, my wrists and ankles chafed from their struggle against the string of lights.

I flip to my back and kick my legs, trying to loosen my binds. A shadow of large black wings crawls across me, a shield from the storm brewing overhead.

Streaks of neon lightning slash across the sky, casting the landscape in fluorescent hues and releasing an acrid, charred scent. Morpheus's porcelain complexion—from his smooth face to his toned chest peering out of a half-buttoned shirt—looks as luminous as moonlight beneath the electric flashes.

He towers over me. His impressive height is the only thing he and Jeb have in common. The hem of his black duster whips around his boots. He opens a hand, a lacy cuff slipping out from his jacket.

"Like I've been telling you, luv"—his deep accent rolls through my ears—"if you relax, your magic will respond. Or perhaps you'd rather stay tied up. I could place you on a platter for my next banquet. You know my guests prefer their entrees thrashing and raw."

I cover my burning eyes and groan. Sometimes when I'm upset or nervous, I forget that there's a trick to my netherling powers. Inhaling through my nose, I think of the sun glistening on the ocean's lapping waves to calm my heartbeat, then breathe out through my mouth. Within seconds, the light strand relaxes and falls away from me.

I flinch as Morpheus forces me to my feet. Weary from their battle with the water, my legs start to give, but he offers no other assistance. So typical of him, expecting me to stand on my own.

"I really hate you sometimes," I say, propping myself against a giant leafy stem for support. The daisy surrenders to my weight without a word, triggering a curious twinge in my gut. I can't imagine why it's not pushing me off or complaining.

"*Sometimes.*" Morpheus drops a black velvet cowboy hat over his blue hair. "A few weeks ago it was a definitive *always*. In a matter of days, you'll be professing your undying lo—"

"Loathing?" I interrupt.

Smiling provocatively, he adjusts his hat to a cocky angle, and the garland of dead moths across the brim trembles. "Either way, I'm under your skin. Either way, I win." He taps long, elegant fingers on his red suede pants.

I fight the annoying impulse to return his smile, hyperaware of what his body language does to the darker side of me: how it curls and stretches warily, like a cat basking on a sunny ledge, drawn to the heat but guarded against slipping off.

"You're not supposed to bring me here in the daytime." I wring out my soaked skirt's hem before moving to the tangles on my head. Gusts catch my hair, slapping slimy strands across my neck and face. Goose bumps cover my skin beneath my clothes. I shiver and cross my arms. "And how did you manage it, anyway? There's only one entrance into Wonderland . . . you can't just move the rabbit hole wherever you like. What's going on?"

Morpheus wraps a wing halfway around me, blocking the wind. His expression teeters between antagonism and amusement. "A magician never gives away his secrets."

I growl.

"And I don't recall agreeing to any particular time of day for our meetings," he continues, unfazed by my grumpiness. "You should be able to visit anytime you please. You have a home here, too, after all."

"So you keep insisting." I break our stare before he can draw me into his mesmerizing gaze. I focus instead on the chaos around us. This is the worst I've ever seen Wonderland look.

Deep purple clouds scud across the sky like fat, gauzy spiders. They leave dark trails, as if spinning webs in the air. The mud beneath my shoes groans and sputters. Brown bubbles pop and rise. If I didn't know better, I'd swear something was breathing under there.

Even the wind has found a voice, loud and melancholy, whistling through the zombie-flower forest that once stood as proud as elms. The flowers used to greet me with snarky attitudes and snooty conversation. Now each and every one cowers, bent at the stems, their wilted arms hiding petals that are studded with hundreds of shuttered eyes.

The multi-eyed netherlings have lost their fight . . . their soul.

Morpheus slides his hands into a pair of slick red gloves. "If you think this is tragic, you should see what's happening in the heart of Wonderland."

My own heart sinks. Wonderland used to be so beautiful and alive, garish and creepy though it was. Still, seeing the land crumble shouldn't affect me so strongly. I've witnessed the gradual decay in my dreams over the past few weeks.

Thing is, I'd hoped it was only imaginary. Maybe this *is* just a dream. But on the chance it's real and Morpheus is telling the truth, I have to step up. It's my place.

Problem is, Morpheus rarely tells the truth. And he always has a hidden agenda. Except for one time when he actually performed an unselfish and uncalculated act for me . . .

My attention wanders back to catch his jaw muscle twitch. A telltale sign that he's lost in thought. It should bother me that I know so much about his mannerisms. Instead, it bothers me that I *like* knowing.

His familiarity is unavoidable. Up until I was five, he visited my dreams as an innocent child every night. When a netherling takes on a child's form in such a way, their mind becomes childlike, too. So we practically grew up together. After I saw him again last summer, we parted ways for a while. He gave me the space I requested. But now he's taken up residence in my REM once more. He's here every time Jeb is gone, keeping me company—even though I don't ask him to.

Sharing that much of your subconscious with someone, you tend to learn things about him. Sometimes you even develop feelings for him, no matter how you try to fight it.

I watch as he clenches his teeth. Beneath his eyes, he bears the same patches I had when in Wonderland. The markings are lovely and dark, like long winding eyelashes, though his are tipped with sparkling jewels. They're blinking through cycles—silver, blue, maroon—a melancholy maelstrom of emotions dancing across his face. I've learned to decipher the colors, like reading a mood ring.

"Don't you think it's time you stop the destruction, Alyssa?"

I trace the two necklaces resting below my collarbone. Lifting

Jeb's locket, I press it to my lips to taste the metal, remembering his vow of commitment in the tunnel. I left him in the water, and he doesn't know where I am. I need to get back to him, to make sure he's okay.

"If you're worried about your boyfriend, he's fine. I can guarantee that." It's not surprising that Morpheus reads me so clearly. He knows me as well as I know him. "You need to concentrate on the here and now."

I glare at him. "Why are you so determined to drag me into this?"

"I am trying to contain the war. She's coming to destroy you one way or another. She was a part of you. Even if it was only for a few hours, she left an impression. As you did on her. You're the only one who's ever defeated her."

I narrow my eyes. "Other than you, you mean."

One corner of his mouth lifts. "Ah, but that was with dumb luck and a vorpal sword. Your strike was personal and, in her mind, treasonous, because of the bond you shared."

"You still haven't proved she's responsible for this. Last I heard, her spirit was in a pile of dying weeds."

"It would appear she's found a healthy netherling body to inhabit."

My spine shudders at the possibility. "How do I know you're not just making this threat up? You've done it before. Invented an elaborate scheme to get me to dive into the rabbit hole. I'm not going to be your pawn again. Where's the proof that you're not just trying to make me come back to stay?"

"Proof . . ." Scowling, he sweeps his wings high, exposing me to the wind again. "Stop acting like a suspicious, petty human. You are meant for so much more than that."

I glare at him through my thrashing strands of hair. "You're mistaken. A human is *exactly* what I'm meant to be. I chose to live up there." I point back toward the doorway. "To experience everything Alice didn't."

Morpheus turns his face to the sky. "I'm afraid you're the one who's mistaken, if you think I'm going to let Wonderland fall to rot so you can play 'pin the male on the virgin' with your mortal toy."

My cheeks prickle with heat. "You were watching us? Wait. You *caused* the overflow in the drainage pipe. You wanted to screw up our date."

Stepping into my personal space, Morpheus closes his wings around both of us. The maneuver effectively cuts off the wind, dims the light, and blinds me to everything but him.

"I'm not the one who put an end to that bumbling attempt at seduction. Jebediah managed that all on his own." Morpheus snatches both of my necklaces from my fingers, holding the delicate links taut enough that I can't struggle without breaking them. "Were he to pay more attention to *you* instead of his precious career"—he drapes the charms over a palm and, using his gloved forefinger and thumb, positions the tiny key in place atop the heart's keyhole—"perhaps then he would be attuned to your needs and desires." Holding my gaze, he makes a show of how the key's teeth aren't the right shape for the heart's opening. "As it stands, he's just not the right fit."

A steady, deep thrum awakens in my mind, like wings thumping my skull. It's the return of my netherling side. No one can bring it to the surface like Morpheus. "Let go," I demand.

Morpheus tightens his grip, defiant. "Has he even taken time to acknowledge the changes in you? To ask why you no longer use bugs and flowers in your mosaics? Or why you've traded your fear of heights for an aversion to reflective surfaces?"

I clench my jaw. "He asked. I'm just not sure how to explain that I keep my mirror covered with a blanket because I'm worried I'll be spied on by a freak with wings."

Morpheus grins. "Says the girl whose wings are always itching to break free."

I scowl, hating that he's right.

"You need a man who knows and understands you, Alyssa. Both sides of you. A partner." He pulls my necklaces—and me—closer. "One who's your equal in every way." The scent of licorice fills my nose; he must've been smoking his hookah before I arrived. My body betrays me, remembering what those tobacco-laced kisses taste like.

He releases the necklaces to cup my chin. His gloves are cold, but the allure of his dark, mystical eyes warms me from head to toe. I almost fall into them, almost forget myself and my choices. But I'm stronger than that now.

I jerk free and shove his chest, hard enough to rock him backward. Even though his duster's hem tangles around his legs, he regains his balance without missing a beat.

Chuckling, he flourishes an arm in a grand gesture and bows. "Game, set, match. Ever, and always, my equal." His smug smirk taunts me with promises and innuendos.

"This isn't a game. You could've *killed* Jeb in that flood!" I lunge at him, but he folds a wing between us to fend me off. Slapping the satiny black barrier, I snarl. "You've crossed a line. Don't bother me during the day again." I start for the doorway. I'd rather face a flooded sewage tunnel than stay here another second.

"We're not done," he says from behind me.

"Oh, we're *so* done."

In some secluded, private corner of my soul, I care about Wonderland more than I dare admit aloud. But if I let Morpheus see that . . . he'll convince me to stay and fight. The last time I faced Queen Red, she left a fingerprint of terror on my heart. Judging by what's happening to the land, her powers are even stronger now than they were then. I suppress another shudder. I'm totally unequipped for a battle of this proportion. I'm only half of the netherling she is, and no match for her.

I never will be.

I'm a few steps from the door when one clap of Morpheus's leather-clad palms stops me in my tracks.

A sinister rustle grows around me, like leaves raking across graves. I turn, but not fast enough. Vines climb my legs, twisting tight. My calf muscles cramp under the pressure. Using my underdeveloped netherling magic, I try to influence the plants. The ivy pulses but refuses to release.

"A shame you've neglected your better side for so long," Morpheus baits me as he steps closer. "If you practiced more often, it would be second nature for you to relax . . . easier for you to coax your powers into submission."

I growl. My top half is still free, so I throw a punch at him, nailing his abs. He *oofs*, but his sneer doesn't waver. With one nod from him, the daisy that I used for a prop earlier reaches out and clamps my elbows. Her hands, both humanoid and plantlike, lock me tight. When I struggle, she hisses a warning.

Biting back a frustrated yelp, I meet Morpheus's fathomless black eyes. "I want to go home."

He fusses with his shirt, smoothing where my fist wrinkled it. "Keep ignoring your responsibilities and you won't have a home left."

I shake my head. "How many times do I have to say it? My home is in the human realm, not here." A half lie. I can't bear to look again at the destruction all around me. But he doesn't have to see how torn I am . . . how torn I've been since last year.

"What makes you think I was referring to *here*?" He leans against a nasturtium stem. The pose shouldn't be threatening, but his wings rise behind him, black and looming against the storm's backdrop, and my skin bristles with apprehension. I try to free my elbows. The daisy is too strong. Even through my long sleeves, her frondlike fingers bite into my flesh.

"I demand to see Queens Grenadine and Ivory," I say.

Morpheus barks a laugh. "You 'demand'? So you're playing the royal card, aye?"

My chest tightens. "The queens are in charge of the portals to my home, not you."

"Oh, but therein lies the problem. Parts of Wonderland have already fallen into Red's clutches, and she intends to reclaim your throne and overthrow Ivory so she might be in charge of both portals. By your absence and apathy, you're giving the witch free rein. You know what a powerless and forgetful fool your substitute, Grenadine, is."

Lightning strikes again, coating everything in eerie light.

The mud beneath me starts to soften, and I sink an inch, then two. I've triggered one of his black moods. That's never good. "You're lying."

"The truth is in the blood. Is your artwork lying?"

I want to lash out at him for spying on me at school, but it won't change the fact that he's right. Even though I can't decipher the violent scenes in my blood mosaics, I can make out enough to know that something is wrong in this world. And that maybe Queen Red *is* behind it.

My body wavers in the mud. I'm sinking even deeper—literally and figuratively.

The daisy releases me from her scratchy grip, and the vines suck me down farther. Cold, gooey sludge squishes up around my shins. I rotate at the waist to plead with the giant flower. "You're my friend. Last time I was here, we played cards, remember? Don't let him do this . . ."

Still silent, the daisy turns her hundreds of eyes toward Morpheus, as if awaiting his instructions.

"Did you forget, Alyssa? The solitary of our kind are loyal to no one but themselves—or the highest bidder." Morpheus steps closer so the toes of his boots are at the edge of the sinkhole. I'm face-to-face with his thighs but can't quite reach him. "You'd do well to reacquaint yourself with their true nature. It might remind you of your own." He claps his hands, twice this time.

As far as I can see in every direction, the flower forest rises, the plants ripping their gargantuan stems from the mud. Leafy arms and legs appear. In the center of each blossom, mouths widen, moaning, to reveal clear, jagged teeth. Their roots, moving like serpents, propel them forward. Soon I'm surrounded by row upon row of blinking eyes.

My heart trips in my chest. The mutants weren't dormant and weak at all . . . they were lying in wait—a trap prepped to spring.

Their roots wind through the mud, and they slide in to share my grave, their stemlike bodies pressing tight—imprisoning me in layers of mossy leaves and petals. I writhe as my arms press against my torso, my biceps digging into my ribs. With the added weight of the flower army around me, I sink another six inches into the mud, now eye level with Morpheus's shins. A flicker of claustrophobia resurfaces. I stifle it, remembering who I am. How I escaped from here once before.

"Oh, come on." My voice sounds steadier than I feel. "If Red couldn't trap me as her puppet, do you really think you have a chance to hold me hostage in a cage of algae?"

One of the flowers hisses, offended by the insult.

Lightning blinks across the sky, and Morpheus cocks his head. "You are no one's puppet, plum. You *are*, however, a hostage. Although you seem confused as to who holds your chains." He crouches, his nose only inches from mine. "I've been very patient." Gloved knuckles glide across my jaw and down my neck. The jewels under his eyes shimmer to an impassioned violet. "But we no longer have the luxury of time. Red has seen to that."

I try to block out how my skin responds to his touch, actually drawing toward him, like hairs rising on an electric current. Pinned in place as I am, all I can do is jerk my head to break contact.

Leaning back on his haunches, Morpheus narrows his eyes. "Release the chains you've put on yourself. Reclaim your crown and free the netherling madness within you."

"No. I chose to be human." Bile burns my tongue as the mud pulls me deeper, as if I were a mouse being ingested by a snake. The sludge rises to my chest, then my throat—a suffocating sensation. I wonder how far he plans to take this bluff.

He drops to his stomach on the ground, wings glimmering like puddles of oil beside him—looking just like he used to as a mischievous child. Chin propped on the back of his fist, he studies me. "I shall not beg. Not even for you, my *precious* queen."

A sharp gust of wind slices through us, knocking his hat off. He snatches the brim before it flies into the cracked sky.

His glowing blue hair whips across his face as he turns back to me. "If you won't stay and save Wonderland, I shall bring my own brand of chaos to the human realm. Fight for us, or face the consequences."

The flowers close in and push me toward him, rough, leafy hands scraping across my neck and cheeks, cinching my hair at the scalp so I can't lean away. He smiles, so close that I feel the heat of his breath on my face.

"I won't let you," I insist. "I won't let you into my world."

"Too little, too late," he murmurs against my humming skin. "By the time they find your body, I'll already be there."

Between the Devil
& the Muddy Sea

Find my body? I want to scream but can't even manage a moan from beneath the leafy hand clamped across my mouth.

Morpheus stands, his duster's hem swirling at his ankles. He settles his hat in place, gestures to the flowers, then transforms into the moth that haunts my memories: black wings, blue body—the size of a bird.

The vines drag me down, and the mud surrounds me like a syrupy, sticky fist. All outside sounds grow muffled. I'm left with only my heartbeat and my whimpers, nothing but vibrations contained by vocal cords and a cage of ribs.

It's impossible to open my eyelids, my lashes plastered against my cheeks so tight they can't even flutter. Each article of clothing con-stricts, as if a layer of glue adheres them to my skin. I'm paralyzed. Not only physically but mentally.

It's too tight . . . too constricting. The claustrophobia I thought I'd defeated a year ago comes back in a crashing wave.

Pitch-blackness. Dead silence. Helplessness.

I struggle not to breathe, terrified the mud will enter my nose. It seeps inside anyway, filling my nostrils. I gag at the squeezing sensation in my lungs as the sludge fills my body.

I attempt to thrash, move my muscles, but barely manage more than a spasm. My efforts draw the mud tighter around me like quicksand.

My heart pounds and panic prickles my nerves.

Don't do this! I cry out in my head to Morpheus. I never thought he would take it this far. Like a fool, I believed him when he told me he cared for me.

How will killing me fix things? I try to reason with him. But the logic goes to work on me, instead. Morpheus doesn't do anything without a reason. He's trying to push me into action. He expects me to free myself.

Morpheus! I scream in my mind once more. My raging pulse echoes back.

The swollen pressure in my lungs is agonizing. Tears burn behind my eyelids but can't escape. My body aches from tensing against the muddy walls. I'm dizzy and confused.

Exhausted, I start to give in to drowsiness. It's safer there, where there are no feelings . . . no fear.

My muscles relax and the pain numbs.

"Would you fight back already!" The shout inside my head rouses me.

I tense up again. *How? I'm trapped.*

"Be resourceful." Morpheus's voice is softer now, gentle yet prodding. *"You are not alone in the mud."*

Of course I'm alone. The zombie flowers slithered away after they pulled me down. No doubt they're on the surface now, laughing with Morpheus. The only thing sharing my tomb are the bugs burrowing around me.

Bugs . . .

All these years I've been listening to their whispers. Yet I never once tried to talk back, to really communicate. Maybe they'd be willing to help, if I just reach for them.

It takes little more than that thought, that glimmer of hope, and a silent plea asking them to dig me out, for something to puncture the mud around me.

Bugs and worms creep along my legs. The pressure eases, and I'm able to wiggle my ankles. Next, my wrists find movement. Finally, my arms and legs are free, and I dig, working my way through the sludge.

Up, up, up. The mud becomes fluid, and I swim my way out. Then something goes wrong. The bugs and worms make a detour and fill my nasal passages. My throat clogs with the creeping, slithering sensations. I gag, my windpipe stretching to accommodate their bodies.

Morpheus shouts again: *"Fight . . . fight to live! Breathe. Breathe!"*

But it's not Morpheus yelling. It's Jeb. And I'm not digging out of a sea of mud. I'm surrounded by water, wet skies, and paramedics. Something other than bugs is being shoved down my throat. I gasp, sucking in oxygen through a tube. Next thing I know, I'm on a gurney covered with sheets and being rolled toward an ambulance.

I shiver. My soaked lashes flutter, the only part of my body that isn't aching too much to move.

Jeb's face hovers into bleary view as he hunches alongside me, fingers entwined with mine. His hair drips on my forearm. His eyes are red, either from crying or from fighting the flood. "Al, I'm sorry." He nuzzles my hand, sniffling. "I'm . . . so sorry." Then he chokes to silence.

I want to tell him he's not responsible, but I can't speak with this tube in my throat—and it wouldn't matter. Jeb doesn't remember who Morpheus is. He would think I'm having an oxygen-deprived delusion. So instead of trying to answer, I surrender to unconsciousness.

⁕·I·⁕

I have the sense of something touching the birthmark at my ankle and a rush of full-body warmth. Then I wake up in a hospital room.

A window stretches across the wall on the right side. Sunset filters through the blinds, settling in a pink haze over a rainbow of beribboned *Get Well* balloons, stuffed animals, flower arrangements, and potted plants on the ledge.

Everything else is colorless. White walls, white tiles, white sheets and curtains. Disinfectant and the fruity notes of Mom's perfume waft around me, blending with the scent of the lilies on the windowsill.

The fresh-cut flowers grumble about their vase being too tight around their stems, but my mom's voice drowns them out.

"He has no business hanging around every day and night," she says. "Go out in the hall and tell him to leave."

"Would you stop?" Dad answers back. "He saved her life."

"He's also responsible for nearly killing her. She wouldn't have been in danger in the first place if he hadn't taken her there for"—

Mom's voice lowers, but I can still hear it—"God only knows what they were doing. If you don't tell him to go home, I will."

Jeb. I jerk, only to have an IV tug at the tender skin of my hand. A sense of confinement rolls over me, reminding me of the mud. Fighting the sick turn of my stomach, I attempt to ask my parents to take the needle out, but my throat is on fire. The tube that was shoved down my windpipe is gone now, but it left its mark.

My parents keep arguing. I'm so relieved to hear Dad defending Jeb, but I shut my eyes and hope they go away and leave me alone with the whispering plants. The flowers will let Jeb in. Especially the vase of white roses. I don't have to see the card to know those came from him.

"Mom . . ." I don't recognize the sound that rattles out of my mouth. It's more like air seeping from a tire than a voice.

"Allie?" Chin-length layers of platinum hair frame her face as she appears over me. She's never looked her age. Thirty-eight years old and not even a hint of wrinkles. Black lashes offset blue irises flecked with turquoise, like a peacock's tail. The whites of her eyes are rimmed with red, a sure sign she's either exhausted or has been crying. But she's still beautiful: all fragile, wispy, and aglow as if the sun shimmers within her. And it does. Magic shines there. Magic that she's never tapped into.

The same magic that's inside of me.

"My sweet girl." Relief crosses her delicate features as she strokes my cheek. The contact stirs contentment in my chest. Throughout most of my childhood, she was afraid to touch me . . . afraid to hurt me again like when she scarred my palms.

"Tommy-toes," Mom says, "hand me the ice chips." Dad obliges and towers behind her five-foot-four-inch frame as she uses a plastic spoon to feed me from the paper cup. The ice melts, soothing my throat. The water tastes like ambrosia. I nod for more.

They both watch in concerned silence as I take enough ice to numb my painful swallows.

"Where's Jeb?" The rawness in my throat returns and makes me wince. Mom's expression draws tight. "He was in the water with me. I need to see that he's okay." I cough for effect, though the resulting pain is real. "Please . . ."

Dad leans down over Mom's shoulder. "Jeb's fine, Butterfly. Give us a second to take care of you. How do you feel?"

I twitch my sore muscles. "Achy."

"I bet." His brown eyes water, but his smile is blissful as he reaches around Mom to pet my head. I couldn't have asked for a better dad. If only my grandparents had lived to see me born. They would've been proud to have a son so caring and faithful to his family. "I'll let Jeb know you're awake," he says. "He's been here the whole time."

It's impossible to miss Mom's not-so-subtle elbow to Dad's rib cage, but her objection doesn't faze him. He rubs a hand through his dark hair and steps out the door, closing it behind him before she can work up an argument.

Sighing, she puts the cup on the nightstand by the bed and tugs a green vinyl cushioned chair from the corner. She sits down close to me, smoothing her polka-dot silk dress.

When she was first released, she wanted to spend every possible minute with me, catching up on all the time we'd missed. We baked together, did laundry together, cleaned house . . . gardened. Things most people consider mundane or unpleasant became paradise, because I finally had my mom to do them with.

One Saturday afternoon, I took her to Butterfly Threads, the vintage thrift store where I work, and we shuffled through racks and racks of outfits.

Most of the clothes there appeal to my style, so we disagreed on almost every option. Until we found a funky satin purple and black polka-dot dress with a lime green belt and matching net slip that peeked out from the hem. I talked her into buying it. But once she got it home, she wouldn't wear it in public, even though Dad loved it on her. She said it made her feel too flashy.

I asked her why she couldn't do one little thing to make Dad happy after all he'd done for her. That was the first argument we had after her release. Now I've lost count of them all.

I can't overlook the significance of her wearing the dress today.

"Hi, Mom," I croak.

She grins and tucks a strand of hair behind my ear. "Hi."

"You look pretty."

She shakes her head and bites back a sob. Before I realize what she's about to do, she collapses, her face pressed to my abdomen. "I thought I'd lost you." The words muffle, her breath broken and hot across the covers. "The doctors couldn't wake you."

"Aw, Mom." I pet the soft fringe of hair at her temple where it's pulled back with a sparkly purple hairpin. "I'm okay. Because of you, right?"

She looks up and lifts her wrist, where her birthmark coils like a circular maze. It matches the one on my left ankle beneath my wing tattoo. When pressed together, a magical surge can heal us.

"I swore I'd never use that power again," she mumbles, referring to last year when she healed my sprained ankle and unleashed an unexpected chain of events. "But you were under so long. Everyone was afraid you were going to stay in a coma."

What little mascara she has on stains her skin in tiny rivulets. The image makes me uneasy—it's too similar to the eye patches I once had in Wonderland. But I shove that thought aside. This isn't the time for a heart-to-heart about what happened last year.

"How long?" I ask.

"Three days," she answers without pause. "Today's Monday. Memorial Day."

Shock closes my already achy throat. All I remember is a deep, dark sleep. It's weird that Morpheus didn't visit my mind while I was unconscious.

"I—I'm sorry for scaring you," I whisper. "But you know, you're wrong."

Tracing the veins on the back of my IV-pierced hand, Mom tilts her head. "About what?"

"My boyfriend."

A grimace tightens her lilac pink lips. She flips my hand over and studies my scars. I asked her a while back why she didn't heal my palms when I was that five-year-old child. She said she was too shocked at causing the cuts to think straight.

"He wanted us to be alone," I continue, "to give me something. A necklace." I touch my neck, but it's gone. Frantic, my eyes dart around the room.

"It's okay, Allie," she says. "Your necklaces are safe. Both of them." There's a tremor in her voice. I'm not sure if it's triggered by my scars or the necklace. She prefers not to be reminded of the madness the ruby-jeweled key unlocks. But she knows better than to take it away after the fight we had over the jade caterpillar chess piece she hid from me a few months ago.

"We went to the old part of town," I say, determined to prove

Jeb's noble intentions, "because he knows how much I like the run-down theater. It started raining, so we ended up at the drainage pipe for cover."

"So there wasn't a convenience store or someplace public you could've gone to stay dry?" she asks in a mocking tone. "Guys don't drag girls into storm drains for anything respectable."

Frowning, I release her hand and tuck mine under my blanket. Hot pain races from the IV to my wrist. "He wanted privacy, but not for what you're thinking."

"It doesn't matter. He put you in danger. And he'll be doing it again if you go with him to London."

I grind my teeth. "Wait . . . what? So you're going to start giving us a hard time now? Of course Dad wants me to have a ring on my finger before I move in with someone. I'm his little girl. But you always told me not to rush into marriage, to feel out my life first. Have you changed your mind?"

"That's not what this is about." She hands me the paper cup and stands, walking over to the flowers on the sill. She strokes the coral-tinged petals of a stargazer lily. Earlier, pink light streamed from between the blinds; now twilight has taken its place, coloring her hair the same purple hue of her dress. "Do you hear them, Allie?"

I nearly cough up my sip of melted ice. "The flowers?"

She nods.

All I hear are the lilies purring in response to her attention. "They aren't talking . . ."

"Not now, but they were while you slept. The bugs, too. I don't like what they've been saying."

I wait for her to elaborate. Mom and I have noticed that we sometimes hear different things. It's as if the plants and insects can individualize their messages, choose to talk to us separately depending on what they have to share.

"They've warned me that the one closest to you will betray you in the worst possible way."

"And you think that's Jeb?" I ask, incredulous.

"Who else could it mean, if not Jebediah? Who else do you spend all your waking hours either talking to, thinking about, or hanging out with?"

My *waking* hours? No one besides Jeb.

But my sleeping hours . . .

I shut my eyes. Of course it's Morpheus. He's already betrayed me, by trying to encroach on my life in the human realm. By trying to force me to go back to Wonderland to fight a battle I'm incapable of winning.

Dread nests inside the back of my skull, making my head throb.

"Jebediah was with you last year when you went down the rabbit hole," Mom says from beside the window. The air conditioner comes on, ruffling the lilies and carrying their sweet scent over to me. "A part of Wonderland might have infected him. Maybe it's been dormant . . . waiting. Waiting to find a way to you."

I huff. "Technically, he was never there. That's not logical."

Mom turns, her skirt rustling as she faces me. "There's no logic to that place. You know that, Allie. No one gets out of Wonderland without some kind of stain. Being there . . . it changes a person. Especially if they're fully human. Has he ever mentioned having strange dreams?"

I shake my head. "Mom, you're making this so much more complicated than it has to be."

"No. You're the one complicating things. Why don't you stay in the States? There are some wonderful art colleges in New York. Let Jebediah go to London without you. You'll both be safe then."

I reach over to set the cup back on the nightstand. "*Let* him? I don't rule him. It was his choice to wait until we could go together."

Her hands clench the sill behind her. "If you want a normal life, you're going to have to break all ties with the entire experience and everything that played a part in it." By the hard set to her chin, I know she's not going to back down.

I don't even try to contain my outburst, even though I know it will kill my throat. "He didn't choose to be there! It's not fair for you to hate Jeb!"

I catch movement in my peripheral vision and jerk my head to find Jeb standing at the open door. We didn't hear him turn the knob, but by the wounded expression on his face, he obviously heard my hoarse shout.

The question is, what else did he hear?

TANGLED WEBS

My dad appears in the doorway behind Jeb. Even though he's an inch shorter than my boyfriend, it's Jeb who looks small and vulnerable lingering at the threshold, as if unsure whether he's welcome to come in.

Mom glances down at her polka dots. Someone coughs in one of the rooms across the hall and a nurse's voice carries over the intercom, the only reprieves from our awkward silence.

"Ali-bear," Dad says to Mom, taking charge of the situation, "I think it's time I show you off in that dress. How about we get some dinner?" He squeezes Jeb's shoulder, then steps around him, patting my ankle on the way over to the window.

Something has definitely changed between Jeb and Dad. They're pals again, just the way they used to be.

"Let's give these two some privacy," Dad says. My mom starts to protest, but the look he gives her makes her force a smile and take his hand. He kisses her wrist.

She lays her phone next to the paper cup on the nightstand. "If you need us, call your dad's cell," she says without looking at Jeb or me. "Visiting hours are over at eight, Jebediah."

Jeb steps inside to let them out. Dad slaps his back encouragingly before closing the door.

Hands in his pockets, Jeb stares at me, dark green eyes full of pain.

"I'm sorry . . ." I struggle to piece together an apology. If he heard what my mom said about Wonderland, there will be questions to answer. Impossible questions.

He shakes his head. "You aren't the one who should be sorry." He doesn't break my gaze as he strides toward me. Dropping into the chair Mom used earlier, he scoops up my hand, laces our fingers, then presses my knuckles to his warm, soft lips. "*I'm* sorry. I promised to always put you first, then I walked away for a stupid phone call and nearly got you killed." His mouth tenses, a press of firm muscle against my hand.

"Oh, Jeb. No." I stroke his face, smooth as silk. He shaved, and considering he's dressed up more than usual—gray khakis and a black short-sleeved Henley—I get the impression he's trying to polish his way into Mom's good graces. The only tribute to his usual grunge rocker clothes are his combat boots.

Yeah, he cleans up nice. Too bad his appearance is the least of Mom's concerns.

My finger traces his chin, and he watches me while I touch him. I pause at the brass labret under his lip. It's about the size of a ladybug, but if you look close, it's shaped like a brass knuckle. I gave it to him a few months ago for his birthday—teasing him that he needed some gangsta hardware to make him look tough.

Even though right now he looks like a little boy, he's always been tough for me. He beat up a guy once just for calling me the Mad Hatter's love slave. He was my rock every time I felt the absence of my mom. And when he followed me into Wonderland—leaping into a mirror without a second thought—he nearly gave up everything to save my life. I really wish he could remember that sacrifice, so he'd stop beating himself up.

"You don't get to be sorry, either," I say. "Dad said you rescued me. So I owe you a thank-you. Now c'mere." Snagging his shirt collar, I pull him close and press my mouth to his.

His long lashes shut, and his free hand cups the back of my neck, fingers weaving through my hair. His closed-mouth kiss is so gentle, it's almost painful, as if he fears I'll break.

He draws back and rests his forehead against mine so the tips of our noses touch. "I've never been so scared, Al. Never in my life. Not even when my dad . . ."

His explanation stalls, but he doesn't have to finish. I know what he lived through. You don't share a duplex with someone and not bear witness to their pain. Unless you *choose* to ignore it.

"What happened in the storm drain?" I ask while holding his hand. "I can't remember anything after the water came."

He looks down at his boots. "When the strand of lights tangled around you, they caught one of my ankles, too, tying us together. I backstroked until I got into the shallower water outside the tunnel, then I reeled you in. But you were . . ." He winces, face paling. "You were so blue. And you wouldn't wake up. Wouldn't move. Wouldn't breathe." His voice catches as he glances at our hands, still entwined. "I tried to give you CPR, but it wasn't working. I've never been so scared."

He keeps repeating that, but he *has* been. There was another time I almost drowned . . . when he told me never to scare him like that again. Another time and another place.

"I keep seeing it, over and over," he mumbles. "It's like a bad dream I can't wake up from."

A dream.

"Wait," I say. "I'm confused. You never lost me in the water? I didn't go away somewhere and then drift back to you?"

"You were never out of my sight." He bites down, causing a spasm in his jaw. "Why did I make you pick up the stuff? If I hadn't left you there, you wouldn't have gotten tangled up." He curses.

"Jeb, stop it. You didn't *make* me do anything."

He studies my face intently, as if sorting through a mental checklist that every feature is still intact. "You must've hit your head when the water first knocked you down. I could see your clothes filling with air bubbles, ballooning around you." His Adam's apple swells on a swallow. "But your body kept sinking . . . I wasn't letting you go." His gaze intensifies on mine. "You know that, right? I would *never* let go of you."

"I know." I nuzzle his palm.

So what happened with Morpheus was a dream after all. Of course it was. He doesn't have the ability to move the rabbit hole. No one does. I didn't use my key to open it. I was floating unconscious in the water. I didn't visit Wonderland, other than in my mind.

Which means what I saw wasn't real. Which means things aren't as bad as he made them out to be.

And best of all, he's not here in my world like he said he was.

For once, I'm glad he was just playing me. I don't have to feel guilty about Wonderland, because everything was a lie.

Is your artwork lying? Morpheus's question buoys to the surface of my mind. My mosaics—are those lies, too? Is he behind them somehow?

I hear the doorknob turning. Jeb must, too, because he sinks back into the chair.

A nurse comes in, an attractive younger woman with auburn hair and jewel-tipped glasses. Instead of scrubs, she's wearing a white nurse dress, like one of those Halloween costumes—although not as short and formfitting. It's the first time I've seen an outfit like that in real life. If not for the American flag pin on her lapel, she could be every guy's librarian and nurse fantasy rolled into one. She writes her name on the dry erase board and introduces herself in a soothing voice.

Jeb and I meet gazes and I smirk.

"Sponge bath?" he mouths in my direction, waggling his eyebrows. I roll my eyes and try not to burst out laughing. His teasing is a good sign. It means he's trying to forgive himself.

Nurse Terri comes to my bedside. Her eyes are gray behind the glare of her glasses. There's a sadness there that makes me want to do anything to cheer her up. Within minutes, I'm standing for the first time. The floor chills my bare feet. Every muscle in my body aches from my fight to swim against the flood. My legs tremble, and I hold the back of my gown, embarrassed about the tubes running in and out of me. Jeb winks, then goes into the hall to look for a courtesy phone.

After he's gone, I use the bathroom, then brave a glance in the mirror. A part of me fears Morpheus will be behind me in the reflection. When he's not there, I'm relieved, until I see the red streak that stands out like flame from the rest of my platinum blond hair—the one reminder of Wonderland's hold on my life that Mom can't ignore. We tried bleaching it, but it won't fade. We tried cutting it, but it always grows back the same vivid hue. She's basically accepted it.

But she would never be able to accept my emotional connection to that place. To accept that, even now, I sometimes miss the chaotic netherling world. If I told her, it would make her crazy with worry.

Fresh guilt simmers inside my chest. Morpheus may have tried to fool me with a fake crumbling Wonderland, but that doesn't mean there isn't something very wrong going on. I can't just turn my back on that world; I can't let it fade to decay and ruin under Queen Red's thumb. Yet I can't abandon the people I love here, either. I don't know how to follow one side of me without leaving the other one behind.

I splash my face with cold water.

Get better, get out of the hospital, and find out the truth. Then I can decide what to do about everything.

Once I'm back in my bed, Nurse Terri returns to offer a handful of herbal cough drops. I pop one in my mouth without hesitation, just to see her smile. The vanilla and cherry sweetness soothes my throat.

She draws some blood for tests. I hold my breath, worried that my essence will come alive like when I'm making my mosaics. Once three plastic vials are filled and capped without incident, I breathe easy again, and Nurse Terri promises to return with broth and crackers.

While I'm waiting for Jeb to get back, the wind picks up outside and whines through the glass panes—a sound I'm used to here in Texas, yet which leaves me uneasy tonight. I stare at the IV in my hand, watching a thin red strip of blood back up into the clear plastic tube. It flutters like a kite string. I'm about to push the nurse's button so I can ask when the needle's coming out, when Jeb steps inside.

"Hey," I say.

"Hey." He closes the door.

Once he's seated, he laces a hand with mine and props his elbow next to my pillow. His free fingers play with my hair where it spreads across the mattress. A spark of pleasure races through my achy body. I'm enjoying being the recipient of his undivided attention so much, I hesitate asking my next question, but I need to know.

"What happened with your interview?"

"We rescheduled," he answers.

"But the two-page spread, that was a big deal."

Jeb shrugs, though his forced nonchalance is transparent.

I bite my lip, searching for a subject change. Something positive. "You and Dad. You're on his good side again."

Jeb winces. "Yeah, but now your mom hates me more than ever."

I study the window behind him. "You know how overprotective she is."

"It's not helping, you lying for me. I heard what you said . . ."

I frown. "What did you hear?"

"That you covered for me. Told her I didn't 'choose to be there.' You and I both know I *did* choose to be at the storm drain. I took you there without even considering all the rain or what could happen."

I squeeze his hand, partly out of frustration and partly out of relief. "That's not why she's mad."

"Why, then?"

I glance at the stuffed animals on my window ledge: a bear, a rather large clown with a boxy-checked hat that covers the top of his head, and a goat eating a tin can with *Get Well* on the label. The clown looks familiar in a sinister sort of way, but I decide it must be the lighting. Shadows drape across all the toys, making them appear to have missing eyes or limbs. It reminds me so much of Wonderland's cemetery that my stomach flips.

"Al." Jeb nudges me. "Are you going to tell me why you guys were yelling when I came in?"

"She just wants me to concentrate on my career, to not get sidetracked. She feels like she lost her shot at being a photographer after being committed. It's not you specifically. It's about anything she perceives as a distraction." I fidget under my covers. A lie shouldn't be so easy to spin.

Jeb nods. "I'm not a distraction. I'm helping. I want you to succeed just as much as she does."

"I know. She just doesn't see it that way."

"After my meeting with Ivy Raven tonight, I should have all the money we'll need to get started in London. That will prove how much I want to help."

My fingers jerk in his. So that's why he shaved and dressed up. To make a good impression on his new heiress client. My mom's warning of betrayal surfaces in my mind, but I push it down. I know I can trust Jeb. Still, I can't seem to control what comes out of my mouth next.

"You're going to leave me for work on the first night I'm awake?" I cringe at the neediness in my voice.

Jeb wraps my hair around his fingers. "Your mom made it clear I should be gone before she gets back. Ivy's in town, so I'm going to meet her and let her choose a painting. She's not in the country very often. We have to take advantage while she's here."

"But it's a holiday. Isn't the gallery closed? Is Mr. Piero meeting you there?"

"He's home with his family. He's letting me use the showroom as a favor."

My lips tighten. I don't like him going alone, though I can't put my finger on why. Maybe it's my netherling side, because the emotion feels animalistic . . . feral. A dark and disorienting instinct that's pecking away all of the trust we've forged over the past year.

Jeb's mine. *Mine mine mine.*

A snarl tugs at my lips, but I suppress it. What's wrong with me?

The stuffed clown flops to the floor with a metallic twang, and Jeb and I both jump.

"Huh," Jeb says as he picks the toy up and rearranges it on the windowsill. He tugs at the oddly shaped hat. "There's something metal under there. Must be top-heavy."

"Who's that from?" I ask.

"The guy who helped on Friday after I pulled you out. I was trying to get you to breathe, and he appeared out of nowhere . . . said he saw an ambulance going down the street and waved it down for us. My cell phone was lost in the flood. He got the help I couldn't give you."

There's something about the clown. Apart from it looking distantly familiar . . . apart from it being bigger than the other toys. It almost appears alive. I keep waiting for it to move.

As it stares back at me, the shadows seem to change its expression—from a smile to an evil sneer. Even the cello in its hand can't soften the image.

I'm not sure what time it is when I wake up. I'm just glad to be awake at all.

The scent of disinfectant reminds me where I am. It's dark. There's no light coming through the blinds or seeping under my door from the hallway. I assume Mom shoved some rolled-up towels there. Sometimes she sleeps better if she seals herself in, a habit she formed while living at the asylum. Each night she'd check every crevice of her room—from the walls to the floors—for insects. Once convinced that none were there, she'd stuff the bottom of the door with her pillowcase.

It's hot, like I'm being smothered by heavy air. I should move the towel away from the door for better ventilation. I kick off my blankets and inch my ankles toward the edge of the bed but freeze in place before sitting up.

The wind shakes the panes . . . louder than earlier. An eerie, vibrating hum that almost sounds like a song. Even the plants and flowers on the windowsill stay silent, as if listening to it. A sudden flash of light blinks across me. It takes a few moments for me to realize that it's lightning. I don't hear any rain. It must be an electrical storm.

The next flash illuminates my surroundings. Thick cobwebs stretch from my bed frame to the windowsill to the ceiling—a morbid canopy, as if a giant spider has laid a trap.

I sit up, and a sticky film suctions to my mouth. Next blink of light and it's even thicker, suffocating me. I scrape webs from my face and scream for my mom, but I can't see her; there are too many strands between us. I yank out my IV and leap off the bed.

Blood flows from my hand, different somehow. It floats upward, a solid strip, forming a glowing red sword. I take it instinctively, slashing at the filaments, cutting my way through the sticky fibers to reach Mom's cot. A thick sheet of spider silk has engulfed her body.

The red glow from my sword reveals stuffed animals and dolls hanging in effigy on the glistening radials all around me, more toys than I remember seeing on my windowsill. They grab my hair and bite my skin as I hack my way and weave toward Mom's cocooned form. An instant before I'm there, the clown drops down from a swinging thread. It plays the cello and laughs, taunting me. What I heard earlier wasn't the wind at all . . . it was the instrument.

I lash out with my dagger of blood, and the toy drops to my feet, its song silenced, though its arm continues to move the bow across the muted cello strings.

Finally, I reach the cocoon. I slice open the white shell, afraid to look. As the sides fold back, it's not Mom's corpse staring dead-eyed at me.

It's Jeb's.

Jeb's face, gray and lacerated. Jeb's mouth that opens and screams. I scream in unison, our combined wails so shrill I have to cover my ears.

In the resulting silence, a voiceless whisper slides into my mind.

"It will end like this, unless you fight back. Rise to your place. Wake up and fight. Fight!"

I wake up, gasping for air. Hair tangles around my face. I comb back the strands so I can see. Moonlight filters through the blinds. There's not a web in sight.

My heartbeat settles as I see Mom sleeping peacefully in her cot. The stuffed animals sit in their places on the windowsill, all but one. The clown hunkers on my nightstand, staring up at me, its hand slowly moving the bow along the cello strings in time with the wind howling outside.

I stifle a horrified moan and shove the heavy toy to the floor. It lands with a strange jangling noise and slumps there, unmoving, yet the message of its muted song still resonates: Morpheus is here in the human realm, and everyone I love is in danger unless I find him, reclaim my throne, and stand up for Wonderland against Queen Red's wrath.

Identity Theft

The clown didn't haunt me again after the nightmare. I stuffed it in the trash under some paper towels and magazines while Mom slept. The toy was more solid than I thought it would be—almost like a toddler—and seemed to wriggle in my arms. It was even more unsettling because, although I can't place where, I've seen that clown before. I told Mom I gave the toy to a nurse for the children's ward, since it was from a complete stranger.

Stranger. The perfect descriptor for Morpheus. He's stranger than any person or creature I've ever met. And, boy, do I have a long line of comparison subjects.

On Wednesday morning Dad drops me at school twenty minutes early.

I'm exhausted. After being discharged from the hospital on Tuesday, I refused to take any of the sedatives prescribed by the hospital's attending physician. Between the pain of my injuries and thinking about Jeb's heiress client and Morpheus's crash-landing into my everyday life, I didn't get much sleep.

"You look pale, even with the makeup." Dad hands me my backpack across the seat as I slide out of the truck onto the asphalt parking lot. "I hope you're not overdoing it."

There's no way to tell him the real reason for my blood-drained face. And his concern is nothing compared to what Mom's been feeling since I've been home from the hospital. She wouldn't let me have any visitors, insisting I needed to rest, so I didn't get to see Jeb or Jenara. Since my new cell phone wasn't charged and programmed, I settled for a short and unsatisfying landline call divided between both of them. Jeb was evasive about his visit with the heiress, insisting we talk about it in person. That did nothing to calm my nerves.

Mom's final words as I left this morning were, "I'm not sure school's a good idea so soon. Maybe take a day off from classes while your car is getting its tire fixed."

Somehow I managed to talk Dad into driving me anyway, and I'm not leaving now. "Dad, please stop enabling Mom's paranoia. Persephone's given me the entire week off from work. I'll get bored sitting at home. I have exams to make up, and there's no way I'm going to summer school. I want to graduate with my class."

I plant my feet in a determined stance. I have to win this argument. If I don't find Morpheus today, he'll come looking for me at home. That's the last thing Mom needs.

Dad's hands tighten on his steering wheel. Sunlight slants through the windshield, glaring off his wedding ring and the silver logo on his work shirt. "Cut your mom some slack. You gave us a real scare. She's having trouble finding her footing."

I bite my inner cheek. "I get that. But her hovering is out of control. The danger's behind me now." *Not true.* It's lying in wait just around the corner. "I'm stronger than you two think, okay?"

His expression relaxes. "I'm sorry, Butterfly. I forget sometimes how much you've grown up over the past year." He gives me a real smile then. "Have a good day. And show those tests who's boss."

"Thanks." I reach in to squeeze his hand before shutting the door. Smiling, I wave as he drives off, though my confidence is forced. I can't stop worrying about what Morpheus has up his lace-cuffed sleeve.

There are rules for netherlings when they breach the human realm. Unless they want to be seen as they are, in all their fairy weirdness, they have to borrow a human's face and body for camouflage—trade places with them. The human has to stay in Wonderland, so there won't be two of the same person running around in the mortal realm, and can't return until their netherling doppelganger no longer requires their image. Only then can they resume their life and identity again.

Which means Morpheus has coerced someone into taking a leap down the rabbit hole. It also means Morpheus may not be recognizable to me, and this gives him a distinct advantage.

As if he needs any more than he already has.

The skies are clear and the sun warms my back. I won the wardrobe argument with my mom, and armed in a dusty-rose tulle miniskirt and scarf, gray corset jacket, paisley tights, and black lace-up knee boots, I head toward the breezeway's door, convincing myself I'm ready to face him.

As I weave through cars—some occupied and blaring loud music, others empty—Corbin's rusted orange 1950 Chevy, Sidestep, comes into view. He and Jenara have their heads together, sharing a few steamy kisses before the bell rings.

Any other time, I'd walk by and give them their privacy, but today I need info on our new exchange student. Jen always has the low-down on everyone and everything at Pleasance High.

A country-and-western ballad drifts from the cracked-open passenger's-side window. I clear my throat and slap the glass with my palm, my fingerless gloves muffling the sound.

Corbin's eyes pop open, and he pushes Jen back, gesturing to me. Jen squeals, opens the door, and drags me into the seat beside her for a hug, shoving Corbin over to make room. He fumbles to salvage the thirty-two-ounce to-go cup that was sandwiched between his hip and the door.

"Sorry," I mouth to him from over Jen's shoulder.

Corbin tips his chin in acknowledgment and offers a shy, expect-ant smile. He's no doubt waiting for me to greet him like I usually do, to tease him about the bromance between him and Jeb. They share a love for cars and have been discussing restorations for Corbin's Chevy. It's too bad Jeb can't seem to find time to work on it with him. *Welcome to my world, Corb.*

"I'm so glad you're here," Jenara says, holding me close. The scent of her shampoo enfolds me. "Seeing you at the hospital . . . the wires and tubes and machines all around you." She breaks us apart to study me, the sympathy on her face visceral. "It was like your worst night-mares had come true."

Even though she's referring to my past fears of being bound and helpless in an asylum, I think about the destruction Morpheus showed me in Wonderland while I was unconscious, and the spider-webs winding through my sedative-enhanced dreams. She has no idea how spot-on she is about nightmares coming true.

"I'm okay now." I pat her wrist.

She brushes a strand of hair off my forehead. "Just don't do anything like that again, yeah?"

"Yeah, yeah." I grin. "You sound just like your brother. By the way, did he say anything about his appointment with that heiress chick yet? He was so quiet last night on the phone."

Jen's black-lined eyes narrow, seeing right through me. "Stop worrying. You're his world . . . his muse. Right, Corbin?"

"Huh?" Corbin lifts his mouth off the straw sticking out of his Coke's lid. "Oh, sure," he says in his deep southern drawl. "He's only got eyes for you." He smirks encouragingly, and the freckles around his nose line up like a pigmented constellation.

The ten-minute warning bell rings, and we pile out of the truck. Jen twists a tendril of pink hair around her finger and secures it over her ear with a pearl barrette that matches the ivory netted skirt layered over her skinny jeans. She hands off her backpack to Corbin. We follow a crowd of students, the three of us locked in our own private conversation.

"So, did Jeb tell you two about the guy who helped him get the ambulance?" I ask. "He said he was enrolling here . . ."

"Yep," Corbin responds after another sip of Coke. "He registered yesterday. A senior from Cheshire, England."

From Cheshire.

"Of course," I say under my breath. Time to find out whose life and identity he borrowed to pull off this charade. "What's his name?" I press.

"M," Jenara answers.

"What? Like *Em*, short for Emmett?"

"Nope. Like the letter in the alphabet."

I don't know whether to laugh or gag.

We step into the breezeway, the tiles slick under our feet compared to the asphalt outside. Our small trio gets hemmed in by other students, and I'm bombarded with questions: *What was it like, almost dying? Did you see any ghosts when you were in the coma? Is heaven like the movies say it is?*

It's weird, but for once, being the center of attention isn't so bad. Being noticed for something other than the way I dress or who I'm descended from makes me feel almost normal . . . accepted.

After our curious classmates get their fill of my guarded answers and move on, Jenara resumes our conversation. "The exchange guy's last name is Rethen."

I frown, feeling out the word in my mind. *Rethen*. It uses the same letters as nether. It's an anagram. There's nothing subtle about Morpheus.

"You should see his amazing sports car," Corbin adds. "Lets anyone drive it who wants to. I drove us to lunch in it yesterday."

I clench my teeth. The jerk isn't even trying to lie low. He's flaunting how close he can get to everyone I care about, how easy it is for him to blend into my world, as a warning to me.

I want to tell them both to stay away from him, but how do I justify the request, since technically I haven't met him yet?

"And Al"—Jen practically beams—"you'll love his style. *Dead-bug chic.*"

"Here we go." Corbin rolls his eyes.

Jen elbows him. "Shut up. Al will totally get this." She loops an arm through my elbow. "He wants to be a lepidopterist or entomologist or something. He's inspired a whole new line for me. Faded jeans, rattlesnake boots, and a cowboy hat with a string of—"

"Moths around the brim," I finish for her, my heart skipping a beat or two.

Jen and Corbin both stare at me in awe.

"How'd you know that?" Corbin asks.

"Jeb mentioned it," I lie, and clear my throat for effect.

"Ah." Jenara's eyes—the same green hue of her brother's—sparkle under their veil of gray eye shadow. "Well, I designed some deadbug fashions during sixth period yesterday. You're hitching a ride with us after school, right?"

I nod.

"I'll show you the sketches later. I used M for the model. He's got this whole hot-androgynous thing going on."

"That's my cue." Corbin taps Jen's butt with her backpack before handing it off. With a practiced arm, he tosses his empty Coke cup into a trash can a few feet away. It lands neatly inside. "Like to see your limey unisex cowboy do that. It's all in the hands." He wiggles his fingers in Jen's direction. "I got *man* skills, babe. That's why I'm starting quarterback."

She huffs. "Really? Looks more like janitorial skills," she teases back.

Corbin laughs and disappears around the corner. Jen gives me a hug and we part for first period.

I settle at my desk. Morpheus is nowhere in sight, although he is the topic of almost every girl's conversation and passed note. I manage to read one over someone's shoulder:

I heard he got in trouble with his rich English family and was sent here to see how regular people live. Viva American peasants! The M *comes from his dad, Mort, but he's rebelling. *drools**

So, not only is he rich, British, and eccentric, he's a bad boy and a rebel. Great. Once again, he's pulling everyone's strings.

I sit through an excruciating three periods—two exams and one review work sheet—without seeing him once. I'm guessing he arranged his schedule contrary to mine so I'll worry about where he is and what he's up to. Another ploy to knock me off balance.

In the basement level on the way to fourth period, I decide to ditch study hall and peek in every door of every senior class until I find him, determined to make contact before lunch. The last thing I want is to face him across a crowded cafeteria.

I slip into the girls' bathroom to wait for the bell to ring and the hall to clear. The small gray alcove is just under the girls' and boys' locker rooms located on the first floor. Faulty pipes run across the dingy white ceiling. Rusty stains branch out like yellow-brown veins, and the scent of mildew hangs heavy on the air.

It's just a matter of time till the pipes spring a leak in the gymnasium floor upstairs and ruin everything, which is why the money our class raised for our senior gift will be used for new copper pipes to be installed this summer.

The tardy bell rings. I wait for voices to fade and doors to shut. Strands of sunshine filter through a hopper window where the wall meets the ceiling. The hinged glass is open a crack, letting in a sliver of fresh air, just enough to make breathing bearable.

A chorus of whispering bugs and plants drifts in, blending into a nonsensical hum. Cobwebs line the windowpane and ripple in the breeze like ghostly handkerchiefs waving at me.

I stare at my reflection in the dusty mirror, focused on the red strip of hair, and imagine the strand moving like the webs—an invisible string drawing it up to dance. As I concentrate, it starts to twine and twist.

My muscles tense. It's not safe, using my powers here at school—entangling pieces of my life I've tried for months to keep separate. If I'm not careful, the end result could be volatile.

Ignoring the sense of dread, I concentrate harder until the wave of magic resurges. My hair sways and spins until it's at a right angle from the platinum strands surrounding it, so much like my horrific dream at the hospital . . . the sword of blood.

As if triggered by my memory, an image begins to stir just behind my reflection. My concentration wavers, and the strand of hair falls limp. There's a blur of white, red, and black checked patterns in the glass, sharpening to the clown from the hospital. It looms there, stretched out of proportion, as if I'm looking into a funhouse mirror. The clown shakes a snow globe in its hands and smiles with teeth sharp and silver like nails. My knees wobble, but I hold my ground, assuring myself I'm imagining it.

If I turn around, it will be gone.

Please don't be there . . . please please please . . .

Gathering my courage, I spin on my heel.

Nothing but walls and stalls. I take a breath, then face the mirror again. The clown in the reflection has vanished.

Maybe Dad was right. Maybe I am overdoing it . . .

A door in the hallway slams, reminding me of the reason I'm hiding here to begin with. *Morpheus.*

This has to be one of his mind games.

I wait for silence and then venture out. I've only made it two steps when the familiar snicker of Taelor Tremont breaks the silence.

Someone shushes her, followed by several girlish giggles and a wicked laugh that I know better than the scars on my own palms.

Curling my hands around my backpack straps, I peer around the corner.

He's there with his back to me, just a few feet away. Tall and lithe. A leather vest and skintight T-shirt across his broad shoulders. Worn jeans hug his legs. Whoever's body he stole is close to his own, although his hair is shorter. I can't see any fringe under the edges of his cowboy hat from the back.

He holds a poster up to the wall that says, TOYS FOR FAIRY-TALE ENDINGS: GIVE A SICK CHILD A HAPPILY-EVER-TODAY. It's a reminder for the charity drive our senior class is organizing from now until Friday. To get in the door for prom, every attendee has to contribute a new toy for a local children's hospital. There's a box for early donations against the wall, already half filled.

Four girls from our senior student council surround Morpheus, offering their opinion on the poster's placement above the box. Taelor and Twyla argue over who gets to tape it in place. Most of the time they're either fighting or competing, yet they claim to be best friends. It's like the symbiotic relationship between a parasitic fungus and its host. I just haven't figured out who's the fungus. Kimber and Deirdre round out the quartet, the bearers of the tape dispensers.

All four are drooling over Morpheus as if he's royalty. Only his second day here and already he's made more headway than me in my entire school career. I bite back a wave of envy.

As if sensing I'm watching, he turns. For one instant he looks like someone else—a stranger. Then, in a blink, it's Morpheus: the patches around his eyes, the jewels that display his every mood tipping the edges.

I whimper as a spread of dark wings lifts behind his shoulders, shadowing my classmates. Gasping, I hide around the corner again, smashed against the wall, backpack sandwiched between my spine and the cold tiles.

I thought I was ready, but to see him in my world, unhinging all that was once normal, revealing everything I've worked so hard to hide . . . it paralyzes me. I hold my breath, ears burning, and wait for the terrified screams when the girls realize what he is—*what I am.*

Instead, more flirty whispers and giggles drift my way.

I work up the nerve to look again. Taelor and the other femmes fatales are ascending the stairs.

"Remember," Taelor says to Morpheus in her most provocative voice, "you promised to let me drive your sexy-hot car at lunch."

The girls disappear from my view.

How could they have missed what I saw so clearly?

Morpheus faces me again, wings spread wide. No one else is in the hall, but my heart pummels my ribs as if we were on exhibition—my secret and his—to the whole world.

Backing up, I duck once more into the bathroom. Before the door can swing shut, he shoves his way over the threshold. Strands of sunlight from the window spotlight his finely lined dark eyes. They're the only part of him that I recognize now. His face and his body, though a strikingly close match, belong to some human guy I've never seen.

He's like a broken vase—delicately angular features with a thin scar that runs from his left temple to his cheek—damaged yet lovely. His skin is golden, very different from Morpheus's alabaster complexion. There's also a dimple in his chin similar to mine. He's about my age and looks like he belongs in high school.

Morpheus takes off his hat, revealing short-cropped hair dyed a blue so vivid it almost glows.

"Alyssa." The voice is his, unmistakably. Deep and sensual with an edge of malice. "You look so much better than the last time I saw you. Although I must admit, you wore those wet clothes very well."

Every part of me wants to shake him until his insides are as jumbled as mine. Just when I thought I had a chance at normal, he comes back and ruins everything. I drop my backpack with a loud thump.

"I can't . . ." My tongue stumbles over the words. "I can't bring myself to ask."

The right side of his mouth lifts—a roguish smirk unfamiliar on the new set of full lips, but every bit as exasperating. "Let me ask *for* you, then." His gaze flits to the rust-stained ceiling. "What is a lovely queen like you"—his nose wrinkles—"doing in a smelly place like this?"

"Stop that." I scowl. "There's nothing funny about what you've done. The guy whose body you stole . . . who is he?"

Morpheus drops his hat on his head and tilts it. A line of dusty white moth corpses wiggles at the brim. "His name is Finley. He's a loner. A failed musician. Found him drugged out of his mind in Grimsby, an old fishing town in England."

"Out of his mind? So that's how you convinced him to go to Wonderland?"

"It didn't take any convincing. He was unhappy with his life here in the human realm. Look how many times he's tried to cut out early." He turns his inner arms. Underneath four twisted leather bracelets are two snake tattoos stretched along his skin from his elbows to his wrists. They manage to hide part of the suicide attempts and needle tracks, but they also hide Morpheus's netherling mark, the one part of him that still remains, even while he mimicks another guy's form.

I think of my own mark beneath my boot on my left ankle, and how it will always be a part of me no matter how many tattoos or layers of leggings I wear to cover it.

My windpipe tightens, making it difficult to breathe. "Didn't you learn anything with Alice? You can't just take him away from the ones who care about him. There will be ripples, consequences."

Morpheus taps the leather braid at his neck thoughtfully. "I chose carefully. He has no one who loves him. I did him a favor. Possibly even saved his life."

My temples pound. "No, no, no. You don't get to make that call. He has a life he's supposed to live here, no matter how miserable it turns out. Something could've been about to change, to bring him out of his slump. You've taken away his chance to redeem himself . . ."

"One damaged soul in exchange for thousands of netherling lives. It's a fair trade."

My frown deepens. As much as I despise his nonchalance and underhanded tactics, I understand his loyalty to Wonderland and his friends there. So why can't he sympathize with my loyalties to *this* world?

"Stop worrying about Fin," he says, his voice softening. "The boy's being well tended to. I gave him to the Ivory Queen for a plaything."

This sets my teeth on edge. "Ivory wouldn't do that."

"Wouldn't she? Have you forgotten how she yearns for a companion? I told her his situation—that he was dying of loneliness in the human realm. That he needed love to heal him. Once you know someone's weakness, they're easy to manipulate. You're intimately familiar with this strategy, are you not?"

Remembering my dream in the hospital—Jeb's screams ringing in my head—I wince.

Morpheus steps closer. "One does what one has to do to protect what they love." His expression is sincere, and something unreadable lurks behind his inky gaze. There's more to that statement than a Wonderland reference. Unfortunately I'm too distracted by his looming presence to analyze it.

I brace my hand against his chest: a barrier. "Look, if you're going to be in my world, there are social guidelines you need to follow. First, there's a thing called personal space. So everyone you encounter, including me, you need to imagine them in an impenetrable box." I gesture invisible lines around me with my free hand. "You don't get any closer than the box's boundaries. Are we clear?"

His chest muscles twitch under my palm; then he steps back, his cowboy boots scraping on the gritty floor. "Apparently, your giggly friends forgot to wear their boxes today."

I shoot him a disgusted glare. "They aren't my friends. And that stunt you pulled out there? Showing your true form for the whole world to see? That is *not* okay. I don't know how they missed it, but you can't do that again!"

He huffs. "Aw, bless, Alyssa. Only you could see that side of me." He catches the strap of my backpack on the floor with his toe and drags it closer. I try to snatch it back, but he's too fast. Unzipping the bag, Morpheus digs through my books and papers. "Had you been studying the fundamentals of Wonderland instead of this pointless mortal brain-rot, you would know how a glamour works." He slides my AP biology book out and flips through several pages, coming to a diagram of the human body. He turns it to face me. "In order for me to become Fin, I had to imprint his form over my own before stepping through the portal into this world. It takes most of my power to hold this mask in place. Were I to let go of the glamour, even for an instant, it would be gone until I could visit Fin again for another imprint." He snaps the book shut with one hand. "But you? There are moments *you* can make out glimpses of truth, penetrate the chinks in my mask and see me for what I am. Because you have learned to look through netherling lenses."

I wish it was that easy to see him for what he is, instead of constantly wondering what he's up to. "Let's just get this over with. I'm tired of the games."

He tilts his head, like a puppy trying to understand its master's wishes. "I haven't been playing any games."

"Right." I consider bringing up the clown, but there's no point in wasting time with his denials. Better to get him off my back by pretending to cooperate. "How, exactly, am I supposed to help with Queen Red so you can return Finley"—I stare him up and down—"back to his life?"

The bell rings, rattling through my bones. Chatter and laughter filter through the window. Moving shadows blink at the bottom of the door as people pass by.

Morpheus tucks away my book and closes the backpack. "I have a lunch date. We'll talk tomorrow. Same place, same time. You have until then to gather your wits and your mosaics. There is something they're trying to tell you, and, with a little magical aid, I can help you decipher it. Then after that we're off to Wonderland."

Twenty-four hours to say good-bye to everyone and everything I love? Not happening. "Wait, Morpheus. We need to talk about this."

"M," he corrects. "And there's nothing to talk about."

I shake my head, annoyed not only with his dismissiveness but with the stupid name he insists on using. "Why didn't you use Fin's name?"

"And chance someone knowing him?"

"Aha!" I point at his nose. "So he does have family."

He snatches my wrist. "Everyone has family in your world, Alyssa. Unfortunately for Fin, his no longer cares where he is. But a fellow like him is bound to have enemies. I don't need trouble. So I took only his image. Not his identity."

"I don't need trouble, either." I jerk out of his hold, grab my bag, and head for the door. "I'm not ready to go back to Wonderland. I have things here to do."

Unconcerned, he turns to adjust his hat in the mirror. "Ah, so you're busy. Perhaps whilst you find time for Wonderland, I shall entertain myself with the lovely little Jen of the pink hair and spar-kling green eyes." His voice is low and suggestive. "Eyes so like her brother's."

Apprehension knots at the base of my throat, and I whip around, casting my backpack to the side. "You stay away from the people I love. Do you hear me?"

When he doesn't answer, I grip his elbow to force him to face me.

Before I can react, he catches my waist and sets my butt on the cold edge of the sink. Face-to-face with his chest, I squirm. He pins me in place with his body, gripping the porcelain behind me—entirely too close for comfort.

"Look at that," he taunts. "Your box seems to have shrunk."

I look behind me but can't back up without falling into the sink's basin.

"If you truly wish to protect those you love," he continues in the same taunting tone, "you will pay heed to what I'm saying. Is your comfort worth more than their safety?"

A realization slams into me, harsh and bitter. "You weren't talking about Finley, were you? *I'm* the soul you're willing to sacrifice for Wonderland. Right?" My eyes meet his, and the resolution there validates my fear.

Playing with the scarf at my neck, he pouts. "War is never pretty, Alyssa."

I suppress a sob. Mom's warning from the flowers and bugs was right. Morpheus is hanging me out to dry. "So, you know I don't have a prayer, and you're still sending me after her!" I shove him, but he won't budge.

"Either you go to her or she'll come to you. Better you contain the fight in Wonderland, where you have the advantage of keeping your family and friends out of the line of fire." He studies my neck where Jeb's heart locket and the key rest atop my scarf. "Remember what almost happened to your boyfriend the last time he got involved, how close he came to—"

"Don't say it," I plead.

Morpheus shrugs. "Simply making a point. Were he to face Wonderland again, he mightn't be so lucky this time."

The sink's edge bites into my hips. "Let me down." Though soft and even, my voice echoes in the hollowness of the bathroom.

Expression serious and intense, he pulls me off the sink, then spins me around, lifts my backpack, and arranges the straps over my shoulders like a mother prepping her child for kindergarten.

"We have a lot of work ahead of us to prepare you for your confrontation with Red," he says, his breath warm against the back of my head. "You are not equipped to fight her yet. But you will be. You're the best of both worlds, lest you forget. All you need is to have faith in yourself."

Without another word, he steps out. The door swings shut behind him.

I look at the waving cobwebs in the window. Considering the less-than-stellar parlor trick I did with my hair earlier, I know he's right. I'm unprepared for any sort of magical battle.

But what if he's wrong, too? How can being half of something be better than being whole? No amount of work or faith can prepare me for facing Queen Red and her heightened powers.

Foreboding creeps into my heart: This trip to Wonderland will be the end of me. By sticking out my neck again, I'll lose more than my normal, everyday life.

This time I *will* lose my head, along with everything attached.

SANCTUARY

Dad says I can have whatever I want for dinner as a reward for acing my two tests today. Considering this could be our last meal as a family, I request his famous maple pancakes and a tall glass of ice-cold milk.

After changing into comfier clothes—navy checkered leggings and a silver tunic sweater—I sneak into the living room to watch from around the corner as my parents cook together, just like they do every evening. Mom sneezes while holding a cup of flour. White dust ends up all over Dad's face, and a food fight breaks out. Before it's over, they're both laughing and covered in pancake ingredients. Dad draws her close and tenderly wipes her lips with a damp washcloth before kissing her.

I ease back into hiding, wanting to smile so much it hurts. Seeing them flirt like kids in love breaks my heart into so many different pieces. They've earned it after all the years they missed together. I just don't want this to be the last time I see them so happy.

When we sit down to eat, the pancakes are light, spongy, and dripping with syrup. They taste like home and comfort and security. I swallow it all down, drowning in the sweetness.

While my parents do the dishes, I escape to my bedroom and feed my pet eels some chopped boiled eggs. Aphrodite and Adonis perform a graceful dance, entwining their bodies, capturing the food as it floats down like they're lovers catching snowflakes on their tongues.

The scene reminds me of the snow globe the clown held in my hallucination today, and just like that, I'm hit with a Wonderland memory; it crashes over me, so vivid I feel like I'm there again: my five-year-old self, glaring at my eight-year-old netherling companion and competitor, driven to near tears as he held a snow globe out of my reach.

It was the time Morpheus and I visited the Shop of Human Eccentricities. He always brought me to Wonderland in my dreams, but we didn't often interact with other netherlings. Unless Morpheus let them, they couldn't see through the veil of sleep standing between us. We could observe them, though, like watching fish swim in a tank.

But that day there was something Morpheus wanted me to learn, so he had temporarily dropped the veil.

"I'm busy," Morpheus teased in his young, cheeky voice, shaking the snow globe in front of me again. "You want a toy of your own? Find a way up on your own." His black wings brushed across my bare foot as he turned his back to explore the store.

"But you're the one who can fly," I grumbled, poking the end of my braid through the space where I'd recently lost one of my front teeth.

When he glanced over his skinny shoulder and rolled his inky-patched eyes, I knew his mind was made up. I looked at my red pajama top. The matching pants were mud stained from an earlier game of tag beneath some giant mushrooms. Morpheus had won that game without even dirtying his white satin shirt and black velvet pants. I was tired of him always winning.

I pouted and strolled around the shop. A woven canopy of branches and moldering leaves made up the ceiling; the floor and walls were decaying stone, and moss peeked through the cracks. It smelled damp and felt cold to my feet.

Solid wooden shelves stood back-to-back to form aisles. The shelves were lined with sparkling new plates, silverware, lamps, toothbrushes, combs, and thousands of other items from the human realm. Our ordinary artifacts were prized collectibles in Wonderland.

A top shelf in the back of the store caught my eye, too high for me to reach. A cheerful muslin rag doll slumped over the edge, eyes the color of cornflowers and a smile kissed with pink glitter. On the seven shelves stacked beneath her, other shiny new novelties sat: a silver Christmas ball; a magnifying glass; a stuffed yellow canary in a cage—so lifelike, I questioned if it were really dead; white crockery jars with happy, smiling ladybugs painted on the front; fancy perfume bottles; a doorknob; and candy keepers made of converted kerosene lamps whose lids were topped with vinyl doll heads. But none of those things intrigued me like the rag doll.

Morpheus had wandered off to another set of shelves, purposely ignoring me.

Hesitant, I padded to the front of the shop, where the clerk, Mr. Lamb, sat next to his cash register. He was an odd-looking creature who appeared to be pieced together from the same curiosities that lined his shelves: raised gray and white patches coated his humanoid face, as if his flesh had mildewed. His lips, eyebrows, whiskers, and hair were made of fungus, green and nappy like worn felt. His body—nothing more than a tattered dress form—had twenty sets of pencil-thin robotic arms and legs affixed to the empty shoulder sockets and torso's edge with rusted nails and hinges.

"Mr. Lamb, I found something I'd like. Please reach it for me?" I pled in my most polite tone.

His flat, open-ended bottom teetered on the bar stool, and he peered over square glasses with eyes as sharp and shiny as wet rocks.

"No," he snipped.

Knitting needles clacked between his brass fingers and toes as he wove butterfly wings into strands of glistening rainbow cloth. With the help of his abundant appendages, he kept adding more knitting needles and was producing bolts of the fabric at an alarming pace. The pile of butterfly wings that had touched the ceiling when I arrived now came to just above his head. I looked at them longingly, wistful for a set of wings, although I knew I would never use them because I didn't like heights.

"My job"—his guttural voice scraped inside my ears like fingernails clawing across a coffin lid—"is to assure the customers don't get bit. It is up to you to capture your own buys. And mind you don't offend the shelves. They're made of tulgey wood. Now step off. I'm busy sewing myself a new dress."

I wondered what was so special about tulgey wood and what he meant about customers getting bit. But I had a bigger problem. The only way to get the toy would be to climb, but my tummy kicked anytime I went high.

I wove through the maze of aisles back to the rag doll. Plush and clean, she looked down on me. Her pretty face promised hours of fun make-believe in my sandbox at home. Something inside me thrummed to life, a subtle assurance that I could meet this challenge.

I cautiously balanced my bare feet on the first shelf, gripping the one above it with my fingers. I made my way up slowly, as if climbing a ladder. Two shelves, four, then six shelves high. The steady clacking of the clerk's knitting needles gave my movements rhythm.

I didn't dare look down. Instead, I focused on my prize, only two shelves away now. The backs of the bookshelves appeared to have holes that showed only in my peripheral vision. When I looked straight at them, all I saw were dark lines in the wood.

At last, I was at the highest shelf. Nervous tremors shook my hands. For comfort, I leaned in to nuzzle the doll's soft yarn hair. She smelled of detergent and vanilla. I drew back, grinning, then spotted a clown next to her, propped against the back of the shelf. Something about its jolly smile called to me. I reached toward it, the fingernails of my other hand digging into the wood for extra balance.

"Ouch, you're pinching!" A shout came from behind the clown, gritty and breathy, like two pieces of sandpaper rubbed together. There was movement where the dark lines I had mistaken for wood grains formed a set of lips. They yawned open to reveal a cavernous hole with splintery teeth and a bumpy gray tongue.

The shelf had a mouth . . .

"Ease up, would you?" it barked at me.

Startled, I almost fell backward but gripped the shelf even harder with both hands just in time.

"Want to play rough, eh?" the mouth screeched at me, its breath as rank as a compost heap. Without warning, jagged teeth—embedded in black gums—snapped out of the wood like an old man spitting up his dentures. Biting down on both toys, the jaw retracted back into the mouth and the rag doll and clown disappeared. The hole vanished, too, leaving only the wood grain and an empty shelf.

Terrified, I lost my balance. Morpheus caught me in midair before I could even scream. As we drifted toward the floor, the mouth and teeth seemed to chase us down the back of each consecutive shelf, catching and swallowing the display items.

"You just had to wake the shelves," Morpheus scolded the moment we landed. "Don't you know that tulgey is the most irritable of all kinds of wood? You'd best hope whatever you wanted to play with so badly doesn't come back to haunt you."

"Come back?" I asked, my heartbeat still scattered from my almost-fall. "But they've all been eaten!"

"No. A tulgey's throat is a two-way portal to another dimension. A place called AnyElsewhere . . . the looking-glass world." Morpheus tapped his fingers on his knee nervously. "If the items that went through are turned away at the gate, they'll be sent back. And once something is spit back out, it rarely returns the same way it left. It's changed. Forever."

"Drat it all." Mr. Lamb's complaint carried from across the room. We couldn't see him for all the aisles between us, but the clack of knitting needles had been silenced and a mechanical whir rang out. Metal feet ground along the stone floor as he came around the corner.

He took one look at the empty shelves, then pointed to the door with several of his brassy fingertips. "Get out!" he demanded. A loud belch from behind us masked the echo of his voice. We all turned to the lowest shelf, where the wood-grain mouth had reappeared. With another belch, it coughed up everything it had swallowed.

The items were mangled—altered nightmarishly. The Christmas ball had withered down to a black coal. A large bloodshot eye opened in its middle, glaring at us. It rolled toward me, but Morpheus kicked it away. The magnifying glass had shattered and blood leaked from the cracks. The silver handle wailed so loudly my spine shook. The stuffed yellow canary—now pale pink and featherless—opened its beak and squawked. Eight wire legs sprouted from the cage's base and shuffled the raging bird toward us.

We backed up. The clerk said a word his mother would've spanked him for and clambered toward the cash register, mumbling something about nets.

Morpheus took flight and left me alone on the ground.

"Help me!" I cried up at him. My heart pounded in my chest, making it hard to breathe.

"I can't always be there to carry you." The jewels under his eyes were a sincere blue. "You must figure out how to escape."

Something pecked my ankle, and I jumped back with a yelp, facing the screeching canary. I shoved the cage over. The wire dome rocked and the metal legs squirmed in midair, like a turtle rolled onto his shell.

More freakish mutations surrounded me.

The white crockery jars spewed up thousands of beetles with snapping pincers, nothing like the smiling ladybugs painted on their fronts. The doorknob had been transformed into an old man's hand and pulled itself closer with bent and gnarled fingers, while the vinyl doll heads on the candy keepers snapped their teeth—tiny and sharp like straight pins.

I took several cautious steps backward, keeping them in my sight as I made my way to the front of the store. "Morpheus!" I screeched again, but now I couldn't even see him overhead.

The mutated items parted to form a path. My rag doll and the clown appeared—their middles stitched together with bloody thread, like a gruesome surgery gone wrong. Instead of four eyes, they had three between them. One eye had been caught in the seam. "Help me find my other eye," the rag doll pleaded. "Please, please. My eye." Her little-girl voice and the clown's distorted laughter chilled the air, and I sobbed.

Blinded by my tears, I stumbled away. Mr. Lamb stood on the counter scooping mutants up in a mass of nets. "Hide, you fool child!" he shouted.

"Do something, Alyssa!" Morpheus reappeared and yelled from above as the creepy mutants encroached on me. "You're the best of both worlds," he prodded. "Use what you have. What *we* don't. Make something that can save us all!"

I dove beneath Mr. Lamb's pile of butterfly wings for sanctuary. The knitting needles were scattered on the floor, and I chanced sticking out an arm to grab some. Inside my frail refuge, I ignored the growls and snaps closing in. I took two wings and held them against a needle, imagining them joining as one, forming a whole new breed of butterfly with a body of metal, lethal and sharp.

The knitting-needle butterfly came alive in my hand, wings fluttering. Gasping, I let it go, and it flew out toward my attackers. For a moment, I was too shocked to move.

The clerk's screeches spurred me again to action, and I made more butterflies, sending them to help the first.

My bug invasion dive-bombed the attacking beetles, herding

them back into their jars; they swooped into the vinyl doll heads and tangled in their hair, ripping it out at the roots.

Soon all the mutants retreated with hisses and snarls.

Inside my hiding place, I imagined that the remaining wings could lift me, attach to every inch of my pajamas. In a matter of seconds, I was floating beside Morpheus. I covered my face, unable to look down.

"You did it," he said and put an arm around me. I couldn't see the pride in his eyes, but I heard it in his voice.

Just before Morpheus dropped the veil of sleep over us again, the clerk started cheering for my metal bugs.

I'd saved him. I'd saved us all.

My aquarium's air pump gurgles, and it shocks me back to the present.

I brace myself against the dresser with my palms, legs weak.

So that's why Morpheus sent the clown, almost an exact replica of the one from the shop. It was a trigger to the memory.

I stumble backward and sit hard on my bed, rattled. Since I was so young when he first started visiting me, and most of his visits took place in dreams, our adventures are stored deep inside my subconscious. He's the master at helping me recall them.

I'm aching to talk to Mom. To find out if she knows anything about the tulgey wood. Maybe she could make sense of why Morpheus wants me to remember it now.

Morpheus and she have a past, too, before his persistence landed her in the asylum. But I don't know if he visited her dreams or if he just contacted her through the insects and flowers. I've often wondered what sorts of memories bind them.

She's never been to Wonderland. The mere thought of going

through the rabbit hole terrifies her—the fear of the unknown. That's why I've never pressured her to tell me her experience. She always seems so fragile. And that's also why it will be up to me to figure out Morpheus's motivations today.

"Use what you have," he said in the memory. *"What we don't."* Once again, he's contradicting himself. If netherlings are as great as he says they are, what could humans have that they're lacking?

I get up and dig through a drawer for Mom's old Lewis Carroll novels, opening the copy of *Through the Looking-Glass, and What Alice Found There.* Unlike Mom's *Alice's Adventures in Wonderland,* where she made notes and comments in the margins—the ink now too blurry to be legible—these pages are clean, old, and yellowed.

I skim over the Jabberwocky poem in search of the tulgey forest, but there's nothing about volatile, gaping mouths in trees that spit things out in nightmarish forms. Flipping to chapter three and the "looking-glass insects," I search for a reference to the looking-glass world or AnyElsewhere, the alternate dimension Morpheus mentioned. Again, nothing.

Finally, I stop at chapter five: "Wool and Water." In it, Alice visits a store. As the scene unravels, I see similarities to the place I visited in my memory, but differences, too. Of course it's not the same as Carroll's version. Things never are. I learned last year that his books are softer, more palatable versions of the real madness of Wonderland.

In the Carroll rendition, a sheep who likes to knit is the store's clerk. In my memory, there's a shopkeeper named Lamb who's fascinated with knitting. The set of bookshelves likes to play tricks just like in the original book, although the tricks I experienced were much more gruesome than the fairy-tale version.

The doorbell rings, and I slam the book shut. I invited Jeb to come by after dinner. Stashing the books in the drawer, I rush into the entryway.

I'm too slow on my still-shaky legs, and Mom gets there first.

Jeb waits under the porch light. We make eye contact; it's obvious he wants to rush in and hold me close, just as I want to run to him. It seems like forever since I've seen him, and the harsh reality is, it could be forever until I see him again.

Mom places herself between us. "I'm sorry, Jebediah. Allie's had enough excitement for one day. You can talk to her on the phone."

I gesture behind her shoulder to get his attention. Holding up five fingers, I mouth the word *Sanctuary*.

He nods my way, politely says good night to my mom, then steps off the porch into the twilight. Mom closes the door and follows me into the living room, where I drag my chemistry book out of my backpack.

"Way to be nice, Mom," I grumble. I don't want to hurt her, but if I don't pretend I'm angry, she might get suspicious.

"Your boyfriend should respect that sometimes you need a break," she answers.

"He's not the only one who should respect that." I rally a convincing scowl. "I'm going to the backyard to study."

Mom and I have spent many afternoons over the past few months working on a lunar garden that shimmers at night. We planted lilies, honeysuckle, and silver licorice. We even have a small fountain that lights up. The flowing water helps to drown out the whispers of bugs and plants. It's one of my favorite places to study and think.

When Mom starts to join me, I turn to face her. "I don't need an escort, *please*."

"You need help with your chemistry vocab," she insists.

I frown. "It's a one-woman job, Mom."

Dad steps from the kitchen with a dish towel on his shoulder. There's still flour all over his clothes. He looks back and forth between us.

I bite my inner cheek, doing my best not to explode. "May I please have some downtime to get my head cleared before school tomorrow?" I direct the question to Dad.

Mom wipes her hands on her apron.

Through the kitchen doorway, the cat clock on the wall ticks away, its tail twitching in time with each second. I can't have her tagging along. There's no way I'm diving into the rabbit hole tomorrow without talking to Jeb first, without being in his arms one more time.

Dad must see how close I am to losing it. "Let her go, Ali-bear," he says. "She hasn't had much time to herself today."

Finally, Mom agrees after insisting I take an extra quilt, "since the evenings are cooler with the wet weather we've been having." But I have other plans for it.

On the patio, strands of twinkle lights glow along a gazebo-like trellis that houses the swing, camouflaging it from the back window.

I fluff up the pillows on the porch swing and strategically place the blanket that's already there over them. Then I balance my book open on top, so if Mom peeks out through the window, she'll see the silhouette through the trellis and think it's me.

Quilt in hand, I take the path away from the porch. The fragrances of flowers are magnified by the damp evening air. Moonlight and the twinkle lights reflect off the pale blossoms and foliage. Everything is relaxed and dreamy. The opposite of how I feel.

I spread the quilt in the darkest corner of the yard, out of view of the back door and window. This is the one patch of ground that isn't overgrown with flowers or plants. A weeping willow's canopy hangs over the fence that separates Jeb's backyard and ours, creating a cave. Mom tried to plant things here a few times, but when they never blossomed, she decided there was too much shade.

Little does she know it's because Jeb and I have spent so many nights under this tree—sneaking out after everyone went to bed—to talk, to count stars, and to do other things . . .

It's our sanctuary.

We're the ones who stifled the seedlings. And I have no regrets.

I lie down and wrap my fingers around Jeb's locket at my neck.

Moonlight streams through the cluster of branches overhead, and the water fountain gurgles. Everything about this place reminds me why I chose to stay in this world last year, why I love being human. And Morpheus wants me to leave it all behind for a battle in another realm.

I'm starting to realize he's right. If it means saving those I love, I have to go.

But first I'm going to tell Jeb. I want him in on this. Maybe because I know he'll try to convince me it's okay not to leave. Not for something so dangerous. Not when I might not make it back.

I want to hear that it's okay to be a coward. Even if I won't believe it.

My hand brushes the key necklace, and the image of a crumbling Wonderland blinks through my mind. My heart hurts—a tearing feeling, as if it's being ripped down the middle.

A cricket bursts into song somewhere to my left. Between chirps, it taunts me. *Courage, Alyssa. Many changes coming . . . mad, mad changes. They'll bring out the queen in you.*

I freeze in place, fingers clamped on both necklaces. A clunk on the other side of the fence silences the cricket. Leaves shake above my head, and several flutter down to tickle my face. I brush them aside to study the shadowy silhouette outside the canopy.

"You look incredible in the moonlight." Jeb's voice, low and silky, is a balm, soothing away the foreboding echoes of the cricket's message.

I tuck the necklaces under my tunic's collar, voice caught in my throat.

Branches part to reveal his face and disheveled hair. He's wearing a sexy, sideways smile. "I know, I'm two minutes late. I deserve a spanking."

I snort, calmed by his teasing. "You should be so lucky." *I can do this.* I can tell him anything. It's Jeb, after all.

He lets himself drop, hanging on to a branch with one hand so he can flip around, feet first. It's a trick he used when we would play king of the mountain in our earlier summers.

In one graceful movement, he straddles me, his weight pressing me into the soft quilt. "This okay? Am I too heavy?"

I tighten my arms around him when he tries to balance on his elbows and knees. "Stay just like you are." He settles back into place, and I twitch my muscles in contentment. Nothing feels as perfect or as safe as being breathless under him.

His hand glides along my rib cage and stops at each bone, like he's checking to make sure I'm in one piece. "Finally, I have you all to myself," he whispers, breath hot on my face.

I bask in the scent of his cologne. "Jeb, I need to tell you something."

"Mmm, can't it wait, skater girl?" His lips nuzzle my neck.

Hearing my nickname breaks me. I pull up his head to kiss him. Just once, before I completely shatter his world. My fingers wind through his hair. He rolls us so I'm on top, and we lie like that: my body imprinting on his, mouths trailing necks, ears, faces. We kiss under the stars, outside of the world's reach, and don't stop until we're both breathless.

Panting, we draw back and stare at each other—overwhelmed by the drama and emotions of the past few days. And it's about to get so much worse.

"So . . ." Jeb breaks the silence. "Is this your way of distracting me so you can steal my king?"

I almost smile at the memory. "Am I that transparent?"

He pulls me to lie beside him on the quilt, brushing hair from my face. "Can't believe we wasted so many summers playing chess under this tree while your dad was at work."

"You're just mad because I always won," I say.

He rests his head on his outstretched arm. "It was worth it. I got to tickle you afterward." He traces my lips with a fingertip. "I liked having an excuse to touch you."

I kiss his finger. "Even back then you thought about touching me?"

"Spending every day surrounded by sketches you inspired left little time to think of anything else."

I suppress a wave of longing for the simplicity of the life we once lived. I had no idea at the time how easy it was.

How am I supposed to tell him I'm leaving? How do we say good-bye to moments like these?

I skim my fingernail along his ear, searching for the words.

He shivers and smiles. "Speaking of my artwork," he says before

I can speak, "we need to talk about Ivy. We were wrong about how much she's willing to pay."

I tighten my lips at hearing the heiress's name. No wonder he was so evasive on the phone. He was counting on that money to help us get started in London.

This is the perfect opportunity. I'll tell him it doesn't matter. That money is the least of what's standing in the way of our future now.

I open my mouth, but Jeb beats me to the punch again. "She's offering ten thousand more," he says as he sits up and brushes leaves from his T-shirt and jeans.

I scramble to sit beside him, mind spinning. My tunic slides off my shoulder, leaving it cool and exposed. "*Twenty thousand bucks? For one fairy painting?*"

Jeb glides a fingertip along my shoulder. "Not exactly. She wants a series . . . three new fairy paintings. *Sexier* ones."

When Jeb paints me, he poses me, evaluates every contour of my body, studies the way the light and shadows skim my skin, which often leads to things other than work. I've missed those sessions. It would be so perfect to start them again. The thought makes me ache even more not to leave.

I swallow, fighting to say good-bye, wishing I didn't have to.

Jeb leans down to kiss my bare shoulder—tender, warm, and sweet—then covers my skin with my sleeve. "You need to know, there's one condition," he says, leveling his gaze to mine. "Ivy wants me to paint a collection of her. *She* wants to be my muse."

℘UPPETS

I shove aside all thoughts of Wonderland and magic wars. "Ivy wants to model for you?"

Jeb was bound to get commissioned for customized portraits eventually, but I wasn't prepared for that to happen *today*.

He watches me in silence.

"What do you mean, *sexier* paintings?" I press.

"Well, she has this amazing costume. She wore it when we met at the studio. It's a little revealing, but . . ." Jeb scrapes his palm down his chin. "It's not a nude series or anything. I told her I wasn't down with that."

I'm grateful for his chivalry, but it's a small comfort. The thought of him being tempted day in and day out by a sophisticated, experienced, half-naked woman makes my stomach churn.

"Al, you just need to meet her. You'll feel better when you see how serious she is about the art. She has some really cool ideas . . . eccentric even beyond the costumes. She's an old soul, like us."

Old soul. Bad enough that she's beautiful and rich. He's not supposed to like her personality, too.

My heart sinks so low I would trip over it if I was walking. That possessive chant resurfaces: *mine mine mine.*

The leaves around us begin to flutter, even though the wind isn't blowing. I concentrate on the willow branches, sending everything I'm feeling into them. They curl around Jeb's shoulders, as if to hold on to him—a puppet's strings to make him do my bidding.

He jumps, and the limbs loosen. Looking up at the swaying canopy, he frowns. He doesn't realize I'm causing the motion, that something is waking inside of me, something I've kept hidden for months. Something I don't want to suppress right now, because the feral anger makes my insecurities seem conquerable, which in turn makes me feel stronger.

As I notice the bewilderment on his face, ice-cold shame washes over me. I stanch my anger and jealousy. The branches go still again.

Jeb's gaze meets mine. "Did you see that?"

My heart pounds. "See what?"

He rubs his hair. "I could've sworn . . ." He stops himself. "Must've been a gust of wind."

I have no response. I'm horrified by how easily my darker side bubbled over—by how much I wanted to overpower Jeb. To control him.

He must see the shame clouding my features because he takes

my hand and laces our fingers together. "I'm sorry to spring this Ivy thing on you. But I need to give her an answer. She's only here through this week. If I turn her down, it could affect my reputation." He studies our linked hands. "Collectors and reviewers might think I'm a one-trick pony."

"I get it," I mumble, trying not to let my emotions control me again.

I wish he'd at least *pretend* this was a hard choice for him, but his expression is hopeful. It's obvious he wants me to say I'm cool with all of this, whether for the money or for the artistic growth. But it hurts, even though I know it shouldn't. I've always been his inspiration, and this just proves he no longer needs me . . . at least artistically.

To be honest, it seems like he's been growing away from me for a while now, and that's what really hurts.

The twinkle lights over the porch swing blink on and off, my parents' subtle hint that I quit studying and come inside. Their timing sucks.

Jeb lifts me to my feet, leans in, and kisses my forehead. "We'll talk more tomorrow." I take a step back, but he grabs the neck of my tunic and the heart-shaped locket underneath to keep me close. "Hey, don't you forget that I love you."

"I love you, too." I hold his hand at my chest. The leaves rattle around us again before I catch myself.

After glaring overhead, Jeb gives me a lingering hug and kiss, then stretches to pull himself into the tree.

"Wait." I snag the waistband of his jeans before he can settle in the branches. None of this has to happen. I can get his mind off Ivy and this commission for good by showing him the truth about Wonderland, about me. "Can you pick me up from school tomorrow?"

Hanging above me, he frowns. "I'm not sure I can leave work that early."

I grind my teeth against the disappointment.

"Okay," he says, as if to placate me. "Okay, I'll find a way."

"Good. Because I'm ready to show you my mosaics."

I only hope he's ready to see them.

✽·I·✽

Thursday morning, I don't take the time to argue with Mom. I choose an outfit she'll approve of—a two-layer organza petticoat skirt that hangs past the knees of my pinstriped leggings—and step into first period as the five-minute warning bell rings. I finish my chemistry test before class is half over, which leaves an excruciating two more periods to sweat over what I'll say to Morpheus about my decision not to leave the human realm until I fix things with Jeb.

Morpheus isn't going to make it easy for me.

Several times between classes, I pass him in the halls with his harem. He walks by without a word, snubbing me, yet each time manages to rake his arm across mine or brush our hands. It's painful in the strangest way.

Finally, fourth period rolls around, and I shut myself in the abandoned girls' bathroom to wait for him. The bell rings, and soon the hall empties.

Sunlight dapples the floor through the hopper window, but the room around me is gray and still. Today the bugs have been relentless in their whispers, as if the cricket from last night is leading them in a revolt:

They're here, Alyssa. They don't belong . . . send them back.

I lean against the sink. "Who?" I whisper aloud, frustrated with the obscure warnings.

As I'm waiting for a response, I hear a rustle inside one of the half-closed stalls. I inhale a startled breath, drop my backpack, and lean down to look under the metal door, careful not to let my hair touch the damp tiles.

"Is someone there?"

No answer and no cowboy boots. Unless he's crouched atop the toilet, it's not Morpheus. Steeling myself, I swing the door open.

A gurgling hiss greets me along with the distorted face of the clown. It's toy-size again and standing on the toilet lid. I screech and stumble back, tripping over my backpack. My elbow knocks the paper towel dispenser open. Squares of brown paper flutter down all around me.

Hopping to the floor, the demented toy scurries after me, razor-sharp teeth bared and snapping. One of its shoes slips on a paper towel and it falls. It crawls toward me instead, never slowing. Heart pounding, I look around for something to use as a weapon—to protect myself from that snarling mouth.

My backpack is too far; there's nothing else within reach. My gaze catches on the dingy white ceiling and the rusty stains branching out like veins. I calm myself, breathing deeply, and imagine the stains are made of twine.

Swerving to avoid the rabid toy, I stay focused on the stains. They begin to peel from the ceiling and drape down. Concentrating harder, I coax them around the clown's arms and legs, stringing it up like a marionette.

I control *it* now.

Fear fading to anger, I make the creepy thing dance in midair, then envision the strings spinning up the toy, trapping it in a cocoon of yellow-brown stains. With a screech, the clown uses its cello's handle to snap the bindings before I can enclose it, then scrambles toward the bathroom door. The toy slips out into the hall, and the door swings shut.

I slide along the wall to the floor, shaking. My rapid pulse beats in my neck. The stains, neglected by my thoughts, retract back into the ceiling, finding their permanent places once more.

I'm shocked, stunned, and ecstatic all at once. The moment I visualized exactly what I wanted the ceiling stains to become, my powers came through in less than a heartbeat. I'm getting better at this.

But why should I have to draw upon that magic in my world? Why is Morpheus's clown still here? Didn't it already serve its purpose?

My cheeks flame and I clap cold palms over them, trying to subdue the adrenaline rush.

Several minutes pass and the door to the hallway begins to open slowly. I fold my knees to my chest, preparing to use my magic again.

The toe of a cowboy boot comes into view, and Morpheus steps in.

Relief washes over me, chased by a flash of annoyance.

Seeing me surrounded by paper towels on the floor, Morpheus lifts his eyebrows. "Building a nest?" he asks. "There's no need to start acting like a bird simply because you have a propensity for flying."

"Just . . . shut up." I struggle to get to my feet, but my soles keep slipping on paper towels. He reaches out a hand. I reluctantly take it and stand.

Before I can break away, he clasps my fingers and rotates my arm in the dim light, observing my sparkly skin. It's a visual manifestation of my magic . . . a result of using my powers.

"Well, well. What have you been up to?" he asks, grinning. There's a glint of pride behind his teasing eyes.

"As if you don't know." I escape his grip, frowning at him as I check over my shoulder in the mirror to be sure my eye patches haven't appeared. "What are you trying to prove?" I ask, relieved to see I still look normal although I feel anything but. "Why do you keep bringing that thing around?"

Silence. His confused frown in the reflection makes me furious. He has the ability to look completely innocent even when I know he's as pure as a pirate.

I turn to face him. "If you didn't bring it here, you had to at least see it."

"It," he says.

"That freak-show toy!"

He smirks, a familiar look on Finley's unfamiliar face. "Well, seeing as there are boxes all over your school with toys inside, I should say yes. Yes, I have seen a toy or twenty."

"I'm talking about the clown you sent me at the hospital. Don't pretend you had nothing to do with that."

"I didn't send you any toy at the hospital."

I growl. Of course he's not going to admit sending it, any more than he would admit bringing it here.

I push by him, glancing out the door. First one side of the hall, then the other. There's no one and nothing besides the charity boxes. I start to step out to dig through the donations. If I shove the proof in his face, he'll have to come clean.

Morpheus grips my elbow and drags me back inside, putting his body between me and the door. "You're not going anywhere. We have mosaics to decipher and a war to win."

I glare at him. "I don't have the mosaics."

"Pardon?" Morpheus asks, the anger in his voice edging me closer to the wall. Paper towels slide under my feet. "I gave you one thing to do. *One.* You've no idea how important they are to our cause."

Squaring my shoulders in determination, I shake my head. "Doesn't matter. I'm not leaving yet anyway. So stop bullying me."

"Bullying?" His true face appears, barely visible beneath Finley's features. The jewels under his eyes flash, as if someone implanted multicolored fiber-optic lights beneath his skin. The dark markings they're connected to are nothing but faint shadows, an echo of the brilliant weirdness that is Morpheus.

"There's no need for me to bully. You *are* coming to Wonderland. Your heart, your soul—they're already there. Try as you might, you will never be able to remove yourself from a world that beckons to your very blood. From a power that begs to be unleashed."

I cringe, thinking of my bizarre dance with the clown minutes ago and my magical mishap last night with the willow branches.

"You will meet me after school," he continues, "in the north parking lot. And bring your mosaics. After we decipher them, we'll decide our next step. No more excuses. You belong to Wonderland now."

I lift my chin. "I belong to myself, and I'm not leaving until I'm ready."

Morpheus scowls, and the hint of jewels blinks a brassy orange—daring and impatient. He studies Jeb's necklace. "You belong to yourself, aye? You expect me to believe this isn't about your human toy?"

"No, this is about the Shop of Human Eccentricities."

His smudged eyes narrow, lit by a glint of interest. "You had a memory, did you?"

"As if you're surprised. You triggered it."

"Ah," he says and pulls back with a dreamy look on his face, neither denying nor confirming my observation. "Those were good times. Mutants, butterfly wings, and tulgey shelves."

I shoot him an irritated glare. "That's just it. What do tulgey shelves have to do with anything? Why that memory?"

He shakes his head. "Why are you asking *me*? Your subconscious was the one that chose to remember it. Perhaps it had less to do with the shelves than how you were triumphant against them. Hmm?"

"Stop dancing around my questions. I want to know . . . since when is being only half of something the best of anything?"

His mouth purses. "Being a full-blood netherling does make Red superior," he agrees, and I suppress a flush of annoyance at his egotism. "But weaknesses can also be advantages in the right hands. Pure netherlings can only use what is in front of us, as it is. Queen Red can animate loose vines, chains, other things. But *you* can create life out of the lifeless by making something entirely different. As a human child, innocent and filled with fancies, you learned to use your imagination. That's something we don't experience."

My head's spinning, trying to absorb his explanation. It fits perfectly with what just happened . . . how I crafted marionette strings out of water stains to trap the toy clown. Also, the metal butterflies I formed in my memory. "I've never understood that. Why netherlings don't have typical childhoods." My statement is more rhetorical than anything. I know better than to expect an explanation.

Morpheus's dark eyes deepen with a wistfulness I've never seen before. "Perhaps that's a discussion we'll have one day. For now, just know that I have faith you can meet Red head-on and win. When have I ever put you in a situation that you couldn't handle?"

I open my mouth to start a list, but he shushes me with a fingertip on my lower lip. My jaw clamps tight as I consider whether it would be worth it to bite him. The one thing that stops me is I'm pretty sure he would like it.

"You always come through victorious," he insists. "With panache."

"No thanks to you," I grumble.

He clicks his tongue. "Stop being cranky. You know what that does to me. Makes it impossible to concentrate." He holds my gaze just long enough for me to see the faint sparkle of fuchsia under his eyes. The color of affection. "The biggest disadvantage to your human side is that you're a slave to your mortal affections and inhibitions. That's what we need to work on before we're off to Wonderland."

My guard goes up—a knee-jerk reaction. "And how do you plan to work on it?"

"Let me worry about the logistics."

At that moment, the bathroom door swings open.

Morpheus draws me close, hands on my waist. I struggle to pull away, but it's too late. Although the light shining from the hall is blinding, I can make out a girl's silhouette and blond hair.

"M?" Taelor's voice breaks the silence. "Why did you want me to meet you here—" She steps into the dimness, a look of shock on her face as she recognizes me.

Morpheus's lips turn upward in a smile of pure satisfaction.

Blood rushes to my face.

He set me up.

Just before I break free he manages to kiss my forehead.

I wipe it away with the back of my hand. A furious scream burns inside my chest, but I stifle it. All I need is to draw a bigger audience. Morpheus would love that.

"I hate you," I mouth silently.

"Sorry, beautiful," Morpheus says to Taelor without breaking our gaze. "Alyssa followed me in. We had some reacquainting to do."

Taelor's mouth gapes. Shock and hatred flash in her brown eyes.

I grab my backpack and shove past, pausing in the hallway to face her. "It's not what you think."

Her mouth finally closes enough to form a sullen smirk. "It never is with you, is it? You have Jeb so fooled. Perfect, innocent little *skater girl*." There's so much poison dripping from her words that I could swear she's been soaking her tongue in arsenic.

Morpheus looms behind her—a silhouette of wings and bravado only I can see. He offers a half bow, the master puppeteer acknowledging his puppet. Taelor's been waiting for a year to get back at me for stealing her boyfriend, and Morpheus has found the perfect way to ensure nothing interferes with his plans to make a martyr of me.

My chest burns. I have no way to convince Taelor of my innocence, so I start for the stairs and concentrate on the forward momentum of each foot, blocking out their conversation. I don't have to hear to know that Taelor is grilling Morpheus for details about how well "acquainted" we are. He couldn't have found a better unwitting accomplice, or one with a bigger mouth.

By the end of lunch, our tryst in the bathroom will be all over school. By the end of the day, Jenara will hear of it. And by tonight, Jeb will know all about my dirty little secret that never was.

BATS IN THE BELFRY

During eighth-period art class, we're working in groups to make decorations for prom. The goal is to create an "enchanted forest" setting for the refreshment area and picture booth.

One student's family owns an apple orchard and provided almost two dozen six-foot "trees" formed of antlerlike branches. For the past two weeks we've been spray-painting them white, sprinkling them with glitter, then transferring them into matching ceramic pots filled with clear glass gemstones to keep them upright.

It was a fun project. Until today.

After what Taelor saw in the bathroom, I can't bring myself to join any of the groups. This is what I get for being a recluse. No one knows me well enough—*really* knows me—to jump to my defense when rumors abound.

I feign a headache because of the spray-paint fumes, and while I'm slouched alone at my table in the corner, I text Jeb. It's against school policy to use your cell during class, but Mr. Mason has stepped out for a minute. His temporary substitute is either terrified of high schoolers or oblivious, because I'm not the only one with my phone in my hand.

I try a little damage control, texting Jeb that I had a weird encounter with the exchange student and not to flip out until I can explain.

I send Jenara a similar message.

She and Corbin ditched school right after lunch to attend his mom's interior design showcase. But it's just a matter of time until someone texts or calls her with the lowdown. Better she hear it from me first.

A fly buzzes around the room and settles on my shoulder. *Fix things, Alyssa.* Its whisper is a tickle in my ear. *The flowers have been compromised. You must stop them.*

I swish the bug away gently. I'm fed up with their obscure riddles. I have enough to worry about.

A few giggles break out at the table across from mine. Four junior girls avert their eyes when I look their way, pretending to focus on the lanterns they're making of stiffened fabric doilies and white LED tea lights. As the girls form domes by tying two doilies together, their giggles escalate. It's the same group that was ogling Jeb last Friday when he came to pick me up on his bike. I'm not sure if they're talking about what Morpheus and I supposedly did, or what an idiot I am to screw around on an incredible guy like my boyfriend. Either way, it's obvious I'm the topic of conversation, just like I have been in every class since fifth period.

My neck and cheeks burn.

The phone hums between my fingers. I click on Jeb's response.

Uh . . . encounter? Details plz.

He sounds either jealous or rushed.

Biting my lower lip, I type the lie I worked up last period: *Turns out his family is good friends with the London Liddells. I'll explain everything when you pick me up.*

I'll do better than explain. I'm going to make a mosaic in front of him. Let him watch my blood's magic in action. Then, once he's past the freak-out stage, maybe he can help me figure out a way to avoid facing Red and still protect Wonderland and the people we love.

My phone buzzes again. *Can't pick U up 2day after all. Interview was rescheduled for this afternoon. Get a ride w/Jen?*

No. I want to scream, to tell him I really need him to drop everything and come see me *now*, but before I can respond at all, the classroom door opens and Mr. Mason comes in. Along with half my classmates, I scramble to hide my phone. Mr. Mason talks quietly to the sub, then sends him on his way.

After sitting at his desk, Mr. Mason fishes an art supply catalog out of a drawer. Against every instinct to hunch at my table and blend into the surroundings, I raise my hand. From behind his pinkish lenses, he spots me and waves me forward.

I start toward the front of the room. A hissing sound stops me in my tracks. It sounds just like the clown in the girls' bathroom. Spine rigid, I turn to see two guys off in the far corner, spray-painting one of the "trees."

I continue forward. My stomach churns as the girls resume their giggling. The gazes on my back weigh heavy and make my steps slow and awkward.

When I arrive at the desk, Mr. Mason looks up and adjusts his glasses. "Alyssa. I've been meaning to speak to you about your mosaics."

Nodding, I gesture to his cabinet. "Right. Should we wrap them in butcher paper for the trip home?"

His jaw drops, but then he regains his composure and stands on his side of the desk, hands splayed next to the catalog. "Your mom didn't tell you?"

"Tell me what?"

"She called me from the hospital after your accident. She'd heard about your mosaic series and wanted to see them, so I took them to her Saturday evening."

My pulse pounds beneath my jawline. *Who told Mom about my artwork?* My blood shuttles even faster to imagine her seeing Queen Red's vicious slaughter in the scenes.

"So my mom has them?"

"Well, she only has three. They were too heavy for me to carry from my car all at once. When I came back for the rest . . . they were gone. Stolen."

A sense of violation chills me. I think of the clown and my sedated, web-filled dream. Morpheus had to be behind all of that, whether he confirms or denies it. So he must've been at the hospital, spying from the shadows, pulling strings. He could've heard Mr. Mason and Mom's call. Which means he stole those three mosaics and already knows that my mom has the other ones. So he asked me to bring them to him for nothing. He's messing with my mind again.

I'm done playing his games. Unless he comes clean with everything, I'm not going anywhere but home today.

"I can't apologize enough," Mr. Mason says. "I don't know how it happened. The car is new. Its alarm system is top-notch. But somehow the thief got the door open without setting it off." His cheeks redden as he picks up the catalog. "I've been looking through all my supply lists, trying to find more of those red-lined gems. I want to buy you some replacements. It can't make up for all your hard work . . . but . . ."

The bell rings, causing me to jump.

My classmates gather their books and bags and scramble out the door. A heavy knot forms in my gut, like I've swallowed a huge rock. All I can think is: *Mom knows*. She knows my head is still in Wonderland, yet she hasn't said a word.

I take the catalog from Mr. Mason and lay it facedown on his desk. "You'll never find gems to replace the ones I used." In a daze, I walk to my table and grab my backpack. "But don't worry. Making those mosaics wasn't as hard as you think."

I leave before he can respond.

There's a buzz in my ears, as if all the bugs hidden inside every crevice of tile and under every locker are talking at once. The sensation fills my head and muffles sounds as I walk through the crowded halls.

Taelor and her crew glare at me when I pass, but it's as if an invisible wall stands between us. Slammed lockers swish like paper fans; chatter and laughter are as small and insignificant as the squeaks of a mouse. I'm removed from everything.

All except my anger . . . Morpheus and my mom are both hiding things from me.

I don't know who told her about the mosaics, but one thing I *do* know is that if Mom's emotionally and mentally stable enough to see my gory artwork and then hide that knowledge without going into a full-scale meltdown, she's not as fragile as I thought.

She and I are going to have a talk about her past *today*.

I step outside, grateful for the warm wind and sun on my face. The buzz in my head gets quieter and fades to white noise. It's like the bugs are preoccupied with something else. Or maybe they're finally giving me a reprieve.

I purposely take the long way around, which costs me a good eight minutes, so the lot's almost deserted. Morpheus is waiting where he said he'd be, next to the Dumpsters, where the cool kids avoid parking.

It looks like he's as much of a social pariah as I am after our rumored bathroom interlude, because he's completely alone, too. Though he doesn't seem to mind. When he sees me, he adjusts a pair of sunglasses, and a taunting grin spreads across his borrowed face.

I think of poor Finley and shudder to imagine the horrors he must be experiencing now, coming down off his high in Wonderland. At least he has Ivory to comfort him.

Morpheus gestures a tattooed forearm at the car behind him.

"A modified Mercedes-Benz Gullwing," he says. "Never seen one of these, I'd venture."

I come to a standstill about three feet away. There's no reason to be impressed. I doubt he paid a penny for it. He probably got inside the owner's head and just drove it off the lot.

The car's body is sporty and black without any sheen, as if someone took carbon paper and rubbed it over the paint. Even the hubcaps and rims are matte black. A peek in the tinted windows reveals red leather seats and upholstery. I pretend not to notice that this ride fits Morpheus to a tee: beautifully gothic, eccentric, and intense.

If I'm going to get the truth about everything from him, I have to get the upper hand. Morpheus thrives on attention, whether it's positive or negative. He revels in my hatred of him, just as he revels in my atypical bouts of adoration. What he can't stomach is indifference. It makes him needy and, in turn, vulnerable.

So that's exactly what he's going to get from me. Complete and utter disinterest.

I make it a point not to meet his gaze and focus instead on the glare in the center of the hood where one vertical strip shimmers like polished onyx. My lips press tightly shut so I don't scream about the mosaics he's had all along.

With my less-than-stellar reaction, Morpheus's smirk fades, and satisfaction unfurls inside my chest. Wearing a downtrodden grimace, he presses a button on the key chain.

The locks clack and pop open. Both doors glide upward as if on a current of air. Once they're fully open, they spread into the sky like wings. The car looks uncannily alive, like a bat in flight . . . or a giant moth.

In that moment, my ruse is forgotten.

Wings.

Morpheus flashes a magnificent smile. A pantomime of his own wings appears—a filmy black haze, almost like smoke—spreading behind him in an elegant arc that both mirrors and overshadows the doors.

"I'll let you drive, luv." His deep voice drizzles through me, liquid temptation. He holds out the key chain and raises his brows expectantly beneath his hat's brim. The jewels under his eyes light up in faint gold shimmers at the edge of his sunglasses.

All I can think of is finding a country road and picking up speed until every tree rushes by and Newton's law of acceleration presses against my chest like cinder blocks. Then I'll open the windows so the wind can rip through me.

Just like flying.

A flicker of excitement ignites in my veins, spurred by the darkness inside me: the darkness that likes to ride Jeb's bike for its power and freedom and sensuality, the darkness that makes the nodules on my shoulder blades itch in anticipation. It's the side I rarely let out to play.

Forget Wonderland, my missing mosaics, Mom's lies, and Morpheus's games. The bad girl wants to play right now. I step up and snag the keys out of Morpheus's hand. "Where to?" I ask.

He smirks. "You decide. Somewhere private, where we can read the mosaics."

I clench my jaw, ready to play my ace. "Which mosaics? The ones my mom has or the ones you're hiding?"

He drags off his sunglasses and answers with a blank stare. It's pretty impressive. He actually appears bewildered.

"You must be certifiable to think I wouldn't figure it out," I say. Before I can step around him to the car, he catches my waist and spins me so my backpack presses his chest.

He pulls me close by my bag's straps and leans down to whisper, "Poor idea of a joke, luv." His hot breath makes the skin beneath my hair tingle. He slips the straps from my shoulders, and I turn around to face him.

"Remember my invisible box, Morpheus." I cross my arms.

"Remember my human name, Alyssa." He frowns and bounces the backpack as if to gauge what's inside. His frown transforms into a worried scowl. "They aren't here."

"Stop with the fake surprise, *M*." I sidestep him, climbing into the driver's seat. The warm leather wraps me in luxury, as if it were made to fit the contours of my body. I click the seat belt into place, catching part of my too-long skirt in the latch. I attempt to open the seat belt to free it, but the bunched-up fabric causes the button to jam. I refuse to ask Morpheus for help. I'll just take care of it later.

The car smells like hookah smoke, which only feeds my annoyance. I insert the key and twist it just enough for the dashboard to light up, and then I acclimate myself with the instrument panel and all its shiny silver gauges and techno-features.

After shoving the backpack into the small space behind my seat, Morpheus crouches next to me. His soles scrape the asphalt as he holds the door frame above his head. "Are you seriously saying that half of your artwork has gone missing?"

I sigh and turn on the radio, watching a display screen the size of an iPad blink to life. "Oh, please. We both know you were at the hospital, spying on everyone."

An alternative rock song thunders through the speakers. The rhythm is skittish and fierce, echoing my mood. I punch a button to lower the volume. "You waited for Mr. Mason to go inside with the first set of mosaics. Then you took the others from his car. Who else could break into the locks without triggering the alarm?"

"Blast it!" Morpheus snarls. Air gusts across me as he shoves away from the car and stands. I watch him rush around to the passenger side until my gaze catches on the faux raccoon tail hanging over the rearview mirror; the stripes flicker from black and red to orange and gray as it swings gently in the breeze coming through the open doors. The tail looks vaguely familiar. I start to reach for it, but

Morpheus drops his long body into the passenger seat and activates the doors to shut. Then he takes off his hat and tosses his sunglasses onto the dashboard.

I don't even have a chance to react before he presses my fingers around the key and forces me to start the car. The motor roars to life with a purr through my calves and thighs, a giant beast ready to perform at my beck and call.

I stare at Morpheus, confused.

"We're paying your mum a visit," he says. "Now drive."

I'm not going to argue with that. I want to talk to my mom about the mosaics, too. Although I'm not sure it should be with Morpheus around. Even if she's less fragile than she looks, I don't know if she can handle seeing him.

I exit the parking lot and take the main street that runs through a residential neighborhood. In about a half mile, it will open up to a suburban housing development surrounded by winding dirt roads and a railroad track. It's the long way to my duplex community.

This route will buy me extra time to grill Morpheus about my magical artwork and why it's so important to him and Wonderland's decay.

Air-conditioning blasts through the vents and flutters my hair. I adjust the rearview mirror to reflect the passenger seat so I can keep an eye on Morpheus. The color-changing raccoon tail swings in and out of my peripheral vision as I drive.

I stop at a four-way intersection with no one else around and turn all my attention to my passenger. "So you're trying to tell me you have nothing to do with my missing mosaics."

He doesn't answer. Instead, he looks straight ahead and holds his hat on his lap, muscles tensed. He's definitely hiding something.

Still staring at him, I start to ease off the brake. He puts a hand on my knee to stall me and gestures in front of the car.

A kid on a tricycle pedals through the crosswalk. My heartbeat shoots into overdrive and a jolt of alarm crashes over me, making my arms heavy on the steering wheel. I would've hit that little boy if Morpheus hadn't intervened. I could've killed him.

"I don't get it," I whisper, my pulse slowing to its normal pace as the boy pedals away safely on the sidewalk.

"Get what, luv?" Morpheus asks, setting his inky gaze on me.

"You could've let me plow over that little boy. You don't care anything about him. He's just a worthless human soul. Like Finley."

He schools his expression to an indifferent scowl. "I didn't wish to muck up my car."

So stunned by his callousness, I momentarily forget I'm at a four-way stop. A Chevy honks from the stop sign opposite us, and I wave the driver on. "You really have no compassion, do you?" I frown at Morpheus's reflection.

He looks back at me in the mirror and returns my frown. His palm is still on my knee, heavy and warm through my leggings.

"You can let go now," I press.

He tightens the clasp of his fingertips before withdrawing his hand. "Pay attention. Driving is a privilege."

"Whatevs, *Grandma M*." I rub my leg to erase the echo of his touch. "I've been behind the wheel a lot longer than you. And I'm not dead yet."

I roll through the stop sign, headed toward the housing development, a plan taking form in my mind. The knowledge that Morpheus loves his car more than a human life has just given me my upper hand.

A sign appears: LUXURY AND AFFORDABILITY: AUTUMN VINTAGE MANORS. Several skeletal roofs jab the sky on the other side of a deserted construction site. A train whistle bellows in the distance . . . a sad, lonely sound.

"This isn't the way to your house." Morpheus's observation lifts my mouth to a smirk.

"Yeah? Well, I've decided to play a little game," I say, baiting him. "You always told me games were fun." Taking the first dirt road, I pick up speed.

Morpheus clicks his seat belt into place and grips the dash, knuckles bulging and white. "I don't much fancy this one." The jewels under his eyes flash faintly—a deep turquoise, the color of turmoil.

I press the gas harder. The bar on the speedometer snaps from twenty-three m.p.h. to sixty-seven in under a minute. Dust swirls all around. I've been down this road with Jeb on his motorcycle countless times. There are rarely any cops here. It's deserted, and a straight shoot for several miles until you hit the railroad tracks. Perfect terrain for driving like a maniac. I give the gas another punch and shoot the speedometer to eighty.

"Bloody hell, Alyssa!" Morpheus grips the console with one hand and the door with another. "Watch out!"

We hit a pothole and the car bounces. My stomach flips as we spin on the dirt. My dad taught me to drive on ice, and that training kicks in. I turn into the swerve. In a matter of seconds I'm in control of the car again.

I try not to smirk at the sound of Morpheus's gasps for air.

My foot gets heavier, and we clip another pothole. The front bumper dips, and we slash through tall weeds. Thistles scrape the car's underside like fingernails as we jostle along the uneven surface.

Morpheus yelps.

Once we're back on the road, I catch a glimpse of him in the rearview. His beloved hat is crushed against his chest between his fists. As much as he's worried about dents and dings, why hasn't he made me pull over and taken the keys?

Then it hits me: It's not concern for the car causing this reaction. It's pure terror.

That's why he lets other people drive the Mercedes: He's afraid to. While imitating Finley, he can't use his wings or transform into a moth. Never once has he had to rely on anything but himself for transportation, and he has no control of his momentum inside a car. It probably feels like he's locked in a tin can, barreling down a cliff, and he can't do a thing to stop it. So . . . better to leave the driving to someone who knows what they're doing.

For the first time since I can remember, Morpheus is totally out of his element. For the first time since I remember, *I'm* the one in control.

All those years he teased and pushed me when we would go flying, all those times he made me confront gruesome creatures and frightening situations until I was paralyzed with fear. He showed me no mercy.

It's time to serve up some crow and get some answers.

Pressing on the gas, I smile—a Cheshire smile.

Brown dust pelts the windows and the sides of the car—loud enough to sound like pea-size hail. Flipping on the windshield wipers to cut through the grit, I let out a hoot.

"This ride is spectacular! Right, Morpheus? Just like flying, right?" He tenses next to me, trying to hide his panic. I glance at him and he's practically green; even the jewels beneath his skin flash a putrid, sickly tone. "What's the matter? Stomach a little kicky? Didn't you always say it's the kicks that let you know you're alive?"

"Blast it! Would you watch what you're doing!" he screeches over the sound of the train whistle getting louder in the distance.

I laugh, returning my attention to the road, where the fork up ahead leads over the railroad crossing and straight to my neighborhood. "Tell you what. I'll take it nice and easy the rest of the way under two conditions. First, you're going to clear everything up with Jeb about what happened today in the girls' bathroom. And second, I want to know the truth about my mosaics. Otherwise . . ." I give the gas a push, and the car leaps forward.

"All right." He smashes the hat with shaky fingers.

"Both of my conditions. Vow it."

He presses his palm to his chest, repeats my conditions, then finalizes the vow with a snarled, "On my life-magic."

"Perfect. Now, about the mosaics."

He slaps his thigh with his hat. "Do you honestly think I'm the only one with the ability to slip undetected into a car with its alarm on? Someone else wants those mosaics as much as we do. She'll do anything to get them."

"She?" I shake my head and slow down to forty miles per hour. "My mom? But she was in my hospital room. How could she . . . ?"

Placing the crumpled hat in his lap, Morpheus gives me a glare that could put molten lava to shame. Then his gaze drifts to the key around my neck.

"Red," I murmur, my temples pounding at the thought. "She's here. She's in the human realm."

Mirror, Mirror

Morpheus looks nauseated again, but this time it has nothing to do with my driving.

"If Red is indeed here," he says, "things are direr than I thought. Both kingdoms have the portals guarded against her. For her to come through, she must be holding a palace hostage—either the Red or the White. Which alters the balance of everything. And if she's seen part of what you know, she's going to want the rest of those mosaics to complete the puzzle. We have to ensure she doesn't get them. We can't let her see your visions first."

I force my eyes to stay forward, only peeking sporadically at the rearview. "My *visions*? What are you talking about?"

He grinds his teeth, and the scar at Finley's temple wriggles. "Since you were the last one crowned of the Red royal lineage, the crown-magic now channels through your blood and yours alone, even when you're not wearing it. This power is at its peak when your kingdom is threatened—it has the ability to show you the future. With the war brewing in Wonderland, the magic is overflowing. Your blood can no longer contain it, and it's found a way to play out on its own, with glass as its receptor. Those mosaics you've made are like bottled visions. And Red doesn't want you to decipher them before she can, for fear you can use them to defeat her, in the same way that she can use them against you."

I tighten my fingers around the steering wheel so hard I almost swerve. "So, if she can get my blood, she can make her own mosaics and read them?"

"No. The magic always chooses a route unique to the crown's bearer. For you, that's an artistic venue. Red is a full netherling; she lacks the ability to set her imagination and subconscious free. You are part human, and an artist. Creation is your power. It's a power she covets but will never have. Although, if she can steal what you've already made and decipher it . . ."

My windpipe tightens as I take the fork in the gravel road. My duplex community lies about a half mile on the other side of the train tracks.

"That's why she would do anything to get them," I answer, dread winding around my heart.

Morpheus nods. "Now do you understand why we need to get to your house?"

In that moment, the railroad crossing arms start to lower and the alarm bell rings.

My intention to "take it nice and easy" is all but forgotten. I shove the gas pedal to the floor, determined to beat the train and get to Mom, too worried for her safety to care about anything else.

The motor roars and the car speeds forward, full throttle, until there's a loud thump in the engine. Shaking and stuttering to a stop, the Mercedes stalls and the engine dies—right in the middle of the train tracks.

The alternator light blinks on. "Oh, no," I whisper. "No-no-no." I grind the key and pump the gas. Nothing happens.

"Start the bloody car," Morpheus says with a desperate glance out the window on his right, where the freight train barrels toward us.

I turn the key, and turn again, but the engine won't start.

"Do it!" he yells.

"I can't! I—I don't know what's wrong!"

The train's whistle blares, no longer lonely but ominous.

"Get out!" Morpheus unbuckles his seat belt. Fingers stiff and trembling, I try to loosen mine, but my skirt is still bunched inside, screwing up the release button.

I sob, and every muscle strains as I put my whole body into pulling at the fabric. Morpheus wedges himself between the console and the seat. First he tries to rip the skirt. When that doesn't work, he yells at me to take it off.

"The zipper is part of what's stuck—" I choke on the realization that we're both about to die. "We don't have time!"

Snarling, he grips his hand over mine and we push the button together, but it won't give. "Use your magic, Alyssa!"

My mind races, trying to think of something to imagine that could get us out of this. But panic climbs my spine into my skull, blotting out all thought. I tremble and slam my forehead against his shoulder. "Just leave!" The shrill scream rips from my throat and over the whistle.

The train's oncoming roar vibrates the car's metal frame, and I scream again for Morpheus to save himself.

Then all sense and sensation fade. The train seems mere yards away, but the only sound I hear is my pulse racing in my ears. Even when Morpheus shouts the words, *"Chessie-blud, a little help!"* it's like he's talking underwater.

I squint to see the raccoon's tail, now orange and gray, disappear into the rearview mirror's glass. A loud clanging bursts from under the hood. The engine roars to life. My hands are locked in place on the steering wheel, but I'm too numb to move. The train is bearing down, only feet away.

Morpheus shoves his leg over mine and gives the car gas. The tires spin, propelling us off the tracks and onto the road on the other side. The train rumbles by, whistle still bellowing, missing us by mere seconds.

Morpheus eases his foot off the gas and pulls the emergency brake. The Mercedes idles quietly. Neither one of us moves. His body is still pressed against my right side, hands gripped over mine on the steering wheel, his rasping breath beside my ear. Sound, sensation, and light sweep back in increments, until everything is too vivid, too bright.

Emotions follow in the wake: delayed terror, confusion, regret . . . too much, too fast. I shake, unable to hold back my tears.

Morpheus puts an arm around me. "You're all right, blossom," he says, his mouth at my ear. "Can you drive?"

I nod and sniffle.

"Good." He scoots back to his seat, then grabs my chin to force me to look at him. "Next time, I expect you to figure a way out. A *netherling* way."

My tears gather around his hand, smudging his fingers with makeup.

"You didn't leave me," I utter in disbelief. "I thought you would leave me."

He releases my face and looks out the opposite window while rubbing his hand on his jeans to wipe off my mascara. "Nonsense. I stayed for the car."

Before I can respond, an orange mist seeps out from the vents. A smile I recognize from my Wonderland memories appears in the vapors.

"Chessie?" I ask. The rest of the hamster-size creature materializes, looking just as I remember: the face of a kitten, the wings of a hummingbird, and the body of an orange and gray raccoon. He flits to the dashboard and perches there, cleaning the oil and grease splotches from his fluffy fur with his tongue, like a squirrel taking a spit bath.

I shake my head. "Wait . . . so it was you? You crawled inside and fixed the motor?" He sneezes, then winks one of his wide green eyes at me.

"Chessie's gift is delineation," Morpheus says matter-of-factly, still looking through his window. "He can manipulate a situation by making a diagram in his mind and then mapping out the best way to solve it. He sees things the rest of us can't, and then he fixes them."

With a swish of his tail, Chessie scurries back into place on the rearview mirror. His top half vanishes, and he's a counterfeit car ornament once more.

I wipe smeared tears from my cheeks. "Do you have any more surprise stowaways up your sleeve?" I ask Morpheus.

Pushing dents out of his hat, he scowls. "I'm starting to fear I didn't bring enough. If there's one thing netherlings are good at, it's cleaning messes."

"Yeah, well, they're pretty good at making them, too," I say.

"Agreed. Some are good at making very *big* messes." He looks pointedly at me and buckles his seat belt. "Roadkill comes to mind. Use a little caution this time. We'll be no help to your mum or to Wonderland if we're dead."

Although I'm shaken, I manage to get us to my house. When we pull into my driveway, I'm relieved to see that everything looks normal and peaceful, at least from the outside.

Once more, I try to tell Morpheus thank you for his bravery at the tracks, but he dismisses me like he did all the way here: *"I stayed for the car."*

I know better. It's not the first time he's done something selfless for me. And I'm starting to suspect he didn't let me hit the little boy at the stop sign because of the same soft side he doesn't like to show.

If only he would be consistent—instead of always turning my image of him on its head.

I shut off the ignition and touch Chessie's swinging tail. "You can come in, if you'll stay hidden." The tuft of fur wraps around my finger like a hairy snake, squeezes, then loosens. The gesture leaves me at peace and warm.

"He needs no invitation," Morpheus scoffs. "If he wishes to go inside, no one will be able to keep him out."

I start to take off my seat belt. "I'm still stuck."

Morpheus eases closer and grasps my hand. "Shall we try to take the skirt off?" he says, his voice provocative. "We have the leisure of doing it right this time."

I'm not sure if he intends all of the innuendos packed into that suggestion, but considering it's Morpheus, I suspect he does.

"Forget it. I'll take care of it myself." I try to jerk away, but he guides my hand to the seat belt. Curling my fingers around the car's key, he uses the teeth to dig my skirt out of the latch while working the button. After a couple of minutes, the fabric pops free, wrinkled but salvageable.

"Thanks," I whisper.

"My pleasure." Eyes meeting mine, he brings my hand up to his lips and flips it to expose my inner wrist. He breathes over my skin—so balmy and close, my veins ache in response. Then at the last minute, he unfolds my fingers, takes the keys, and drops my hand. Before I can even get my bearings, he's back in his seat.

I press on my wrinkled skirt with my thumb, wishing I could iron out my emotions as easily as the fabric.

"Look . . ." I find my voice again. "I'm sorry for scaring you by driving so crazy. I shouldn't have played on your fears like that."

He opens his door. As it glides upward on its hinges, he sets his feet on the ground and looks over his shoulder.

"You wish to apologize?" He grins. "Whyever for? Everyone has something that can be used against them. You set aside your innate compassionate nature and used *my* weakness to get what you wanted from me. That was well played. You followed your instincts and let down your inhibitions without my even having to coach you. That is good. For the only way you'll be able to defeat Red is by learning to be merciless. Compassion has no place on any battlefield . . . magical or otherwise." He eases out of the car. He sways as if to get his bearings after the earlier drama. "You know how to manipulate me, and I know how to manipulate you. That makes us even."

No. We'll never be even.

We'll always be trying to outdo each other. I won't say it aloud, any more than I'll admit that I like it that way; that some primal, powerful side of me craves the challenge and always has.

"Wait." I get out of the Mercedes, grab my backpack, and press the remote to shut the doors. "Before we see my mom, we need to get our story straight. You're an exchange student from school. You're interested in seeing my art. That's how we'll bring up the mosaics she has."

Forearms propped on the roof of the car, he stares across at me, a hint of the jewels under his dark eyes glittering beneath the shade of his hat. "And what if she sees the truth beneath the mask? She shares your blood."

"We'll deal with it," I answer, although I know it won't be that simple.

We start toward the garage, but a shout from next door stops us.

"Hey." Jen jogs up with a dress bag over one shoulder and her sewing tote hanging from the other. I completely forgot we had plans to do last-minute alterations on the prom dress she made for me. She looks Morpheus up and down. *"M?"*

She appears puzzled but not mad, which means she still hasn't heard about our supposed lunchtime liaison.

"Hey, Jen." I play with the backpack's strap on my shoulder, keeping my eyes averted from Morpheus. "Did you get my text?"

"Oh, sorry," she answers. "My phone died during lunch. It's charging at home." Her attention wanders back to Morpheus, that curious glint still there.

"Good afternoon, green eyes." He tips his hat and gives her a heart-stopping smile.

"Uh, hey." When she turns back to me, her cheeks are flushed the same pink as her hair. "Wasn't my bro picking you up today?"

At least I don't have to invent an excuse and lie even more than I already am. "The magazine rescheduled his interview. Mor . . . *M* offered to drive me. He's an old friend of the family." Yeah, *old* is an understatement; and *friend*? That doesn't quite cover it. "I mean, his family has known ours for years." *Plagued* is more like it. My gaze drops to my feet. "I brought him by to say hi to my mom, okay?"

"What's with you?" Jen asks. "You act like I caught you guys making out in his car."

Morpheus laughs. "Timing truly is everything, isn't it?"

"What does that mean?" Jen turns to him.

Morpheus holds my gaze. "Had you been just a few minutes earlier, you would have caught us. I had my hands in Alyssa's skirt."

Jen gives Morpheus a look that could kill, then frowns at the wrinkles around my skirt's zipper. "What's going on, Al? Why are you such a mess?"

I suppress the urge to punch Morpheus. "I found out that Mr. Mason lost three of my mosaics," I say to soothe Jen's accusatory scowl. "I was upset." I swipe at my dried mascara tracks for emphasis.

Jen's expression softens a fraction and she dabs at the smeared eye makeup with her thumb. "But what's that have to do with your skirt?"

I glare so hard at Morpheus that heat radiates from my eyes. It's my own fault. I made him promise to fix things between me and Jeb but not Jenara. Which means he can still use her to screw with my world. "It got stuck in the seat belt, and he had to help me get it out."

"Oh." Jenara snorts. "*Hands in her skirt.* That's frackin' hilarious." There's an edge to her sarcasm as she turns back to Morpheus. "Word to the wise. I wouldn't use that joke with Jeb. He doesn't have my sense of humor . . . in fact, he has a 'pound first, ask questions later' policy."

"I'm aware of his overprotective tendencies," Morpheus says.

"How's that?" Jen asks, wrapping the dress bag around her neck like a feather boa. "You only met my brother once. And that wasn't exactly on a good day. Al was halfway drowned."

Morpheus takes off his hat and swirls the brim in his hands, an obeisant gesture. He pulls it off beautifully; only I know he's faking. "Of course. What I saw was care and concern." Morpheus's gaze flits to mine. "It's obvious he'd go to the ends of the earth for her."

Nostalgia tightens my throat. "And I'd do the same for him."

"That's why you guys are so great together." Jen smiles and weaves an arm through mine, my easygoing best friend again. "So, are you ready to see the dress? Fresh from the dry cleaner and waiting for the final touches."

Morpheus returns his hat to his head and angles it, completely at ease. How can he be so calm? Jen being here complicates things even more. I'm going to have to corner my mom and convince her to go along with my lie about Morpheus being a family friend. And to do that, I'll have to be honest about who he is. Pile on Queen Red's possible presence in our world and the battle I'm totally unprepared to fight, and I'm almost at my wit's end.

Sweat beads at my hairline as I lead the way to the garage, then punch the combination into the keypad. Morpheus pauses to look at the buckets filled with gardening items.

Jen stops next to him. "Al used those buckets to make traps, to capture insects for her mosaics. Back before she started working with glass gems."

Morpheus doesn't answer, just stares at the buckets. "You know, those aren't nearly as comfortable as they look," he says with a sour frown on his face.

He's referring to the night he spent inside one as a moth a year ago, but Jen can't possibly know that.

She snickers. "Really? Did the bugs tell you that? You talk to them?"

"They undoubtedly told Alyssa," he answers, "but she chose not to listen."

Jen laughs.

My face burns as several bugs hidden throughout the garage chime in to scold me:

We told her, all right . . .

She never listens. Even now, we're still trying to tell her . . .

The flowers, Alyssa. You don't want them to win any more than we do.

You are a queen . . . stop them.

I thought the insects and flowers were on the same team. Together, they have served as my connection to Wonderland for years. Now they're fighting with each other?

It must have something to do with Red's rampage.

Jen edges by and steps through the garage entrance into the living room. Morpheus tips his hat in a maddening gesture, then lets me go through the door first.

It's a relief to shut out the bugs, but it's short-lived when I notice the living room is empty. Musty dampness blasts from the wall unit air conditioner. The wood paneling makes the room appear small and dark. Clean towels and rags wait to be folded on Dad's favorite chair—a ragged corduroy recliner with daisy appliqués, where my mom used to hide her Wonderland treasures. Those have been gone for a while now, all but the Lewis Carroll books in my bedroom.

"Mom?" I drop my backpack on the floor and peer into the kitchen. The scent of chocolate chip cookies drifts from cooling racks on the counter.

"Wonder where she is," I say absently, but my guests have wandered to the back hallway, where my bug mosaics decorate the wall.

Dad hung them up after they won some ribbons in the county fair. He refuses to take them down now, no matter how many times Mom and I beg. He's sentimental in the worst way, and we can't explain our aversion to the artwork, so he always wins.

"Told you she was talented," Jen says, adjusting the tote straps on her shoulder.

Morpheus nods in silence.

Jen gravitates to her favorite piece: *Winter's Heartbeat.* Baby's breath and silvery glass beads form the image of a tree. Dried winterberries dot the end of each branch so it looks like they're bleeding, and shiny black crickets form the background.

Morpheus taps the berries gently, as if counting them. "Looks like something from a glorious dream." He glances over his shoulder at me. There's pride and nostalgia in his voice.

That very tree is in Wonderland, studded with diamond bark

and dripping rubies from its branches. Morpheus took me there in a dream when we were both children. I crafted the image years later, as a way to free the subconscious memory.

All my mosaics represent Wonderland landscapes and suppressed moments with Morpheus. No doubt it feeds his ego to know that he inspires my art. Or *haunts* it.

Haunts is a better word . . .

"Okay. C'mon, Al." Jen heads to my bedroom. "Prom's tomorrow. This dress isn't gonna fix itself."

Before following her through my door, I stick my head into my parents' room. Mom's not there or in the master bathroom. It's weird. Her perfume lingers as though she was here minutes ago. She's always home after I get out of school. She doesn't drive, so someone would've had to pick her up.

Or worse, someone forced her to leave.

I signal to Morpheus. He traces a fingertip just above the blue butterflies of *Murderess Moonlight*, careful not to touch them, completely absorbed in his study until I clear my throat.

He looks up. "Did you need something, luv?"

I glance over my shoulder into my room. Jen opens her tote and lays out measuring tape, sewing chalk, a thimble, and a box of straight pins on my bed. When I turn back to Morpheus, he's already moved on to the last bug mosaic.

"Red hasn't been here," he says before I can even voice my concern. "Everything is much too tidy. You know how chaos flourishes in her wake. Besides, she wishes to see into your mind. Had she found your house, these masterpieces would be gone."

This allays my fears momentarily. But I still can't bring myself to leave him alone. "Morpheus," I whisper.

He glances at me again.

"Don't mess anything up out here. Promise."

He frowns, as if offended by the suggestion. "I vow it. Keep your friend distracted, and I'll look around. Perhaps your mum left a note."

Not without some hesitation, I leave him to explore and step into my room, closing the door for privacy. Sunlight streams through my slanted blinds, revealing dust motes in the air. Everything's in its place: my cheval mirror in the corner, Jeb's paintings on the walls, my eels skimming in their softly humming aquarium. Yet the hair on my neck won't lie down. Mom's perfume is stronger here than anywhere else in the house. It's almost like she's standing in front of me, but I can't see her.

I shiver.

"Yeah, that was my reaction, too." Jen grins as she slides the dress from its plastic sleeve. "It turned out even better than the one in the movie, right?" She hugs the dress to her torso.

The gown is exactly as I envisioned it, and I let out an admiring sigh.

When Jen and I were brainstorming our "fairy-tale" costumes for prom, there was one thing I knew: I was not going to wear a princess pageant gown or some sequined, skintight Tinker Bell number.

My mind kept returning to a dress from a cheesy horror movie that Jeb, Corbin, Jenara, and I watched called *Zombie Brides in Vegas*. The gown was delicate and backless with a fitted bodice and flowing skirt—elegantly tattered and stained with bluish gray mildew from the grave. It appealed to me in ways I couldn't explain.

As my accomplice in all things morbid and beautiful, Jen insisted on making a replica. Using some images we found online as examples, she drew several sketches, then gave a copy to our boss at the thrift store. Persephone looked for similar wedding gowns at estate sales each time she went shopping for inventory and finally found one for twenty bucks: strapless, white, satiny, sequined, and pearled . . . a paragon of vintage charm. It even had a long, sweeping train. Best of all, it was only one size bigger than what I wear.

With scissors, a few tightened seams, an airbrush tool from Jeb's studio, and dye the color of faded forget-me-nots, Jen turned out a masterpiece.

She cut triangles out of the hem to create scalloped edges. Then she cauterized the raw satin so it wouldn't fray, leaving the scallops crinkled like wilted flower petals. For the final touch, she airbrushed dye—enhanced with glitter—along the cut edges, across the sweetheart neckline, and also at the seam where the bodice and skirt converge in a cascade of pleats.

The result is shimmery, shadowy, and moldering.

Jen rotates the dress back and forth so the flower-petal edges swish. I feel a pang of something I haven't felt in years: the thrill of playing dress-up.

"Uh-oh. We're in trouble," Jen teases, picking up on my unspoken reverence. "Is that excitement I see? Alyssa Gardner, looking forward to wearing a gown and tiara and hanging out with her peers? Definitely a sign of the prom-pocalypse."

Smirking, she spreads the dress out on the bed and shakes a netted periwinkle underskirt out of a plastic bag. It reminds me of the iridescent mist that lingers on the horizon after a storm, just before the clouds clear and the sun emerges.

"Gotta tell you, Al. I'm really glad you're not backing out."

She's wrong. I am backing out. But not because I want to.

None of this is helping my frazzled nerves. I'm worried about my mom, my blood mosaics, and Red . . . I'm worried about telling Jeb the truth and leaving him alone to spend time with Ivy instead of me. I'm worried about *everything*.

The last thing I should be doing is pining for a silly dance.

I can't just keep pretending everything's normal and okay.

"So, let's see those boots," Jen says, referring to the pair of knee-high platforms I found online about a month ago.

Moving mechanically, I drag them out of the closet. After stripping down to bra and panties, I tug the underskirt over my head and arrange the elastic at my waist. Then I step into the dress, and Jen zips up the back.

Seated on the mattress's edge, I slip my left boot into place over my tattooed ankle and run my hands along the synthetic leather. It's the same faded blue-gray as the dye on the dress, with three-and-a-half-inch soles and utility buckles that run the length of my shin—the perfect foil to all things princess.

"What do you think?" I ask Jen halfheartedly once I get both boots secured and my periwinkle fingerless lace gloves pulled up to my elbows.

Her smirk is both proud and conspiratorial. "I think all those poser frog-princesses are going to hatch tadpoles when they get a load of you." She bursts into a fit of laughter while helping me stand. I do my best to fake a carefree laugh, but it feels flat and transparent.

Jen adjusts the clear elastic bra straps she sewed on to keep the bodice in place and sets a tiara made of artificial forget-me-nots and baby's breath on my head. She was meticulous down to the last detail, even draping fake spiderwebs along the flowers to hang over my neck and upper back like a veil.

When she turns me to face the mirror, my breath catches. Her admiring reflection over my shoulder says she's every bit as impressed.

The dress looks exactly like I hoped it would, yet even better because she modernized it by scalloping the front hem so it would touch the top of my knees and spotlight my boots. With the addition of the netted slip, the back of the dress barely drags on the floor so I won't trip while dancing.

Or I *wouldn't* trip, if I really was going to prom.

I drag Jeb's locket from my bodice. The key necklace catches on it and pops out, too. Studying them both, I'm struck by how the chains are tangled together, inseparable, like my two identities have become.

Jen repositions the tiara. "Now tell me what *you* think."

I'm determined not to disappoint her, knowing I'll be leaving her soon, that all her work was for nothing. So much of her time went into this masterpiece, and so much of her affection for me. "You're a genius," I whisper. "It's perfect."

She fluffs out the back. "Just wait until you're wearing the mask."

I glance at the half mask of white satin laid out on the bed, airbrushed to match the dress.

"You're going to look like one of Jeb's dark fairies come to life. I wouldn't be surprised if you two end up being crowned king and queen."

Her words take me back to a time I wore a gown dripping with jewels while translucent butterfly wings sprouted from behind my shoulders, a time I was crowned as a real dark fairy queen. I can't decide which title—the high school or netherling one—comes with more prestige, scrutiny, and pressure. That moment in Wonderland changed my future and my past . . . who I am in the present. I thought prom night would be just as life altering. Jeb and I were finally going to be together in every way.

But it was all a lie. He doesn't know the real me—he only knows half of me. I haven't made peace with the other half yet. Until I do, how can I hope to truly connect with anyone?

I have to stop wasting my time, craving an experience that feels so far out of reach now.

"How's Jeb's tombstone tux coming along?" I ask, trying to keep myself from spiraling into a funk. I'm supposed to be distracting Jen, after all.

"Just needs a little more distressing," she answers with a comical lift of her left eyebrow. "And to think you used to say you wouldn't be caught dead at prom. Now you'll have to eat those words because you guys are going to be the hottest dead couple there."

In the mirror, I notice that the red strand of hair has caught in the spiderweb veil, looking too much like the blood sword I used to free Jeb's cocooned corpse. I bite back the whimper climbing my throat.

Pinning a pleat next to the zipper to tighten a small gap in the waist, Jen peeks around me in the mirror's reflection.

"This M thing is weird," she says, digging through her pin box. "I thought you didn't know anyone in London. And he never mentioned to Jeb at the storm drain that he knew you. Yet he's a family friend." She clamps her teeth down on some straight pins and continues to mold my bodice to my waist, taking pins from her mouth as needed.

"Well, my mom met him when she was a kid."

Jen's eyes widen, and my tongue locks up. I can't believe I said that.

"I mean his *dad*. My mom met his dad. M and I had never met, so he didn't recognize me that day."

Liar, liar, wings on fire.

"Ah," Jen mumbles around the pins. She tugs at the dress to ensure the pleats are secure, spits the pins she didn't use back into the box, and stands. "Well, I think our limey cowboy is drooling for your bod. Things are going to get real interesting once Jeb gets here. Guys have a way of sniffing stuff like that out."

This is the perfect segue to tell her about the bathroom episode. The perfect time to cough up yet another lie and cover my tracks again. "I don't think he likes me like *that*. He's just kind of . . . eccentric."

Jen picks up her sewing stuff and laughs. "Whatever you say, queen of denial."

Before I can even answer, either to lie or to finally tell the truth, she's out the door.

Weighed down by all the secrets I've been carrying for almost a year, by all the new ones piling up, I stare at myself in the mirror, hoping to find something other than the dress to like. Because right now, I'm not my favorite person.

Dust motes float around my reflection—tinted a glowing orange by the sun. They drift like pieces of scattered magic. I wanted to be an anti-princess for prom. I nailed it by looking like a netherling—the antithesis of all things fairy tale.

It hits me that maybe this is why Mom doesn't like the way I dress, because it makes me look like them.

My stomach drops. It's not Morpheus forcing the elements of my two worlds together. It's me. It has been all along. And I'm starting to realize it's not so much a choice as a necessity.

I'm so lost in thought, I barely notice the dust motes coming together, forming a miniature feline-shaped silhouette in midair. Beating wings shake me out of my trance.

In a blink, Chessie hovers beside me, his sharp-toothed smile inquisitive and contagious. I smother a yelp and rush to shut my door, locking it in case Jen gets back before I can convince him to disappear.

Satin and netting rustle around me as I spin to face him. "We can't let anyone see you," I whisper. "Let's find a place to hide. Okay?" I hold out my gloved palm.

He perches there on the lace, a warm bundle of glimmering gray and orange fur, like embers on ashes. His big green eyes watch me as I carry him to my dresser and open a drawer. I settle him atop some soft socks and pat his tiny head. Before I can close the drawer, he launches back into the air—wings a blur. Smile widening, he beckons with his front paw, then wriggles through the glass of my cheval mirror, his tail the last thing I see before he vanishes.

For an instant, the reflection shows his destination: a metal bridge over a dark, misty valley and a quaint village on the other side. Then the glass splinters and crackles, showing only broken images of me.

In spite of my inner alarms, I reach a hand toward an intersection of cracks and jerk back upon contact. Even though I knew to expect the broken glass to feel like sculpted metal and look like an intricate keyhole, it still startles me. It's been so long since I've traveled via mirror.

In the human realm, one mirror can take you anywhere in the world, as long as there's another mirror big enough to fit through at the destination you're aiming for.

In Wonderland, they travel by mirror, too, but their rules are different. The glass there can spit you out anywhere in the netherling realm, whether there's a mirror on the other side or not.

The one rule that is constant is that you can't take a mirror from one realm to the other. The only way to come into the human realm from Wonderland is via one of the two portals—one located in the Ivory castle, and the other in the Red. And the only way to get to Wonderland from here is the rabbit hole, which is a one-way entrance.

Knowing all that, I shouldn't be nervous. Wherever Chessie wants me to follow is here in the human realm, at least. Fingers trembling, I take aim with the key at my neck. Jeb's heart locket dangles just below. Seeing it makes me imagine what he would say in this situation.

Chessie is Morpheus's right-hand cat. This might be a trick . . .

I should just take a peek. Stick my head in but keep my feet planted firmly in the here and now.

"Envision where you wish to go," I say, using what Morpheus taught me. Closing my eyes, I picture the bridge and village I saw before the glass cracked. Then I insert the key into the hole and turn.

When I look again, the glass is liquid. The window of water opens to reveal the metal bridge. Stars shine down on the river beneath it, glistening and welcoming. Wherever this leads, it's beautiful.

A woman catches my eye in the distance. She walks along a grassy knoll toward the bridge. I choke on a startled breath. Even in the moonlight, I recognize the black and fuchsia tracksuit. She was wearing it this morning when I left for school.

Mom.

Shattered Images

Seeing Mom inside the mirror makes my heart flutter as fast as Chessie's wings.

"How did you get in there?" I ask, knowing she can't hear or see me. I touch the key at my neck; I could've sworn it was the only one we had. Maybe Red lured her in?

I yelp out loud at the thought.

But on second glance, Mom doesn't look upset or scared. She carries an oversized burlap bag on her shoulder—the one we used to stuff with beach towels, plastic shovels, and buckets for picnics at the lake. That was back when I was little, before she was committed. I loved those picnics . . .

Her stride is determined as she heads toward the bridge. She's up to something. Something she *wants* to be doing. When Chessie's glowing form appears next to her and perches on the bag's straps, Mom doesn't even startle, as if she was expecting him.

It's too much. I don't care where they are; I have to get in and see what's going on.

"Want it with all your heart," I remind myself. "Then take the plunge." I lift my boot and shove one leg into the cool air on the other side, stiffening when someone jiggles my bedroom doorknob.

"Al, what's with the locked door?" Jen says from the other side. "Jeb's here and it's getting ugly. He got a call from Taelor at work. He and M are in the driveway . . ."

No. I can't do this now. I have to see what Mom's up to. "I'm busy!"

"Busy?" Jen screeches from the other side of the door. "Are you freaking kidding? Jeb's going to kill him! You need to get out here, now!"

"Crap," I mumble. As if triggered by my broken concentration, the portal ripples like water filling up a bucket. If I'm going through, it has to be now, before it closes. I fight with myself, desperate to solve the mystery of my mother but feeling the pull of my life here.

The hesitation costs me my chance. The faux liquid glosses over to reflective glass again. I jerk free an instant before it closes, shutting me off from my mom and all the secrets she's been hiding.

❦ I ❦

I don't take the time to change out of the dress or tiara. As I scramble down the hall, Jen fires questions about what happened at school. I have no clue how to answer, so I push past her and sprint out the front door onto the lawn, expecting a bloodbath.

Instead, both guys are standing in the shade of Morpheus's opened car hood. Neither of them realizes they have an audience.

Jeb must've come straight from his interview. He's still in his photo-shoot clothes: black jeans, a black short-sleeved knit polo that hugs his muscles, a long-sleeved burgundy tee underneath, and a Japanese-design necktie draped loosely where the buttons open.

"So, it died on some random street?" he asks without looking up.

Morpheus nods. "Stopped rather inconveniently, in fact."

I purse my lips at the understatement.

Jeb leans his elbows on the car's frame and pokes at the engine. "Not sure what caused it. This model has a single serpentine belt for everything, so when it fails, the whole engine stops. But if that had happened, it would've been close to impossible to get it started again." He digs around, getting grease on his hand. "Yours looks a little worn, though. You'll need to change it soon."

Morpheus taps his hat's brim in thought. "I was afraid of that. What does something like that run?"

My breath winds tight inside me. I should be relieved that they're not trying to kill each other, but my mind can't quite wrap around it. With my mother having an outing in the mirror, it's too much weirdness all at once.

I turn to glare at Jen as she steps up beside me. "You said they were fighting," I whisper.

She shrugs.

Morpheus must've kept his vow and smoothed things over with Jeb somehow. Which leaves me clear to take care of Mom. Nerves on edge, I start to go back inside.

Jenara clears her throat.

I spin, locked in Jeb's and Morpheus's gazes.

They stand there gawking for what seems an eternity. Late-afternoon sun beats down, making the layers of fabric hot and itchy. With everything so quiet, I'm painfully aware of the absence of whispering bugs. Once again, they seem to have abandoned their posts. Lately, they're either griping about the flowers or just . . . silent.

Jeb shuts the car's hood. I bite my lip as he closes the distance between us, wiping grease from his hands on a bandana that he drags from his pocket.

"Wow." His eyes run the length of me, then meet my gaze, relaying a message as gruff and hungry as anything he's ever spoken aloud: *I want to touch you so bad, it hurts . . .*

His study of me has never been this intense. My legs feel like softened clay.

He takes my lace-clad hand and pulls me into a hug.

"How am I supposed to wait until after prom with you looking like *that*?" he whispers against my ear, then kisses my temple.

The sentiment leaves me breathless. If only I could enjoy it. I peer over his sturdy shoulder to catch Morpheus watching. He drags off his hat, and the glint in his black eyes tells me he approves of the dress, too.

I frown, screaming at him with my eyes: *Stop wasting time! Get my mom out of the mirror! Find Red so we can send her back!*

"The perfect fairy bride," Morpheus says, making it obvious he can't hear my thoughts this time. "All you're lacking are the wings."

Jeb's arms tense around me. There's the friction I expected to see between them when I came out. They're both on their best behavior, but that peace could snap at any moment.

Jenara shifts so she blocks Morpheus's view. "Speaking of wings

. . . Mr. Entomologist, I have a costume question for you for Alyssa's gown. What say we get some cookies and do some brainstorming?"

He follows her, giving me one last glance over his shoulder.

The instant they're gone, Jeb whispers, "I thought they'd never leave," then leans in to kiss me.

I sidestep him and edge toward the door.

He frowns and follows. "You're mad that I didn't pick you up from school. I cut the interview short to get here. I have to meet the reporter later to finish the questions. Doesn't that count for something?"

His wounded expression twists me up inside. "Yes. I mean, no, I'm not mad. I thought *you* were mad. Jen said that Taelor—"

"Mort clarified things." Jeb tucks his bandana away.

"Mort? He lets you call him that?"

"I didn't ask permission."

I tilt my head in thought. "So everything's cool with you guys?"

"You texted that you had an 'encounter.' So when Mort said that he wanted to make Taelor jealous by pretending to come on to you, and that she exaggerated the details because it backfired and ticked her off . . . well, his explanation fit. Too bad he made an enemy out of Tae, though. She's not a girl you want to cross."

"Tell me about it," I mumble, picking up my pace across the lawn with Jeb in tow. "You should hear what she's spreading around school."

"Well, he's going to clear all that up tomorrow. Old family friend or not, Mothra had no right to use you like that."

My feet stop dead, entire body freezing at the nickname. Jeb can't be starting to remember Morpheus's ability to become a moth. He wasn't technically *in* Wonderland to make those memories . . .

not anymore. Unless Mom was right at the hospital, when she said no one ever leaves Wonderland unscathed. Does his subconscious somehow remember something he no longer experienced?

"What did you just call him?" I ask, my voice shaky . . . hopeful.

"Mothra," he answers. "You know, Godzilla's archenemy. Because the guy's moth crazy." He gives me a sly grin. "C'mon, you couldn't have missed his hat. And that car? Gullwings look like moths when both doors are up."

"Right." Of course he doesn't remember. My thoughts return to Mom and her secrets. "We should go in so I can change."

"Wait." Jeb takes my hand and twirls me so my flower-petal hem ripples. When I'm facing him again, he shakes his head. "Mort was right. You're like a fairy on her wedding night. Let me enjoy the fantasy a little longer." His plea is so silky sweet, I can almost feel it on my skin. He kisses my gloved hand.

We've stopped where the grass ends just before the porch's first step. Morpheus's laugh carries through the door. The sound transforms Jeb's expression from admiring to fierce.

"When I got here, I was ready to kill him." I follow his line of sight to his motorcycle haphazardly parked on and off the driveway's incline. He didn't even take time to put down the kickstand. "I had him pinned against his hood, threatened to give him another scar on his face."

It's strange, to finally be the center of Jeb's undivided attention, but now I'm the one who's torn. One part of me tugging toward the house, and one part wrenching toward him.

Jeb catches my hand and holds it against his chest. "He said I could do anything to his face. Just asked that I didn't mess up the car. It's the only thing he has left of his dead dad." Jeb traces his thumb over the lace that hugs my wrist. "I saw his scars, Al. Those tattoos can't hide them. Did you know about the suicide attempts?"

I nod, reluctant to encourage his pity for Morpheus, yet knowing I can't possibly explain that those scars belong to someone else.

Jeb glances at Morpheus's car. "He told me his dad died hating him. And the main reason he came to the States was to meet your mom. To try to see his old man through someone else's eyes. To make peace with the memories." When Jeb looks back at me, his expression is filled with empathy, and my chest cinches tight. It's unfair that Morpheus is exploiting vulnerabilities Jeb doesn't even realize he's aware of. But I have no right to judge, because I'm a user and a liar, too.

"So as long as he's respectful to you," Jeb says, oblivious to my inner turmoil, "I'll do my best to respect him."

His tone is tight and pained, but he's in control. He's been working hard not to be violent like his father was. And I'm proud of him, because he's grown into an honest and compassionate man in spite of everything his dad did to wreck him emotionally. I've also never felt more unworthy of him.

I draw his hand up to my lips and kiss the tattoo where his wrist peeks out from his sleeve. What would he think of me, if he knew how deceitful I'd become? It might as well be me in that mirror in another part of the world, as far away as I feel from him right now.

"Hey . . ." He breaks his hand free and lifts me onto the porch. With him still standing on the lawn, we're at eye level. "You're too quiet. You would tell me if there was more to the story, right?"

There is more. I have to find out why my mom's in my mirror, and I have to defeat a psychotic magical queen . . . I'm just not sure how to tell you.

My eyes water.

Jeb's frown evolves into a grimace. "Why are you crying? Was Tae being straight?" His eyes blaze. "Did that jerk have his hands on you? Did he kiss you?"

Dang it. "No, it wasn't like that. It's just, maybe you can see now how I feel about Ivy. Why I'm hesitant."

He squints. "That's totally different."

Looking down at my boot buckles, I scramble to say the right thing—to hurry and fix this so I can rush to my room and fix everything else.

Jeb steps onto the porch. "Al, it's business. That's all. And I already told her yes."

My emotions do an about-face—from worried to indignant. "I thought we were going to discuss it."

"She went back to Tuscany this afternoon and won't be returning until the end of the month. I had to give her an answer before she left. This is for both of us—don't you see? It'll pay for our first year in London and then some. It's real money—proof I'm not a loser."

"Of course you're not a loser." I stifle the sob that climbs my throat. "You're the most talented artist I've ever seen."

"So are you," Jeb says, pushing us apart to watch me closely. "No more tears, okay?"

I sniffle. "But you're tired of painting me." I'm so pathetic. Mom is somewhere across the other side of the world, and here I am crying to my boyfriend about being his model.

It's just that right now, he's the only stable world I have left. And I'm about to walk away from him, even though it's the last thing I want to do.

"Tired of . . . ?" A wrinkle bridges his eyebrows. "Are you kidding? I'll never get tired of painting you. This dress"—he strokes the pearls and sequins across my ribs—"it's inspired a whole new series: Fairy Bride's seduction by moonlight. We'll start it after prom."

Right. My nonexistent prom. I bite my inner cheek to keep from screaming.

Jeb bends his knees so our foreheads touch. "I can't wait, you know," he says, his thumb skimming under my shoulder strap, leaving my skin tingling. "I'm going to check out the art studio Ivy's renting tonight. It has a loft. I'm thinking it might be the perfect place for us to get some privacy after the dance."

But I won't be here, I ache to say.

The front door opens, stopping me from blurting out everything—the whole truth.

"Hey, lovebirds," Jenara teases. She offers Jeb a cookie, then studies us, as if sensing she's interrupted something. "Sorry, but Al's mom showed up."

"She did?" I ask.

"Yeah, she's inside. She was in the backyard gardening and didn't know we were here."

The pulse in my neck kicks into overtime. She must've returned through the mirror. I have to find out where she went. "Wait . . . you left her alone with *him*?"

Jenara wipes crumbs on her fashionably ripped jeans, looking confused. "Who, M? He made a beeline for the bathroom before I saw her."

A loud crash followed by Mom's scream shatters the quiet afternoon. I drape my skirt's train over my arm and leap across the threshold with Jen and Jeb on my heels.

Morpheus stands at my bedroom doorway, looking in with a studious expression. I step around him toward my mom, cautious. She's on her knees amid a glittering spray of glass on the floor. My cheval mirror lies beside her, an empty wooden frame.

Tucking a necklace into her tracksuit's jacket, Mom lifts her gaze to mine. I can't even form the words to ask her where she got the key. She seems so small and frail, swallowed up by her tracksuit. The sun reflects off the broken shards around her, spattering the black fabric with prismatic dots of light.

I crouch down, careful not to get cut. "Are you okay?"

She keeps one arm behind her. "I was trying to move your mirror . . . it hit your dresser. The glass broke." She watches our audience. "It's his fault."

At first I think she's referring to Jeb, until Morpheus steps inside.

"That's a wretched lie," Morpheus says, then sits on the bed. "You broke that looking glass before I even came down the hall. I'd say you did it on purpose, though I can't imagine why."

"Hey . . ." Jeb's the next to come inside, an irritated yet baffled scowl aimed at Morpheus. "Show some respect."

Morpheus returns the scowl and stands so they're eye to eye. "A person must *earn* my respect."

Jeb's lips curl. "You're starting something you can't finish, moth boy. You're a guest here. Don't forget that." He pushes by, oblivious to the shadows of wings that lift behind his opponent.

Mom gasps, proof that she *does* see the wings, that she knows our guest is not who he's pretending to be. I suspect she's known from the moment she saw him in the doorway.

Jeb kneels and touches my mom's hidden arm. "Can I see your hand, Mrs. Gardner?" His voice is noticeably softer now.

As if in a trance, Mom offers her palm. Blood drizzles from a gash that starts at the base of her thumb and stops at her pinky.

My stomach knots. "Mom, you're hurt!"

Jen squeaks, covering her mouth. It doesn't matter that she can sit through a twenty-four-hour slasher movie marathon; she can't stomach real gore. It reminds her of scenes from her childhood. "I'll get some bandages." Trembling, she heads to the bathroom.

"You're going to need stitches," Jeb tells my mom as he helps her up and leads her to my bed. He wraps her hand in the clean side of his bandana. She seems numb to everything, and my whole body aches with worry. I start picking up the shards of glass.

I should be alone with her, comforting her, pressing my birthmark to hers so she'll heal. But how do I get rid of everyone? I curl my fingers harder around the glass I'm holding, trying to get a grip on my crazy out-of-hand life.

Morpheus steps aside and turns his back on Jeb and my mom as they sit down. He snatches a Kleenex from my dresser and offers the tissue, gesturing with his chin to my clenched hand.

Blood drips from the curve of my fingers, spattering on the shards at my feet. My forefinger stings. I turn it over to see a scratch no bigger than a paper cut. I must've been holding the glass too tightly. I wrap the Kleenex around my finger to stop the flow and keep the blood from getting on my gloves.

My breath catches when I look at the floor again. My blood hops from one piece of glass to another, like a pebble skipping on water, leaving thin streaks behind. When it's done, the result of all the lines is a red arrow pointing toward my closet.

I left the door slightly ajar when I took out my boots earlier. Through the crack, I catch a hint of movement inside. Two glowing pink eyes stare back from the shadows.

Intimate Strangers

I'd know that piercing pink gaze anywhere. It was one of the first creatures that greeted me and Jeb when we jumped into the rabbit hole last year.

"Rabid White," I mumble under my breath. Morpheus appears as rattled as I am at the netherling's appearance. Which means this isn't one of his stowaways.

Last summer, Rabid swore his loyalty to me and Queen Grenadine as our royal advisor. He could be here to warn me that something's gone wrong in the Red kingdom. Maybe he startled Mom, and that's why she broke the mirror.

I'm suddenly grateful Thursday is Dad's weekly inventory day at work. He won't be home until after seven. Maybe I can get this mess cleaned up before then with some help from Morpheus. And I'm not just talking about the glass . . .

Jen rushes in with the medicine box, and I hurry over to help bandage Mom's hand, keeping one eye on the closet. As if he knows he's been spotted, Rabid backs deeper inside. His antlers catch on some hangers, which clang together.

Jeb looks over his shoulder at the sound while holding my mom's palm so I can tape the bandage. "Did you guys hear—"

"I can drive her," Morpheus interrupts, crunching glass beneath his boots on the way to the bed. He offers his hand to my mom. "Alyssa and I, we will take you for stitchings."

Jeb shakes his head and stands. "No, I should drive, since you're having car trouble. Give me your keys, Mort."

Mom snaps out of her lull and stands up next to me. "Alyssa can drive." She hands the blood- and grease-stained bandana back to Jeb. "Thank you both for all you've done, but Mort is like family. He can help us take care of this now."

The ease of her lie takes me aback. She and Morpheus must've had a few minutes together before we all came in. It's the only way she could know our cover story.

The wounded look on Jeb's face catches my attention and pricks at my heart. If only he knew the truth . . . how much Mom hates Morpheus and how hard it is for her to pretend otherwise.

"Sure, we'll get out of your way." Jeb takes his sister's sewing tote after she gathers up her stuff.

I walk them to the front door quickly, antsy about leaving Mom alone with our otherworldly visitors—although I'm starting to suspect she's less intimidated by them than I once thought.

Jenara takes her tote from Jeb and steps onto the porch. "I have to close Butterfly Threads, but you can bring the dress by after. It'll only take a few minutes to finish those alterations."

I nod, wishing I *would* be wearing my gown someday again.

Jen squeezes my hand, her features softening. "I know you're worried about your mom. But her mind is strong, or they wouldn't have released her from the asylum. She said it was an accident. I'm sure it was. Everything will be fine, okay? Text or call if you need me?"

"Thanks." I squeeze her hand back, touched, even though she's so far off the mark about my concerns.

After his sister leaves, Jeb puts both arms around me and pulls me close. "You sure you don't want me to follow? Mort's car isn't reliable."

I study the vein throbbing in his neck and press it with my fingertip to feel his accelerated pulse. "It's not his car you don't trust. It's him."

"He had no right to talk to your mom like that. He's a disrespectful jerk."

You thought the same thing the first time you met him, I want to confess. It hurts so much that I no longer share those memories with him . . .

I force words over the lump in my throat. "I love you for worrying. But I promise, we'll be fine. I'll call my dad and have him meet us at the ER. Okay?"

Jeb doesn't answer, and he doesn't look inclined to leave.

Desperate to get back to Mom and heal her hand, I say the one thing I know will make him go. "Shouldn't you go meet the magazine guy? You said he had a few more questions."

The expression on his face matches how I feel inside—torn. "Let me know how your mom is. *Call.* Don't text. I want to hear your voice."

"I will." He starts to leave, but I catch his arm. "Thank you for being here. For helping."

"I'll always be there for you." He gives me a bone-melting look, then kisses me good-bye.

I've barely shut the door when Mom stomps to the kitchen.

"And don't touch me again!" She shouts over her shoulder in the direction of the living room. As she walks around me, she unwinds the bandage from her hand to reveal a healed palm.

Morpheus enters the kitchen from the living room side. "You've become such an ungrateful chit, Alison," he says, not even sparing me a glance. "I'm not going to stand by and watch one of my own bleed to death."

He tosses his hat onto the table. Sunlight streams from the windows, and his netherling form is vivid underneath Finley's full-body mask. His wings are high and looming, his eye patches dark, and the jewels flash from red to black.

"Allie could've healed me just fine," Mom rebuts.

I grip the door frame and study them both, speechless, as Mom uses a spatula to transfer cookies from the racks to a sealable container, as if the things that have happened in the last hour are just everyday occurrences.

Why isn't she freaking out about Morpheus? Shouldn't she be asking him why he and Rabid were in my bedroom instead of quibbling over her healed hand? Or better yet, shouldn't she be telling me where she went via my mirror, and where she stashed my mosaics?

Mom licks a melted chocolate chip from her finger and points at Morpheus. "This isn't like the past. I'm older. Wiser. I don't need your help anymore."

Her eyes are the bluest they've ever been, and her cheeks burst with color. She radiates energy and strength. Morpheus brings something dormant to the surface in her, just like he does in me. I have to wonder what was really between them, if he once said he loved her like he said to me. Maybe he seduced all of my predecessors.

The thought makes my stomach churn.

"You don't need me, aye?" He moves closer to Mom, but not as close as he usually stands to me. It's like he's respecting her invisible-box boundary. He snatches a cookie from the container and sits on the edge of the table with a phantom flourish of wings. "Well, I suppose you're right. You certainly put my information to good use. I told you about her mosaics so you could keep them *safe*. Then I learn from Alyssa that you asked the bumbling teacher to bring them out in public and leave three of them exposed. I'd say you bloody *do need my help*." He shoves a bite of cookie into his mouth for emphasis.

"Wait a minute." I step into the kitchen, my mind out of sorts. "Morpheus is the one who told you about my artwork? You knew he was here? I thought I was protecting you . . . all the while you were hiding things from *me*."

Lips pressed tight, Mom tosses the cookie sheets into the sink and turns on the water. "Without a complete set, they're useless," she replies, answering Morpheus but ignoring me. "I took care of the three I have. I hid them somewhere safe. Where none of you netherlings would dare to touch them."

Her words remind me of what I saw in my cheval mirror. "Is that why you were inside the reflection . . . next to that bridge? Was my art in the bag?"

Mom spins to face me, frowning.

"Ah." Morpheus looks back and forth between us. "Alison went to the iron bridge, aye? Brilliant strategy, skipping off to London like that."

Iron bridge . . . Morpheus once told me netherlings have an aversion to iron. It warps their magic somehow, though he's never given details.

"It's the only way I could keep the mosaics safe," Mom says, as if reading my mind.

"Of course," Morpheus taunts. "Did you visit our favorite haunts in Ironbridge Gorge while you were there? Did you take a train ride and relive some lost memories?" He narrows his eyes. "That's why you broke the mirror. To cover your tracks."

She returns her attention to the pans in the sink. "If only I could shut down the portals to and from Wonderland," she mumbles, more to herself than us. "Then Red and anyone else who wants to hurt Allie would be stranded in the nether-realm with no way back. Just like it should be."

"As if you would let that happen." Morpheus replaces his hat. "You speak of us like we're a different breed. But you're the same. Fierce . . . manipulative . . . and a touch mad. You're more netherling than human, Alison. You couldn't handle not having a way back into your heart's home."

I slam my hand on the counter to get their attention. "Would someone tell me what's going on?"

Silent, Mom scrubs at some baked cookie residue with a sponge. Water and soap slosh across the front of her and down the counter.

Morpheus dabs his mouth with the corner of the tablecloth. "Alison's fooled you into thinking she's a helpless little rosebud. But it's all an act, Alyssa. Your mum is ruthless, and she would've made a spectacular Red Queen. She wanted that ruby crown, in fact. Came so very close. But she met your father . . . failed to fulfill the tests. Otherwise, she would never have given up, would never have stayed in the human realm. And you, little luv"—his gaze locks on my face, jewels blackest black—"would ne'er have been born."

My tongue is thick and heavy like stone. All the questions I need to ask are wedged beneath it. I back into the entryway where the shadows offer solace, putting distance between me and Morpheus's ugly accusations.

No. Mom *can't* have wanted to be queen. That would mean she knows the truth. That everything we talked about the night I got back from Wonderland—the tender moments we shared in the asylum when I told her that our family wasn't cursed after all—was an act. That would mean she's been *pretending* to be clueless.

If that's the case, what else has she been lying about?

I press a hand to my mouth. Morpheus is trying to come between us. I won't let him.

"No," I say. "You . . ." I point to Morpheus. "You told me I was the first since Alice to dive into the rabbit hole."

He raises a finger. "Not so. What I said was you were the first since Alice who was cunning enough to discover the rabbit hole on your own and leap inside. I led your mum to the rabbit hole, and she let me carry her down. She wasn't quite as resourceful as you. I believe that was her downfall, ultimately. That and her complete and utter lack of loyalty."

Mom scowls in his direction.

I swallow a sob. "But Sister One, in the cemetery that day . . . she said I was the first to come forward and try for the crown."

The look that passes between Mom and Morpheus is full of knowing.

"Perhaps because your mum never made it quite that far?" Morpheus offers the answer up as a question. A sure sign he's covering something.

"It wouldn't matter," I respond. "Sister One was keeping track of my progress the whole time I was in Wonderland, because of what she stood to gain if I passed the tests. She would've been doing the same with Mom. No." I direct my next words to my mom. "You've never been there. You thought the Liddells were cursed. You didn't know the truth, didn't know what the tests were for. Not until I told you. Right, Mom? Right?"

She wipes her hands dry on a dish towel and starts toward the doorway. "Allie," she says as she steps across the threshold, "let me explain."

Morpheus follows her, his mouth on a severe slant. "You owe her more than an explanation. You owe her an apology for deceiving her all these years."

"You're one to speak of deception." Mom seethes.

"Oh?" In a graceful flash of movement, Morpheus backs her to the wall without even touching her. Again, he keeps that distance between them, some invisible line he won't cross. "You let *me* take the blame for Alyssa being pulled into Wonderland, for the disorder in her life. But it was you who turned your back on your commitments. You made a conscious choice that affected the future of any child you and *Tommy-toes* would ever have. It's time you admit it."

In the dimness, Mom's platinum hair glows and writhes like slivers of living moonlight—as evocative as the plants in our lunar garden caught in a breeze. I'm paying such close attention to her,

I don't notice what's happening with Morpheus until he growls.

The moths on his hat's brim flap, as if resurrected. They lift the hat off his head, and he has to leap for it. The corners of Mom's lips quiver, fighting a smug smile.

She's manipulating their wings.

I suppress the scream building in me, unable to deny what's right in front of my eyes: the magic inside her that I thought had never been tapped is alive, because she's been to Wonderland . . . and back.

I remember first meeting the flower fae in Wonderland, how they mentioned that I looked like "you know who." I always thought they were talking about Alice, or maybe Red. But that wasn't it at all. They were talking about my mom.

I press my spine into the wall hard enough to pinch my wing buds. "The smudged writing in the *Alice's Adventures in Wonderland* book," I say, barely above a whisper. "Morpheus didn't blur it. It was you. You didn't want me to figure out you'd been there."

Morpheus drops his hat into place again. He leans against the wall a few feet from me, one boot heel propped on the baseboard. "Your mum wanted to work with me from the very beginning, when she was thirteen and heard the nether-call. That's how badly she craved the power of the crown. All I had to do was find a way she could accomplish the impossible tests in King Red's decree. So for three years, I worked on an alternate route of obstacles to fulfill his requirements by playing on the definitions that he'd written out, getting her approval on each step—"

"You were going to let Queen Red live inside you?" I interrupt, staring at Mom in disbelief.

"Not quite," Morpheus snaps. "Unlike you, Alison planned to use her wish as I instructed, to banish Red from Wonderland forever.

And we wouldn't even be in this sorry predicament had you chosen to do the same instead of saving your boyfriend's insignificant mortal life."

I want to scratch off the jewels under his eyes for saying that, but I can't move.

Morpheus waves a hand. "It doesn't matter now. I made the ultimate mistake, by not having her vow on her life-magic to finish what she started. Alison's a traitor. She backed out because she met your father. 'Tis telling, though. How she kept all of the heirlooms, taking precautions so no one else could follow the clues I'd given her. Perhaps she wanted another chance to try for the crown one day."

"That's not why, Morpheus," Mom hisses. "And you know that."

He shrugs. "We could ask Rabid. He was there."

I shake my head. "Where *is* Rabid?" In all the craziness, I'd forgotten we left him alone in my room.

"I tied him up," Mom answers. "He's being entertained by your eels. Electroshock therapy. Penance for his role in what happened to you last summer."

I gasp at her callousness and start for my room, but Morpheus steps into my path.

"He's fine," he assures me, a hand on my shoulder. "Electricity has no effect on our kind."

I shake him off. "Well, it can't be good for my eels!" I shout. "They have to be terrified!" Morpheus and Mom both look at me like I'm losing it. If I am, they're the ones to blame. "Get Rabid out. Tell him I demand to know why he's here."

Morpheus raises his eyebrows at me. Then, with an admiring glint in his eye, he removes his hat and bows. "As you wish, Your

Majesty." He passes a meaningful glance to my mom. "You might try telling your daughter the truth for once. Were you able to decipher any of the mosaics before hiding them?"

Mom shrugs, a sour expression on her face.

"Share what you saw . . . along with everything else you've been hiding. She won't survive Red's attack unless she's equipped with the truth." Morpheus offers me one last glance—jewels flashing the gentle blue of compassion—then replaces his hat. His boots clomp across the linoleum floor.

Once his footsteps are muffled in the living room carpet, I give Mom my full attention, waiting for that explanation. "The mosaics," I blurt out, though it's not at all what I want the answer to.

She returns my stare with one of her own. "I only had a chance to decipher one. There were three Red Queens fighting for the ruby crown, and another woman's silhouette watching from behind a wall of vines and shadows—someone invested in the outcome . . . someone who had a deep stake in it all. I could see her eyes. Sad, piercing. I was in a hurry. That's all I had time for."

There have been three Red Queens since last summer: me; Grenadine, who I appointed to rule in my stead; and Red herself.

That leaves the question of the fourth player, the one in the shadows.

Mom watches my expression as I flip through the possibilities in my head. Her scowl softens to a sympathetic frown, and she looks like the woman I once knew: the one who made me Jell-O ice-pops when my throat was sore; the one who kissed my hurts away and sang me lullabies; the one who had herself committed to save me from Wonderland.

But the mom I'm remembering is not her at all. This mom's hair is still glowing, her skin glistening like snow under starlight. This mom . . . this *netherling* . . . is a stranger to me.

"You were in Wonderland," I say, voice quivering.

"It's not like he said, Allie," she murmurs. "I smeared the clues on the pages. But it was because I met your father and wanted to put an end to the quest forever." She wrings her hands in the dish towel. "I was trying to decide what to do with the heirlooms. That's why I hid them. I couldn't just toss them away—I had to figure out how to fix it so none of our descendants would ever end up in Wonderland again."

Her answer echoes hollow in the small entryway. Her words send a cold, crackling sensation down my spine. "You knew about the tests. Even worse, you *caused* them. Because of you, Morpheus came up with all those crazy things I did in Wonderland. All so you could be queen. Then you left him high and dry, and I became your substitute."

Mom kneads the towel. "We made the plan before you were born, Allie. I—I didn't know it would turn out like it did . . ."

"Seriously?" The word comes out high-pitched and pinched. "You're missing the whole point! You've been to Wonderland and you never bothered to tell me! You lived what I lived. Do you have any idea how much I needed to know that? To know I wasn't *alone*?"

Her expression falls, but she stays maddeningly silent.

"Why didn't you tell me that night at the asylum, when I spilled my guts to you?" The sobs I'm holding back pile upon one another, and my throat hurts more than when I had a breathing tube shoved inside. "Or earlier than that. If you'd just been honest from the very beginning, when you found out I could hear the bugs and plants." I let one sob loose. It breaks apart into two. "It could've changed everything. Wonderland wouldn't be in this mess, because I wouldn't have gone and screwed it all up."

Mom clutches her dish towel like a lifeline. "It's not you who caused this. It's Red."

"But I *unleashed* her," I growl. "And because of that, it's my responsibility to fix things."

"Sweetie, no . . ." She drops the towel and reaches for me.

Jammed in the corner, I can't escape, so I slap her hand away instead.

"Allie, please—" Her voice breaks.

Her wounded voice barely registers. All I see is a traitor. The lilies in my hospital room had been referring to her. *She* was the one who would betray me in the worst possible way.

"You're unbelievable," I say through gritted teeth. "You planned to fix things for all of us, huh? You, the one who's so *afraid* of everything Wonderland related. You, who thought our family was cursed until I told you otherwise. You, who stepped into my mirror today, with a key you've kept hidden not for months but for years. Why? Because you wanted to go back again someday and be queen? Were you even planning to tell Dad before you left him?"

She opens her mouth to respond, but I plow ahead before she can.

"All this time you've been riding me about my clothes and my makeup . . . it wasn't because I looked too wild or immodest. It was because I looked too much like a netherling. It reminded you of everything you lost. Right?"

She sniffles but doesn't answer.

"You hammered into my head how you don't want me to make the same mistakes as you . . . to fall in love too young and lose my shot at being an artist. I couldn't understand why you didn't try to start over again now that you're out, to have the career you've always wanted. But it was never about your photography. Dad kept you from becoming queen. And now I have the crown. You must really resent us."

"No, Allie . . ."

I'm deaf to her. I can't hear past the lies. "How can you hold a grudge against someone as amazing as Dad? He was faithful for *eleven* years. He stayed true to you and waited for you to get well. All those nights he sat alone in the living room . . . pining for his wife . . . staring at those stupid daisies that hid all of your secrets. He deserved the truth, Mom." Another sob escapes my throat. "We *both* did!"

Tears race down her face in the dim light.

She went to the asylum to protect me when I was a child—those memories threaten to soften my anger. But how can I truly know why she did what she did? Maybe she just didn't want me to become queen instead of her, and that's why she tried to sever my connection to Wonderland. Maybe it's her in the mosaic. She's the one in the shadows, watching and waiting to get her chance to steal the crown.

The blossoming mistrust smothers any last traces of compassion, and I hurl the cruelest insult I can think of. "I don't know who you are anymore. But I do know one thing. You're a bigger liar than Morpheus ever was."

ℭOLLISION ℭOURSE

I can't face Mom's devastated expression, so I brush her aside, gather up my dress's train, then make a beeline to the back hall.

She stays behind, her soft sobs ringing louder than any scream . . . louder than the train that almost crushed me earlier today. Maybe it would've been better if I had been crushed. That pain would've been instantaneous and then gone. It wouldn't linger and eat away at me like what I'm feeling now.

Poor Dad. I can't believe how dishonest she's been with him—the man she vowed to love and stay with forever. And I'm becoming just like her, lying to the guy I love. Which is something I never wanted to do again . . .

Mom's footsteps drag heavily across the living room; then the back door slams. Instead of coming after me, she went to her garden to commiserate with her chatty plants. It's fitting. They know her better than I ever did.

I sag against the wall outside my bedroom, willing myself to stop trembling before I face Morpheus. Chest tight and eyes stinging, I peek through the door.

There are a few puddles around the aquarium's base. The eels seem okay, gliding through bubbles as if nothing happened.

On my bed, Rabid White is wrapped in a bath towel. The only part of the bunny-size netherling that shows is his bald head: pink doelike eyes set within wrinkled, albino skin. Fuzzy white antlers rise behind his humanoid ears.

He's so out of place here. He needs to go back. Problem is, with my cheval broken, I don't have a mirror big enough to send him into London and through the rabbit hole. The netherling world once again has me under its thumb with all of its one-way tickets. The portals from the Red and White kingdoms only lead *out* of Wonderland. The rabbit hole only leads *in*. I just wish there was some way around the rules.

I also wish I could be as carefree as Morpheus.

He sits Indian style in front of Rabid in an oddly endearing scene, like one friend comforting another. He's tucked a pair of earbuds into Rabid's humanoid ears. The creature's ancient face fills with wonder as he bobs in time with the music.

A wave of affection washes over me, for Rabid and Chessie, and all the netherlings in Wonderland—followed quickly by anger at Morpheus. He let me believe he used my mom's mind to approach me so young because he was desperate to be free of his own curse. I made peace with that, empathized on some level. One of the things he and I have in common is our fear of being constricted or imprisoned in any way—mind, body, or spirit.

Now I suspect he wanted revenge on Mom for backing out of their deal. That's something I can't forgive.

Morpheus offers Rabid something shiny and silver to play with. It's Jen's thimble. She must've missed it in her hurry to pack and leave. Rabid tries to eat it, but Morpheus stops him.

"Warm it with your eyes," he instructs.

Rabid sharpens his glowing irises until they radiate red heat. Under his concentration, the thimble turns a soft orange.

Morpheus places the tiny inverted cup on one of the four prongs of Rabid's left antler. The orange glow seeps down his fuzzy horn and evaporates every drop of water in its path, as if the heat is traveling through him.

"Now, we only need seven more to warm and dry you," Morpheus says, then laughs as Rabid clacks his bony hands together in applause.

I don't know what to think, seeing my dark tormentor caring for one of his own—gentle and teasing. He's like that with me sometimes, too.

I fight the tears building at the inner line of my lashes. I'm utterly alone and confused, but a queen doesn't let her vulnerabilities show.

As I step in, I clear my throat.

Morpheus looks up. His true likeness fades beneath Finley's masquerade, although an echo of his jewels remain. They blink a hazy lilac-gray, the same hue of my boots. It's the color of bewilderment, as if he's sympathizing with my turmoil. As if he didn't have a hand in it all.

"What did your mum tell you about the mosaics?" he asks.

"Why is he here?" I sidestep his question, pointing at Rabid. I'm not sure I can trust Morpheus with anything my mom said, or my mistrust in her motives.

Before Morpheus can respond, Rabid notices me. His pink eyes grow to the size of half-dollars.

"Majesty, ever and always yours!" The netherling sheds the towel and knocks the thimble off his antler. The scent of fishy water and dusty bones hits my nose.

Rabid scoots to the edge of the mattress, plops to the floor, and bows. The earbuds pop out and tangle in his antlers. Morpheus catches the tails of the creature's wet waistcoat to stop him falling face-first into the glass-speckled carpet.

"Penitent be I." Rabid laces his skeletal fingers together in a prayerful gesture. The white, foamy saliva that earned him his name dots his lips.

"Why are you penitent?" I ask, cautious.

His glowing gaze drags across the shards sparkling on the floor. "Broke your gateway I did *not*."

I frown. "I know. My mom did that."

The creature bows his head. "Betrayed my kingdom . . . so says Queen Grenadine." He offers a red piece of ribbon tied in a bow.

Grenadine was born an incurable amnesiac. The bows she wears on her toes and fingers are enchanted with the ability to remind her of important things she wouldn't otherwise remember.

A whisper greets me as I press the velvety ribbon to my ear. *"Queen Red lives and seeks to destroy that which betrayed her."*

The fingerprint upon my heart, the one Red left as a warning last summer, flares—a sharp jolt that pushes the air from my lungs. I drop the ribbon and it flitters away. I meet Morpheus's gaze. He lifts an eyebrow, making the scar on Finley's temple curl.

"What does this have to do with you?" I ask Rabid, struggling to keep the quaver from my voice.

"Imprison me you will, Queen Grenadine said." He lifts his hands toward me, bones grinding as he waits to be handcuffed. "Chains for you I'll wear, Queen Alyssa. Contrite I'll be." He falls to his cadaverous knees.

I wince when he lands hard on the broken glass but check myself. Bones aren't susceptible to superficial cuts.

Morpheus removes his hat and stands, towering over Rabid.

"What do you know about this?" I ask him.

A shadow of wings distorts the air behind him, like a wave of summer heat radiating off an asphalt road. "He helped Red find a body to inhabit. He's the reason her spirit survived."

I snap my attention back to my kneeling subject. "Why would you do that? You swore your allegiance to me."

Rabid shudders, and his bones sound like tree branches clacking together. "Other obligations tainted good intentions . . ." Groaning, he keeps his head low. His antlers block his face.

"As you know, Red saved his life once," Morpheus clarifies, dropping his hat onto his head. He runs a finger along the moths draping the brim. "Rabid had to repay his debt to her. Only she could set him free."

"Free?" I ask.

"Free to be your faithful subject," Morpheus explains. "He made a trade. Red's life for his loyalty. In order to be true to you forever after, he had to betray you one last time."

Logic wrapped within nonsense. Par for the course for Wonderland. "So is Red here?" I ask, fighting a clench of dread in my chest.

Rabid doesn't answer. Everything that's happened today—Taelor seeing me and Morpheus, the mosaics going missing, the near-death car ride, my mom's betrayal— hangs over me, a noxious cloud of black emotion. The power inside me begs for free rein, promising to *make* him talk. To make him obey.

I surrender to it: envision the earbuds lifting and swaying like cobras. The song that's playing grows loud and screeching. Rabid plugs his ears, howls, and backs up. The buds follow and strike. Though they have no fangs or venom, they're vicious in their pursuit.

Wearing an amused expression, Morpheus steps back to allow Rabid to scramble onto the mattress. The black cords slither up the edge behind him.

"The insects, listen you should!" Rabid yelps as the cords strike and wrap around his antlers, yanking him to his stomach atop my quilt. "Please, Majesty!"

I hold up my hand, and the earbuds go limp.

"I said, *Is Red here?*" The power behind my voice surprises even me.

Rabid shakes his head no as Morpheus helps untangle his antlers. "A flower she chose to be. Lead the forest in a revolt. Amplifying pastries for all. Thorns the size of dragon talons. First, they wake the dead. Shake the foundations, free the consecrated." Frothy white saliva drizzles from the corners of his lips. "Then divide and conquer the living. Enslave them all."

Terror, as dark as a raven's wing, casts a shadow across my thoughts. So that's what the bugs were trying to tell me. They weren't referring to the flowers here in the human realm but to the ones in Wonderland. Queen Red has gathered a giant flower army.

"It won't work, will it?" I ask Morpheus as he adjusts the volume on the earbuds and coaxes Rabid to listen to the music once more. "The cemetery is hallowed ground. Right? No full-blooded netherling can step inside the cemetery gates. That's what you told me."

Morpheus sweeps the towel off the bed and crosses to my aquarium, blotting up the puddles. "That's true for those of us who *live*," he answers without turning, "but Red is a dead inhabitant in a living body. She's no longer held to the natural laws of our world."

His flippant use of the term *natural* in reference to Wonderland almost makes me snort.

"Red can cross the boundaries of the cemetery gates because part of her belongs there already," he continues. "If she made it inside, she could free the dead, for she knows the secrets of the maze. But she would have to get through the Twid Sisters. That wouldn't be easy."

"I remember." My feet jitter as I picture both the twins' spidery bottom halves beneath their gowns. Sister One has her charms, but Sister Two . . .

I faced her side of the cemetery, felt the cold chill of blades along my neck as she threatened me with her mutated hand. I stood under her trees ornamented with toys possessed by the spirits of the dead. I'll never forget how their eyes pierced me with agony.

"When the twins stand united," Morpheus continues, "they are the two most formidable netherlings in all the land. The only way for anyone to defeat them is to put them at odds so they aren't working together. Since both twins hate Red for her successful escape last year, it's doubtful she could break them apart." He says the word *doubtful* quietly while tracing the glass of the aquarium. His profile is troubled as my eels follow his finger, mesmerized.

Morpheus loves his world. It's why he's so adamant about getting my help. I've seen the destruction in my dreams, and the violence in my mosaics. It would be heartbreaking for such a beautifully unique and bizarre land to succumb to Red's schemes.

Nausea winds through me. This entire disaster is my fault. I made it possible by drying up the ocean last year, by giving the flower fae a path into the heart of Wonderland, and by freeing Red's spirit from the cemetery so she'd have access to a new body.

I stumble toward my bed, almost tripping over my dress. Morpheus is at my side in an instant and steadies me until I'm seated next to Rabid.

Rabid drops the earbuds to the floor, scoots close, and pats my gloved hand, brittle fingers snagging on the lace. "Majesty," he croons. "Please . . . no exile for Rabid of the family White. Ever your loyal subject. Stay with you always." He reaches inside his wet waistcoat and offers a key that looks just like mine with a ruby on top.

"You're not staying here," I answer, wrapping his bony fingers around his key. I point to the closet behind us. "Get back inside until we can figure out a way to get you home."

Rabid's pink eyes lose their shimmer, as if a curtain of cotton candy has fallen across them. He tucks his key into his coat's inner pocket and shivers. "Rabid wet be."

Touched by his discomfort, I pick up the thimble and give it to him. "Dry yourself off and keep quiet in there."

The light in his eyes reignites. "A prize to keep! Generous are you!" He presses the thimble into place on his antler, scoots across the bed, drops down, and shuts himself in the closet, leaving me alone with Morpheus.

"You said *home*." Morpheus looks down at me, expression hopeful. "You admitted it. Wonderland is your home."

I shake my head. "I meant *his* home."

Didn't I?

I shake the doubts from my head, suspicious again of Morpheus's part in all of this. "You were with the flower fae in my dream when I was drowning." I look up at him pointedly.

He steps back, scowling. "Obviously Red hadn't yet bribed them to aid her cause. Stop finding reasons to doubt me. We need to work together."

My fingers trace the pearls on my dress, letting the slick, cool bumps soothe me. "I don't know how to work with you."

"You did when we were childhood playmates," he answers, his expression as close to humble as I've ever seen it.

My fists clench around the fabric of my dress. "Before I knew you were a liar. You and my mom. That's all netherlings do. The only people I can depend on are . . . *people*. My dad, Jeb, Jenara. Humans haven't let me down. Not like you have."

His black eyes soften to a depth of emotion that surprises me. He actually looks wounded. "Perhaps because you hold me to a different standard. You won't give me the benefit of the doubt, as you do them. You act as if I've never done right by you."

My attention drops to my gloved hands. He trained me to know the Wonderland creatures, to understand how to survive in the nether-realm. He stood by me in the car earlier, facing down a train . . . and it was not the first time he looked death in the face so I wouldn't have to.

He has moments of courage, tenderness, even selflessness. But he'll put anyone or anything at risk in a heartbeat if it gets him something he wants. I lift my eyes to meet Morpheus's gaze. "Earn my trust."

"How?" he asks.

"By telling me the truth. What went on between you and my mom? Did you seduce all the Liddell women? Did you tell them the same pretty words you told me?" I curl my legs beneath my dress, feeling small and vulnerable for even asking.

Morpheus scoots aside some glass with his boot and kneels. He takes my hand in his. "I've known but three generations of Liddell women. Counting the ones in London, there's been twenty or so. Most were oblivious and unreachable—they didn't hear the nether-call. The others weren't strong enough to face their lineage without losing their minds. As for Alison, she and I were business partners. There has never been more than that between us. There's only one Liddell I desire, only one who earns my undying devotion." He works a fingertip into the lace at my elbow and drags off the glove. "The one who was my truest friend . . . who took my place and braved the attack that was meant for me."

I hold my breath as he trails his thumb along the scars on my palm.

"But I didn't know what I was doing," I insist. "I was just a naïve kid who wanted to protect her pet bug."

"I don't believe that." He holds my hand in his. "Self-sacrifice is innate in you. Your mum wanted the crown for the power, but you faced Wonderland's tests to save your family; just as you faced the bandersnatch for Chessie; and then Red . . . you faced Red, all alone, for Jebediah. Can you not face her one last time, with me by your side, for Wonderland?"

I try to drag my hand free of his, but he holds me tighter. "Please, that's enough."

"It will never be enough," he insists, guiding my palm to his chest so I can feel his pounding heartbeat. "I will not stop until you're reigning over the Red court forever. Until you're back with us where you belong."

"I don't belong there."

"You do. Because of who you are. *What* you are. One half brimming with dark curiosities and a fierce appetite for all things mad. But the other half whimsy and light—filled with courage and loyalty." He bites his lower lip, a gesture so minute I might've imagined it. "Nothing can break the chains you have on my heart. For you *are* Wonderland."

The endless depth of his eyes is at once ominous and tranquil. Light glints off the glass around him on the floor, speckling his face as if he's cloaked in stars. Somewhere there's a memory of him like this—an enchanted child sitting beneath the nether-realm's constellations and telling me the same thing: *You are Wonderland. That is your whole; accept it, and you can rule our world . . .*

The memory, like this moment, is a living thing—lapping at my soul, hot enough to burn, yet chilling to my blood.

"Alyssa," Morpheus murmurs. "We were children together. I've waited for your return more years than your mortal knight has even known you existed."

I can't bring myself to meet his gaze again . . . can't bring myself to face him or the temptation he's awakened. I want to give in, to embrace him and Wonderland and its endearing yet macabre creatures, to seize all of the deranged beauty and power that waits for me there and never let go.

But that isn't right. That isn't the future I have mapped out. I belong with Jeb and the people I love, here.

I pull my hand out of Morpheus's. Only the aquarium's hum and the sound of bubbles racing up the filter break the silence.

Morpheus sighs. "Enough indecisiveness. It is time for us to go to Wonderland."

"I won't leave until I find a way to tell Jeb the truth," I say. "I want my future with him to be based on honesty. He *has* to know why I'm gone . . . where I am. When I'll be back."

Morpheus's frown is soft but stubborn. "You've already waited too long, trying to ignore what's happening. If Red isn't already here, she will be soon . . . and all the mortals you love will be in danger. Is that what you want?"

I groan and bury my face in my hands. "Of course not," I answer into my fingers.

"It is your place to step up and be the queen. Red cannot win," Morpheus insists. "It's not a game this time. It's life and death."

It's not a game this time.

This time.

I drop my hands to the edge of the bed and push myself up. He follows my lead, appearing puzzled. Although I barely come to his chest, a surge of resentment makes me feel taller by at least six inches.

"What you called a game *last* time was life and death to me." I can't suppress a snarl. "It was you and Mom who made me jump through all those hoops. The two of you together should have enough magic to fight Red. Why is it my responsibility to throw away all my plans and risk my life again?"

Morpheus's mood flashes from gentle to formidable in a matter of seconds. He grasps my chin so I can't look anywhere but at him. The touch surprises me, because Finley's hands aren't soft and ethereal like Morpheus's usually are. They're callused and human, like Jeb's.

"You are just as responsible as we are," Morpheus says. "For not following my instructions to the letter. You chose to listen to mortal sentimentalities over netherling genius. The same mistake she made when she chose your father. You disappointed me once, Alyssa. Dare not do it again."

I drag my chin free. "*I* disappointed *you?*" I'm so tired of his arrogance. "You should go. I'm really done looking at your face."

He grins—a malicious flash of white teeth. "You mean Finley's face."

I cringe, thinking once more of the human guy trapped down in Wonderland. "Get out," I insist. "I want you gone before my dad gets here."

When Morpheus doesn't budge, I animate the earbuds to strike at his boots.

He kicks them away. "Lacks imagination, little luv. You'll have to do better than that to defeat me. And those antics won't even put a dent in Red's armor."

He's right. But I'm emotionally and physically spent. There's an ache that starts in my heart and goes all the way through to my muscles, bones, and blood.

"I need time to think, to rest," I whisper. *No more revelations, no more arguing.* "Leave. And don't visit my dreams tonight."

Morpheus huffs and starts for the door. "As if I could in this form."

He's almost in the hall when I grab his elbow. "What do you mean?"

Tensing against my fingers, he turns. "My powers are spent retaining this blasted glamour of Finley. I haven't been in your mind, dreams or otherwise, since you were unconscious in the water."

"You're lying."

He rounds on me, slaps a hand to the door frame overhead, and pins me between him and the wall. "What makes you think I've been in your dreams?" Underneath the sinister fathoms of his eyes, his jewels glimmer yellow-orange like goldenrods, the shade of apprehension.

"First off, because you sent the clown to the hospital."

"I already told you I didn't send any toys."

"But it's been everywhere you've been. It was in the mirror at school, shaking that snow globe from my memory of the Shop of Human Eccentricities. And then there's the blood sword I dreamed about—that had your fingerprints all over it."

He leans closer. "You had a dream about your blood? Why didn't you tell me this?"

"Because you already *knew*." I dig my nails into my palms, wanting to strangle him.

"No, Alyssa. I did not. That dream could be symbolic, implanted in your mind by your crown-magic. Perhaps your blood will be used as a weapon . . . possibly against you."

"No. You said Red can't use my blood because she's not human."

Jaw clenched, Morpheus squeezes the door frame. "You are the most vexing creature I've ever had the misfortune to know!"

I glance down at my boots. There's a tickle at my ear as he catches my red strand of hair and tugs it to get my attention.

His expression softens. "I have never once claimed to be trustworthy," he states matter-of-factly. "But there's something I can say with all honesty. I have always pushed you toward your best."

I huff. "Right. Even if it means I end up dead."

He shakes his head. "Not so. Our fates are entwined. *That* is the one abiding truth from our time together. It makes sense I would want to see you succeed."

Jerking my hair free, I shove his chest with a fist. "Nothing about you or Wonderland makes sense. And the 'one abiding truth' is that life was so much easier when I'd forgotten your massive ego and that other world ever existed."

A tremor shifts through his features, first fragile, then severe. His muscles twitch under his T-shirt, sending a tingling sensation through my knuckles. "You want me nonexistent?"

Before I can respond, he steps back and flips the hat from his head. Then he drags off his vest and his T-shirt, dropping them all on the floor at my feet. Once he's peeled off his necklace and bracelets, he stands there facing me in only jeans and boots.

Finley's chest and abs are tanned, toned, and scarred. Another tattoo—an angry skull and crossbones—slashes his pecs, but I see through all of that to Morpheus's smooth porcelain skin.

I watch him warily. "W-w-what are you doing?"

"I'm clearing the way for my massive ego." His long legs close the space between us. He catches my waist. I wriggle to get free, but he lifts me until I'm flush with the wall, my chin almost touching his.

I swallow and level my gaze, pushing against his muscled shoulders.

He leans close as if to kiss me.

I stiffen. "Morpheus, don't."

He hesitates, curses, and then lowers me. My gown's netting and satin catch between him and the wall. When my feet finally touch the floor, the dress is bunched around my thighs, revealing more of my bare legs than I like. I push the fabric down, blushing.

He smirks, and I lunge to slap the smugness off his face. Without missing a beat, he sidesteps me and ends up at the center of the room.

"I suggest you stay where you are, *Your Majesty*," he says before I can move again. "Wouldn't want you to get caught in the cross fire."

His fingertips burst into orbs of light as he lifts his hands. Blue electric filaments reach to every corner of the room. The glass on the floor jingles and hops, as if an earthquake is shaking the house. My eels dive into their hiding cave, and Rabid whimpers from the closet.

The shadow of Morpheus's wings looms high behind his shoulders, then enfolds him, like a moonflower closing when the sunlight torches its petals. He's quickly surrounded by a cloud, thick as fog and scented of hookah smoke, with echoes of blue lightning within.

In a blink, his wings fully manifest and slice the smoky haze, peeling it back to reveal him in his true state: flawless, pale skin, masquerade-style patches curved like ivy beneath his eyes. The teardrop-shaped jewels flash bright and blinding through a rainbow of colors, so many moods they can't be read.

Finley's cropped hair has transformed to a mass of blue, shoulder-length tangles, messy from the static of the magic still emanating from Morpheus's fingertips. His wings spread out behind him—at once intimidating and majestic.

All traces of the glamour are gone. It's Morpheus in the flesh.

I lean against the wall, my wing buds itching to join him in his metamorphosis. The tattoos have vanished from his forearm, and his birthmark shimmers a soft blue, coils of magic writhing like a snake beneath it.

My fingertips twitch, remembering how they touched him there last summer . . . how he healed me.

With a grand flourish, he extinguishes the electric pulses from his hands.

"We shall see how you fare without me." His voice is gritty and raw. "My guess is you won't even make it through school tomorrow before you're on your knees begging for my return." He tosses his car keys on the floor atop the hat and other pieces of clothing.

He transforms into the large moth and hovers in midair. His voice ignites in my mind: *"I won't be seeking you in your dreams, tonight or any other. You will have to find me now. I'll be hiding among lost memories. Sleep tight, luv."*

Then, with a flutter of wings, he's out of my door and out of my life—gone as fast as he stormed into it.

PROOF

The instant Morpheus leaves, I'm slammed with regret. The more I think about it, the more it seems clear: He hasn't been in my head once since he showed up wearing Finley's image. Even in my dream at the hospital, it wasn't his voice I heard. It was a whisper that could've belonged to anyone. Even me.

He was telling the truth. He opened his heart, and I gutted it. All he wants is to save Wonderland, and I can't stop acting like a coward.

Sunset filters through my blinds and reflects off the glass on the floor, casting soft pink designs onto the walls. The serenity is out of sync with how I feel. I can't bring myself to pick up the mirror's pieces. So much has broken today. So many things, I don't know how to begin fixing them all.

The sound of snoring distracts me from my guilt and leads me to my closet. Rabid is curled in a ball on the floor. Some clothes have fallen off their hangers, and I arrange them over him for camouflage. He smacks his lips and snuggles deeper into the bed of shoes and belts. As creepy-weird as he is while awake, he's adorable when he's sleeping—vulnerable, even.

His safety is my first priority. I need to send him back through the rabbit hole. We can't risk Dad or other humans stumbling upon him.

Butterfly Threads has full-length mirrors along the walls. If I take Morpheus's car before Dad gets home this evening, it will buy me some time before I have to explain what it's doing in our driveway.

I can smuggle Rabid into the store. He's the size of a rabbit. He'll fit inside my backpack. We can get there before Jen closes and locks the doors. I'll take my prom dress, then suggest that I close up so she can leave early to finish it.

The plan's foolproof. But the question is, what happens *after* I send him back? Morpheus is gone. That means I have to go to Mom, have to try to trust her. Maybe she has some idea how we can stop Red and her zombie flowers.

Also, it's time to tell Jeb everything like I've been wanting to all along. And Mom's going to help me convince him, whether she likes it or not.

I grab my backpack from the living room and stop to peek at her out the back window. She's sitting in the grass beside a clump of silver licorice, whispering all of her secrets into their feathery ears. Tears roll down her face.

If only she could confide in me or Dad as intimately as she does them. All these years they've known a side of her that we never have. I bite the inside of my cheek, because even I'm not too far gone to realize how ridiculous it is to be jealous of a plant.

Back in my room, I slide two schoolbooks from my backpack and lay them on my desk, leaving only a half-empty bottle of water and my cell inside. I call Jeb so I can lay out the groundwork for him to come over later. The phone goes to voice mail. Afraid to leave a message with my voice so shaky, I text him instead.

I tried to call like you asked. Mom's OK. I pause. I can't tell him via a text that I'm off to work so I can send a bald, skeletal creature through the looking glass. Instead, I improvise.

I'm tired . . . going to study, then take a nap. Txt me when you have time. I need to see you tonight.

A percentage of what I said is true. I *am* tired. I need a shower to rejuvenate myself.

Inside Mom's pink-and-pearl-toned master bathroom, I take off my prom gown and underthings. I step into the shower and twist the faucet head to massage. The heat works its magic on my aching bones and muscles.

Scented like a sugar cookie, I step out and dry off. My mind is clear, but my body is still heavy and sluggish. There isn't time for makeup or blow-drying, so I twist my wet hair into a loose braid that leaves only my red strand to hang long and wavy in the front. I slip into some skinny jeans—vertical stripes of deep red and black running the length of the stretchy denim. They were a Christmas gift from Mom. It's the first time I've worn them. Jeans and no makeup. She'll be so proud.

As soon as I've dragged a black, holey T-shirt over a purple tank and knee-high lace-up boots into place, I loop my necklaces around my neck.

In my room, I put my gown away and drape the dress bag at the foot of my bed, then crawl under the covers—clothes, boots, and all. It doesn't matter that the sheets are damp or that they smell of old bones and aquarium water. I'm too exhausted to care.

Through bleary eyes I peer at the clock on my nightstand. The red digital numbers glare 6:15 P.M. I fumble with the buttons to set the alarm for 6:45.

Just a quick catnap . . . I can fit that in before Dad gets home . . . then I'll be rested enough to take Rabid to Butterfly Threads.

The moment my eyes close, my mind kicks into overdrive. I keep wondering: Could Morpheus be right, that my blood might be used as a weapon against me? He is a creature of dreams. He knows how to interpret them. And since he wasn't behind the clown, who was?

Who triggered that terrifying nightmare that ended in Jeb's cocooned corpse?

If only Nurse Terri hadn't sedated me that night, things wouldn't seem so muddled. If only she hadn't had those sad eyes that made me want to please her.

My breath sticks inside my lungs.

Mom's interpretation of my artwork resurfaces: three Red Queens fighting for the ruby crown, and another woman watching from behind a cluster of vines and shadows. *I could see her eyes. Sad, piercing.*

Nurse Terri . . . she was dressed in that white costume uniform. She stood out. Maybe she was a Wonderland denizen in disguise. She had access to my room, could've brought the enchanted clown inside. She would've heard about and had access to the mosaics in my art teacher's car . . . and my blood.

But if she was a netherling, I would've seen glimpses of her true form through the glamour like I did with Morpheus.

It's all so confusing. But one thing's for sure: There's another player in this game. Someone in the human realm who doesn't belong. I can't go back to Wonderland and fight a battle while my family and friends are unprotected here with a mysterious netherling on the loose. The fact that they might've already had contact with her gives me goose bumps.

If I go through the mirror to the iron bridge in London, maybe I can decipher the mosaics Mom hid and figure out who I'm up against. I squeeze the key at my neck, debating if I should call Morpheus back.

He won't come. I hurt his pride. He told me I have to *find* him now. He said he'd be hiding among lost memories, whatever that means.

Yet another riddle to solve on my own.

Strangely, it's that thought that lulls me to sleep, as if I've been preparing my whole life to handle all of this myself. Come to think of it, maybe I have.

※ · l · ※

"Butterfly?"

I startle awake at Dad's voice in the darkness. Light slants from the cracked door where he's peering in.

It takes several seconds to shake the fuzziness out of my head, to remember where I am . . . what I was supposed to get done before he made it home.

The low rumble of Rabid's snores from my closet releases a spring in my spine. I sit up, yelping in hopes of awakening my hidden guest.

"Whoa. Didn't mean to scare you." Dad comes inside and shuts the door partway so my eyes can adjust. He sits on the edge of my mattress and rubs my head, just like when I was little. Rabid's quiet now, so I sigh, contented.

"Why are you wearing your clothes in bed?" Dad asks.

I scrub my face and yawn. "Clothes?"

"Are they from yesterday? Your mom said you weren't feeling well, so I left you alone. But I know you've got one final left. I just wanted to check, in case you were up for going to school."

"School?" I'm like a parrot, mimicking everything that's said to me.

I glance at my glowing clock: 6:20 A.M. Only then do I notice that I set the alarm for 6:45 A.M. instead of P.M.

My empty stomach turns over. I've been asleep for twelve hours. Morpheus kept his word and didn't haunt my dreams, and I slept soundly. Too soundly. Now I'm not going to have time to send Rabid back or look for my mosaics before school.

My rested brain kicks into overdrive, formulating a new plan. I could leave early and use the full-length mirrors in the girls' locker room. That would mean tucking Rabid in my backpack and taking him with me to school. The thought of mixing more of Wonderland with my real life rattles my nerves, especially because I still have Morpheus's mess to clean up with Taelor and the other students.

But it doesn't matter. There's no time to lose.

Dad leans over to turn on the lamp. "Something keeps crunching under my feet . . ." He flips the switch before I can stop him. He gapes as he sees the glass sparkling on the floor. "W-w-what happened in here?"

Busted.

I suppress a groan. "Mom can tell you."

It's shameful how quickly I sell her out, though on some level I feel vindicated. Let her justify the broken mirror. Let her be the one under the microscope. She's proven herself adept at lying for years.

Dad crouches beside my bed, careful not to kneel in the glass. He's not in his work clothes yet, which means he's been making breakfast. Mom must still be asleep.

He touches a shard with dried blood on it. "Allie . . . did you cut yourself?"

"No. Mom—" I stop talking in midbreath. He's staring at my palms. Of course. This reminds him of the time she cut me. "Dad, it's okay." I toss off my covers and scoot out of bed.

His stunned gaze drops to my boots.

I reach down and adjust their laces, as if it's perfectly normal to wake up wearing them. "Mom bumped my mirror while she was dusting. It fell against my dresser. She cut herself a little, but she's fine now. It was . . . more like a paper cut, you know? Superficial."

The concern doesn't leave his expression as he picks up shards piece by piece, careful not to get sliced. "I didn't notice any cuts. Why didn't she tell me about this?"

"Maybe she figured I'd already cleaned it up." I bend to help him, but he lifts a hand in a forbidding gesture.

"Let me take care of this, Allie."

He's always done this—he's always taken care of us, cleaned up our messes. And we've done nothing but keep secrets.

Once he drops the final piece of glass into my trash can and sets my empty mirror frame upright, he turns to me. "I'm sorry, sweetie. It's just . . . I was afraid it was happening again. She used to break mirrors a lot. On purpose. She wouldn't allow one anywhere near you since you were a tiny baby."

The sun creeps up, and the orangey pink light softens Dad's edges, making him look as young as Mom does. He's never talked much about how it was when Alison started "losing her mind." It had to be horrible for him.

"Dad . . ." I touch his arm, stroking his tattered sweatshirt.

He lays his hand over mine. "I couldn't bear for it to start again. I can't be away from her anymore."

Nodding, I brave a question. "Did she ever try to explain her aversion to mirrors? Did you ever ask?"

He sits on the edge of my bed. After another puzzled glance at my boots, he shrugs. "It was a *looking glass* thing. Her explanations weren't sane."

Of course her rantings would sound demented to someone who didn't know the truth. Why didn't she prove it to him when I was little, show him her powers? She had years to find a way to do it.

"If she had given you some real proof that Wonderland existed," I say, going out on a limb, "you would've believed her . . . right?"

He shakes his head. "The blood on her hands when she cut them on the mirrors. The blood on our baby girl when she attacked her with the garden shears." He looks up at me, his expression pure agony. "Allie, that was tangible. That was real. That was all the proof I could handle. You just don't *know*." He rubs his face, hiding his eyes behind his palm. "She kept screaming that she had to fix you. Like you were something she could glue back together. But she was acting so erratic, so high-strung—and she had just hurt you, so . . . I couldn't let her near you. That was the last straw, but things had been bad for a long time before that. Even *I* started having nightmares about Wonderland. I knew we had to get some help . . . you needed one parent who was sane. One who was safe."

So that was why Mom didn't heal my palms. My grudge against her thaws an infinitesimal degree.

Dad bends over to pick up my dress bag. It must have fallen to the floor last night. He lays it across his lap.

"Did you actually see her bump the mirror?" He runs a fingernail along the bag's zipper. "I mean, it doesn't make sense. She would've had to throw it against the dresser to cause that much damage." He glances at the trash can. "Maybe she should talk to her doctor."

His suggestion makes me bristle. I won't have her tied up in a straitjacket or drooling under sedatives again. I love her, regardless of the rift between us, and she's suffered enough for a lifetime.

"Wait, Dad." I sit down next to him, feeling out my options. "I'm going to tell you something . . . I just don't know how you'll react." Staring down at the earbuds on my floor, I consider animating them, having them wrap around his ankle like an amorous cat.

I stare so hard, my eyes sting.

"Allie, you're making me nervous. What's going on?"

My heartbeat hammers loud enough that I hear it in my ears. I'm so close to breaking loose, so close to showing him my magic. The earbud cords tremble—a movement so minute, only I can see it. Then I lose my nerve and look at my eels instead, breaking my concentration.

"Mom and I had a fight yesterday," I mutter. "I—I pushed her, and she fell into the mirror. That's what made it hit the dresser. That's why I shut myself up in my room. And she told you I wasn't feeling well to cover for me so I wouldn't get in trouble. I'm really sorry."

Dad's skin flushes dark pink. "You *pushed* your mother?" His gaze deepens with disappointment and apprehension—a look that makes my confidence shrink to the size of an ant. "What's with these violent outbursts?"

"Outbursts? This is the first one."

"It isn't. I heard you yelling at your mom in your hospital room. Was this over Jeb again? Did you sneak out last night to see him? Is that why you're wearing your shoes in bed?" The color in his face isn't a blush anymore. It's bordering on purple.

I stand up. "No! None of this is about Jeb." I can't have him doubting Jeb again, not now that they've finally worked things out. "I took a couple of sedatives after my fight with Mom. I guess they kicked in before I had time to undress." A full-blown lie.

When he keeps watching me, unconvinced, I add, "I hate that we fought, that I almost hurt her." Even more, I hate that I'm defending her when she should be defending herself to both of us.

Dad's fingers drum the dress bag—unconsciously keeping rhythm with the nervous twitch in his eyelid. "What was this fight about? It had to be big, to make you push your mother into a mirror."

"Well. I didn't *exactly* push her . . ." I want to say more but draw a complete blank.

A look of discernment crosses Dad's face. "Wait. It was over the car, wasn't it?"

"Huh?"

"The Mercedes that was in our driveway when I got home."

"Uh . . ." I don't know what to say. Mom's apparently told him something, and I have to go along with her story.

"Your mom said you wouldn't give her the keys when she asked for them."

I glance over at the corner behind my door where Morpheus's vest, shirt, and hat lay crumpled last night. They're gone, along with his keys, and Mom just handed me my alibi on a silver platter. "Did she tell you she tried to take the keys from me and I wouldn't let go?"

Dad's gaze hardens. "No."

"They slipped out of my hand and caught her off balance."

"You mean that's how she fell into the mirror?"

I nod, despising myself with every move of my head.

Jaw clenched, Dad stares into me. "Look, I agree with your mom. It's generous of that exchange student to offer you his car until Gizmo's tire is fixed, but you can't drive it. If you were to get even a dent in it, he could turn around and sue us for more money than your college education is worth."

"All right," I whisper, relieved the explanation for the car is out of the way. But that's the only relief I get because now Dad's looking at me like I'm a stick of dynamite he needs to defuse. "Dad, I get it."

"I don't think you do," he says, shaking his head. "I'm guessing you think your mom got overemotional about the car."

"Like she does about everything," I mumble.

"Well, this time she has a reason. When we were first dating, I had a wreck." He glances down to where his toes wiggle inside his woolly socks. "It was in a sports car . . . not as nice as the one in our driveway but similar. I took a curve too fast and hit a tree. The car was destroyed. I was in a coma for months."

My breaths become shallow. I can't risk inhaling too deep and missing even a word. This is something sacred, a part of their history they've kept from me.

"I know you wish I'd talk more about my mom and pop," Dad continues, though the change of subject throws me.

"No, Dad. I get why you don't like to."

"It's because of the wreck, Allie."

I stare dumbly at him, trying to connect the dots. "They were in the car with you?" He never told me that's how they died . . .

The dress bag crunches as he crosses his ankles. "Well, no. It's because of the wreck that I don't *remember* them. If it wasn't for your mom, I wouldn't remember anything about my childhood. She put a photo journal together for me so I would know my parents' faces, since they had passed away before I met her. I couldn't remember that I have no sisters or brothers, or cousins or relatives who were interested in knowing me. I didn't even remember meeting your mom. That's how bad the damage was. Is. My life before I crashed that car, before your mom . . . it's just gone. As if I never lived it."

There's a prick in my heart, like a thorn piercing me from the inside out. "Dad, I'm sorry." The apology feels inadequate. Memories are such precious and priceless things. It's always made me sad to think about Jeb losing his from Wonderland. But this is so much worse. "You never told me."

"You already had a messed-up childhood. I wasn't going to add anything to that. You needed at least one parent who had a semi-normal past. Right?"

I shrug, though I don't know if I agree. Maybe if we'd both been honest all along, we could've helped each other.

"So, do you see now?" he asks. "Why she doesn't want you driving that car? It's too easy, when you have unharnessed power at your fingertips, to forget you're not invincible. To make rash decisions that can affect your whole future."

His words are so perfectly cut for me, they could be the missing pieces of my own thoughts and fears.

"I want you to work things out with her before you go to school," he says, in a final tone. "And I want you to make a better effort to get along with her. She's been trying so hard with you." His jaw clenches. "Make me proud, Alyssa."

Alyssa. He hasn't called me by my first name alone since the time I came home in ninth grade with a C in geometry. It's worse than if he'd yelled at me.

"All right," I mumble.

"You better get ready for school," he says. He stands and drops his keys on my bed. "You can drive my truck. I'll call someone to take me to Micah's Tire Repair. They're supposed to be done with Gizmo this morning. Oh, and I parked the Mercedes in the garage last night to keep it safe. Bring your friend home after school to pick it up. Okay?"

"Okay," I say, though I have no idea how I'll accomplish that.

Dad looks like he's about to leave. Instead, he stops to lift the dress bag from my bed. "Is this what I think it is?"

At first I have no idea what he means—I'm not even sure *I* remember what's in the bag. Then I nod.

He opens the zipper, tugging out the mask and a corner of the dress.

"So you were serious about going to prom tonight?" He looks suspiciously close to happy again. He's wanted me to go to a school dance since I was a freshman. He signed himself and Mom up to be chaperones the minute he heard I'd told Jeb yes, but it's obvious he never believed I'd follow through until now.

He lays the bag back on the bed and glances at the flowery tiara pinned on the hanger. His famous Elvis smirk appears. "You're going to wear a crown? Aw, Allie, you'll look just like a princess. Just like when you used to play dress-up." His goofy grin is pure nostalgia, and it makes me want to cry. He strokes the mildew-tinted lines of the mask. "Well . . . a princess who's been through a bit of a rough patch. I like it."

"Thanks." I attempt a smile as I wrestle the dress back into the bag and zip it closed, hating that I'll disappoint him yet again when I don't show up for the dance tonight.

A worried wrinkle appears between his eyebrows. He catches my hand and drags me close for a hug, tucked safe under his chin. I snuggle into him, my daddy . . . my champion. And the love of Mom's life. It's amazing what she did for him, putting that photo journal together, giving him his past back. That doesn't sound like a woman who resents her marriage. Maybe she really did choose Dad over the crown. Maybe there really was more to the story. I need to give her the benefit of the doubt and hear her out—if we ever get the chance to discuss it again.

"Listen, Butterfly," Dad whispers against my head. "You haven't seemed yourself, but I get it. It's the end of school. You have tests, prom, graduation, and on top of all that, you almost drowned. It's understandable that you feel a little unhinged. Maybe you need to talk to someone other than me or Mom."

A burning sensation rises in my esophagus. I push back enough to glare up at him. "What, like a psychiatrist? No, Dad. I'm not going crazy."

"That's not what I meant. You could go to your school counselor. You just seem to be teetering a little. We can put you right again. Let us know what you need."

My 6:45 alarm buzzes and we jump.

I crawl across my bed to shut it off. "Can we talk about this later? I should get ready."

"Sure," Dad says. He stalls outside my door. "There are scrambled eggs in the kitchen. And don't forget to apologize to your mom before you leave. I'm going to take a shower, to give you two some privacy."

I promise him I'll fix things. I do want to talk to Mom, for so many reasons, but the instant Dad shuts my door, I know that I won't follow through. Not this morning . . . but hopefully later today, after I take care of my royal advisor.

I cram Dad's truck keys into my pocket, then throw open my closet. Rabid's standing there with his skeletal hands intertwined, thimble dangling cockeyed from an antler prong and mismatched socks hanging off his ears. For one weird moment, he reminds me of the White Rabbit I always read about in the Carroll tales.

In spite of my emotional uproar, I can't stop the smile that breaks on my lips. "Thanks for being quiet. You did good." I pat his bald head.

He blinks bright pink eyes at me. "Rabid White, hungry be."

Opening my empty backpack, I wave him inside, hoping netherling stowaways like eggs for breakfast.

INVASION

Turns out netherlings do like eggs, at least the buttery kind my dad makes. After Rabid and I have breakfast, I scoop some extra into a Tupperware bowl. Along with a bag of Mom's cookies and a bottled water, I put the bowl into my backpack to keep my royal advisor occupied on our way to school.

For such a small creature, he has a huge appetite, and a huge knowledge of the inner workings of Wonderland's politics. During the drive, he sits out of view on the floorboards of the passenger side, head poking from the backpack zipper. He answers every question I ask as he gobbles up eggs.

According to Wonderland law, there are three ways the blood

heir of a netherling queen can relinquish her throne once she's been crowned: death, exile, or losing to another blood heir in a magical tournament. I turned my throne over to Grenadine, but that doesn't count as an official abdication. She can only be a temporary substitute, since she's not of our lineage. Now that the kingdom's in trouble, it's up to me to step back in, take up the crown, and defeat Red. It's like Morpheus said while we were in the car: I'm the only one who can release and wield the magic that is now a part of my blood.

So I'm stuck for life, which is another fact Morpheus failed to mention before he placed that thing on my head last year.

Then again, now that I'm coming to terms with my netherling inheritance and responsibilities—and how they're entangled with my mortal side—I'm not sure I *would* give up my crown-magic to just anyone, even if I could. The recipient would have to want what's best for both Wonderland and the human realm.

If only I could divide myself in half and be two people: The human side could stay here with Jeb and my family, and the netherling one could reign over Wonderland, keeping the peace with an iron fist.

It's 7:20 when I pull into the north parking lot, forty-five minutes before the first bell. I park Dad's truck next to the Dumpsters where Morpheus waited for me after school yesterday.

The lot is abandoned except for two vehicles, both of which I recognize. One belongs to the principal, and one is Mr. Mason's new car with the annoyingly ineffective alarm system.

Even though Morpheus stayed out of my head like he said he would, I can still sense him in the background, watching how I handle things. Just like when we were kids together. As mad as he was when he left, I'm confident he wants me to succeed. Not only that, he *wants* me to find him. He doesn't do anything without a reason. It must be important for me to discover where he went on my own.

I just need to figure out what he meant by "hiding among lost memories."

Before I go in, I try to call Jeb one last time. It's not like him to be so quiet. I'm starting to wonder if he got my text last night at all. But if he didn't, why hasn't he called to check on me and Mom? Doesn't he care? At least Ivy's out of town, so I don't have to torture myself worrying about her.

Jeb's phone goes to voice mail again. This time I leave a message. "I'm at school. Text me. I need to talk to you."

I stare at my phone. Something's still bothering me: Nurse Terri.

Pleasance University Medical Center doesn't have an employee directory online. On a whim, I do a search for nurse uniforms along with the name of the hospital. An announcement pops up, posted on the News page from a week ago:

During Memorial Day weekend, in tribute to fallen veterans, Pleasance University MC will be reinstating vintage nurse and doctor uniforms. Any employee who has lost loved ones in past wars and wishes to participate should contact Louisa Colton in human resources for available sizes and styles. Rentals paid for by Catholic Family Services Board and supplied by Banshee's Costume Boutique.

I close the link. That explains Nurse Terri's costume on Monday and possibly her desolate, sad eyes. Maybe I jumped to conclusions about her. She was so nice and helpful. But what about the clown and my stolen art from Mr. Mason's car? Could there have been another netherling around that I didn't see?

After zipping Rabid into my backpack along with my phone, I start toward the back entrance. The classroom windows glow yellow, muted by the closed blinds and that hazy light of post sunrise. The building looks just like it always does, even though everything is different inside, at least for me. Morpheus saw to that.

I skulk through the deserted breezeway and inhale the scent of yeast and sweet spices wafting from the cafeteria. The sounds of screeching zombies and annoying theme music drift out of my backpack. I made the mistake of showing Rabid how to play a game on my phone. Muscles tensing, I unzip my backpack, take the phone out, and mute it before handing it to him once more.

I duck into the dark gymnasium and use the flashlight on Dad's key chain to find my way to the girls' locker room, treading carefully so my boots won't leave black streaks on our mascot—the giant blue and orange ram painted in the middle of the wooden floor.

As I curve around the partition entrance to the locker room, the stench of old socks and musty tile stings my nose. With a flip of the light switch, a fluorescent glow buzzes to life overhead, and I face a panel of full-length mirrors.

I unzip my backpack. Rabid clambers out, his mouth stuffed with cookie. He punches buttons on my phone in a last-ditch attempt to kill the zombies in his game. Gently, I pry the cell from his skeletal grip and tuck it into the backpack.

"Are you ready?" I ask, though it's a rhetorical question. On the way to school I gave him direct orders to go straight to the Red kingdom and stay by Grenadine's side until I return to help her.

Rabid fishes in his coat. His thimble clatters to the cement floor. He picks it up and starts to dig again for his key.

"It's okay. I got this." I hold mine up on its chain and stare into the closest mirror, picturing the Thames sundial trail in London. An image of the sundial statue boy that hides the rabbit hole from human eyes blurs in the glass—projected by my memory.

I wait for the mirror to splinter. As soon as the cracks appear, my heartbeat kicks into overdrive. I'm right where I was a year ago, standing at the doorway to madness. Only this time, I know exactly what's waiting on the other side.

Pushing past my hesitation, I press the key into the juncture of crinkles shaped like a keyhole. The portal ripples open, and a cool breeze swishes through my hair, scented with grass and flowers.

I take Rabid's craggy hand. We're just about to step through, when I pause. The ground around the sundial appears to be moving, as if it wasn't grass but a dark and angry sea, its waves thrashing against and underneath the sundial's stand.

"What is that?" I mumble.

Rabid leans in, his bones clattering. "Fire pincers. Pinch you, Majesty."

I lean closer and realize it's a sea of fire ants—shimmering a deep black and red—invading the rabbit hole. There are enough to cover the ground for what looks like the length of a football field—thousands upon thousands of them.

I wonder if anyone on the sundial tour is seeing this.

I don't have time to look around and find out; I need to get Rabid down the rabbit hole. There's no safe place to step. It doesn't matter that ants chat with me on a daily basis; they still won't hesitate to attack with their pincers if they're angry or determined, especially if I stand in their path. And these are fire ants. The most aggressive and painful of their kind.

If I didn't have to be quiet in the locker room, I'd shout out to them. They can't possibly defeat Red's zombie-flower army. Yet it's obvious they're on their way to try.

Unexpected voices from the gym shake my concentration. I jerk free of the mirror, closing the portal. Then I shuffle Rabid into the backpack and scoot it into a locker.

"Stay hidden until I see what's going on out there," I say and hand him the bag of cookies. "When I get back, we'll come up with some way to make peace with the ants."

The locker door won't latch shut with the backpack in the way, so I leave it open a crack. After turning off the light, I peer around the partition wall into the gym.

Multibulb fixtures beam down from the ceiling. I blink at the brightness, taken aback by the flutter of activity along the floor. A handful of students carry in white, glittery trees and doily lanterns. More follow with giant plastic tubs of lacy white tablecloths, crepe paper, and other party decorations.

My stomach drops. It's the student council and prom committee, setting up for tonight's fairy-tale masquerade dance. Could I possibly have worse timing?

Some of the bigger guys fold the wooden bleachers and roll them against the walls to leave the rest of the floor free for dancing. Most of the girls putter around on either side of the gym, setting up the snack area and the makeshift stage where the band will play, announcements will be made, and the prom king and queen will be chosen.

I groan as more students saunter into the gym. Any possibility of sending Rabid through the mirror before school is shot. Someone could walk in just as we step inside. I consider hiding in a shower stall till everyone's gone, but movement in the crowd stops me in my tracks.

"Hey, you!" Taelor shouts, holding up her arm.

She's the last person I want to talk to. I sink farther behind the partition, then exhale a relieved breath when I realize she's not yelling at me. She waves her arm again at a dark-haired, baby-faced sophomore in the corner diagonally across from where I'm hiding. He stands next to a tree he placed on the floor, and before he can look up, he's surrounded by Taelor, Twyla, and Kimber.

"We have to leave space for the park bench where the couples pose for pictures," Taelor scolds him. "The tree goes on the other side of the gym, by that long banquet table where the snacks will be."

The boy stares at her, dumbfounded, either stunned by her beauty or shocked to be addressed by a senior.

She sighs and starts dragging the tree in its pot, completely oblivious of the streaks it and her black cowboy boots are making on the high-buffed floor.

Wait. *Cowboy boots?* That's a first.

Even her dress looks carefully chosen to impress an entomologist: a silvery mini with fluttery sleeves that look like wings. Maybe she's hoping Morpheus will mistake her for a moth and pin her to his corkboard.

I almost smirk at that. I'd heard a rumor that she broke up with her original date to prom after M asked her to go. I never thought to ask him if it was true, but it sounds like something he would do—lead her on just for the fun of it. She's about to be disappointed.

"Ugh." She whimpers when she's a couple of yards away from me. I slink farther into the shadows of the locker room but keep her in my sights. Her arms—tanned and toned from incessant tennis and volleyball practice—shimmer under the lights as she tugs at the potted tree. "This thing is heavy."

Blushing, the sophomore snaps out of his trance and jumps in to help, winning a stunning though sarcastic smile.

"Thanks, Superman," she purrs and releases her side of the pot.

I can almost see stubble sprouting on his chin as he fast-forwards through puberty, following at her heels.

I duck behind the wall when they pass by.

"Al?"

Jenara's voice brings me out again. A basket hangs on her arm. Lanterns thump together inside. She threads string through a few to form the garlands other students are hanging on the trees.

"I thought that was you lurking back here," she says. "What's going on? I didn't see your name on the sign-up list."

"I didn't exactly sign up for this," I say, meaning it on so many levels.

Jen smirks. "Yeah, me neither. It's part of my penance for defacing the prom posters. As if posters have faces." She snorts, then sobers when I don't respond. "You never brought your dress by last night." Her meticulously lined eyes narrow with concern. "Is your mom . . . ?" The question trails off, falling silent beneath the hum of the busy students in the background.

"No, she's fine." Reluctantly, I ease out of the safety of the shadows and into the gym, trusting Rabid to stay hidden. "Something came up when we got home from the emergency roo—"

"Whoa!" Jen interrupts as I step into the light. "What's with the au naturel?"

Only then do I remember I don't have any makeup on. It's the first time since I was a freshman that I've shown up to school without wearing my armor.

Against every instinct to run, I take a lantern from her basket and some string to start my own garland, nostalgic for the times I would string moth corpses with Morpheus in Wonderland—back when I didn't have to wear armor. "Sheesh, Jen. Make me feel like a troll, why don't you?"

She drops her lantern strand back into the basket and squeezes my forearm gently. "Hey, you know I didn't mean it like that. You've got the perfect complexion and bone structure to pull it off. It's just not . . . *you*. And your hair"—she flicks the red strand hanging free from my messy braid—"did you sleep with it like this?" Before I can answer, she inhales a sharp breath. "Oh, my gosh."

The basket slides off her arm and tips over, and lanterns roll onto the floor. Ignoring the mess, she grabs my shoulders.

Her lips tremble on a half smile. "No way. You finally *did* it!"

Her outburst echoes louder than the chatter around us. Several of the students turn in our direction. Twyla and Deirdre pause in the act of setting a navy blue sign with silver foil letters on an easel next to the picture cove. They whisper and point; then Twyla heads to the gym's entrance, where Taelor's too busy digging through boxes of donated toys to notice us.

"Way to be subtle, Jen," I say, frowning.

She glances over her shoulder and lowers her voice to a whisper. "Sorry. It's just . . . this is so huge!"

"What are you talking about?"

"You spent the night with Jeb. Right? That's why he wouldn't answer his phone after he went to the studio. Why he didn't come home last night. Ha! I knew once he saw you in that dress—"

"Jeb didn't come home last night?" It's my turn to interrupt. Heat rushes to my cheeks as I realize how loud I spoke. Even more of our classmates are watching us now. Taelor's tuned in, too. She and Twyla wind their way through the crowd. By the pompous look on Taelor's face, I'm guessing she heard what I said.

She's the least of my worries. I drop my lanterns to the floor with the ones gathered around Jen's feet.

"I wasn't with him," I whisper to her. "You think he spent the night at the studio?"

Her face falls. "I—I just assumed."

"You don't know for sure? Didn't your mom go ballistic?"

"She worked the late shift at the convenience store and crashed as soon as she came in. I didn't even know he was gone until I walked by his room this morning. His bed hadn't been slept in. You know he never makes it up."

My first thought is Ivy. What if she only *said* she was going out of town? I know Jeb would never cheat on me. But it's not my mind behind the thoughts, it's my netherling instincts. They *know* something is off.

Maybe it's never been just that I'm jealous of Jeb painting Ivy. She appeared at the most inconvenient time, when Morpheus started haunting my dreams with news of Wonderland's demise. She has to be a real person—I've looked her up—but I've never actually met her. So a netherling could've kidnapped her and could be wearing her imprint as a glamour like Morpheus did with Finley's. Maybe it's the same someone who's in the shadows in my mosaic, and the same someone who's been taunting me with the clown.

My blood chills. I grab Jen's arm. "We have to find him . . ."

She nods and we start for the entrance, but the volunteers surround us, looking between us and Taelor. There's no clear path to the gym door. Rage starts to build inside me. *Get out of my way,* I want to scream, but everything shuts down the minute Taelor steps into full view.

She holds a toy in her hands—my stalker clown, complete with miniature cello and strange, squared hat.

The walls seem to shrink.

"Nice, Alyssa," Taelor says, stepping into my personal space. "We ask for new toys, and you bring this piece of secondhand junk. What's it stuffed with, rocks?" She drops the clown at my feet. It hits the floor with a metallic clang. The red, black, and white checked outfit is dirty and smudged.

"Where did you get that?" I manage, my voice trembling. I can't look away from the toy for fear it might move. That beady black gaze gawks up at me—mocking.

"Don't play dumb. Your name is on a piece of tape on its back." Taelor rolls her eyes when I don't respond. "Leave it to you to be cheap. This isn't gonna get you in the door tonight. The signs specify *new* toys. Not thrift-store rejects. And by the way, what's with you? Did you sleep in the locker room? This is even worse than your usual mortician style."

It takes me a second to catch on that Taelor's referring to my wrinkled clothes and lack of makeup. But I can't respond with the clown still staring up at me.

Jen steps between us. "At least Al's fashion sense isn't dictated by her flavor of the week." She gestures to Taelor's cowboy boots.

A few snickers break from our spectators. Taelor glares over her shoulder at them. "Don't you all have stuff to do? Could've sworn there are assignments posted on the task sheet. Did you forget how to read?"

As the students disperse, Taelor exchanges a smug grin with Twyla, then turns to me again. "So, Jeb was out all night, huh? Maybe he's sick of you cheating on him."

The clown at my feet holds my gaze and my tongue.

Jen doesn't wait for me to answer. "Al didn't cheat on him, Tae-ter. British bug boy was trying to get your attention. So lay off."

"Your brother might be gullible enough to believe that load of bull. But I'm not."

"Really? Then why are you still trying to impress *Mort*?" Jen presses.

"Because he's dead sexy, and his car is worth more than your house," Taelor snaps.

Jen grits her teeth. "You little—"

"Stop." I tear my gaze from the clown to face Taelor. "Why don't you go find someone else to annoy." I want to give her a speech about having some self-respect, about not valuing a guy for his net worth but for how he treats you. But I have to get to Jeb, because something's very wrong. "I need to go."

I push Taelor aside.

She pushes back. "A little late for that."

The students who earlier thinned out gather around again, though they keep a safe distance.

"You didn't volunteer to help," Taelor snarls. "So what were you doing hiding in the locker room? Looking for some way to ruin prom again?"

"What are you talking about?" My eyes feel hot and dry and my heart pulls toward Jeb. "I don't have time for your prom fantasies."

"Fantasies?" Her face flushes, making her even prettier, if not for the hate in her eyes. "Aren't fantasies supposed to be happy? There's nothing happy about being crowned queen of prom when your king has left the dance so he can be with another girl. Bet you loved hearing how I stood onstage by myself." Her jaw clenches tight. "The *one* time I got my dad to chaperone something, and all he saw was me looking like a total loser."

I shift my feet, an uncomfortable heat rising along my neck. "Jeb knows he didn't handle things well, and he's sorry. He's tried to apologize."

She huffs. "I don't need his pity."

"Get over it already, Taelor," Jenara intervenes. "It was just a stupid dance."

"To you, maybe. Not when your family—" Taelor's lips press tight, as if reshaping her words. "I just want to make one more good memory before I leave this place forever. So stay out of it this time! Don't ruin my life again!"

Her words hang in the air. When she sees everyone's widened gazes, she covers her reddening face and darts toward the locker room. For one second, her perfect mask cracked. I'm used to being under scrutiny at school, but this is new for her.

My heartbeat hammers as I remember that Rabid is waiting inside the locker room, a sitting duck. I'm torn between him and searching for Jeb, but I choose what's closest at hand and start toward the locker room and Taelor.

"Oh, no, you don't." Twyla grabs me from behind.

Jenara intervenes. A shoving match breaks out between them. Some students head for the door, while others pick sides and shout encouragement.

Things are escalating too fast. My head throbs as I sprint to catch up to Taelor. I snag her elbow and spin her around a few feet from the partition entrance.

Her eyes are watery. She's vulnerable, like the kid I used to play with in elementary school. I'm struggling to find the right words to keep her out of the bathroom when someone's shrill scream pierces my eardrums.

I glance around to check on Jen. Everyone's attention, including hers and Twyla's, is on something over my shoulder.

"What is that?" one student shouts, pointing.

Fearing the worst—that Rabid is standing there with all of his netherling creepitude hanging out—I follow their gazes.

"Ants!" someone else yells as a rush of black and red races across the threshold toward us.

My throat cinches tight. *It can't be. I closed the mirror portal.*

Scrambling, our classmates stampede out the entrance, leaving only me and Taelor. We back up simultaneously. The invasion swirls around us, trapping us.

"Al!" Jen shouts from the doorway.

"Stay out!" I yell.

"I'm getting help!" she screams back and disappears down the breezeway.

The ants are chanting, but I can't hear them over Taelor's yelps. She stomps her feet, killing and maiming several.

I plug my ears against their agonized screams.

They retaliate, circling us tighter.

"Back off!" I yell at them. "She was just scared . . . she won't do it again."

"Who are you talking to?" Taelor shouts, lifting her leg to stomp some more.

"Don't." I put a hand on her thigh, then pick up a garland of lanterns. By shuffling the globes through the infringing army, I'm able to brush the bugs aside without hurting them. Once a path is cleared, I seize Taelor's arm and clamber onto the banquet table, forcing her up alongside me.

She breaks out of my hold once she's standing on top. "You planted them. That's why you were in the locker room."

"What?"

"You've always been a bug freak! This is a prank. You were going to release them tonight, weren't you?"

"No! I . . ." My tongue can't complete the denial, because what would it offer as an explanation? The truth?

"Look," Taelor snarls. "I'm sorry I told everyone your Liddell secret! How long are you going to hold the grudge?"

"Shut up!" I shout, dropping the string of lanterns on the table between us. "I need to hear them!"

She stares at me, eyes boggling. I glare back while listening to the ants:

Run . . . run . . . run! The rabbit hole's undone!

They weren't running *toward* us, they were running *from* something, until Taelor started attacking. A faint scraping sound jerks my attention back to the locker room. Five spindly fingers wind around the entrance. They're shadows, but at the same time they're not—all black and drizzly as if made of thick liquid.

The droplets trickle down the wall to form puddles on the floor, dark and shimmery like oil. Nails the size of talons erupt from each fingertip, spreading to birth more drippy fingers. In seconds, a blanket of hands clamps the entire length of the threshold. They grip and pull, as if they can't get through, as if a huge weight holds them back on the other end.

My entire body goes numb. I don't even *want* to know what all those oozing appendages are connected to.

"Do you see that?" I whisper, mostly to myself. I hope Taelor doesn't acknowledge me. This is one time I would prefer to be hallucinating.

Her attention doesn't budge from the ants underneath us, our oasis shrinking as they swarm closer.

"See what?" she snarls. "The millions of creepers you let loose? Yeah. I see them. We need a king-size can of Raid!" She kicks a line of ants making their way onto the table's top. The lantern strand catches on her heel, and she stumbles. As she tries to right herself, a globe rolls under her foot, and she teeters.

"Taelor!" I reach out but miss her by an inch. She falls backward onto the table, head hitting the edge with a sick thump. Her eyes go dull before rolling shut.

"No no no." I drop to my knees, keeping the shadowy hands in my peripheral vision. I stroke her cheeks gently. "Taelor, can you hear me?"

As if satisfied she's defeated, the ants retreat toward the gym door.

Save our realm, Alyssa.

Send the trespassers away.

They siphon into the breezeway, and I leap down. With their whispers gone, the gym falls silent.

I whip around to face the shadow hands and choke on a strangled breath. The clown stands just inside the locker room entrance. It has a hostage: Rabid White. The clown's cello's bow is wedged between his fleshy chin and cadaverous neck.

Far above them, dark liquid dribbles from the threshold. The fluid runs down the clown's face, blackening its eyes and teeth.

"Majesty, sorry I be . . ." my royal advisor whimpers, his hideous face remorseful.

His key dangles from one hand, the empty cookie bag in the other. Some crumbs dot the floor around his feet. He must've opened the portal, tried to bribe the ants so he could get to Wonderland like I wanted him to. Instead, Wonderland came to us.

I'm starting to think Wonderland has been here all along, seeping in ever since my accident. That was when the possessed clown appeared. Red could've found it in the cemetery and sent it after me.

I can't let that demented plaything take Rabid.

"Let go of him!" I yell.

With a laugh as eerie and haunting as an out-of-tune cello, the clown squeezes Rabid tighter around his neck.

The oily shadows claw at the threshold, gouging marks on the painted cement wall. Whatever they're attached to on the other side won't let them through. They release a garbled rush of shrieks and moans, more disturbing than what I've heard on the third floor of the asylum, where patients cry out in padded cells.

The noise rakes across every nerve ending in my body and echoes through my bones. I slump to the ground, covering my head until it fades to silence again.

Depleted, I barely have the energy to look up. A giant black form pushes through the doorway, shoving the clown and Rabid aside. It explodes into a flock of shrouds, constantly changing shape like wisps of living smoke. They screech as they fly up to the rafters and wriggle into the bulbs, filling them with inky fluid until each one ruptures. The lights snuff out in a domino effect.

I yelp and roll Taelor's unconscious body from its perch to the ground, then drag her underneath the table to shield us from shattering glass. When the last bulb bursts, the room dims, leaving only the glow from the breezeway slanting through the gymnasium entrance.

More shrieks hammer my ears. One of the shadows slinks along the floor to the gym doors, trailing a greasy black streak behind. It disengages the doorstops to swing them shut, leaving us in complete darkness.

The clown hisses. Terror prickles through my backbone, and I pull Taelor closer, holding her like a security blanket. Her breath is warm against my neck and her pulse seems strong. It's better she's out cold. I could never explain what's happening around us.

"Rabid, what are those things?" I shout, needing to hear his familiar voice in the darkness, needing to know he's still there.

"The mome wraiths . . ." His soft answer is at odds with the loud shudder of his bones. *"Outgrabe."*

FIRE WITHIN

All mimsy were the borogoves;
And the mome raths outgrabe.

It's from the Jabberwocky poem. *Mome wraiths.* The pronunciation, "wraith" instead of "rath," doesn't even faze me. Morpheus has mentioned them before.

The word *rath* was misspelled and mispronounced in the Carroll poem. In reality, they're wraiths—gloomy, phantasmal creatures. *Mome* means far from home, so they're lost, seeking their way back. *Outgrabe* is the sound they make, a mind-curdling shriek.

That's all I remember. I can't let them escape into the rest of the school to terrorize the humans. I have to hold them here until I can figure out how to defeat them.

Their howls and wails scatter my thoughts. Gusts of cold air swoop by my face, rife with the scent of menace and clammy sweat. I hold Taelor against me, letting her expensive perfume flush the stench from my nose. I never expected to feel so protective of her. But she has no defense other than me. The responsibility is overwhelming.

The clown's laugh erupts again, demanding my attention.

Rabid screams: "Majesty!" His plea echoes from the depths of the locker room, and I know that he's gone—taken somewhere out of my reach.

"No!" I shout.

I can't just sit and do nothing. Going against my resolution to stay with Taelor, I prop her along the table's legs and blindly crawl around, patting the floor and praying I don't touch something that grabs back. My hand slides through an oily puddle, and I wipe the goop on my pants, then resume the search. Finally, a lantern rolls under my fingers.

I drag my prize under the table. After fumbling for the light's switch, I flick it on. A soft amber glow seeps through the doily patterns, creating a luminary effect. It would be beautiful, if not for the gruesome scene it reveals.

Thick, oily sludge runs down the walls, then gathers in small puddles along the floor. Phantom shapes skim through the air, dipping and diving—like ghouls in a graveyard. Each time they touch the floor, they leave a black streak behind. It's like I'm locked inside a Halloween movie. All that's missing are the crumbling tombstones.

My gut twists with fear. "Morpheus. Come back, please." I

mumble the request, hoping he'll hear me. Hoping he's not too mad to listen.

Underneath the phantoms' shrieks, Morpheus's silence rings even louder.

"Morpheus! I need your help!" My scream echoes off the walls. The phantoms hiss in response, and one lunges under the table, splitting in half to form a pair of floating gloves filled with disembodied hands. They grab Taelor's ankles to wrestle her away from me.

"Stop!" I drop the lantern and hug her from behind, fingers laced under her arms and around her chest. She becomes the object of a supernatural tug-of-war. Using my weight, I pull so hard, her boots slip off. My back thuds against the table legs. The gloved hands spin through the air in the opposite direction, then reunite to their original shapeless form.

I search for the lantern again, only to find that the other phantoms dragged it away. The one that attacked Taelor must've been a decoy so they could steal my light. They ooze into the holes in the lacy pattern, filling the globe until the light is extinguished.

The black void is as heavy as a wet quilt. I hold Taelor's limp hand. Maybe Morpheus really has turned his back on me. I never thought he would leave me trapped with no way out. Even if he's furious enough to want me to suffer, surely he'll come around. He needs my help to save Wonderland.

As if in answer to my thoughts, a glowing light appears in the locker room's doorway, small and sparkly like the lit fuse on a Roman candle, bobbing in midair. It dodges the plummeting wraiths on the way over, then perches atop Taelor's knee.

The brightness fades, taking shape: two inches tall, feminine curves, lima-bean green, and naked all but for the strategic placement of glistening scales. Coppery bulbous eyes study me. It's like being in a staring contest with a dragonfly.

"Gossamer," I say, as surprised as I am relieved to see her. She was once Morpheus's most beautiful and treasured sprite before she betrayed him. Either she's here on her own or she's made amends.

"Queen Alyssa." She bows, and her furred wings tremble. She looks over her shoulder at the wraiths. "It is a dark time," she says in her tinkling voice.

"It is," I answer, trying to keep my voice steady so I'll sound regal. I fail miserably. "Did Morpheus send you?"

"Indeed," she answers. "He heard your call."

I inhale deeply, reassured that he hasn't completely abandoned me. "So what do I do? How do I defeat them?"

"You need not defeat them. Simply lead them home."

"To Wonderland?"

"To its foundation. Children's dreams are the infrastructure of Wonderland. You are versed in the Lewis Carroll tale and his poetry: *A childish story take, and with a gentle hand, lay it where Childhood's dreams are twined in Memory's mystic band . . . thus grew the world of Wonderland.*"

We both duck as a wraith skims by.

"Uh, yeah," I mumble. "That's a little different than I remember." Not that I'm surprised.

"In either version, the truth is there, if you but look for it. There are two halves to each child's dream. The borogoves are the frivolous and mischievous half and are used by Sister Two within the cemetery to distract and entertain the angry spirits. But wraiths are the nightmarish and horrific half. They guard the rabbit hole, keep anything that belongs in Wonderland from escaping, or retrieve by force those things that already have. They're tucked within the soil, and something violated their resting place."

I remember my dream with Morpheus in Wonderland while I was drowning, how the mud seemed to breathe and bubble beneath my feet. Could that have been a collective of wraiths? Then I think of the ants, how they're masters at moving more dirt than any other organism, including earthworms. They must've disrupted Wonderland's foundation, awakened the defense mechanism to prevent the flower army from breaching the hole.

Gossamer's wings flutter in a misty blur as she hovers in front of my face. Her green flesh shimmers. "Wraiths are much like lost children, since they are born of children. They're fearful, vexed creatures, unless they're tucked within their resting places. Once disturbed, they only wish to do their job so they might return to safety again. They crave the security that their brighter halves, the borogoves, once provided. Which is why they're drawn to the light and to you. Your crown-magic forbids them to touch you, but they think you bid them here. Since they've found nothing that belongs to Wonderland, they are confused. They expect you to lead them back to safety, to light their way."

I stare at the swirl of formless beings just behind Gossamer's glowing body. They bob close to us, as if trying to decide whether Gossamer belongs in Wonderland or here. The light she emanates must be hypnotizing them—confusing them.

"So that's why they busted the overhead bulbs and stole my lantern? They were trying to get close to the light?"

Gossamer nods. "You must show them the way to the rabbit hole."

"Why can't you? Let them follow your glow."

She turns up her nose at the suggestion. "I haven't the ability. The light you choose must be powerful enough to illuminate their footsteps so they will return to their place, while at the same time erasing their footsteps, so they will not follow them back."

I moan. Another riddle. "They don't even *have* feet."

Gossamer lands on my thigh, where my oily handprint from earlier is still damp. She drops to her hands and knees, tracing the shape with a palm the size of a ladybug. "Footprints are unique to every creature."

I glance at the oily streaks they've left upon the floor and walls.

"Use what my master taught you," she says. The affection in her voice indicates that Morpheus has forgiven her. It also gives me hope that he'll forgive me. "Send them home." She takes to the air.

The phantom shapes close in as she floats away. I cover my head with my arms. Even knowing they're forbidden to touch me doesn't ward off my fear. "Wait! Don't leave me. Tell Morpheus I'm sorry I hurt him. Tell him I need him here. Please, it's important!"

"I *must* leave. Before the wraiths take me forcibly. And Morpheus is seeing to Rabid's safety. Do you not consider that important?"

Ashamed, I let my silence answer for me. I was one step away from getting on my knees and begging for his return . . . just like he said I would.

"He wants you to find him when this is over." Gossamer flutters into the locker room, leaving me alone to take care of Taelor and the wraiths, the two sides of me now entwined inexorably. I was delusional to think I could ever keep them separate.

The school's 8:05 warning bell rings, and someone jiggles the handles on the gym doors. Shouts escalate from the other side.

"It's stuck," the principal hollers.

"I'll find the janitor," a teacher answers back.

My temples throb—thoughts bouncing around like Ping-Pong balls in my head—as I attempt to formulate a plan.

The wraiths wail and shriek, agitated by the human voices. They flap and ruffle through my hair, sucking my breath away in gasps. They rip through Taelor's fluttery dress and leave the sleeves in rags. I slap them away and shout. They cower, but I know their retreat is only temporary. They're becoming less like frightened children and more like volatile monsters the longer they're stuck here.

I have to send them back before someone from the Pleasance High staff opens the doors and experiences full-blown cardiac arrest.

I consider grabbing a strand of lanterns to try to "light their way," but they'll only rupture the lightbulbs. How am I supposed to lead these creatures home if they keep destroying my efforts to help?

In that moment I feel my netherling sense awaken, like a flutter behind my eyes, revealing the logic behind the illogical: Only one thing can stand up to living shadows, and that's living *light*.

Flames can breathe. They also have the ability to eat away certain kinds of oil, like kerosene. If the oily streaks left by the wraiths are flammable, that could be the answer to Gossamer's riddle.

In this realm, lighting footsteps while erasing them would be impossible and nonsensical, but not in Wonderland. And now that Wonderland has crossed our borders, it's reasonable and makes perfect sense here.

My idea is mad and dangerous. I could end up burning down the school. But I'm out of options; not to mention the thought of having so much power at my fingertips is too tempting to resist.

My body thrums with anticipation and a hunger to meet the challenge head-on. To prove to Morpheus I can handle this, that he was right to put his faith in me.

I scramble out from under the table and stand in the darkness, plugging my ears against the wraiths' shrill screeches. Eyes closed, I concentrate on the lantern garlands hanging on the trees and the ones still scattered across the floor. I can't see them, but I know they're there, and I envision the tiny lightbulbs animating, breathing and burning like real candles. My pulse becomes slow and steady, and in the resulting peace and darkness, I give life to the lifeless.

When I open my eyes again, the lanterns glimmer with a flickering orange glow. Wraiths hover over them but don't attack, as if awaiting direction.

Now the fire has to make contact with the oily streaks. I coax the candlelight to grow within the lanterns until they erupt to balls of flame. The strings between each lantern catch fire, like a dragon float in a Chinese New Year's parade—lit up in oranges and yellows and reds.

Building on that image, I imagine the blazing strands can move. They slink from the trees—the spray-painted branches igniting in their wake—and slither along the ground to join the others already there. They spread out until no puddle or streak is left untouched.

In seconds, the "footprints" catch fire and the wraiths fall in line.

"Go home!" I yell at them. "There's nothing here to be collected!"

They follow the fiery trails back into the locker room. The oily streaks burn away as they go, erasing each greasy line. As the last phantom swoops around the partition and the sound of cracking glass drifts from the locker room, a sense of accomplishment washes over me.

I did it. I led Wonderland's lost defenders home while rescuing my classmates and teachers.

All that remains is the cleanup.

The gym is on fire. I should be afraid. Instead I feel a sense of pride. This is my creation, born of my magic.

The blaze from the trees spreads to tablecloths and crepe paper—a chain reaction so brilliantly spectacular and terrible, I ache to be a part of it . . . to devour and destroy, then relish in the plunder.

I could do it. I could stand here amid the flames, let them lap at my skin, and laugh in a death-defying haze—because they belong to me. I could watch the world crumble and then dance, triumphant, in the snowfall of ash left behind.

All I have to do is set the power free. Escape the chains of my humanity, let madness be my guide. If I forget everything but Wonderland, I can become *beautiful pandemonium.*

The flames rise higher . . . tantalizing . . . tempting . . .

Smoke fills the room, gray and sylphlike, lovely in its deadly grace. It trails into the fire and forms what appear to be wings—black and magnificent. A man's silhouette fills out the image, two arms reaching for me.

Morpheus, or a mirage?

My mind trips back to our dance across the starlit sky in Wonderland, how amazing it felt to be so free. What would it feel like to dance with him in the middle of a blazing inferno, surrounded by an endless power that breathes and grows at our will?

The school bell sounds—three consecutive rings—the signal for a fire alarm. It doesn't affect me. Let the humans run from the flame. I'll walk straight into it.

Relishing the heat that magnifies with each step, I move closer to the shadowy wings and beckoning hands, only pausing as a faint sound breaks through my euphoria.

Taelor is coughing.

It makes me hesitate. Makes me listen. Makes me remember.

She didn't get out with the others. *She's in danger.*

I shake off the netherling tendrils wrapped around my mind, shut down my tyrannical desires. The smoky wings and silhouette disappear. I'm not sure they were ever there. In spite of the heat, I shiver, appalled at how easy it was to almost abandon my humanness.

I can't see Taelor for the flames rising between us, but I hear her coughing. Either she's waking up or her lungs are instinctually flushing out the pollutants. Whichever it is, she needs my help. I gulp down scorched air. My eyes sting and blur.

In order to get Taelor to safety, I have to kill the fire I gave birth to. I pause for a split second, frozen by a bizarre maternal anguish.

If I could make it rain, I could destroy the flames quickly. Douse them before they feel any pain. I remember the moldy girls' bathroom where I met Morpheus, in the basement beneath the gym. Those faulty water pipes are right under my feet.

I envision the rusted conduits coming alive, stretching and bending awake, like a salamander rousing from hibernation inside a decaying log. Flexing metal thumps the underside of the floor and radiates through my boot soles. Water pools around me, seeping between the wooden slats. Metallic pings echo as the pipes snap. Spurts of water hiss through every crack and split in the floor, shooting straight up, then coming down to douse the flames.

As the inferno shrinks and the gym gets darker by the second, I race through the water, my wet, cold clothes sticking to my skin. I skid to a stop beside the table.

Taelor grunts and rubs her eyes. I help her up and prop her against the table's edge. She coughs again. I won't leave her side. She can barely stand on her own.

The main doors fly open with a thud. A handful of firemen step inside with flashlights flaring. They pause at the door, stupefied by the sight of the gym.

Their waving lights expose my rampage: scorched wood, paper, and paint; sooty puddles along every inch of the floor; and somewhere under it all, the school mascot warped beyond recognition, blistered and black.

"What happened?" Taelor mumbles, her bloodshot eyes taking in our ruined surroundings. She's up to her ankles in black water. Her boots lie in a smoky heap a few inches away, the stink of cooked leather enough to make me gag.

Instead of trying to answer, I slump on the table beside her.

I'm like the flames. Used up. Burned out. And I haven't even begun to fight, because the battle I just won against Wonderland and myself is nothing compared to the accusations I'm about to face, and the answers I don't have.

※ · I · ※

The wind blows through my tattered braid as I stand between Dad's truck and Gizmo. I gulp down the last of my water, then toss the bottle into the Dumpster behind me. My gaze takes in the mid-morning sky, then drops to the plumbing trucks parked beside the school's back entrance.

The soft buzz of bugs hums in my ears:

Well done, Alyssa . . . just one more war to save us all.

Every muscle tenses at their warning. It's true. I'm nowhere close to safe yet, and neither are the people I love. Jeb is my priority now. I've wasted enough time here.

The fire trucks and police cars left five minutes ago. Their flashing lights still burn on the back of my eyelids. Or maybe it's the flames. Maybe that inferno will never leave my memory. An indelible reminder of the moment I lost sight of my humanness and ruined my school career and my relationship with my dad in one fell swoop.

Dad had just picked up Gizmo from the tire place when he got the call from my principal. He could never have anticipated what awaited him on the other end of his cell.

"If you get home first," he says, "you wait for me to get there. I want to be the one to tell your mother you've been suspended. All right?" The cautious restraint in his voice grates, as if he's afraid to yell at me. He thinks I'm too unstable to handle any real emotions.

He looks defeated, hunched against the truck in his work uniform. He's convinced—like everyone except Jenara—that I collected a ton of ants to sic on the entire student body. Then I accidentally set fire to the gym while trying to regain control of my prank gone awry.

Dad isn't sure it was an accident at all, although he never said that to the police or me. I can see it in his eyes. He thinks I broke the mirror in the locker room, just like the one in my room. He doesn't buy the theory that the mirror was hot from the flames and when the icy water ran over it, the glass busted, like what "happened" with the busted lightbulbs.

At least I didn't have to try to explain the water. According to the firemen, the heat warped the wooden slats until they pressed against the rusted pipes and snapped them. It was a stroke of luck.

Luck. *Right.*

I'm anything but lucky.

I didn't deny the accusations about the ants, because on some level, I am responsible. Dad is done suggesting I talk to the school counselor; he's already made an appointment with a psychiatrist. He sees the broken mirror as the beginning of the same downward spiral Mom took. This time, I'm the mindless victim.

"Alyssa." Dad presses for my answer to his question.

"I know," I answer. "If I get home first, Mum's the word." It's a joke, but he doesn't laugh, probably because he's never met a certain smug netherling who's always referred to Mom in his cockney accent. I cough in the awkward silence, my throat raw from smoke inhalation.

"You should count your lucky stars the school thinks this was an accident," Dad says, proving that even if he didn't get the joke, he sensed my sarcasm. "And that they took your good behavior over the years into account. A one-day suspension for nearly burning down the gym? Accidental or not, they could've pressed charges, and then you'd be taking your final exam in juvie instead of at home."

I nibble my inner cheek. Of course I'm glad that I won't end up with a criminal record of vandalism. I'll even get to attend graduation on Saturday and receive my diploma with my classmates, on one condition: I don't show up at prom tonight.

Taelor's father offered to hold the dance at Underland now that the gym is ruined. In the most shocking twist of all, Taelor opted not to press charges against me. She must remember on some level that I tried to help her. All she asked was that I be put under a temporary restraining order prohibiting me from coming within fifty feet of her family's underground center.

I'm exiled from my own senior prom. Last year, I would've

thrown a party to celebrate. This year? I'm actually disappointed. Even though I knew in my heart that it would never be.

There's a battle with my name on it, and I can't procrastinate any longer. If I don't get down the rabbit hole fast, Queen Red and her army could come through a portal next—if they're not already here—which would make what happened in the gym look like a *Disney on Ice* show.

"Take these." Dad doesn't even cast a glance my way as he hands me the keys to Gizmo. "And be sure to clean your face before she sees you. Your makeup is a mess."

There must be soot on my skin, considering I didn't wear any makeup. "Can't you help me clean it off?" Anything to get him to look my way.

He keeps his gaze averted. "Use your car mirror." The snub aches more than a scolding word or disappointed look would have.

Dad turns his back to unlock the truck and gives me one last instruction. "You won't be leaving the house today or having visitors. You're going to finish your last test. And you still have an apology to give to your mother. Go straight home. Understood?"

I nod. It's not an actual lie. After all, he didn't specify *which* home.

I made good use of my time, sitting in the nurse's office while Dad had a conference with the principal and the counselor. I got the address of Ivy's studio from Mr. Piero and entered it into my cell.

As soon as I leave this parking lot, I'm tracking down Jeb, finding my mosaics and Morpheus—begging on hands and knees if necessary for his help—and meeting Red head-on in Wonderland.

So yeah, Dad, I'm going home.

Just not to the one you have in mind.

Starving Artist

After answering a concerned text from Jenara in which I promise to find her brother, I wait for Dad to pull out of the parking lot first so he won't follow me. I can't let myself think about how furious he'll be or how much he'll worry when I don't show up at home. If I do, I will never have the guts to do what needs to be done.

In an attempt to look busy, I take down my braid and rub my fingers through my hair to loosen the waves. I lean toward the rearview mirror to clean the smudges off my face. One look and my stomach flips.

It's not soot at all. My netherling eye patches have returned—a more feminine version of Morpheus's, without the jewels. It must've happened when I started losing touch with my human side. No wonder everyone was looking at me so weird in the school office.

I'm braving another glance at the marks when I notice a gray and orange striped tail hanging from my rearview mirror.

"Chessie?"

The fuzzy appendage twitches.

Dad gives me a pointed glare as he's backing out, and I pretend to dig a Kleenex from my glove box. As soon as he's on the street, I check the parking lot to make sure I'm alone, then tap Chessie's tail. It wraps around my finger and dissolves into an orange mist.

When the feline netherling materializes, I hold out my palm. He perches there—furry, wiggly, and warm.

"Let me guess. Morpheus wants me to find him," I say.

His shimmery green eyes study me for a minute before he flutters to the driver's-side window. Breathing over the glass to fog it, he etches the letters *m-e-m-o-r-y* with a clawed fingertip.

I put my key in the ignition. "I know. He's waiting among lost memories. Look, I don't have time to figure out what that means right now." The motor roars to life. "Jeb needs me."

Chessie shakes his head, then breathes another stream of fog across the windshield in my line of vision. This time he draws a picture of a train and a set of wings.

I sigh. "Yes, you saved me and Morpheus from the train. I remember. Thank you. Now, go back and tell him he's going to have to wait a little longer." I wipe away the condensation from the windshield with a Kleenex.

Chessie flaps around me. The downy white tufts above his eyes furrow.

I wave him toward the dash and slide on a pair of sunglasses. "I'm not changing my mind. I'm doing this first. You can come, but only if you don't distract me."

The tiny netherling plops down on the dash, arms crossed. His usual toothy smile curves to a frown, and his long whiskers droop. As I pull onto the street, a pickup passes. The driver stares at Chessie so hard he almost misses his turn.

"You're going to have to look more . . . inconspicuous," I tell my passenger.

Releasing a teensy sigh that sounds like a kitten's sneeze, he crouches on all fours with his tail curled behind him, lays his wings flat against his back, and loosens his head so it will bob—a perfect imitation of a bobblehead car accessory.

I'd laugh if I wasn't so worried about Jeb.

It takes twenty minutes to find the studio. It's located at the end of a lonely dirt road eight miles south of the same housing development Morpheus and I passed yesterday.

I park on a dusty plot of land that doubles as a driveway. As soon as I kill the engine, Chessie reaffixes his head and flits to his perch on the rearview mirror, hissing.

I remove my sunglasses, scared enough to hiss myself. A half dozen dying mesquite trees surround a run-down cottage with a flat roof. Their trunks and branches are gnarled. A few of them appear to have grown into the cottage walls, as if they're attacking the place. It's not a welcoming sight.

Weathered wooden slats form the front and side walls. The only part of the cottage that looks new is the door, which is painted a deep red with shiny brass hinges and an oddly shaped knocker. The whole door seems out of place against the rotting background.

There aren't any windows—at least from the front. How could

there be enough light for painting in a windowless cottage? I'm starting to think I made a wrong turn until I notice Jeb's Honda lying next to what might've been a rabbit hutch. It's more like a pile of kindling and wire now.

Seeing his bike on the ground validates my worst fear: He's been here all night. He's either alone and unprotected, or not alone—and that might be worse.

Dread and guilt wrap around my heart. I should've told him the truth from the beginning. If he'd known since last summer, he would have been prepared.

My cell phone rings, startling me. It's Dad. I turn off the ringer but send him a text:

I'll be home soon. Try not to worry. I just need to be alone, to figure out some things.

He'll be furious and will start looking for me immediately, but at least maybe he won't worry as much.

I drop the phone into my backpack and turn back to the cottage. I shouldn't feel intimidated by this run-down building after what I just faced at school. But there's a possibility Red is here—one of the few netherlings even Morpheus fears. To think of Jeb facing her alone makes me shiver.

The wind kicks dirt across my windshield in a gritty scatter of brown. Chessie hisses again—a reminder that at least I'm not alone.

"I have to go in," I say to him.

He grabs his tail and twirls, wrapping the appendage around his body and face to hide.

"Well, do you have any better ideas?" I ask.

He peers out, fogs the window again, and writes *Find M* with the tip of his tail.

I narrow my eyes. "We'll find Morpheus after we take care of this. Now, are you coming?"

Chessie frowns, his fur puffed up like a frightened cat's. He shakes his head.

"Fine. Stay out here by yourself, then."

The instant I open my door and step out, Chessie's fluttery wings touch my ear. He lights on my shoulder and ducks underneath my hair.

Relief rushes through me. He may be little, but he's magic, stealthy, and adept at fixing things. It's better than going in by myself.

I hold his tail for comfort as I walk to the door. Dirt clods and pebbles crunch under my feet. The bugs whisper all around. I can't tell if they're cheering me on or warning me; there are too many voices to pick apart.

After stepping onto the crumbling porch, I pause and stare at the brass knocker. It's in the shape of a pair of garden shears.

Goose bumps erupt across my flesh. I look down at my scarred palms. Whoever put this knocker here knew I would come . . . they're playing games with me. I grit my teeth. It doesn't matter. I'm not leaving without Jeb, no matter how menacing his captor is.

The knob turns easily, and I push the door open but stay on the porch to look in. The place appears to be abandoned, and it occurs to me there's one outcome that could be worse than finding Jeb here: not finding him at all.

I stick my head in farther. The scent of paint and a pungent metallic odor hit me first. Then something else . . . sickly sweet and fruity . . . familiar enough that it makes my mouth water, but I can't place it.

Sun rays stream from the ceiling where skylight panels make up the roof, giving the place a greenhouse effect. Cobwebs flecked with bug corpses drape from the glass and hang to the floor in places, glistening like grotesquely jeweled wedding veils. There's one big room—not counting the loft to the left and a bathroom to my right, where a tall chest with fifty or more minidrawers stands just inside the open door. The canvas-covered walls are taller than they looked from outside. There's no furniture, other than the portable scaffolds propped against the walls, so the sun's reflection hazes off a dusty wooden floor.

The result is bright and ethereal . . . almost heavenly. Now I can see why Ivy chose this studio. I tiptoe around some art supplies, leaving the door ajar behind me. Chessie tenses under my hair.

There are paintings everywhere—three on easels covered with drop cloths, others on the canvas walls. I spin to take them all in, the wooden floor slick beneath me.

My breath accelerates as the paintings' subjects become clear: garden shears and a child's bloody hand; an octopus being swallowed by a clam; a rowboat afloat on a romantic river of stars; two silhouettes skimming on boards down a cliff made of sand; bleeding roses and a box with a head inside. Memories that Jeb and I made in Wonderland. Memories that no longer belong to him. Yet I'd recognize that morbidly beautiful style anywhere. He painted perfect renditions of our journey. He had to be working nonstop all night.

Somehow he's remembered everything.

I back up and hit a rolled piece of canvas with my heel. I open it, revealing a painting of Jeb breaking into Mr. Mason's car in the hospital parking lot, a nurse waiting beside him in a white dress.

I rock in place, feeling dizzy.

So Nurse Terri *did* play a part in my stolen mosaics—and Jeb helped her?

I remember Morpheus's words: *"Do you honestly think I'm the only one with the ability to slip undetected into a car with its alarm on?"* He was right. Even some humans have that ability, if they know enough about cars.

But there could be an innocent explanation. Mr. Mason's car is new, and Jeb has never seen it. The nurse could've lied and told him it was hers . . . that she had locked herself out. Once he had her car unlocked, he left. Then *she* stole my art—maybe under the orders of another netherling. That might explain how I never saw a fae form through her glamour.

That has to be how it happened, because Jeb would never betray me.

Morpheus was right about something else, too. I do hold him and Jeb to different standards. In the same situation, I would never give my dark tormentor the benefit of the doubt.

"Jeb!" I yell, struggling to suppress a sob. "Are you here?"

No answer, just the echo of my desperation.

Chessie weaves his way out of my hair.

"He's in the loft . . . he has to be." I say it aloud to comfort myself, although it doesn't work. I climb the ladder. The rungs creak under my weight.

I stop once I'm high enough to see the upper level. The fruity, sweet scent is strongest here. There's a large glass decanter turned over on the floor, droplets of what appears to be dark purple wine leaking from its wide mouth.

Jeb wouldn't have been drinking. He almost never drinks, and especially not while painting.

Everything, including the barren wooden walls, is covered with thick, opaque webs full of bulges. There's a minifridge and a floor lamp in the far corner. A box mattress sits next to the railing. I shake off the sudden image of my nightmare in the hospital, of Jeb's body bound in web on a cot. This mattress might be dusty and old, but there's nothing lying on top of it.

In fact, it doesn't look like anyone's been up here for years. I start to climb down, but then I spot something—the black polo and Japanese tie Jeb wore to his photo shoot yesterday—spread out in the corner closest to the ladder. Holding my breath, I return to the top two rungs, then reach out and grasp it. As I drag the shirt toward me, my three stolen mosaics come into view, hidden underneath.

I slap my hand over my mouth. The sound reverberates in the empty room and brings Chessie up beside me.

Just like at school, I can't make out much, other than what appears to be a ravaged Wonderland and an angry queen. I wonder how Mom was able to read anything else into them.

Chessie buzzes around me, as if trying to tell me something.

Morpheus said the feline netherling's gift is mapping out the best way to solve puzzles, then fixing them. Maybe that applies to magical artwork, too.

"Do you know how to read these?" I ask Chessie. "You were perched on Mom's shoulder in my mirror—to help her read them, right?"

As if he's been waiting for me to connect the dots, he dissolves into orange sparkles and gray smoke. He drifts like a cloud over the glass beads and acts as a filter, bringing clarity to the lines of the mosaics. Once he's in place, it's like watching a monochromatic film play out: First, there's a giant spider chasing a flower; in the next mosaic, one Red queen is left standing amid a storm of magic and chaos; and in the last one, there's a single queen whose upper half is wrapped in something white, like web.

Disturbing clues I can't quite fit together.

Shaken, I descend the ladder, leaving the mosaics where I found them.

On the floor, I hold Jeb's shirt up in the sun. Something dark is caked all across the front. The scent reminds me of blood. I suppress a moan.

"We have to find him." I slap stray tears from my face and toss the shirt aside.

Chessie hovers around one of the covered easels. Maybe the remaining paintings will tell us where Jeb is now.

I nod, giving my netherling companion permission to do what I'm too scared to do myself.

Holding a corner of the cloth in his paws, he flits his wings and drags it away. Instead of canvas stretched over a frame, there's a pane of glass streaked with red paint so fluid, it dried in drizzles. I study the runny lines, the image unmistakably more of Jeb's handiwork.

The same coppery scent that was on Jeb's shirt overpowers me. Following a hunch, I scrape off some of the red paint and touch it to my tongue. Nausea follows in the wake of the salty-metallic flavor.

Blood.

My mind tumbles to a dark, terrible place, but I haul it back and hold myself steady. Jeb needs me to be strong. I can't imagine him draining his veins for paint like he did last summer in Wonderland. But he survived it once. He will again. He's okay. He has to be.

I look closer at the painting. It's familiar beyond Jeb's style. It's an abstract version of one of my mosaics—one of the ones now hidden somewhere under a bridge in London. Chessie helps me remove the cloth from the second one. It's also a glassy rendition of my artwork. The last easel holds a clean pane next to three empty plastic vials. The same ones Nurse Terri used to take samples of blood at the hospital.

My blood.

Morpheus pointed out that even if Red had access to my blood, she didn't have the imagination to set the visions free. Since I'm partly human and an artist, creation is my power.

Jeb's an artist, too. And he's fully human. Morpheus was right about my blood being used as weapon against me. And Jeb unwittingly wielded the sword in the form of a paintbrush.

Once again, he's caught in the middle of my identity crisis.

My eyes well with tears, but I don't have the luxury of time to cry.

Chessie blinks at me, waiting, and I give him permission to help decipher the artwork.

He uses his magic veil again to animate the glass paintings: What was a stationary queen on a rampage in Wonderland becomes three fighting queens, just as Mom described. They move across the glass, using magic and wit to one-up each other and gain the crown. Another woman spies from behind a cluster of eight spindly vines.

Chessie rakes his paws through the residue left on the first pane of glass and smears it on the next glass painting, as if transferring his magic. This time, only two queens are left to battle for the crown, while the third is eaten alive by some vile creature. The mystery woman who was watching from behind the vines retreats. As she leaves, the vines go with her. They appear to be coming out of her bottom half. She's not hiding behind a plant at all—the appendages are a part of her. And the top half is too humanoid to be a zombie flower, so it can't be Red.

Chessie materializes and lands on my shoulder. I'm too numb to even thank him for his help. There's little satisfaction in our discovery because I can't understand what any of the mosaics mean. All I do know is that they're proof that Red has used my blood to gain the upper hand in our battle. Even worse, Jeb has been in her clutches and is now gone.

My heart hurts—a pain that sucks the breath out of me. Unable to stand on my trembling legs, I sit hard on the floor, knees curled up to my chest. It's like my sternum is caving in. All this time I was trying to protect Jeb from my past by hiding it. And now he's been swallowed by my future.

I know I need to think beyond this world, to what this means for Wonderland. Red is one step ahead of me. She's seen five of my six mosaics. I can only hope she wasn't able to interpret them, because they show the results of a war that is only just starting to play out. She wants to alter the ending to her benefit, and I need to find the last mosaic so I can be a step ahead.

But she's got Jeb.

I hold his locket to my lips to taste the metal, burying my face behind a curtain of hair. Our plans for London, our life together. His chance at being a world-renowned artist . . . it can't be gone.

If it is, I don't know how to go forward.

The door slams shut, making me jump. I shove my hair back and look up.

I nearly scream when I see Jeb standing there. I'm off the floor in an instant. He's wearing his black jeans from yesterday, but that's all.

Even his feet are bare. Sunlight shimmers on the dusting of chest hair between his pecs. His olive skin glistens with sweat, and colorful paint smudges his torso, covering several of his scars. There's not a hint of magic to him, yet he's the most spellbinding thing I've ever seen.

I'm about to tackle-hug him, but my netherling senses give me pause. Something's not right. He hasn't acknowledged me.

A dusty white rabbit wiggles in his arms, wrapped up in the long-sleeved T Jeb had been wearing under his polo. Judging by the grass tangled in Jeb's hair, he's been outside chasing the animal. He's so intent on his catch, he doesn't notice anything else.

"Jeb?"

"I need more paint," he says, but the words aren't directed to me. "She didn't leave enough." His voice is rough, like it hurts him to talk. He rubs the rabbit's ears, seemingly oblivious to the way it's struggling to get free . . . to how it's wriggled out of the shirt he had wrapped around it and is leaving bloody scratches on his chest and arm. "I've got to have more. To prove that I'm an artist."

Everything about this is wrong. The way he's talking, the way he's moving.

I step closer, cautious. He's in a trance of some kind.

I notice his mouth, the unnatural color of his lips: dark purple.

I look around for Chessie. He's hovering up by the skylights, watching Jeb with wide, curious eyes.

Jeb holds the rabbit in front of his face, one hand braced around its neck. "It'll be so fast, you won't feel a thing."

I react without thinking. "Jeb, stop!"

My scream startles the rabbit. Its back claws thrust and leave a welt on Jeb's chin. Cursing, he drops the animal, and it hops by me.

I dive out of the way as Jeb races after it, pounding the floor with his bare soles. He skids into the easels and knocks them over. The glass panes fall and bust into glittery shards.

It's a strangely familiar scene. Jeb is so determined, so focused. I was where he is once, chasing a mouse across a table that was set for tea, driven by an unquenchable appetite. There are so many different kinds of hunger. Mine was for food and experiences I had never lived. Jeb's is for his art, and to prove he's the best.

He manages to regain his balance, pursuing the rabbit as it darts from one side of the room to the other, so relentless he doesn't realize he's about to run through the glass and gouge his feet.

"Jebediah Holt!" I've never used his whole name before. It feels dry and unnatural on my tongue, as if I've been licking cotton. He cocks his head and slows down enough for me to lunge at him. His shoulders hit the wall. I crash into his chest, and we both grunt with the impact.

"Al?" He cups my face tenderly, trying to come back, though still far away. "I'm so . . ."

"Hungry," I offer, smelling the same familiar fruity, sweet scent that first hit me when I came in the door. That's what was in the decanter on the loft's floor. Jeb's been drinking Tumtum juice. Red used it to channel his desire to prove himself into a gluttonous frenzy of artistic passion. That's why he painted all night nonstop and never called, texted, or went home.

Only one thing can cure him of the effects of the juice, and that's to eat a handful of Tumtum berries whole. "Chessie," I say, holding my voice from trembling, "Tumtum berries. Try the minifridge."

Chessie zooms up to the loft but comes back in a few seconds, empty-handed.

The rabbit bounds by, gracefully hopping across the glass without cutting itself. I fall on my butt as Jeb pushes me aside and heads straight through the shards. I can't get up fast enough to stop him.

I concentrate on the glass on the floor, magnetizing it so it clumps together like a crocodile's scaly tail. It sways out of the way each time Jeb's soles come near it. With the path cleared, Jeb gains on the rabbit.

The prey hops toward the door. I scramble up and get there first, just in time to throw it open and let the frightened animal escape. I slam the door shut and press my lower back against the doorknob, blocking Jeb from following his would-be blood donor.

"Get out of the way." Jeb's voice is raw. His eyes lock on mine, but he can't seem to focus. It's like he's looking through me. His jaw twitches and he grinds his teeth.

"Chessie!" I screech. "Berries!"

Chessie buzzes to the bathroom and disappears into a half-opened drawer. The wood rattles as he winds his way through the contents and into the next drawer. Only forty-eight more to go.

Jeb grips my arms, fingernails gouging my tender skin through my sleeves, muscles straining as he tries to move me away from the entrance. He's always been able to lift me as if I weigh nothing, but this time, I imagine the doorknob behind me being a fist and envision its fingers uncurling, just like the doorknob that morphed into an old man's hand in my Shop of Human Eccentricities memory. Cold metal spikes cinch and curve tight around the waist of my jeans, holding me in place.

Jeb strains harder, frustrated.

Desperate to bring him back, I tug him down and kiss him, gentle and coaxing.

Come back to me, my lips say.

He clamps his mouth shut and keeps struggling to move me aside. There's a small ripping sound as the metal fingers at my waistband start to lose leverage. I grip Jeb's bare shoulders, dragging his body close so there's no space between us. His torso presses mine, and I kiss his throat. Even through my layered shirts, the unnatural heat of his skin scorches me.

He tenses, and I feel the change. It's not surrender; it's a redirection. His hands drag up along my rib cage, stopping under my arms. I lose all concentration on the doorknob, and the fingers release me, transforming back into the knob. My feet lift as Jeb pins me to the door.

There's nothing gentle about his expression. His raging hunger is focused on me now.

More drawers rattle in the bathroom.

"Chessie . . . hurry." I can only mumble the plea. Being under the scrutiny of Jeb's eyes—the brightest green I've ever seen them—makes my bones melt to liquid.

Chessie flits from the chest of drawers and sifts like smoke through cracks in the skylights. He must be going out to use my car mirrors. He'll have to go through the rabbit hole to find some berries.

But I'm not sure I care if he finds any or not. At last, I'm the center of Jeb's undivided attention, and I like it.

A low rumble escapes his throat as he initiates a kiss this time. Our tongues touch, then wrestle. Enough Tumtum residue remains in his mouth to ignite heat in my abdomen. He tastes of defiance and wildness, of things both wicked and sweet. He's the flavor of Wonderland interwoven with all things Jeb. I urge him to deepen the kiss. He wraps my legs around his waist, moving on instinct—

no romance, no caution, only lust motivated by a potent fairy drug.

I'm lost to sensation. This is the raw passion he only reserves for his paintings. He's not suppressing his wants or needs to protect me; he's not worried I'm fragile or breakable. He's starving, daring me to match his fierceness.

He knots his fingers in my hair and his labret scrapes my chin hard enough to leave welts. His kisses burn heavy like a brand and I brand him right back.

He catches my wrists, smacks them to the wall, and holds them there. He abandons my lips, both of us panting as his mouth glides along my neck, teeth bared against my jugular vein. A painful twinge makes me break a hand free and shove at his face. There's blood on his lower lip. I touch my stinging neck where he broke my skin, shocked.

Jeb runs his tongue across my blood on his mouth. His face changes. He's never been rough enough to leave imprints on my skin; hurting me must've brought him back to himself. Still holding me against the wall with his body, his hands move to my neck.

I expect comfort or an apology. Instead, he clamps his fingers around my throat, shutting off my air supply. I grapple with his wrists, but he's too strong. The breath locks in my lungs; I can't force it out or drag any more in.

I dig my fingernails into his skin and squeeze my legs around his waist, trying to get his attention.

"Paint," he mumbles, licking the blood on his lip again. The distant look has returned to his eyes, tinged with murderous intent. Cold dread slashes through me.

In his mind, I'm the rabbit.

This is what Mom's flowers were predicting. My death at his hand. He'll never forgive himself.

I have to stop him.

I try to force a sound from my throat to shake him out of his trance, but his grip is too tight. His thumbs clamp harder around my windpipe, fingers pressed to my vertebrae. The bones ache under the strain.

I panic . . . can't concentrate . . . can't evoke my powers. . . can't even focus.

Black fuzz creeps across my vision.

"I have to finish what I started," Jeb says, mechanically. Maniacally. "It'll be so fast, you won't feel a thing."

PEREGRINATION &
NEGOTIATION

Jeb's viselike grip tightens on my neck.

My body goes limp just as a gust of wind rushes by.

"Playtime's over." Morpheus's gruff command snaps my eyes open. My heart kicks my sternum, thumping at the chance to stay alive. I never thought I'd be so happy to hear that cockney accent.

He breaks Jeb's grip and drags him away from me. I slump to the floor on my knees, holding my neck as I cough and wheeze. I whimper with each painful inhalation, relish the burn as it rushes through my bruised windpipe and into my aching lungs.

I want to plead with Morpheus not to hurt Jeb, but I'm too weak. Everything is throbbing, from my neck to my legs. I push myself to sit against the wall and bury my face where my arms cradle my knees, trying to stop trembling.

The sound of grunts and growls forces me to look up.

Morpheus kneels over Jeb's supine form. He holds him down with a knee on his chest, stuffing Tumtum berries into his mouth. Surprise and relief surge through me. He's helping Jeb instead of hurting him.

It's like watching a James Bond movie. Morpheus—in a black trench-coat-style blazer that hangs to his thighs, gray tweed pants, a dark gray vest, skinny red tie, and black pin-striped dress shirt— could pass for a punk-fae secret agent who's captured his villain. His thick blue waves touch his shoulders from under a gray tweed flat cap, and his wings drape down his back and across the floor, fluttering sporadically as he keeps his balance against Jeb's resistance.

Of all the upheavals I've experienced over the past few days, this is by far the most mind-twisting: My dark tempter becoming my knight, and my knight becoming my persecutor. I know the reversal is temporary, but I'll never be able to forget the way that hungry light fired Jeb's eyes to such a vivid green . . . or the way it felt when he broke loose of his inhibitions and demanded I give as good as I got. I don't want to forget, because we were rivals, yet at the same time partners.

Until he tried to kill me.

The berries take effect, and Jeb stops struggling, inch by inch, until he's motionless.

"Once you've had a little nap," Morpheus says to him, voice brutal and clipped, "we'll discuss those marks you left on Alyssa's skin." He pats Jeb's cheek with a black leather glove he drags from his pocket but can't hide the rage bunched up in his jaw muscles.

Chessie appears next to my face—a flurry of wings, fur, and paws. He perches on my shoulder and tenderly nuzzles my neck where Jeb bit me.

"Thank you for getting Morpheus," I tell him.

My voice is sandpaper and rust. My cough brings Morpheus over, his expensive black dress shoes coming to a halt beside me. They're all I can see of him, until he kneels. He's been smoking his hookah, and the scent enfolds me.

"Watch over the mortal, would you, Chessie-blud?" he says, appraising me as he tugs his leather gloves into place over berry-stained fingers.

The tiny netherling leaves my shoulder and perches atop Jeb's resting form.

I strain my neck to look into Morpheus's eyes, and my broken and bruised skin pounds. Sun from the skylights shimmers behind his silhouette—a halo of yellow light.

"I'm so glad you didn't hurt him," I mumble, unable to talk above a hoarse whisper.

Morpheus's frown is fierce. "Had it been *anyone* other than the boy who bled himself dry for you in Wonderland," he answers, "I would have killed him with my bare hands—no magic required."

There's a chilling grimness behind his gaze, and I let myself acknowledge what I've been denying: In his own way, Morpheus is my knight, too. He just has more muddled motivations than Jeb—not always unselfish and honorable, but vigilant. I have to give him that.

"You were right," I say, swallowing my pride. "About my blood being used as a weapon against me. About me holding you to a different standard. I should've at least tried to trust you. I'm sorry. I'll work on that."

"See that you do." Although his words are harsh, the expression on his porcelain-pale face is anything but. It reminds me of the netherling playmate from my past, eager to win my trust and adoration. Willing to do anything for it. He doesn't have to say I'm forgiven or that he's touched by my apology. Both of those emotions blink through his jeweled patches in colorful flashes.

I proceed to tell him everything I know—what I saw in the paintings Jeb made with my blood and glass, my mosaics in the loft. And I tell him that I suspect Red is here in the human realm and playing games with me.

He shakes his head. "That doesn't sound like her. She's not one for subtleties."

"But the garden shears on the door," I insist. "They were there to scare me."

He looks genuinely baffled. "I didn't come in the door. I came through a crack in one of the skylights. Are you sure that's what you saw?"

"Go look for yourself if you don't believe me."

"I believe you, but it makes no sense. She would've wanted you at her mercy—unprepared. She was using your boyfriend not only for his imagination, but for his tie to you. He was bait. She lured you here, so she must've planned to be here, to vanquish you. But something spooked her, and as much as I'd like to think it was you, I know better."

My heart drums at the thought of who or what could've spooked someone as powerful as Red. "Do you think it was the mystery woman in my mosaics? The one who's hiding in the shadows? The one with the tentacles . . ."

"Perhaps the answer is in your final mosaic. We need to find it. But first, let's have a look at your battle scars." He cups my chin, thumb running across the welts left by Jeb's labret. "You managed to make me come back without begging. I suppose you're proud of yourself."

His gentle teasing slows my heart rate down, calms me. "You came back for *me*? I figured you were just missing your car."

Morpheus's lips quirk—an almost-smile. He tips my chin up to get a better look at my neck. The action stretches my bruised muscles and I yelp.

"Sorry, luv." He winces and releases me, then taps the skin around Jeb's bite mark. His gloves feel cool and soothing. "I do think you'll live, though." His attention shifts to my face, respect sparking in his dark gaze. "Appears you've had a busy day of magic making."

I scrub at my eye patches. "You already knew that. You had Gossamer and Chessie watching over me."

"So I might stay away until you found me. But as always, you're determined to be the crimp in my plans."

"Well, if it makes you feel any better," I say, holding my neck where I can still feel the burn of Jeb's handprints, "I did figure out where you were, so I would've found you."

Morpheus tilts his head. "Is that so?"

I nod, then point at Jeb's paintings all along the walls. "When I saw Jeb's lost memories, they reminded me of what Chessie drew on my windows on the way here: a train, and you. And the word *memory*. After my mom went to London through my mirror, you asked her if she took a train ride and relived lost memories. You were waiting at Ironbridge Gorge, right? That's why you sent Chessie. You expected me to go there and find my mosaics, and you knew I would need his help to read them."

"Impressive."

"Is that why you wanted to lure me there? For the mosaics?"

"Partly. But I wanted you to ride the train most of all."

I furrow my brow. "So the train is real?"

Morpheus slides off his flat cap. His glowing blue hair appears to move and reach for the air, as if thrilled to be liberated. "What's your definition of *real*?"

I look around the room, stopping at Jeb's sleeping form. "It's ever changing."

Twirling the hat on his fingertip, Morpheus nods. "As it should be. There's an underground tube passageway close to the bridge that was deserted and sealed up years ago by humans. Netherlings have a freight train that runs through it, specializing in very precious cargo. There are passenger cars available for those who have a personal stake in the merchandise. I arranged tickets for us."

"You mean you were planning to go, too? You're afraid of riding in a car. How's a train any better?"

He shrugs, his frown sheepish. "The train doesn't exactly *move*."

"But you said it runs through the passageway."

He waves his hand in a dismissive gesture. "You would have to experience it to understand. There's something there you need to see. A memory in the cargo that doesn't belong to you but has shaped you nonetheless. A memory that's been lost for years, that needs to be found before you face Red."

His answer whets my curiosity. "I don't understand. The cargo in the train is *memories*?"

"Lost memories."

"But how . . . ?"

"Let's just say that the human concept of a freight train is as misguided as the human concept of a hat." He offers me his cap.

Puzzled, I take it. It's the first hat I've ever seen him wear that doesn't have moth embellishments. I hold it up in the sunlight. The texture doesn't feel like tweed. It's silkier and seems to breathe and move under my touch. I meet Morpheus's gaze, confused.

With a wink, he takes the cap back and places it on his head. In a subtle gesture, he waves a hand over the hat's crown. The tweed transforms from cloth to living moths. They burst off his head and flutter all around us, then, at a whistle from Morpheus, they reunite, scuttling into place like puzzle pieces to form the hat again.

I grin, and he beams with pride.

"So what kind of hat is that?" I ask, unable to resist. He's adorable when he's showing off his wardrobe—like a puppy doing tricks. Although I remain cautious, knowing in the blink of an eye he can become a wolf again.

"My Peregrination Cap," he answers.

"Huh?"

His smile widens—baring white teeth. "Peregrination. An excursion . . . a journey."

"So, why don't you just call it your traveling cap?"

"Then it wouldn't be much of a conversation starter, would it?"

I raise an eyebrow. "Um, the fact that it's made of living moths might give you something to talk about."

Morpheus laughs. For once our relationship feels comfortable, friendly. So unlike his usual flirting and threats.

"About the train," I say, breaking the genuinely nice moment.

He opens his mouth to answer, but a moan interrupts him. Jeb is rousing. Morpheus starts to get up to check on him.

"Wait." I grab his tie. Even through his shirt, I feel the strong curve of his collarbone beneath my fingers. It takes me back to how he looked in my bedroom: shirtless and perfect—wings spread high like those of some sort of celestial being—elegant power and pulsing light. Unabashed, unashamed, and confident. All the things that I crave to be.

My pulse beats rapidly against the bite on my neck. "There's something I want you to do, before Jeb wakes enough to know what's going on."

Morpheus kneels again. "What? You want I should kiss your ouchies?" The dark purr of his voice is more teasing than seductive.

I roll my eyes. "I want you to heal me."

He scowls, all playfulness gone. "Oh, no. No. Jebediah will face what he did to you."

"He would never have attacked me like that if he hadn't been under the influence of the juice. Why would you want to rub his nose in it?" I make a frustrated noise. "You were the one forcing me to keep him oblivious about everything. What's changed?"

"You need to acknowledge the dangers of him dabbling in a world beyond his ken. The Tumtum juice made you voracious, but it made him murderous. He's a liability. If you involve him in this war, he will be your downfall. This I guarantee."

My mouth gapes open. I can't believe I was pouring out my heart to him just moments ago. "No. You want Jeb to doubt himself. You want him to believe he's turning into his father. You're going to manipulate him, because that's what you do. You use people's weaknesses against them."

He studies me, long black lashes unblinking in silent affirmation.

"Well, I won't let it happen," I say. "Now *heal* me."

Morpheus snarls and tries to pull away, but I refuse to let go of his tie.

He raises his wings, casting giant blue shadows over us. If he uses them, he can break free and refuse to do as I ask. Then again, I might do better in a battle of wills now that my powers are getting stronger. A tendril of excitement unfurls inside my chest, just considering it.

We stare each other down. To my surprise, he relaxes his wings.

"What is it worth to you?" he asks.

I release his tie and frown. It's a trick question.

"Jebediah's peace of mind," he reiterates. "What's it worth?"

"Everything," I say, knowing it's a mistake the second I admit it.

With a thoughtful frown, Morpheus sits back, legs crossed, and places his hat in his lap, coaxing the moths that form it to separate and flutter in place atop his thighs. After removing a glove, he raises his hand, and strands of blue light drizzle from his fingertips, connecting to the insects. He wiggles his fingers, and, guided by their magical harnesses, the moths fly in a circle like a miniature carousel.

His expression becomes dreamy, glowing blue from the light. "One day and one night," he says without looking up, preoccupied with his toy.

I swallow. "What?"

"That's the price." He still doesn't look my way. The magic from his fingers accelerates, and the moths follow suit. "If I help you protect your trophy boy's frail psyche, you give me one day and one night as soon as this battle with Red is behind us. Twenty-four hours with me in Wonderland."

I study him. *He can't be serious.*

As if spurred by my silence, he withdraws his magic, and the moths flock together, reuniting into the hat. He puts it on, and his gaze locks to mine. His jewels flicker between passion and defiance—an evocative and intimidating combination. "Fair warning, I intend to make good use of that time. I will be gentle, but I will not be a gentleman. You will be the center of my world. I'll show you the wonders of Wonderland, and when you're drunk on the beauty and chaos that your heart so yearns to know, I will take you under my wings and make you forget the human realm ever existed. You'll never want to leave Wonderland or me again."

The thrum starts at the back of my skull, a resurrection of my netherling side, almost as powerful as what I felt at the gym while standing in the flames. But my human side nudges me—a warning. Morpheus is the most magical and captivating creature I've ever known. And, other than in dreams, I've never spent more than a few hours alone with him at a time. How could I resist the darkness he summons inside me for an entire day and night?

I glance under his left wing to check on Jeb. His feet twitch, and he rolls to his stomach, mumbling. He'll be fully conscious within minutes.

Morpheus's gaze falls to the handprints on my neck. "Give me an answer or I wake your boyfriend and let him bask in his newest masterpiece."

"Okay," I murmur. I might never make it through a battle with Red in the first place, so the day with Morpheus might not ever happen. Who knows if I'm the final queen left standing in the mosaics? Maybe I'm the one whose torso is covered in web, or the one who's swallowed by some unnamable monstrosity.

It's something I have to consider. If I don't survive, I don't want Jeb to be tormented by the thought that he hurt me, that he inherited his father's violence in any way. That's one gift I can give him.

"Vow it," Morpheus says. "And make the words count."

Cheeks hot, I hold my palm over my heart. "I vow on my life-magic to give you one day and one night, the moment we defeat Red."

"Done." Expression unchanging, Morpheus removes his remaining glove.

When he starts to peel off his jacket, I get up on my knees and shove at his lapels, hurrying him. Together we drag the sleeves down his shoulders. Despite my efforts to be businesslike, I find myself overcome by the intimacy of undressing him with Jeb lying unconscious on the floor. If he were to wake and see this . . .

Two slits open in the back of the blazer to release Morpheus's wings. One of them grazes my hand, causing my own wing buds to tingle behind my shoulder blades. I fidget. He watches my reaction intently. My stomach knots as I take his wrist and unbutton his shirt cuff, pushing the sleeve to his elbow to reveal the birthmark on his forearm. His skin is soft and warm.

I release his arm and untie my boot to expose the netherling mark on my ankle.

Morpheus rocks back on his heels and studies me. "Of all the times you've undressed me in my fantasies, I never remember feeling this . . . unfulfilled."

"Please, Morpheus," I beg upon hearing Jeb stir in the background.

"Ah, but those delectable words," Morpheus says with a provocative smirk, "those are always in the fantasy."

I glare at him. "You're unbelievable."

"And *that* sentiment is reserved for the end."

"Shut. Up." I drag his forearm over to match it to my birthmark.

He pulls free before we make contact. "A moment, please. Allow me to bask in your devotion." He's referring to my ankle tattoo.

I blush. "I've told you a hundred times. It's only a set of wings."

"Nonsense." Morpheus grins. "I know a moth when I see one."

I groan in frustration, and he surrenders, letting me press our markings together. A spark rushes between them, expanding to a firestorm through my veins. His gaze locks on mine, and the bottomless depths flicker—like black clouds alive with lightning. For that instant, I'm bared to the bone. He looks inside my heart; I look inside his. And the similarities there terrify me.

I avert my eyes, breaking our mental connection. My neck stops throbbing, my throat soothes, and my limbs feel languid. I relax against the wall.

Morpheus's pale skin flushes, and he lifts his arm off my ankle. There's something new behind his eyes—*resolution*—and I know I've just signed my soul away.

Crouched beside me, he weaves his fingers through my hair on either side of my face, his expression changing to reverence. "You were magnificent today, little blossom. My one regret is the same as yours. That we didn't share a dance in the flames."

I gasp. He *was* at school this morning, luring me into the fire, daring me to give over to the darkness. Before I can react, Chessie flies between us in the same instant Morpheus is jerked away.

"Get off of her!" Jeb flings him across the room, surprisingly strong for someone who was unconscious seconds ago. Morpheus hits the floor and rolls, wings acting as a cushion. His hat slaps the wall, dispersing into the moths once more. Some fly up to the skylights, others toward the closet, and the remainder flutter to the loft.

Jeb staggers, struggling with his balance. In wide-eyed wonder, he watches Chessie buzz along the ceiling with the moths. "That's no costume."

"Bloody genius observation." Morpheus stands and shakes out his wings.

"What . . . is . . . that thing?" Jeb asks, staring at Morpheus now.

"You don't remember?" I respond. I motion to the paintings around us. Jeb turns on his heel to take them in, then pales. "Agh!" He grabs his temples, crumpling to a fetal position on the floor.

Horrified, I kneel down, dragging his head into my lap. He wails.

"Jeb, open your eyes, please."

He grips his temples with white-knuckled hands—face scrunched up in pain.

"What's wrong with him?" I shout to Morpheus.

Morpheus brushes himself off leisurely, as if Jeb's screaming were a trivial inconvenience. "Those weren't his memories he painted. They were yours, held within your blood. Some residual blood on the paintbrushes must have gotten mixed in with the regular paint."

Jeb moans and curls into a ball. He convulses—his chest and arm muscles contracting.

My body twitches and aches in sympathy. It's like barbed wire wraps my joints and tendons, tightening with Jeb's movements. "What's happening to him?" I whimper.

Morpheus looks up at the moths bumping against the ceiling's glass panes, unconcerned. He squints in the sunlight. "Seeing your memories has made his subconscious aware that there are holes in his own. It must be an excruciating sensation, having Swiss cheese for your brain. Now, if you don't mind, I need to remedy my hat."

I struggle to contain the rage rising in me. "Who cares about your stupid hat! For once think of someone besides yourself!"

My outburst catches Morpheus's attention. He looks at me curiously, almost detached.

"Help Jeb. *For me*," I urge, feeling only a sliver of guilt for exploiting his affections. After all, he's the one who taught me how to use people's weaknesses.

There's a crack in his veneer of indifference. He strides over, kneels down, and cups his palms around Jeb's temples. Blue light pulses through Jeb from his head to his bare feet, and he relaxes.

Clearing his throat, Morpheus stands and walks away. "I made him sleep. His dreams will keep him out of pain for now. But the only way to save him from madness is to reunite him with his lost memories. That means a train ride. And I am not getting on any train without my Peregrination Cap."

With Chessie's help, he coaxes the frightened moths down from the skylights, rebuilding his hat piece by piece. Enough insects are still missing to leave noticeable gaps. He and Chessie head toward the bathroom to search for more.

I clench my fists until my nails leave imprints on my skin, fighting the urge to yell at him for his vanity, but it won't do any good. Morpheus is Morpheus. At least he made Jeb comfortable.

I push back a lock of dark hair hanging over Jeb's eyes, then lean down and kiss his forehead. "I'm sorry. I should've told you everything. I'll never keep the truth from you again."

I make the promise even though it means I'll have to tell him about the deal I made with Morpheus, and what precipitated it. Jeb will end up knowing that he attacked me, so I made the deal for nothing. But I can't lie to him anymore.

I stretch out my leg and catch Jeb's discarded shirt with my heel. After dragging it over, I fluff it into a cushion. He mumbles my name subconsciously as I ease his head onto the makeshift pillow. I cover him up to his shoulders with a drop cloth to keep him warm.

"We're going to fix you," I say, stroking his hair.

I stand and retie my bootlaces, impatience building in my blood. Jeb needs his memories, and I still have to decipher the final mosaic so I can face Red. The first point of business is to find a mirror big enough to climb through.

But Morpheus is too stubborn to leave without his hat. While he's busy sifting through drawers in the bathroom, I head to the ladder. I saw at least two or three moths fly up to the loft.

Two moths flitter in and out of the sunlight as I arrive on the upper level. They perch atop the box mattress. Scooping them up, I release them over the railing, sending them down to Chessie.

"There's one still missing," Morpheus says from the ground floor.

"It's here," I answer. "Caught in some web."

The insect cries as it jerks against the sticky tangles, helpless and frightened. Whispering comforting words, I work it free, careful not to damage its wings. As soon as I turn the moth loose, I notice something in the far corner where the web is thickest. I edge closer, eyes adjusting to the shadows.

A sick feeling rolls through me as I recognize the outline of a body—a cocooned corpse.

"Uh, Morpheus . . ." I can barely murmur the words.

As if reacting to my voice, the corpse moves under the thick white fibers. The air in my lungs freezes. I lift my foot to step back just as a hand rips through the web and snatches my wrist with a grip as cold as ice.

Sweet Poison

A scream tears from my throat.

Adrenaline surges through me, and I pry the cold fingers from my wrist. Morpheus flies to my side. We exchange a glance, then examine the cocooned webbing along the wall. Together, we break through and release the form from its shell.

A woman slumps into Morpheus's arms. She smells fruity and delicate—like pears. Her skin sparkles with the sheen of moonlight over a frosted lake, and giant feathery white wings drape behind her shoulders.

She's an ice swan and a queen entwined. I'd know her anywhere.

"Ivory," I whisper. I can't imagine why she's here, trapped like this.

Morpheus pales. He lifts her and carries her to the mattress, kicking aside the lamp on the way. He lays her down gently. Off-white lace peeks out from the web clinging to her dress. Waist-length silvery hair wraps around her long, elegant neck.

Seated on the edge of the bed, Morpheus peels a sticky gossamer coating from her nose and mouth. She gasps for breath. Her white lashes and eyebrows twitch, glistening like crystals.

I drop to my knees in front of Morpheus's feet, holding her hand as she coughs herself awake.

"Don't try to talk, Your Majesty," Morpheus insists, though I sense tension along with the concern in his voice. "Alyssa, could you get her something to drink? Surely you have water or some such in your car."

"No." She furrows her brow at Morpheus, then focuses on me. The black markings on her temples glitter in the sunlight, veined like a dragonfly's wings. "Queen Alyssa, forgive me." Her faded blue irises are almost colorless.

I squeeze her fingers to comfort her. "For what?"

"For endangering your mortal knight. I never anticipated things getting so out of hand. We will find him . . . we'll get him back."

She's obviously confused. There's no telling how long she's been encased in that web. I cast a glance through the rails. Jeb's lying on the floor. Chessie buzzes around him, keeping watch. "He's not lost. He's downstairs, sleeping."

"Sister Two didn't take him?" she asks.

"*Sister Two?*" Morpheus appears as shocked as I feel. Then he groans. "The door knocker. The mystery woman in Alyssa's mosaics. The one hiding in the shadows . . ."

"Of course," I whisper, seeing the vision again in my mind. The eight living vines connected to her lower torso. They weren't tentacles. They were spider legs. The door knocker wasn't about the scars on my palms. It was a tribute to her mutated hand.

"But why would Sister Two be involved?" I reason aloud. "Why would she be at the same cottage where Red was holed up? She despises Red for escaping her keep in the cemetery last year."

"Red was never here," Ivory answers.

Morpheus clears his throat, and their gazes meet in some silent understanding.

"So *Sister Two* was holding Jeb prisoner?" I ask. "*She* gave him the Tumtum juice, forced him to paint all night? Why would she do that?"

Ivory tries to answer but coughs again.

Morpheus nudges my shoulder. "The water, Alyssa."

Ivory swallows hard and tightens her fingers through mine as I start to get up. "That won't be necessary. Her questions deserve answers."

Morpheus frowns. "I don't think this is the time."

"When else, Morpheus?" Ivory scolds. "She is in deeper than any of us now. Sister Two left that door knocker as a warning to both of you. She knows of her twin's betrayal from all those years ago." Ivory's eyes settle on me. "And Alison's betrayal."

I struggle to make sense of her cryptic words. "You mean how my mom tried to become queen? Why would Sister Two care about that?"

"Blast it!" Morpheus scoots off the bed and crouches next to me on the floor. He props his elbows on the mattress and cradles his temples in his hands, massaging with his fingertips. "So the twins are squabbling . . . that leaves the cemetery only partly guarded. If

Red breaks into it, she'll have her spirit army. Then she'll come here. This wasn't supposed to happen."

Ivory's lips and cheeks deepen from white to pale pink. "You should've stayed in Wonderland . . . faced Red, like she wanted."

"You know why I couldn't." A tremor shakes his chin almost imperceptibly. "So who told Sister Two the secret? There were only three of us who knew."

Ivory frowns. "No, there were four. Red knew. Sister One has a foolish habit of confessing secrets to her dead spirits when she tends them, and that was well out of the boundaries of our vows not to tell a living soul."

"Perfect," Morpheus snarls.

"Red tried to invade the cemetery this morning," Ivory continues. "The sisters captured her and were preparing to exorcise her spirit from the flower fae so they could seal her in a toy for eternity. But Red told Sister Two the secret about Alison to distract her. Sister Two turned on her twin in a rage, and Red escaped. Sister Two came here to find a replacement for what Alyssa's family has stolen from her, one way or another. Those were her final words as she wound me in the web."

I shake my head. "I don't understand. Is she still mad about Chessie's smile or how I accidentally helped Red escape last year? But what's that have to do with my mom?"

"What Sister Two seeks compensation for wasn't an accident," Ivory answers. "And the payment will be steep. She intends to take your mortal knight for reparation."

I still don't understand what exactly is going on, but the fear clutching at my heart overpowers any curiosity. "Jeb was outside when I got here," I say, trying to talk over my terror. "That must've saved him. She thought he was gone."

"Yes," Morpheus says. "The boy escaped by chasing a white rabbit. There's poetic irony in that, aye?"

We turn our combined glares on him.

"Simply trying to lighten the mood." His expression sours.

"There is nothing lighthearted about Sister Two's threats," Ivory scolds. "Alyssa's mortal knight is in true danger now."

"Now?" I huff. "We've been in danger from Red for a week. She's been stalking us. At school, at the hospital. And she's been masquerading as an art collector—that's how she got Jeb out here."

Neither one responds.

I look back and forth between them. There's something they're not telling me, and I'm tired of ambiguous revelations. "This is *my* world you've invaded, my life being screwed up, and my loved ones in the middle of it all. I have a right to know what's going on."

"She does," Ivory insists.

"She knows all she needs to know," Morpheus says.

"Curse you, Morpheus." Ivory says exactly what I'm thinking. "These human lives we trifle with. There is a heavy price to be paid." She rolls to her side in a rustle of lace and satin so we can't see her expression. "Will I never learn? Time and again . . . you offer me glimpses of love and companionship, and I am too weak to turn you away."

Morpheus reaches around me and tips her chin in his direction. "That's not entirely true. You were the one offering glimpses of love this time." He dries her ice-encrusted tears with a knuckle.

Another private moment passes between them, a look I can't

quite decipher, as if he's relaying a message to her mind. I'm so used to being the recipient of his silent messages, it's unsettling to sit on the outside.

"What's going on between you two?" Suspicion wavers in my vocal cords.

"You're supposed to be working on that lack of trust," he reminds me.

I stare at him until my eyes itch from not blinking.

Ivory pats my hand. "You misunderstand. I gave Morpheus a glimpse into his future. Something I saw in a vision."

"That's enough, Ivory," he says, a threatening edge to his voice that makes the hair on my neck bristle.

She blinks twice. "In gratitude for my help, Morpheus offered me the gift of companionship, but not his own. A young man from your world, who needs my love as much as I need his."

"Finley." I'd almost forgotten the pawn Morpheus stole from the real world. "Is he okay?"

She nods. "He's safe in my palace, as a ward of my knights. Though he came with a stipulation. I owed Morpheus a favor, so that's why I am here. Nothing is ever free with him. Nothing."

"Exactly why we have this trust issue," I answer her but shoot a glare at Morpheus.

He traces a split in the mattress, ignoring me.

Ivory gives him her hand, and he helps her sit up. She takes my elbows, coaxing me to join her on the edge of the bed.

As Ivory strokes the ends of my hair, her voice becomes gentle. "There is *one* thing you can trust about Morpheus. He is loyal to you. It is his desire to be with you that drives him to these desperate schemes."

Morpheus stands in a rush of wings and rustling clothes. His shoulders droop as he turns his back to us. "There is nothing desperate about enlisting Alyssa's help. It is her *place*. She is the bearer of the ruby crown. Wonderland is as much her home as ours, no matter how she denies it. I had to make her see."

I push off the mattress. "By lying?"

Morpheus responds with silence, not even glancing over his shoulder to acknowledge me.

Blood rushes to my cheeks. I'm more furious with myself for believing in him than anything else. I move to the loft's railing and look pointedly at Ivory, an ugly theory taking form. "The real Ivy Raven. She's never even seen Jeb's artwork, has she?"

Ivory shakes her head.

"You didn't need her imprint for a glamour. You just needed a legitimate name in case we checked up on her. It was you who showed up to meet Jeb at the art gallery." I grit my teeth. Neither of them deny it. "He was so blown away by your amazing 'costume.' And you weren't even wearing one. You kept him here last night. Why?"

Ivory looks at the lace and webs sweeping the floor at her feet, long lashes veiling her eyes in a white curtain. "Only those with royal blood can see through Chessie's filter and decipher visions. Morpheus needed me to read your mosaics. And since your mother hid the others, he had to arrange for replicas. We were running out of time."

My stomach drops. "Why the big hurry? You've already said Red isn't here."

Morpheus's muscles tense at the statement, but he stays maddeningly silent.

Ivory answers, "Morpheus needed to know if Wonderland could be saved if he ignored Red's threats. She had given him an ultimatum: Surrender to her and meet his death, or watch his beloved nether-realm fall to rot at his feet."

I think of Queen Grenadine's ribbon that spoke to me in my bedroom: *Queen Red lives and seeks to destroy that which betrayed her.* "It was Morpheus she was after, not me. He's the one she thinks betrayed her."

Stoic, Morpheus kicks the carafe that once held the Tumtum juice. It rolls along the floor and stops beside my stolen mosaics. "I escaped her Deathspeak without her getting the throne. In her mind, I recanted our deal and owe her my life."

Glancing at Jeb's prone, dreaming form downstairs, I curl my hands into fists. "You vowed to tell me the truth about my mosaics. You lied."

Morpheus grunts. "You never specified *what* truth. So I told you the truth about their origins . . . their power. And I never once said Red had them. You were the one who supplied her name."

My legs feel shaky. I slide to the floor, my spine raking along the railing. "So Red called you out—a bully on a playground—and you ran. You brought your fight to my world."

"*Your world,*" Morpheus huffs. He faces me, his exquisite features hardened to a defiant scowl. "I showed you the truth in your dreams, the havoc she was wreaking. But because it didn't cast a ripple in this stagnant little human pond you call home, you ignored me. You put it out of your mind. Talked yourself out of believing it. I knew you would care nothing about my well-being. But I hoped . . . I hoped you would fight for Wonderland."

I want to say that I would've fought for him because I owe him.

Because I remember what he did for me. Because a part of me cares about my childhood friend, even about the selfish, charismatic, and frustrating man he's become. But I wouldn't have been in Wonderland for him to rescue in the first place if he hadn't lured me down on false pretenses last year. And I wonder, would I really have faced the one creature that terrifies me most, to save someone who was once so careless with my own life?

"Don't you dare turn this on me," I say, maybe as much to myself as Morpheus. "This is about you, what *you* did."

"I did the only thing I could to bid a reaction from you. The stolen mosaics, the vials of blood, the spellbound nurse, and the haunted clown—"

"Aha!" I point at him. "You can't deny that lie. You said you never sent a toy."

"Herman Hattington isn't a toy. He's a thespian of the highest order, due to his ever-changing face. And I didn't send him. He went to you of his own volition, as a favor to me."

I bury my head in my hands. That explains the clown's weird, heavy hat; it was the metal conformateur that's a part of the hatmaker's skull. "I suppose Rabid was helping you, too." That possibility hurts worse than any other.

"No," Morpheus answers. "His loyalty to you is sincere. His part in this was purely accidental."

"What about the nightmare?" I ask, looking up.

Morpheus shakes his head. "Your own subconscious manifested that tidbit, with a little help from the hallucinogens we put in your sedatives."

"Why?" I growl.

"I had to make you believe Red was putting your boyfriend in jeopardy so you'd return with me to save Wonderland. The only way I can ever get your attention is by placing your mortal toy in danger. It was working brilliantly, until once again the human muddled things up."

"You jerk!" My muscles coil and I scramble up to lunge at him. I expect him to fold a wing between us to block me. Instead, he steps forward, wings high and open. He holds out his arms—daring me to tackle him—egging me on. Ivory catches me around the waist and hauls me down beside her once more.

I struggle to get out of her embrace. She holds me with a force that's surprising for someone as delicate as an ice sculpture.

"You came swooping in here today, pretending to be the hero," I seethe to Morpheus. "When all along it was your fault Jeb was in that state to begin with. And now he's in real danger."

"It was only to be a few paintings on glass," Morpheus answers, his voice far too calm. "The juice was supposed to make him more focused until he finished. I never anticipated he'd become crazed, or that you would find your way here and he would put his hands on you . . ." There's a slight shift in his features—something menacing. "I never imagined, if Ivory left him for a few hours, that he would go off on a tangent and paint your memories—the very ones he lost. He's trapped in a hell crafted by his very own hands." Morpheus's gaze narrows. "But no. It's more at your hands, is it not? You've had a year to tell him everything. Had he known, he wouldn't have been such an easy target for me, and perhaps he wouldn't be in danger from Sister Two now."

I break free of Ivory's hold but can't move off the bed. Morpheus is right. Jeb's vulnerability is my fault.

"How do you do that?" I ask. "How do you always turn everything around on everyone else? Manipulate even those who know better than to believe you?"

Morpheus shrugs. "That's my power. My magic. *Persuasion.*"

"No. Your power is poison." My pride raises its head again. "Just so you know, there's something you'll never persuade me to do."

He studies me, smug. "What's that?"

"Love you."

Morpheus's jewels turn pale blue, the color of anguish, and I revel in the knowledge that I cut him.

"Never say never," he murmurs.

I match his stare, eyes stinging as if venom seeps through my irises.

He looks away first, steps over to the ladder, and dives, graceful black wings spread wide. He lands lightly in the middle of the floor. He waves to his moths, reuniting his hat, then kneels to hoist Jeb onto his shoulder around his left wing.

I leap to my feet and scramble back to the railing. "Put him down!" I screech.

"He's not safe here," Morpheus answers, gathering Jeb's shirt and boots with his free hand. "We must find a mirror and get him to the train. You wish to try to haul him out to the car yourself?"

I swallow a rebuttal. As arrogant as he is, he's right: I need his help to find the train.

"The keys," he presses.

Frowning, I chuck them toward him. Chessie zooms up and catches them in midair.

Ivory stands—all lace and elegance. She moves behind me, her wings low like a feather cape.

Morpheus looks over my shoulder at her. "Go back through the rabbit hole and protect your castle. Warn Sister One that her twin has crossed over to the human realm. She'll need to keep a close watch on the dark side of the cemetery. Alyssa and I will follow soon. We've little time to waste."

"Right," I say. "Now that you've managed to lure one of the creepiest and most venomous netherlings into a world of helpless humans, we don't have much time, do we?"

Morpheus resituates Jeb on his shoulder. "We're not at a complete disadvantage, Alyssa. Sister Two has a weakness, as we all do. She has a blind spot. Once she's cornered her prey, she notices nothing else around her. So, since there are two of us, we can work as a team to defeat her and send her back to Wonderland."

"Right," I answer. "And then you'll be the big hero again. For cleaning up a mess that you caused to begin with."

Morpheus doesn't answer. He strides out the door. Chessie looks up at us once, then follows.

"Perhaps you were a little harsh with him," Ivory says.

Hands clenched at my sides, I face her. "Jeb is the target of a black-widow woman big enough to eat a horse, and now he's catatonic and can't even defend himself. Not to mention all the humans who almost went up in flames today, all because of Morpheus's stupid plan."

"He never expected Sister Two to become involved. And he had nothing to do with the events at your school. The bugs caught wind of Queen Red's alliance with the flower fae. They feared she would lead her army into your world after she destroyed all of Wonderland, where they would feed on insects and humans alike. They released the wraiths in an effort to protect their home from Wonderland invaders."

"Technicalities," I answer. Her calm rationalizations are only making me angrier. "Doesn't it ever bother you? How he always gets by on those? He couldn't use his magic because of the glamour, so he had you and Hattington and the nurse do all his dirty work. Which meant that each time he told me he wasn't doing those things, he was able to lie to my face—guilt free, in true Wonderland form."

"He wasn't guilt free. He has been in torment. It was not his original plan to use your mortal knight."

"Right. I'm sure it was to sacrifice his own life for all of Wonderland, because he's an old-school martyr like that."

She frowns, her pale pink lips shimmering like flower petals in the sunlight. "That *was* his plan."

I want to laugh, but the sincerity within her frosted eyes stops me. One thing I've learned about Ivory, she's always honest when confronted. "All right. Convince me."

"A week before Morpheus started visiting your dreams again, he came to my castle and told me of Red's ultimatum. He asked me to use my crown-magic to look into your future, to assure that if he did as she asked and gave himself up to Red, she would be satiated and you and Wonderland would be safe forever. What I saw . . . it changed everything for him."

She holds out her palm, and a bubble appears. It's the size of a softball, only luminous and clear. "Vow to me you'll never tell anyone what I'm about to show you."

I stand mute, staring at the bubble as a blurry image begins to form inside.

"*Vow* it," Ivory presses.

I make the pledge. Two life-magic vows in one day. I'm becoming a pro at netherling negotiations without even trying.

Still holding the bubble, she bends down beside my mosaics and scrapes off a small residue of gray powder left from Chessie's sparkle cloud of earlier. She swipes it over the crystallized bubble, which animates a scene that's startlingly familiar. Not only can I see it, but I can hear, smell, feel, and taste it.

I'm crowned and seated on a throne at the head of a table, hosting a feast with mallet in hand, prepared to strike the main course dead. The scent of clover wine, moonbeam cookies, and baked fruit wafts from sparkling platters and crystal glasses.

Gathered around are a mishmash of creatures, some clothed, others naked, all more bestial than humanoid. They are my subjects, and my heart brims with affection for them—for their weirdness, for their madness, for their loyalty.

We talk and tease and bargain with the main dish. Maniacal laughter echoes in the marble halls, sweet to my ears.

There's movement at the banquet hall's entrance. A child with my eyes tumbles in—all wings and blue hair and giggling innocence. Holding his hand is Morpheus, wearing a ruby crown.

The Red King. My king.

The bubble bursts and takes the vision with it, leaving nothing but the sound of my gasp and wisps of gray smoke behind.

"You see," Ivory says, "once Morpheus knew that one day you would belong to him and he to you, that you would share a child, he was no longer willing to die to save Wonderland. But he's insecure about your feelings for him. He feared you would refuse to help. So he made a new plan, however flawed it was."

I'm reminded of that first day in the bathroom at school, the words Morpheus said: *"One does what one has to do, to protect what they love."* I knew there was an underlying meaning; I just had no idea how soul-deep it went.

I'm having trouble breathing. "A son," I say, recalling every detail of the child's perfect face.

Ivory's smile is blinding. "A most unique creature. The first child to be born to two netherlings who've shared a child*hood*. Wonderland is founded on chaos, madness, and magic. For so long, innocence and imagination have had no place there. As a result, we haven't had children, at least by your world's definition. And because of this, we've lost the ability to dream. But Morpheus experienced those things via you, each time you played together in *your* dreams. Through your child, Wonderland will thrive with new magic and strength. Our offspring will become true children once more; they will learn to dream again. And all will be right with our world."

"No," I murmur. I put my theoretical son out of my mind. I'm not ready to make that sacrifice. All I can think of is Jeb, my family and friends, and my future in the human realm. "That can't be right. I chose to stay here." I look down at the spot where Jeb was earlier and feel so empty.

Ivory catches my hands and clasps them. "You can still have a future with your mortal knight. You can marry him. Have a family and children, here."

My head spins. None of this makes any sense. "How?"

"Just as you have two sides to yourself, you have two potential futures. One day, the mortals you love will grow old and die. You, also, will age outwardly, and will have to go through the illusion of death. But your crown grants you an eternity in Wonderland. You'll be restored to the age you were when it was first placed upon your head. Your second future, your immortal netherling reign over the Red kingdom, will begin. And as you saw, Morpheus will play a very pivotal role."

I feel like someone sucker-punched me. "I can't be with someone I don't trust. Who doesn't trust me, either."

She places a hand on my shoulder. "You will learn to understand one another, to read one another. Morpheus is rarely honest with his words. His actions are where the truth lies. There may be many, many years between now and the vision you viewed. Something will change the way you see him. Perhaps a bevy of small things along the way, or possibly another grand gesture you never thought him capable of. Whatever it is, it will alter your relationship forever." Ivory steps back. "Alyssa, you've been given a chance at two lives and two loves. That is nothing short of a miracle. Cherish the gift for what it is. I shall see you soon, in Wonderland."

Her wings arc above her head, high and beautiful. She folds them over herself, and then, in a poof of white light and sparkling powder, becomes a swan and soars gracefully out the door.

I clench my jaw, emotions reeling. My heart breaks to think of outliving Jeb and all the people I love: Mom, Dad, Jenara, and Jeb's and my children. It's a mind trip I couldn't grasp even on the best day. And today's been the worst one ever.

Then, beyond the sadness that overshadows my future, there's the terrible confusion of my present.

How can I truly be with Jeb, knowing that one day I'll marry Morpheus? How can I give Morpheus the day I vowed to him and be true to Jeb, knowing what Morpheus knows?

I sit hard on the mattress. Morpheus bargained for those twenty-four hours because he doesn't *want* me to have my mortal life. He doesn't want to wait, or to share me with any other guy. He plans to start our future immediately.

I clasp the heart locket at my neck, struggling to separate its chain from the ruby-tipped key. I won't let him take my time with Jeb away. I refuse.

There's a rustle in the doorway. I stand and glance down to see Morpheus at the threshold.

"We should go," he says.

"No," I snap, too overwhelmed to say anything else. I want to hate him for all his lies, but Ivory's vision keeps imprinting our child on my mind's eye. Morpheus had motivations. They were pure—regardless of the lies and deceit it took to justify them. There is nothing black-and-white about him. He's a chaotic portrait made of every shade of gray.

With a flourish of dark wings he appears beside me in the loft. "What do you mean, no? We haven't time for nonsense, Alyssa."

"Release me of my vow," I say, forcing myself to meet his gaze. "We both know I'll never have feelings for you. So why even play this game? There's nothing between us." If I can say it to his face, maybe it will be true.

He leans in so his wings cast us both in shade, and his jewels flash a blinding red. "I'll prove you wrong. The moment this war is over, when I have you to myself for twenty-four hours. You'll never again question what we have between us."

"No. Deal's off."

"Fine. Break your vow. Lose your powers. Then you'll have no one to blame but yourself when Sister Two takes Jebediah into her web."

My nightmare flashes through my head: Jeb wrapped up, a corpse.

I growl and barrel into Morpheus. He catches me and backs me to the wall where the webs are thickest. He winds me like a top until my arms are pinned to my body by a sticky blanket. I struggle, but Sister Two's web is as strong as twine.

Morpheus bends his knees so we're at eye level. "Why do you insist on binding your heart within these chains? For once, just be still and *listen*. Listen to the nether-call."

Before I can even ask what he means, he skims his licorice-scented lips across my forehead—just shy of touching—his warm breath dragging across my left eye patch, then down a cheek, toward my mouth. The corner of my mouth tickles as he passes over it; then his breath stops to hover across my chin.

His palms rest against the wall on either side of my head. He lets the web serve as his hands, his breath serve as his lips, holding me immobile and kissing me without ever touching me. My eyes flutter closed as his lips skim a hairbreadth away from my lids. His familiar lullaby ignites in my mind, but there's a new verse:

"Little blossom trapped in between, wearing malice like a queen; hide the truth, be cruel and tart, still all the more, you rule my heart."

I try to shut him out, but the song drags me back to Wonderland, to landscapes now ragged and wounded.

Tears burn behind my eyelids as I witness the destruction.

The restlessness wakes within, that thumping in my head. The more I try to resist, the more my blood burns—anger for Wonderland's ailing skies and terrain, compassion for its ragged soul.

Morpheus finally touches me, bringing my thoughts back to the loft. Hands cupping my face, he coaxes my eyes open with his thumbs at their edges. He pulls back, and his gaze meets mine, sending a message deep into my heart.

Release your chains, Alyssa. Set your magic free.

In reaction both to his silent plea and to my fury over Red's rampage, my wing buds itch and pinch until the pressure is unbearable.

I cry out in startled surprise as they burst from my skin, ripping my shirt and slicing through the cobwebs. The webs cling to the wall and my chest—a draping of thick gossamer that serves as a shirt in place of the one I lost.

I'm free, and I step away from the wall, my wings both heavy and light.

Morpheus watches me. His jewels are the deepest purple I've ever seen—triumphant and proud. His mouth curves to a slow-burning smile.

"Beautifully done, My Queen," he says, stepping back and adjusting his hat. "You are at your most powerful when you stop resisting what's in your blood." He walks toward my mosaics, then stalls next to them, glancing at me. "One thing more: Wonderland and I are the same. You love one of us, you love the other. You are Wonderland, too. Which means we are the perfect fit, in more ways than you can even imagine. On our day together, I'll take great pleasure in showing you all of them."

My heart is pounding so hard I can't speak around it.

Morpheus picks up my mosaics then steps to the edge of the loft. He tosses Gizmo's keys at my feet. "Don't take too long. Your mortal boy's memory needs a jump start. And Wonderland is waiting."

He falls backward off the ledge and leaves me standing there, my body humming with power: a full-fledged netherling queen—freed of my webby cage, yet spellbound by a devil's almost-kiss.

TURBULENCE

As soon as Morpheus shuts the door behind him, I peel the web from my chest and wrap up in a drop cloth to cover my bra. A rope from the scaffolding serves as a belt around the waist and holds my wings plastered to my back under the sheet.

I feel like Quasimodo in a toga.

Morpheus left his trench-coat-style blazer on the floor. It would be ideal with the wing slits, but I refuse to give him the satisfaction of wearing his clothes. A peek out the door reveals him lounged against Gizmo, wings draped over the car's hood in all their inky glory. It's a good thing we're on a deserted road.

He's wearing my shades, and the ends of his hair blow in the breeze. He chats with Chessie—cool, calm, and self-assured. He doesn't even look nervous about what's ahead of us: facing Red and Sister Two. He's too busy gloating.

I hiss in frustration. I want to be furious that he made a liar out of me about my feelings, and even angrier that he goaded my wings to appear, since I'm stuck trying to hide them until they fade back into my skin. But I have to admit, embracing the reality of my power is heady. I'm finding it difficult to hold a grudge when he was only trying to show me how strong I really am.

When it's in fact what he always does.

Still, I can't let him think he's won. If he *is* my king in some unfathomable, immortal future, we will be partners. But queens have dominion over the kingdoms. I have to prove I have a penchant for manipulation that can rival his.

I gather my keys and Morpheus's blazer, then tuck the glass decanter into the back of my makeshift belt between the bulge of my wings so it's hidden.

When I step out of the cottage into the dusty air, Chessie flutters over and lands on my head. He digs his paws into my hair and kneads my scalp like a kitten.

Morpheus regards my outfit as I hand him his jacket. "So, we're off to ancient Rome, then?" he teases.

"I'd lose that smile if I were you." I jingle the car keys in his face. "Your life is in my hands, *lest you forget*." My imitation of his cockney accent is actually spot-on, and I let myself bask in it.

"Sorry to disappoint, luv." He tosses the jacket into the passenger seat. "I plan to fly this time around."

He transforms into the moth, his hat exploding into a spectacle of smaller moths that take to the air. Morpheus perches on the hood of the car. My sunglasses rest on the metal beside him, catching a glint of sun. I pretend to reach for them, but before he can guess my intentions, I catch one of his wings instead. He flutters, trying to break loose, his one free wing batting my hand.

I draw out the decanter and stuff him into it, careful to fold his wings. I don't want to hurt him. I just want to *better* him.

Once he's settled inside, I shove a paper towel into the bottle's neck. No need to worry that he'll smother. After all, he spent that night in a bug trap last year and survived.

"Looks like you're going to have some turbulence on your flight," I tell him through the glass.

His voice fills my head, an angry, scolding growl. When I don't respond, he yells Chessie's name. Chessie flits over to the car and sits on the side mirror, licking his paw, amused and uninterested in taking sides.

I hold the decanter up to get a closer look at Morpheus. "Game, set, match, *luv*. You do realize that my human side defeated you, right? No magic required."

Unlike a real moth that would beat itself against the glass walls until exhausted, he hangs under the curved neck, dignified, glaring with his bulbous eyes. If he had a mouth instead of a proboscis, I'd be able to tell if he's snarling or beaming with pride. Knowing him, it could be either. Most likely, it's both.

My chest swells with some small satisfaction.

I put on my sunglasses. The frames are warm from the sun, but the heat isn't enough to keep me from shivering when I see Jeb curled up on his side in the backseat. Morpheus dressed him in his shirt and boots, and that small kindness earns my winged rival a secure seat for the drive.

Jeb mumbles something as I tuck the decanter into the curve of his knees. It's the best place to keep the glass from rolling around. I kiss Jeb's head, then slide into the driver's seat.

It's difficult to find a comfortable position while sitting on my wings. I finally shove them over to my right, which makes a lumpy, irregular form under the sheet. I'll have to take the side roads to get into town because if anyone were to see me, they might think I'm hiding a dead body.

Chessie pauses on the dashboard, blinks twice in my direction, and disappears through the rearview mirror, getting a head start on London and the rabbit hole.

For the rest of us, Butterfly Threads will be our first stop. There are full-length mirrors across the walls, and plenty of clothes, although I'll have to make some creative adjustments to fit anything over my wings.

It's only ten after twelve. When Penelope's understaffed, she closes the store from noon to one for her lunch break.

I tuck Morpheus's blazer into my backpack, then check my cell. There are two texts from Jen and three voice mails from Dad. First I respond to Jen:

Found Jeb. Deets later. He's safe. Be home in a while . . .

Next, I listen to my dad's most recent voice message:

"Allie, I'm worried. Enough thinking, okay? Come home. We'll talk. We can fix things."

His voice is tight. He's freaked, without a doubt, but apparently he's home and, judging by the "*I'm* worried" line, hasn't told Mom about what's happened yet. Good, because if she found out about the events at school, she'd put two and two together and do something impulsive. I don't need her in danger, too.

Dad said we could "fix things." I know what that means: When I get back, I'll be grounded. Shut off from my car, phone, computer, and friends until Monday when he can take me to Mom's psychiatrist. I wonder if he even plans to let me graduate with my class on Saturday.

There has to be some way to fix this, but I don't have the time or brainpower to waste on it now. After Red is defeated and I get Sister Two off Jeb's back, I'll return from Wonderland and make things right somehow.

If I survive the war.

All of the guilt, fear, and doubt form a lump in my vocal cords. *I hope to see you and Mom soon, Dad,* I text—meaning it with all my heart.

I take a deep breath and turn off the phone.

❈ · I · ❈

We arrive at the strip mall at half past noon. I use the alley behind Butterfly Threads. It's a safe place to leave my car while we're gone halfway across the world.

Gravel crunches under Gizmo's tires as I come to a stop a few Dumpsters down from the shop's back door, angling the car between a box compressor and a nine-foot brick fence to hide it. Persephone's red Prius is absent from its usual curb slot, and all the shop's lights are off. If we hurry, we'll be gone before she gets back from lunch.

I take off my sunglasses, grab Morpheus's decanter, and climb out of the driver's side. I'm not looking forward to releasing him, but I need him to help me carry Jeb and unlock the store's back door.

His buggy eyes stare at me through the glass. He's tinged green, which means that those bumpy shortcuts took their toll.

I stand between the Dumpster and the bricks for privacy. Holding a breath against the stench of baked trash, I look around to ensure we're alone in the alley. The hot sun glints off a car grille in the distance, but there's no one inside it, so I unplug the jar.

Morpheus squeezes through the neck and balances on the rim, as if getting his bearings. He launches into the air—a flutter of wings and blue static—then transforms in front of me into an ominous silhouette that blocks the sun and chills my skin.

"My Peregrination Cap," he grumbles, straightening his tie and vest while wavering on wobbly legs.

I gesture to the layer of moths crawling around on Gizmo's roof. "We lost a few of them to the wind. Sorry."

"Brilliant." Scowling, Morpheus walks over and sweeps his hand across the insects, coaxing them to form the hat. They manage all but the brim. He puts it on anyway and turns to me.

I bite my cheeks in an effort not to laugh.

He narrows his eyes. "Don't get too cheeky, little plum. Though your prank may have been irresistibly wicked, I'm still in the lead by a set of wings." He glances over my shoulder at the slipping drop cloth.

The netherling in me nudges until I no longer want to hide what I am. I glance around the deserted alley, then twist the belt so it holds the sheet secure across my front but opens in back. My wings splay high and free behind me, opaque white and glimmering with rainbow-colored jewels similar to the gems under Morpheus's eye markings.

His wings rise, mirroring mine, and we face one another, silently calling a truce. *For now.*

We take the back door to the storeroom. Air-conditioning greets us, along with the lavender scent of Persephone's latest obsession: holistic aromatherapy in the form of wickless soy candles.

Morpheus slumps Jeb against the wall and shuts the door as I flip on the light switch. A thousand tiny bulbs light up, all strung together on one wall like a cobweb made of amber Christmas lights.

"I'm growing weary of toting your baggage around, Alyssa," Morpheus gripes as he pushes Jeb to a sitting position. "And his clothes are a mess. You might consider letting him wear my jacket."

I shoot a grimace his way, set aside my backpack, and kneel in front of Jeb. "It's your fault he has to be asleep and that his clothes are shot." I work Jeb's bloody shirt off and tuck it in my bag so I can replace it with Morpheus's blazer. Biting my lip, I trace the cigarette-butt scars along Jeb's bared torso. I've often wished he could replace all those bad memories with the good ones we've made together since. But now, more than ever, I realize how important every memory is, bad or good, because they shape who we become.

Jeb's deadweight arms are awkward and difficult to thread through the jacket's long sleeves. It's unsettling to see him immobile. He has such a strong, active body and is a master at everything he uses it for—riding his Honda, skateboarding, painting, rock climbing, or even making me feel . . . *amazing*. Seeing him so vulnerable reminds me of the danger he faced in Wonderland last summer, and what lies ahead for both of us now that I've brought him into this again.

I try to move fast. He's broader through the shoulders than Morpheus, but the wing openings allow enough give that I can still button the jacket just below his sternum. I skim my fingers through the hair on his chest, wishing I could talk to him.

"If only you could hear me," I whisper, more to myself than Jeb. "If I could make you understand how sorry I am."

Morpheus taps a foot beside my thigh. "I suppose now might be the time to tell you I could arrange for him to be awake in a dream state that would keep his conscious pain at bay."

My jaw drops and I look up at him. "What? He could've been awake this whole time and not been miserable? What's *wrong* with you?"

Morpheus purses his lips. "Hmm. Have Jebediah mooning over you in a half-awake dream state, or have him unconscious and drooling. What do they call that here? A no-brainer."

I clench my teeth. "Morpheus! I swear, you are the biggest—"

"Tut." He rolls up the cuffs on his black dress shirt. "Don't say anything I'll make you sorry for. In all honesty, I've rather had my fill of your nagging for a bit. I could use a distraction."

"The feeling is *beyond* mutual." I scowl at him.

Smug, Morpheus waves glowing blue fingers across Jeb's forehead. "Dreamer awake, but stay undone; your thoughts are but shadows eclipsed by the sun."

Jeb grumbles but doesn't wake.

"It will take a few minutes to kick in," Morpheus says, then wanders off to examine Persephone's personal shrine to the 1990s movie *The Crow*. He stares into the eyes of the life-size cutout of Brandon Lee as if staring in the mirror.

"Let me find something to wear, and we'll go," I call over to him.

"You should hurry. Once Jebediah wakes, his dream state will be temporary. Reality will start seeping into his psyche, so we're on borrowed time."

"Okay," I answer.

Morpheus returns to his appraisal of Brandon Lee. "Not bad. If he only had wings."

I shake my head dismissively, then make my way to the racks filled with funky and gothic clothes waiting to be wheeled out to the main floor. Persephone's collection of window-dressing props adds a creepy air: a skeleton with only one leg occupies a busted antique chair, bony arms crossed over its chest like it's a crypt-keeper; a roll of canvas for backdrops; a trunk filled with shattered masquerade masks and threadbare costumes; Styrofoam wig heads sporting an assortment of wig colors and styles; and some electrical items including more strings of lights and a miniature smoke machine.

I stop at a rack of damaged merchandise. Not my first choice for a trip to London, but since Persephone will be throwing most of them away after writing them off on her taxes, it's the *best* choice, so I don't feel like I'm stealing.

I find a three-quarter-sleeve minidress of stretchy purple velvet, with fitted bodice and flared skirt. Turquoise lace trims the cuffs and hem. It hits at my thighs, the perfect size for a tunic to go over my ripped jeans. There's a tear in the left shoulder seam. I unravel it further until the slit will accommodate my wing and then tear the other shoulder on the right side to match.

After tossing a quick look at Jeb, I duck into the tiny bathroom off to the left, close the door, and set my backpack on the floor. I loosen my belt, and the drop cloth slips away, so I'm standing there in only my bra, jeans, and boots. Cold air rushes over me from a vent above the sink. The tiny fluorescent light barely illuminates the room and wreaks havoc with my reflection.

I skim my fingers through my tangles, shocked at how wild I look.

I'm every bit a netherling: eye patches, unruly, wavy hair that appears to move as if alive, and a sheen of glitter on my skin.

Most awe-inspiring of all is how my wings rise behind me, shimmery and frosted—a haze of jewels and gossamer.

Last year, I stood here, terrified of becoming who I thought my mom was—a crazed woman, bound in a straitjacket and occupying a padded cell. Now here I am, a completely different person than I was: half netherling, half human, but still wholly confused.

Who am I, really? Powerful but broken, like my mother? Or am I something more? A queen destined to rule Wonderland with the most enigmatic and frustrating of all netherlings at my side, to have a son who will in some warped way be a gift to that mad world?

I can't. Not yet. I snap my gaze to my boots. No more staring in the mirror. No more conjecturing. It's overwhelming, even terrifying, to know my life has already changed so much. I can't imagine it changing so drastically again.

I need to be reminded of what's normal. What's safe. And Jeb represents all of that. I need to fix him, to get back to real life. A life with no more secrets between us.

Dressing myself with wings proves a challenge, but the stretchy fabric helps. When I finally step again into the storeroom, Jeb's standing against the wall wearing a confused expression, though he doesn't appear afraid or in pain.

My heart gives a little jump to see him awake and alert, even if it's in a dream state.

Morpheus is missing, and *The Crow* display looks different. I try to place what's changed, but a shuffling sound in the shop's main room distracts me. I assume that's where Morpheus went, probably to check out the mirrors on the walls. I should make sure he isn't seen by any passersby through the front windows, but I'm so thrilled to finally have a chance to talk to Jeb, I can't bring myself to leave yet. It was yesterday afternoon when we last had a lucid conversation, but it seems like forever ago.

"Jeb."

He jerks to attention as he notices me. The black blazer fits him even better when he's standing, pulling open across the front to display more of his chest. The fabric glides down the thighs of his jeans. He pushes off the wall, studying me like I'm a painting. I shiver under his appraisal—not sure how to react after our earlier encounter. I know he won't hurt me, but . . .

He walks over, cautious, as if I'm a shy animal that might spook easily. Or maybe it's him that could be spooked.

I stand my ground. I'll have to camouflage my wings and eye patches somehow before we go to London, but I don't want to hide them from Jeb. Not anymore.

I flinch as he reaches toward my neck.

"Al?"

I melt. There's nothing but the gentleness and love I've come to expect in his voice. No murderous intent or crazed edge to his gaze. I tackle-hug him, just like I wanted to the instant he showed up at the cottage.

He stumbles backward two steps, but his sturdiness prevails. He steadies me and returns the embrace, hands searching for a place on my back that isn't blocked by my wings.

"This is different," he whispers, yet he doesn't sound disturbed or freaked out. "Of all the times I've had this dream, we were never in the storeroom."

I draw back and study him, smiling. Morpheus wasn't kidding when he said he'd be in a dreamlike state.

He returns my smile, and his labret sparkles. Even in the dimness, I can see the red welts on his chin from the rabbit's claws.

"I'm so sorry." I stroke the raised lines with a fingertip, though I'm talking about so much more than his physical condition. "Does it hurt?"

He lets me fuss over him all of a nanosecond before pulling the macho act. "Nothing ever hurts when I'm with my fairy skater girl." His gaze doesn't leave mine as he grabs my hips and drags me close so there's no space between us. "You know I love you like this." He skims my eye patches with a fingertip, his breath hot on my face.

The confession is beautiful, but I wonder if he'll feel the same when he's no longer in a trance.

"I'm ready," he says. There's a sweet insistence in the words that makes my throat dry. He's a toned-down version of the starving artist I faced before, and I'm once again the center of his world.

"Ready for what?" I ask.

"For you to wrap me in your wings," he answers, voice gruff. "And for me to show you how to fly without ever leaving the ground."

He nuzzles my neck, and a blush heats my skin. A quiver of pleasure surges through me, from my toes to my wing tips, but I push him to arm's length, hands wrapped in his lapels. Morpheus said this dream state is temporary. We have to hurry.

"Listen, Jeb. This dream is different. There's about to be a lot of weirdness." I inch backward toward the entrance to the main floor where Morpheus is so we can go.

Jeb follows me, head cocked, a provocative intensity in his eyes. "Bet I can handle anything you throw at me."

"Wouldn't be so sure if I were ye, dream-boy." A woman's murmur

comes from outside the door, dry and husky, like leaves scraping tombstones.

There's a *whoosh* behind me, and I spin at the threshold. All I can see is web.

Sister Two.

I nearly choke on the pulse battering at the base of my throat.

Gossamer filaments shroud the entire main room—shadowy strands strung from ceiling to floor. It's like looking inside an albino pumpkin before the membranes are scraped clean. The web coats clothes racks and the checkout desk, even the display window, cutting off the daylight. The result is an eerie, misty gray light, as if storm clouds have settled outside. I squint, unable to pinpoint where the spidery grave keeper's voice originated.

"Morpheus!" I shout.

No answer.

"Who are you yelling at?" Jeb comes up behind me and touches my wing. A tingling sensation pulses through me.

I turn and shove him toward the bathroom. "You're in danger. She can't find you." I push him inside. He stumbles over my backpack but regains his footing.

Questions fill his eyes as I slam the door between us.

"Hey! Let me out! Al!"

I hold the knob tight and look around the room, and pausing on Persephone's prop skeleton. Taking a breath to calm myself, I coax him to move as if he were a marionette who requires no strings.

Creaking and rattling, he hops over on his one foot and sags beside me, awaiting my command.

We trade places, his bony fingers holding the knob as I look around dumbly.

"Don't let him out or let anyone in but me," I tell him over my shoulder, not even sure the bag-of-bones understands. I'm still getting used to this magic stuff.

Jeb's door pounding grows louder.

I gulp down my fear and step again into the main room, stopping short of a drapery of webs.

"Welcome to my parlor, said the spider to the fly." The whisper smells of fresh-dug dirt and is cold against my ear. My soul shrinks.

I look up. Sister Two hangs upside down overhead. She hisses, and I retreat, my breath rapid and uneven.

She's not even trying to hide her gruesome form under a dress. Her top half is a woman—lavender lips, translucent face all bloody and scarred, a curtain of silvery gray hair hanging almost to my nose. Her bottom half—a black widow's abdomen the size of a beanbag chair that could seat six people—balances on a strand of web connecting the ceiling to her spinnerets. Eight shiny spider legs curl around it, strangely graceful, like some grotesque circus acrobat dangling from a rope.

Snip, snip, snip. The sound is my only warning. I duck out of the way as her scissor hand slices the air inches from my face.

I dive to the floor and crawl behind the checkout counter, staying low to avoid dangling webbing.

"Morpheus!" Fear ices through me. "Where are you?"

"He won't be answering, little fly." Sister Two scurries down the wall behind me, the clawed, pointed tips of her legs tapping like raindrops. "He left ye, like the coward he be. It's jest the three of us, here to settle yer mother's debt."

Her head tips toward the storeroom, where Jeb is still knocking and shouting.

"You're lying," I say, trying to ground her attention on me again. "Morpheus wouldn't leave me."

"I found him in the other room. He shrank to the moth, and I chased him here." She lifts her normal hand, the one encased in a rubber glove, and waves it. "Then, poof. He doesn't be here anymore, does he? He found a way out. Too bad for ye."

I scramble backward from behind the counter, gaze locked on her gray-blue eyes, daring her to follow. I have to get her as far from the storeroom as possible, have to keep her focused on me as her prey. That's the only way she'll forget Jeb.

She scurries after me. I trip over the edge of a rack. While trying to right myself, one wing catches in a sticky web. I'm stuck. My heart thuds against my sternum.

Sister Two grows taller, her jointed, sticklike legs stretching up in one smooth motion. She leans over until we're nose to nose.

I won't let my panic get the best of me. If I'm going to keep Jeb alive, I have to stay the center of her attention.

"Why are you here? What debt does my mom owe you?" I ask, remembering how the same question was sidestepped by Ivory and Morpheus at the studio. I'm ready for answers.

"Aw, curious now, are ye?" Drawing back, she laughs—like a rusted screen door swinging on its hinges. Strands of hair hang over her eyes, and she brushes them aside with her garden-shear hand. Blood drizzles from a freshly made cut, but she doesn't seem to notice.

"I should've killed her when I had the chance, and then ye wouldn't have been born to steal the smile or release Red's sprit. Like mother, like daughter. Though her thievery was more egregious than yours. She took the boy with the dreams."

The boy with the dreams?

Gossamer said something about dreams when explaining the wraiths and borogoves—that they balance each other.

"The borogoves?" I ask. "You use them in the cemetery to soothe angry spirits."

"Aye. Dreams don't be a renewable resource, mind. And as our kind can't dream, we steal humanlings, those young enough to still have an imagination. They provide the protection for the rabbit hole, and peace for me garden."

My stomach drops. "You steal human *children*? You kidnap them?"

Sister Two's eyes narrow. "Is that disdain I smell on yer breath, child? Yer mother was so like ye, disrespected the way things had to be. Rules are there for a reason. For the survival of our world, some have to suffer in yers. And vice versa, aye?"

I'm too stunned to respond. I want to love Wonderland with all my heart, but how can I love a place that takes children from their homes?

"There have been other humanlings since that boy," Sister Two continues, her bloody face euphoric. "But he was different. Even as he aged, his dreams were *magnificent*. The ten years he was mine, I had such tranquility among me wards." She works off her glove, using her teeth. The rubber sheath pops off, exposing scorpion tails in place of fingers and stingers in place of nails.

I suppress a gag.

My mind races for some way to keep her talking. "Who was this boy?" Although, in some private, horrified corner of my soul, I'm starting to think I already know.

Curling and uncurling her venomous fingertips, Sister Two bows over me. "What difference does a name make? He's long gone now. Ye can die without that answer, just as I've lived without it. All ye need is the knowledge that I'll take yer mortal knight to be our new dreamer. He has an artist's mind. I've seen his work. He'll give me spirits many years of peace and entertainment."

"No, please. Don't hurt Jeb . . ." I try to break free of the web, but it only tightens around my wing. Cold panic sluices through my blood, making me shiver.

"Aw. Don't ye worry, little fly, he'll never know he's suffering." Sister Two's palm rakes my face. I grip her wrist and wrestle her, but those eight legs give her a better center of gravity.

"Back off!" I snarl through gritted teeth, mind shifting into netherling mode. I remember her blind spot and silently call my skeleton marionette in from the storeroom to attack her from behind. "I won't let you have Jeb without a fight." I wince as a stinger presses my cheek, about to break the skin. Poison wells from the tip and drizzles down my face.

"I be counting on that, devil-bug," Sister Two says. "I like me food to have some bite."

"You want bite?" Morpheus's voice interrupts from somewhere on the other side of the room, breaking my concentration. Bones rattle in the storeroom as my skeletal puppet falls limp. "Take me in her stead."

My heart soars . . . only to seize again when I realize what he's just offered. I can barely make out his silhouette through the webs, standing in front of the display window: his body, his wings.

"Morpheusssss." Sister Two shoves me backward, unintentionally freeing my wing of its trap. I swipe the poison from my face and regain my balance.

Morpheus's wings flap slowly and cautiously. "Right here, my lovely wretch. I was feeling neglected. You were aiming all that beautiful fury at the wrong insect. After all, I'm as responsible as Alison for stealing the boy. You must know that by now."

Hissing, she scuttles toward Morpheus.

"Alyssa," Morpheus says, unmoving from his position, "you have a trip to take. Everything you'll need is in my jacket."

Wait . . . that was why he insisted I put the jacket on Jeb, so I'd have the tickets if we got separated. It had nothing to do with Jeb's bloodstained shirt. He thinks I'm going on the train without him.

"No," I insist. "Not without you."

"Would you sacrifice the mortal you love for the netherling you hate?" he asks, and the conviction in his voice hurts as bad as a blow. I don't know what's more excruciating, the fact that I've told him I hate him enough times to make him believe it or that I'm starting to realize how far it is from the truth.

I hesitate, wishing I could rescue both of them. It's a risk, and if I fail trying, Jeb doesn't stand a chance against Sister Two.

Morpheus, on the other hand, does.

Eyes stinging, I sprint toward the storeroom. I make the mistake of throwing one last glance over my shoulder. Sister Two casts a web that covers Morpheus's silhouette, and I scream.

He shouts, "Go, Alyssa!" His voice is strained and muffled as she twists him toward her like she's reeling in a fish, building a cocoon around him on the way.

I turn because I have to, because Jeb needs me and Wonderland is running out of time. Although every pounding step I take rips my heart further down the middle.

LONDON BRIDGES

There isn't time to hide my wings.

For safety, Jeb and I stay in the bathroom and take the mirror above the sink to London. He's cooperative, not even asking questions as I twist the key into the crackled glass and open the portal to the bridge in the distance. Wooden slats partially block the view, as if a gate is closed just on the other side of the mirror.

I climb onto the sink and reach inside to push it open, then I plunge through. The motion sickness is as bad as the first few times I traveled via mirror. I guess it's been too long.

Once I have my balance, I stand to face the London side of the portal—a six-foot-tall garden mirror that has two wooden panels giving the illusion of a gated entrance. There's no one else around, and I breathe a sigh of relief.

The sun hangs low on the horizon, streaking orange across a clear sky. A village sits on the other side of the river, complete with busy streets, people, and charming buildings set so close they could be Legos snapped together. Trees cover the hill I'm standing on, casting shade in thick patches of blue on the grassy ground. A brick cottage hunkers a few yards away from me. Though it looks abandoned, the garden is vibrant and flourishing.

Gardenia, larkspur, and hyacinth fill the air with sweet scents. Bees and butterflies flutter around the petals and leaves. Their unified whispers tickle my ears:

You're not the first to trek this ground. Your mother was here before you.

Yes, she was. Yesterday, when she hid my mosaics. I'm about to ask if they happened to see exactly where she hid them on the bridge when Jeb ducks through the mirror wearing my backpack. He sways but takes the disorientation in stride, thinking it's all part of the dream.

If only it *were* a dream.

I fight the prick of tears behind my eyes again. Morpheus has to be okay. I can't believe he gave himself up so I could take Jeb with me. Of course he wants me to find the final mosaic. He wants me to save Wonderland. Maybe there's even a deeper plan, some secret scheme. I can't be sure where he's involved.

Still. It took courage. And he also alluded to having a part in stealing Sister Two's dream-boy. If the dream-boy is who I think he is, it changes everything I've ever thought about my mom . . . about my life . . . even about Morpheus.

"Hey," Jeb says, touching my cheek. He draws back his hand and studies a tear I didn't realize had escaped. "This can't be right. You're never sad in my dreams."

"It's nothing." I rub my face. "It's just the rain."

He looks up. "There's not a cloud in the sky." Then he levels his gaze on our surroundings. "Where is this place? I've never imagined it before."

"Maybe this is my dream." I attempt to ease his mind. "Yeah. You're sharing mine."

He stares at me, expression doubtful. We need to start heading for the bridge before he fully wakes up, but I wait one minute longer, hoping Morpheus will come through the portal. Sister Two can't find us. He was careful not to reveal where we were headed.

When he doesn't show up, I stifle the twinge in my chest and swing the wooden gate shut again to camouflage the mirror.

I grab Jeb's hand and weave his fingers with mine. "Let's go."

"Just a second." He catches my elbow with his free hand. "My stomach's growling. That's weird for a dream, isn't it?" There's a new inquisitiveness behind his eyes. "What's really going on?"

He's coming out of his daze, and when he's conscious, he'll be too savvy to fall for any more lame excuses. We don't have much time before all the pain of unremembered and unreachable memories comes crashing in on him. I decide to take the train ride before searching for the mosaic.

Morpheus said the abandoned station is somewhere beneath the ground. I'm not sure where the secret entrance might be. I had hoped Chessie would be here to lead the way.

"Everything will make sense soon," I answer Jeb. "I'll find us something to eat once we get where we're going. Trust me. Okay?"

He nods, but a shadow falls over his expression. I have to hurry before he curls up into a ball again. The bridge is so far. I'm not sure he'll keep it together for the trek. If only I could fly him there without being seen by the people on the other side of the river. But even if it was nighttime instead of early evening, he'd be too heavy for me. I know that much from past experience.

Before I can do anything, I need to figure out how to find the underground train station.

"Help me look through your pockets," I press Jeb. "There should be tickets in here somewhere." They might have directions or maybe a map on the back.

Jeb frowns, as if just noticing the jacket he's wearing isn't his, but digs through his side pockets without asking whose it is. He drags out a handful of mushrooms with caps the size of dimes.

"Are these glow-in-the-dark gummies?" he asks. There's a hint of apprehension behind the question.

I don't answer, afraid to tell him that they're real and from Wonderland. They're fluorescent and small, which makes them look like candy. Some are neon orange and others are lime green, but all are solid and smooth on one side and speckled with tiny pink dots on the other—miniature versions of the mushrooms in Morpheus's lair.

I search the inner pocket of Jeb's lapel for the tickets. Something crinkles beneath my fingertips, and I draw it out. I unfold the piece of paper. It's a sketch similar to the ones Mom had tucked in her *Alice's Adventures in Wonderland* book. This one has a caterpillar sitting atop a mushroom, smoking a hookah.

The puffs of smoke form legible words:

One side makes you taller, the other side shorter.

It's from the scene in Lewis Carroll's tale when Alice complains to the caterpillar that she wishes to be taller and he suggests she eat the mushroom to grow but leaves her without telling which side does what.

I crumple the piece of paper, frustrated that everything always has to be so difficult.

"Where are the tickets?" I vent to no one in particular. "He said everything we need is here."

A large monarch butterfly flitters over on a breeze and lands on my shoulder. One flapping wing tickles my neck as she whispers: *The ticket is your* size, *silly. You could never fit on the train as you are.*

I stare at the bulbous-eyed insect.

"Don't try the candy," Jeb says, making me turn back to him. "It's stale." He's chewing something.

"Jeb!" I grab the mushroom pinched between his finger and thumb. Half of its cap has been bitten off, leaving only the speckled side. "Spit it out!" In my haste to get closer to him, I knock all of the mushrooms out of his palm. They scatter on the ground.

He swallows and meets my gaze. Before I can react, he starts to shrink and doesn't stop until he's the size of a small beetle—the similarity enhanced by the tiny backpack on his shoulders.

That's all it takes to bust his dream trance. He rolls into a fetal position and screams. Even as tiny as he is, the sound scrapes through me like claws. I crouch to scoop him up, but the butterfly swoops in and snatches him with her legs. She hovers just out of my reach, at eye level.

"Hey, give him back!" I jump to my feet but refrain from swatting her. The backpack tumbles off him and hits the ground. If Jeb falls from that height, it could kill him.

The monarch gracefully dances in midair and whispers: *Your boy makes a far better flower than you.*

"Huh?" I ask.

Any wise flower knows: Stretch for the sunlight and shrink from the shadows.

And then she's off toward the bridge with my groaning boyfriend in tow.

In full panic mode, I'm about take to the sky and risk being seen by the entire village, when everything starts to make sense: The ticket is our *size*; to get on the train, we have to be small. That's what the mushrooms are for. According to the butterfly's riddle and Jeb's transformation, the side that faces the sun and becomes freckled will make you grow, and the side that faces the shadows and is smooth will shrink you.

I shove all the remaining mushrooms in my jeans pocket except one. I've done this before, but with a bottle that said *Drink Me.* My clothes and everything touching me shrank, just like Jeb's did.

I nibble off half of the mushroom's cap, taking care not to ingest any of the speckled side. My first taste is sweet, like paper soaked in sugar water; then a fizzy sensation leaves my tongue numb.

My muscles contract, my bones narrow, and my skin and carti- lage tighten to hold everything together. The surroundings shoot up around me, flowers becoming the size of trees, and the trees the size of skyscrapers. Tall fronds of grass bend across me. It's like I'm in a jungle.

As soon as my metamorphosis is complete, I shake off the nausea, swing the backpack over one shoulder, and use my wings like I've been itching to for months. I clench my shoulders and arch my spine, my muscles falling into a rhythm with almost no effort. Just like skateboarding, it feels natural.

My hair slaps around my face. Up, up, up, through the strands of grass and looming flowers until my boots skim the tops of the giant trees. The height is exhilarating, and I'm little enough that no one can see me from the village.

I catch up to the butterfly. Jeb moans and droops in her hold. As if choreographed, we descend on a current of air. I follow her into a crack in the brick foundation of the iron bridge. We maneuver through the hole and burst out into a deserted elevator passageway where arriving train passengers used to wait for rides up to the village. The muffled sounds of cars and people overhead drift in through vents. I hover in midair next to the butterfly, keeping Jeb in my sight.

The tunnel is lit with moving chandeliers, rolling like miniature Ferris wheels across the curved, stone ceiling. As they come closer, I realize they're actually clusters of lightning bugs, harnessed together. Each rotation illuminates dingy tiled walls and faded advertising from the 1950s. The posters are giant compared to me—as big as buildings.

The train, on the other hand, is just the right size, and it's now obvious what Morpheus meant about it not being a form of transport. In a shadowy corner, a rusted tin train set is tucked within a pile of toys—some wooden blocks, a pinwheel, some jigsaw puzzle pieces, and a few rubber jacks. The playthings were either forgotten or abandoned by children waiting with their parents at the elevator decades ago. A large sign hangs over the pile. The words LOST AND

FOUND have been marked out and replaced by the phrase TRAIN OF THOUGHT.

Boxcars, flatcars, and passenger cars connect to an engine and caboose, perfectly scaled to our current size. Through the shadows, I can barely make out the title *Memory's Mystic Band* painted in black letters across the red engine.

The butterfly deposits Jeb next to one of the passenger cars. I hurry after her, trying to remember how to land. The car door opens. Something that looks like a walking rug wearing a black conductor hat steps out and drags Jeb in. I skim the dirt with my boots to slow my momentum, dropping the backpack. I'm unable to thank the butterfly as she leaves, too busy keeping my balance.

I skate to a stop as the carpet creature shuts the door.

"Wait!" I cry, sprinting toward the train and clambering onto the car's platform.

After I pound on the door several times, the shaggy creature opens it.

He blocks the entrance; I can't see around him into the train. "State your name and your business." His high-pitched voice crackles and snaps as he speaks.

The car's amber glow illuminates his form: six sticklike legs—two sets serving as arms—compound eyes, crisscrossed mandibles that click when he talks, an oval-shaped thorax and abdomen hidden under a hide of shag carpet.

"Bug in a rug . . . is that it?" I ask.

His mandibles droop as if he's scowling. "I prefer 'carpet beetle,' *madam*. Just because I stumbled into the tulgey wood and was swallowed and turned away at AnyElsewhere's gate doesn't give you the right to talk down to me. You think *you'd* fare any better as a reject?"

He sniffs, or maybe huffs—it's hard to tell with his many moving facial features. "You certainly don't act like someone who wishes to board this train."

"I'm so sorry. I didn't mean to offend you." In my Shop of Human Eccentricities memory, toys and objects were spit back out of the tulgey wood shelves in mutated forms. I had no idea the same thing could happen to *living* things, too.

"You act like I'm the queerest thing you've seen come out of those woods." The carpet beetle drags a vacuum attachment from a holster at his side and flips it on. It whistles and hums, sucking dust from his carpeted coat. "Have you never met the carpenter ant?" He raises his voice over the noise as he cleans himself. "Her whole body is made of tools. She has a saw for a hand! Try making her acquaintance without losing a finger. Or the earwig? Entire body is an ear. Feeds herself through a dirty old ear horn. Least I'm pleasant to dine with. And that hornet fellow . . . blows out your eardrums with a trumpet call each time his wings flutter. I'm by far the most palatable of the looking-glass rejects. And the cleanest, to be sure." Satisfied with his vacuuming job, he turns off the attachment and secures it in the holster once more.

Looking-glass rejects = looking-glass insects.

Another near-consistency with the Wonderland novels. Carroll mentioned bread-and-butterflies, rocking-horse-flies, and snap-dragon-flies. Maybe they had all been spit back out of the tulgey woods in strange and awful forms.

"Now, last chance," the carpet beetle says. "Name and business. Make it quick." He turns the pages of a small journal with a spindly foreleg, cradling the book with two others. "I've passengers already on the manifest, waiting for their ride. Time's a-wasting."

"I'm Alyssa. I'm here with one of your passengers. The human boy you just pulled in." I try to peer around the bug's fluffed-out body to see where Jeb is, but he blocks me.

He closes the journal. "Did you say Alyssa? As in Queen Alyssa of the nether-realm?"

"Yes . . . that's me," I answer cautiously.

"Well, why didn't you say so from the get-go? I've been expecting you. This way." The bug moves, two of his forelegs gesturing me inside.

I step in. The passenger car is resplendent, ceiling aglow with more firefly chandeliers, although these don't roll. Crimson velvet hangings line the walls. Red and black tiles cover the floor. The front section has rows of empty white vinyl seats like those on a typical passenger train. The back is divided into private rooms, outer walls shiny black with red closed doors—three rooms on either side with a narrow center aisle separating them. I follow the conductor down the aisle.

"Morpheus said you'd be coming on behalf of a mortal guest," explains the beetle.

My heartbeat skips, hopeful. "You mean Morpheus is here?"

"*Was* here," my host responds. "This morning. Haven't seen him since."

My hope fades. "But he told you I'd be bringing a mortal? How could he have known?"

"Nay. I didn't say that. He told me you'd be coming *on behalf* of one. Told me the lad's name, so I could ready his memories for transfer."

"Jebediah Holt, right?"

The beetle stops next to the first two rooms and turns to face me, scratching the carpet under his hat as if puzzled. "Never heard that name."

"He's the boy who came with me. The one the butterfly dropped off a few minutes ago. Where is he?"

"The boy who came in before you . . . ah, yes. He's in this room here."

The conductor points to the first door on my right. There are brass brackets on each door with removable nameplates. Jeb's is marked *Nameless*. I reach for the knob, but it's locked. I try to force the door open, leaning in with one winged shoulder.

"Now, we'll have none of that." The conductor grabs my wrist with his spiny leg, and I shudder from the cold, prickly sensation.

I pull away and frown. "I need to make sure he's okay."

"He's about to be."

"Shouldn't you at least put his name on the door?"

"His memories can find him on their own now that he's here. They've been waiting for him, after all. But since you are to view memories that aren't yours, we needed a name to coax them in."

I look over my shoulder at Jeb's door as we walk down the aisle. I don't want anyone else's memories; I don't need to know any more secrets; I just want to make sure my boyfriend's all right. My throat tightens as we come to the last room on the left. I force myself to look at the name in the bracket: *Thomas Gardner*.

Even though a part of me suspected as much, I gasp, holding my hand at my numb lips.

The conductor opens the door and leads me into a small, windowless room that smells like almonds. On one side, an ivory tapestry hangs above a cream-colored chaise lounge. An ornate brass floor lamp stands beside it, casting a soft glow. On the other side there's a small stage complete with red velvet curtains that appear ready to part at any moment to show a silent movie on a silver screen.

"Have a seat, and the show will begin shortly," the beetle instructs.

"Right. The show." I settle into the chaise, arranging my wings on either side of me. There's a small table to my left holding a plate piled with moonbeam cookies on a lace doily. My mouth waters as I grab a handful. I scarf down three before I realize the bug is staring at me with his compound eyes.

"Sorry," I say between gulps. As I speak, silver beams radiate from my mouth, reflecting around the room. "I was hungry."

"Yes, well, that's what they're there for. Just expected royalty to have a bit more couth is all."

I cover my mouth to hide a hiccup. Light flashes from between my fingers.

The beetle clears his throat. "You get to choose which head to ride in." He looks at his passenger manifest. "Would you prefer your mother or your father?"

"My mother? I thought this was my dad's memory," I ask, confused.

"It's a memory they share. So there's a residue of your mother's insights imprinted on his. Whomever's eyes you watch it through affects the perspective."

I bite my lip. This is my chance. A unique opportunity to understand what took place all those years ago, why Mom made the choices she made. Everything will be the truth, because memories don't lie.

"I want to see it through my mom's point of view." I croak the answer, not sure what's about to happen or how it's possible to step into another person's past.

"Noted." The conductor scribbles something in his journal, then punches a button on the wall with his spindly leg. The stage curtains open, revealing a movie screen. "Picture her face in your mind whilst staring at the empty screen and you will experience their past as if it were today."

He turns a dial that snuffs out the lamp and then closes the door, leaving me alone. I do as instructed, envisioning Mom's youthful face, picturing her as she looked in photographs from years ago when she and Dad were dating, when she was sixteen, the age she was when she went to Wonderland.

An image comes to life on the screen in vivid color, but instead of staying in its place, it stretches toward me . . . reeling me in. I feel my seams fraying—my cells and atoms breaking up and floating apart, then re-forming on the screen. I'm looking out of my mother's eyes, sharing all of her thoughts and sensory cues.

We're in the garden of souls. She's alone, following Morpheus's instructions, only two squares away from becoming the queen.

I had no idea she ever made it this far . . .

"Harness the power of a smile," she whispers to herself. "Where are you, Chessie?"

I recognize the surroundings, although they're new to her. She took a wrong turn and hasn't realized it yet. A stale-smelling chill hangs on the air, and snow blankets the ground. Everything is silent—not at all like the cries and laments I remember from my visit. Dead weeping willow trees, slick with ice, are hung with an endless array of teddy bears and stuffed animals, plastic clowns and porcelain dolls, clinging to the branches on webby nooses. Each one holds a restless soul, yet all of them are sleeping peacefully.

Mom's on a mission to win the crown. It's all she's been thinking of for the past three years. The determination in her pounding heart overpowers her fear as she treks farther into Sister Two's lair than I ever went, far past the trees and slumbering toys. She's seeking the source of the glowing roots that connect every tree and branch. The light pulses with a steady rhythm, like a heartbeat.

She's led to a shelter of ivy. Inside, there's a thick sheath of web alive with light and breath. She draws closer, morbidly intrigued by the humanoid form wrapped inside. The glowing roots are attached to its head and chest, siphoning the light from the creature.

Glancing over her shoulder to be sure she's alone, Mom peels gossamer threads from the creature's face. Her breath freezes in her lungs. It's not just humanoid, it's an actual human. A boy who looks close to her age.

My dad.

But she has no idea she's going to love him. Not yet. All she knows is, he's beautiful.

She traces his features with a fingertip. His lashes tremble, and his eyelids open to reveal soulful brown eyes. He doesn't seem to see her. To see anything.

But in his eyes she sees the same loneliness she's faced her whole life, bouncing from foster home to foster home while struggling to hide her differences from those around her. Here in Wonderland, she feels like she could find a place, be accepted, although it's not the same for him. He's lonely and afraid, even if he's in a trance and doesn't realize it. One can't hide loneliness like that.

Snow crunches behind Mom, and she turns to face Sister One— the good twin.

The netherling's translucent skin is flushed, and she's out of breath. Her long, peppermint-striped hoop skirt is soaked with snow at the hem. "You weren't to come here," she scolds Mom between breaths, shoving tendrils of silvery hair off her face. "You must wake the dead in my gardens. I was to get the smile for you."

Mom swallows. "Who is this?"

Sister One glances at the cocooned victim. "My sister's humanling. His dreams keep her spirits' discontent at bay. Surely Morpheus has told you how the cemetery works."

Mom clenches her jaw. "Knowing how things work and seeing them in action are two entirely different things."

Sister One stands taller, exposing the tips of her eight legs beneath her skirt. "Keep your eye on the prize, little Alison. If you're to be queen, you must accept the way of our world. Some things cannot be changed without terrible consequences."

Mom looks back at the teenage boy. "But he's close to my age. Morpheus said when they get too old to dream, your sister poisons them and gives their bodies to the pixies."

"Aye. The pixies use the bones for our stairways, and the flesh feeds the flower fae. Everything serves a purpose. Nothing is wasted."

"Nothing but a human life." Mom's surprised by her own reaction: disdain and disgust. She thought she could accept the dark and gruesome rituals of this place, but her heart softens. "Let me have him. She's going to dispose of him anyway. Let me take him back to the human realm and give him a chance to live."

"Contrary that! I'm already to face the wrath of my sister for the smile I'm to steal for you. And you wish me to cross her further by taking her most prized pet? She treasures this humanling above all the hundreds of others she's had. I'm not sure she plans to ever dispose of this one. She might use him until the day his heart stops and he's a dreamless corpse. Sad, that. But it's just the way of it."

Mom straightens—determined. "How is this any different from what you're already doing? You're stealing for Morpheus, right?"

Sister One purses her lips. "Not for free! In exchange for something valuable. Hardest part of my job, tracking down stowaway souls. He knows it. I never wanted to cross no one no how, especially my sister, but for those souls . . ."

Mom holds her hand over her heart. "I can pay you. If you let me take the boy, I vow on my life-magic that when I come back to claim the crown, I'll put all of my royal resources behind you. My guards will be at your disposal to track down delinquent souls anytime you catch wind of them. You'll never be forced to make deals with anyone again."

Before I can hear Sister One's answer to Mom's proposition, the scene stretches around me, then blurs as I'm dragged out of the memory and dropped back into my seat, surrounded by darkness. I barely have time to catch my breath before another memory flips on, bright colors smearing across the room to pull me inside.

My mom is in the Ivory Queen's glass castle, next to the portal, waiting to step into the human realm. Morpheus stands beside her, carrying my dad over his shoulder. Dad floats in and out of consciousness. He's dressed in a frilly white shirt with slits at the shoulders and a pair of black pants, too long by a couple of inches. His bare feet stick out of the hems, twitching.

Ivory faces them, regal and glistening like the crystals of ice on her glass walls. "You did the right thing by bringing her here, Morpheus. Your goodness shall be rewarded."

He rolls his eyes. "That has yet to be seen."

Ivory smiles affectionately at him. "I will personally assure that it is."

He holds her glance long enough to make her blush before she turns to my mom.

"In order to protect the boy's sanity and our realm," Ivory explains, "I had to erase his memories. All nineteen years of his life, even from before he was captured by Sister Two, since we don't exactly know when or how he stumbled in. When memories are 'unmade' by way of magic, the void left behind is unbearable to humans. So best he never knows he had them to begin with. Were he ever to see a netherling in true form, or even just glimpse their magic, it could make him realize he was missing something. And then a ripple effect would begin. Do as Morpheus says. Abandon him in a hospital and come back to claim your crown. Forget you ever saw him."

My mom nods, but something is slowly changing in her heart. Something she's not even aware of yet.

She and Morpheus step through the portal into her bedroom. He drops Dad on her bed, then starts back toward a tall, flat mirror hanging on the back of her door.

"Morpheus," Mom says, sitting on edge of the bed, "I want to at least find his family. We can look at his memories. Go to the train . . ."

Morpheus glances over his shoulder at her, wings low. "You've given him a chance to live. That's enough. It is more than any of us would've done."

Mom pushes back a strand of Dad's hair with a trembling hand. "But just to leave him alone? He'll be so lost."

Morpheus turns on his heel to face her, jewels flashing red. "We are out of time. We need to get you crowned before all hell breaks loose in the cemetery. By the end of the day Sister Two will realize the boy's gone and buckle down her security. Then there will be no stealing Chessie's smile or Queen Red. Wash your hands of the boy. Don't make me regret helping you, Alison."

"But that's exactly what I did." Mom's voice speaks out of sync with what's happening on-screen, and suddenly the lamp flips on beside me. The curtains fall to cover the screen, and I'm slammed back to reality, slumped in the chaise lounge.

I turn to see Mom standing by the wall next to the closed door. She's barefoot, wearing my favorite polka-dot dress, and carrying her canvas tote on her shoulder. I have no idea when she came in or how long she's been reliving the memories with me.

"I made him regret it," she says again, "and now look what's become of us all."

She crumples to the floor in a puddle of purple satin and lime green netting, pretty legs curled beside her, and eyes filled with enough remorse to launch an ocean of tears.

Second Sight

I can't contain the sobs clogging my chest. I jump up from the chaise and cross the room in four steps. Dropping next to Mom on the floor, my wings sweep out to one side of me. She opens her arms and I cling to her, clutching the slick fabric along her ribs, face pressed against her breasts and surrounded by her perfume.

"It's okay, sweet girl," she whispers and kisses my forehead, leaving behind a warm smudge. "It's all going to be okay."

I hug her tighter. I should be the one comforting her, but right now I'm that little five-year-old child watching my mommy leave for the asylum. "I thought it was because of me." I choke on the words. "But you had yourself committed for Dad, too."

Mom's body trembles as she takes a ragged breath. "After you were born, everything changed. I kept messing up, letting things slip. He started to have dreams about Wonderland . . . his mind was seeking memories that were no longer his." She strokes my hair behind my ear. "Your father was special to Sister Two. He somehow got into Wonderland on his own as a child. She found him, and for the first time, she didn't have to steal a humanling for her cemetery. She's never liked that part of her job. Not that she feels guilty for it." Mom's voice is bitter. "It's just an inconvenience."

I lick away the tears lining my lips. "And he doesn't remember anything?"

"It's as if he never lived it. That day I cut your hands"—her voice breaks, buried beneath the sound of both our sniffles—"I wanted to heal you. But I couldn't. Not without shattering all that remained of his peace. I had to get away. From you both. To keep you safe."

I nod against her. "I'm so sorry for doubting you. For saying those horrible things." Wet streams scorch my cheeks and under my nose.

"No," Mom mumbles, her breath comforting on the top of my head. "I'm the one who's sorry. If only I'd told you the truth from the beginning. But I kept hoping the nether-call would pass you by. And when it didn't . . . I panicked. I didn't know what to do. I just knew I didn't want you to get trapped there."

Ivory's vision of my future flashes through my mind. Funny, but I didn't feel trapped in that future. I felt happy, powerful, and treasured. I want to share that epiphany with Mom, but I vowed not to tell anyone. Maybe it's better this way. It's one secret I'll never have to feel guilty for keeping, because I can't afford to lose my powers by breaking a life-magic vow.

Mom's hand glides from my back to the base of my right wing.

She skims a finger over the gossamer surface. It sends a tickle through my shoulder blade.

"What made them manifest?" she asks. There's no scolding or anxiety like in the past. Just curiosity.

My snuffles echo as I try to figure out how to answer. What can I tell her about Morpheus, who's lied and manipulated me and yet managed to coax me into my wings anyway? How do I answer that, when Jeb is down the hall, tormented by half-remembered moments he never lived in this reality? It feels like a betrayal somehow.

I hold my necklaces against my chest. "It doesn't matter," I answer. "They're a part of me. Just like the streak in my hair. Just like the magic in my blood. Traits from your side of the family. It's time I embrace all of it. It's time we both do."

Mom squeezes me tighter. "I can teach you how to reabsorb the wings into your skin. The eye patches, too. It's an ability only half-lings have. There's a trick to it."

It's bizarre to be talking to her about netherling traits the same way we would talk about fashion or makeup. "Maybe later. I'm kind of happy to have them right now."

She presses her lips to the top of my head, and I rub my heart locket and key together between my fingers to make a scraping, metallic song. The irony hits me: It must've been so hard for her to learn to accept her human side, just as it's been for me to accept my netherling one.

I force us apart so I can see her face. She's used her magic recently. Her skin glitters and her hair moves like an underwater plant. I touch a platinum strand. "I don't understand. You made a life-magic vow to Sister One and broke it. How do you still have your power?"

"I never broke the vow." She smirks. "It's all in the wording. I told her *when* I came back to claim the crown. Technically, I never did."

Her knack for word wizardry surprises me—she thinks just like they do, takes everything said as literal, twisting it this way and that until it means what she wants it to mean. Morpheus was right. She would've made a magnificent Red Queen.

"You gave up your crown for Dad." I can barely look at her now without picturing her as royalty. "Turned your back on something you wanted with all your heart, for a guy you didn't even know."

She taps the dimple in my chin, the one that's always reminded her of Dad's. "That's not true. The second I looked into his eyes, I knew him. And later, when he woke up on my bed, confused and scared, he looked at me. He held out his hand. Calm. Like he'd been waiting forever to find me. Like he knew me, too."

"So you pretended that he did know you."

Her smile softens. "I made up a story about his past so he could have a future. But he's the one who gave *me* a future. Accepted me, loved me unconditionally. He's always felt like home. Something I have never felt in my life anywhere else. Everything paled next to that. Even the magic and madness of Wonderland."

Tears burn my eyes again. "It's kind of like a fairy tale."

She looks down at the polka dots on her skirt. "Maybe. And you're our happy ending." Her gaze returns to mine, filled with love. She blots tears from my cheek.

We clasp hands, and the moment spins out between us. I'll never let this memory be damaged . . . never forget how it feels, right now, to look at her and know her, to understand her—through and through. Finally, after so many years.

Now I want to understand Dad, too.

"Do you regret it? Not looking into Dad's past . . . not finding his family?"

Mom fidgets. "Oh, but, Allie, I did."

"What?"

"I watched a few of his memories once, when I was pregnant with you. I finally understood the true importance of family, because I had one. And I wanted to give your father's back to him. I was even willing to tell him he'd had amnesia when we first met, that I'd lied about knowing him. Just to see him reunited with them."

She grows quiet.

I touch her hand. "Mom, tell me what you saw."

Rubbing her nose, she sniffs. "Your father was nine when he stumbled into Sister Two's keep. So I looked a year before that, expecting to see him in a typical little boy's life. I was hoping to learn his last name, hometown, something." She shakes her head. Her hand clenches beneath mine.

I wait, afraid to prompt her. Unsure if I want to know more.

"I must not have looked far enough," she continues. "But I'll never look again. He's been places, Allie. Even as an eight-year-old. Places humans aren't meant to go. Places netherlings hope never to be sent."

My throat goes dry. "What do you mean?"

"The looking-glass world—AnyElsewhere. Did Morpheus ever tell you about it?"

"Not enough." *Obviously.*

"It's where all of Wonderland's exiles are banished, where Queen Red was supposed to go, before she escaped. There's a dome of iron that surrounds it, holding them all in, and two knights who guard each gateway, one Red and one White. The place is Wonderland on steroids. The creatures"—her face pales—"the landscapes, they're wild and untamed, mutated beyond anything you can imagine. It's no wonder your father's dreams were so captivating to the restless souls. His experiences from that place probably fed their hunger for violent frivolity to the brim. Not to mention how formidable his nightmares must've been. The rabbit hole was never safer than when he was providing the mome wraiths."

Discomfort slinks into my bones as I consider the wraiths I tamed in the gym. To imagine Dad's nightmares as any more ghastly than those makes my skin crawl. "How could he have found his way to the looking-glass world as a child? I thought the only entrance was through Wonderland, the tulgey forest."

"Morpheus once told me there's another way in, from the human realm. There's a way to open mirrors without keys, an ancient trick that only the anointed knights know."

I stand, needing to move or I'll throw up. "So, you think when Dad was a kid, he got inside through a mirror and ended up crossing AnyElsewhere all the way to the other gate that leads to the tulgey wood . . . inside Wonderland?"

Mom shrugs. "That would explain how he fell into Sister Two's keep. The answer is in his lost memories. But I can't watch them again. It felt like I was betraying him. Viewing pieces of his life that he would never have access to. That's not right. No. We just have to move forward. We're his family now, and that's enough."

I sit again and try to digest everything she's told me. The quiet becomes unbearable. I'm hyperaware of the time passing, and of Jeb in the next room filling his head with lost memories. There's nothing I can do now about my family's messed-up past, but there's still a mosaic to find and a battle to fight.

"You're right," I say to get us back on track. "We need to move forward. Why are you here? Did Dad tell you what happened at school?"

She nods and plays with the straps on her tote bag. "I knew he was keeping something from me. I finally got it out of him. He wanted me to go with him to look for you because he was afraid to leave me alone. But I insisted on staying behind in case you came home. When he left, I called for Chessie. He led me here."

"But we don't have any mirrors at home. And you don't drive."

"I have a mirror in the attic, Allie. A netherling always has an escape plan. Surely that's one of the first lessons Morpheus taught you."

I smile sadly. I hope he remembered his own lessons. I hope he had an escape plan to get out of Sister Two's web.

I consider telling Mom that he lied to me, that it's his fault everything is such a mess in the human realm, but after seeing what he did for my dad and watching my mom betray him—no matter how happy I am that she made those choices—it doesn't feel right to let her rake Morpheus over the coals.

I understand now, why he needed me to experience Dad's memories for myself. He knew I wouldn't have believed him if he just told me. It's so hard for me to accept the good in him.

Though that's starting to change.

I see why he hid so much from me about the tests last summer. Why he kept me in the dark as I fulfilled his plan, bit by bit. He was honest with Mom in the beginning, and she made him believe she'd be the one to help him. Then she backed out at the last minute.

He wasn't about to take the chance I would do the same, not with his spiritual eternity in the balance. Although it doesn't excuse everything he's done, it does make his motivations sympathetic. More human than he'd ever dare admit.

"What's in the bag?" I ask as Mom tugs the canvas straps toward us.

She pulls three mosaics from the tote. "Chessie said you found the others, but he wouldn't tell me where." She waits, as if thinking I'll fill in the blanks. When I hold my tongue, she continues. "These are the ones I had hidden."

My blood races, and I get on my knees to help her lay them out. "Mom, you're the best."

She beams.

Some of Chessie's sparkly silt remains on them. I copy Ivory and smear the residue around on the one mosaic I have left to decipher.

The animation shows some sort of celebration. A crowd of creatures weaves through barren trees. A few have crowns; others have beaks or wings. All of them wear masks. Some glide and float, as if standing on magic carpets. Chaos erupts when feral toys bust out from the shadows, attacking the creatures.

An uneasy dread uncoils in my chest as the image blurs away. I look at Mom, who's watching over my shoulder.

"Red," I murmur.

She tucks the mosaics away in her bag again, her mouth pressed into a worried line.

"I was wrong." I nibble my lip. "I thought that the one I hadn't seen yet was the end of the war. But that was the first one I made, Mom. It's the catalyst. You've been to Wonderland. You saw places I haven't seen yet. Can you tell me where the party is?"

"It looked like a forest," she answers, her voice shaky. "But I didn't recognize it." She rubs her temple. "I don't understand how

Red could release the restless souls. Sister Two isn't one to let her guard down. Especially not since she lost your father."

I gulp. Mom doesn't realize Sister Two has discovered who stole her prize in the first place.

I take both her hands in mine, putting on a brave face so she won't see my fear. "Sister Two's not in Wonderland to watch her side of the cemetery. She's here. She knows you stole Dad all those years ago."

Mom pales. Her fingers go limp, and for a minute I think she's going to faint. "She's coming after Thomas?" she whispers.

"Dad's safe. No one knows who the dream-boy grew up to be, other than Morpheus and Ivory. Sister Two just wants revenge." I try not to let my voice waver. "She has her sights on Jeb."

"No." Mom's face falls even more. "I'll help you protect him."

The offer means so much, considering how she's always tried to keep me and Jeb apart. I think now I understand. He reminded her of Dad in too many ways: a young mortal man with a noble heart at the mercy of a cruel Wonderland.

"It's okay," I say. "Jeb's here with us on the train. He's getting a chance to relive last summer. He'll be safer with the memories intact."

"It should never have come to this." She's about to break into tears again.

We don't have time for any more regret. I stand and offer her my hand. "I think Morpheus hoped I would forgive you if I saw Dad's memories. He hoped you would forgive yourself, and we'd find our way back to each other. He wants us to work together. It's the only way we'll have the power to stop Red and send Sister Two packing. Are you up for it?"

She clasps my hand and nods. In the time it takes her to stand, the fear and trepidation fall away from her face. She looks determined, regal. Her confidence feeds mine, and we step out the door arm in arm.

I run smack into Jeb's solid chest. He's against the wall on the other side of our door. One look at his face and I know he's remembered everything.

He doesn't move, doesn't acknowledge my mom, just stares at my wings, then at the netherling patches around my eyes.

Mom squeezes my arm. "I'll keep the conductor occupied. But don't take long. We have to find out where Red's sending her army." Before walking down the aisle, she touches Jeb's shoulder.

He meets her gaze, and an unspoken understanding passes between them. Then she makes her way to the front of the passenger car and whispers something to the conductor, coaxing the beetle outside.

Without a word, Jeb takes my hand and leads me toward his room. Expression set in stone, he guides me in and closes the door behind us. It's identical to the room I was in, only Jeb's cologne mixes with the almond scent and his plate of cookies is empty except for some crumbs. The theater curtains are still drawn open on the stage, as if it's ready to start playing his memories again.

I watch him and shiver, unbalanced by his silence. As hard as I try, I can't talk, either. What would I say? How do I explain a year-long lie so life-altering?

He steps close, traces the patches around my eyes with the lightest touch, then surprises me by spinning me around. He touches my wings, arranges them with gentle veneration, as if they were the train to an heirloom wedding gown. He draws me close to his chest and nuzzles the tangled hair bunched at the back of my head.

"I never got to touch them," he says, voice muffled. "Not once. But he did, didn't he?"

How do I answer that? I'm glad my back's to him, that he can't see my face, afraid of what my expression would say.

He strokes my wings—featherlight—affecting every sensory receptor in my body. "Tell me that's all he touched, Al." He opens his palms along the veinlike cross sections, letting them graze the jewels.

My heart skips a painful beat. "I kissed him." It's brutal to admit it out loud, but I can't lie anymore. "I was trying to get my wish back, so I could save us."

Jeb makes an anguished sound, somewhere between choking and growling. I need to see his face—even if that means him seeing mine.

He steps away from me, leaving my back and wings cold. I turn, and his muscles tense. With a snarl, he shoves the chaise lounge and sends it scraping along the wall. It knocks over the table and shatters the empty plate. My body goes rigid at the sound.

"Morpheus." Jeb bites down on the name, as if trying to chew it up. "He visits your dreams and flies with you. How can a human compete with that?"

"This isn't a competition," I say. "I made my choice."

"Is that why you lied for so long?" He won't meet my gaze, concentrating instead on his boots. "Because you made your choice?" His jaw clamps so tight I can see the muscles twitch beneath the skin. "No. You lied because I'm just a skater. Just an artist. I have nothing to offer. He can give you a world of magic and beauty." His eyes slowly trail up to mine. They're like a forest trampled by a storm. "A world that you were born to rule."

Words bottle up inside me. I'm so furious, I want to shake him.

How is it possible he watched everything play out yet overlooked the most important part of our journey? What we learned about ourselves, about each other?

No. He's going to watch those memories again a second time, and I'll make sure he sees what I see.

I sidestep him and turn the dial on the wall to dim the lamp. The screen lights up. This time, I'm pulled into *his* point of view, seeing things from Jeb's eyes. Fighting the flower fae, defeating the octobenus, figuring out how to wake the tea party guests.

There are things that are new to me, like him rolling me over to face him while I slept in the rowboat, stroking my hair and promising to keep me safe. Or how the sprites lulled him to sleep while we were apart at Morpheus's mansion, how they tried to make him forget me, but my face kept surfacing in his dreams. And how hard he fought to escape when Morpheus shrank him and put him in the cage, while I was being forced to win the crown.

Then the most dreaded scene comes, the one I've only imagined in my darkest nightmares.

Gossamer slips into Jeb's cage, her size matching his. Seated atop a wedge of pear tottered on its side, she tells him my fate. I feel his terror and helplessness as he leaps up, so desperate to get to me he pounds his head against the cage until his skin is gashed.

"Would you die for her, mortal knight?" Gossamer's words stop him.

Hands clenched to the bars, he looks at her, blood drizzling into his eyes—burning. "If it will send her home."

Gossamer stares back, unblinking. "Are you willing to go beyond death? To be lost to everyone, even yourself, in a place where memories wash away with a tide as dark as ink? For in order to free Alyssa, you will have to take the Ivory Queen's place in the jabberlock box."

There's a moment when he hesitates. I feel it: his heartbeat stumbling for self-preservation, his mind racing to find another way. Then, his heartbeat slows, resolved again.

"Yes. I'll do it."

"And so you shall." Gossamer flies him out of the cage, leading him to a pewter box the size of an armoire.

Jeb strokes the giant white-flocked roses on the outside of the box, studying Ivory's face as it bobs to the surface. He draws a knife from his pocket. Rolling up his sleeve, he runs the flat side of the blade across his arm as he considers the roses. His canvas. His shoulders slump, defeated. "It'll take every drop I have."

"Is that not the true meaning of sacrifice? Giving more than you ever thought you had, to save the one you love?" Gossamer asks from behind him.

His jaw tightens. "Is there a paintbrush?"

The sprite hands him one.

He concentrates on his hands. They're fidgeting against his will. "I—I can't stop shaking."

Gossamer squeezes his wrist. "You can. You are an artist. And this is the most important piece you will ever create."

Jeb dabs at the beads of sweat inching along his forehead. "My old man never thought I'd accomplish anything with my art."

Gossamer smiles sadly and hovers in midair to give him room. "Then with every stroke, you will prove him wrong."

Jeb grinds his teeth against the pain as the snow-white roses turn red with each sweep of his brush.

The image flicks off, the curtains drop, and the lamp snaps on.

Jeb and I face each other.

"You tell me," I say over the emotions piled like rocks in my throat, "how can anyone compete with *that*?" Tears gather behind my eyes, but I hold them at bay. "*Just an artist.* You painted my freedom with your blood. *Just a skater.* You flew across a chasm on a skateboard made of a tea tray to get me to safety. You don't need magic, Jeb." I touch his face, and he leans his stubbled cheek against my palm, all of his anger and hurt seeping away. "You held your own against everything that was thrown at us, using only human courage and ingenuity. You're my knight. There's nothing left to prove anymore. Not to your dad, not to my mom, not to Morpheus, not to me. You've already proven you're the guy I always knew you were. The guy I love."

Urgency darkens his eyes. He drags me roughly to him, kisses my eye patches, then glides his lips to mine, his thumbs against my temples, caressing sweetly. He tastes of moonbeam cookies—almonds, sugar, and enchantments.

He pulls me into his arms and holds me so tight my lungs can barely expand. I nuzzle the soft hairs where the jacket opens at his chest. Even with our frayed emotions surfacing, being wrapped in his warmth is still the safest place in the world. I never want to leave.

"What happened after that?" he asks against the top of my head, his voice so hoarse it chills my momentary bliss. "I need to know what you gave up to get me out of the box. It had to be more than a kiss." He pushes us an arm's length apart. "You have to tell me, Al."

I lead him to the overturned chaise lounge. He flips it upright and we sit. I tell him everything: how I used my one wish, how I battled Queen Red, and what Morpheus gave up for me, so I could return home. Then I break down and tell him how Morpheus has come back. How he tricked me. But I can't say why, because I've made a life-magic vow.

"So Red is back, too," Jeb mumbles.

"She plans to destroy Wonderland. I'm the only one who can stop her."

The dread on Jeb's face makes my blood run cold. "Why you? Let Morpheus face her."

"Morpheus isn't here to face her. He put himself between Sister Two and us, so I could get you to safety." A sharp jolt of worry stops me short. Why hasn't he shown up yet?

Jeb scrubs his face with a hand. "Okay. Set aside the fact that he's done one or two noble things. He dragged you into this, using me to do it. You walked away from that world. You chose our side of your blood. Chose to stay here. But he didn't respect that choice, and he manipulated you into his plans again. You can't go back there. You nearly died the first time, masquerading as one of them."

Everything else Jeb says falls on deaf ears as the word *masquerading* echoes in my head like a gong.

My mosaic.

The creatures weaving through barren trees, some wearing crowns, others beaks or wings. All of them wear masks. It's a masquerade. The wings and beaks and crowns are part of the costumes. Fairy-tale costumes. The forest is made of props, probably whatever trees they could salvage from the burned-out mess I left behind in the gym. The creatures gliding on magic carpets are people skating.

Underland.

And the senior class's collection for the orphanage—the perfect cover for an army of undead toys.

My face burns. "We have to get my mom. Now." I catch Jeb's hand and force him to stand, towing him to the door.

"Why?"

Queen Grenadine's ribbon flickers through my thoughts again, along with its odd wording: *Queen Red lives and seeks to destroy* that *which betrayed her.*

"*That* which betrayed her," I say, weighing each word. "Red wants revenge on the life I chose to live over her. In her mind, *that's* what caused me to betray her. My normal teenage life. She's planning to attack prom!"

STING

We lost track of time while on the train. Night has already fallen over London when we fly back to the garden mirror beneath the dim glow of starlight. Mom can't use her wings without ruining her dress, so she and Jeb ride on moths and I carry the backpack. On the way, we make a plan for prom.

To keep Dad home and safe, Mom's going to slip him some of my sedatives. No one from school has seen my gown except Jen. Once I have my mask on, I should be able to sneak by, and Mom's already signed up on the chaperone list. Jeb still has a key to Underland from when he worked there last year. He's going to smuggle us in before the other kids and chaperones arrive. I'm surprised he hasn't put up a fight about my part in the plan. Maybe because his sister could be in danger. Whatever the reason, it's great to have him watching my back without standing in my way.

If we don't find anything suspicious before the party starts, we'll just blend into the crowd and guard the mirrors on the dance floor wall. Hopefully we'll stop Red before she can come through and start a war. If we keep this first mosaic from coming to pass, maybe the other events will never take place. The biggest challenge will be our impaired vision. Underland is strictly glow-in-the-dark.

At the garden mirror, we nibble the neon-glowing mushrooms to return to regular size. I reabsorb my wings, and we plunge through the portal to Mom's attic mirror. It's a little after four in the afternoon. Three hours till prom.

We climb down the ladder into the garage. The overhead door is open and Dad's truck is in the driveway behind Morpheus's Mercedes. There will be no pretending we've been here all along. Even worse, Gizmo is in its spot, so Dad's been to Butterfly Threads and knows I was there. I don't know how he got Gizmo home or who helped him. My pulse slams in my neck, wondering what else he's discovered and how many people are involved.

Wind carrying the scent of moisture slices through the garage, rattling old newspapers gathered in the corner. Storm clouds are rolling in, making it darker than it should be. I shiver.

Jeb takes my hand and kisses the back of it. "It'll be okay," he whispers and sets my backpack outside the door.

Mom steps into the living room with Jeb and me trailing behind her.

Dad's standing at the threshold between the kitchen and the living room. The lamp next to his recliner is on, but he's outside the circle of light. Shadows muddle his features as he holds the phone to his ear. When he sees us, he hangs up and comes all the way in, expression somewhere between relief and anger.

"I've been looking for you both for almost two hours," he half shouts. "I was about to call the police. Where have you been?"

Mom rushes to him. "It's okay. I found Allie next door." She takes the phone and gives Jeb a pleading look.

"What?" Dad asks. "How's that even—"

Jeb steps up. "It's true. Al's been with me."

My dad frowns, giving Jeb's clothes a once-over. "But I came by your house earlier this afternoon. Your mother said you weren't there."

Jeb exchanges glances with me. "We just got in a few minutes ago. Before that, we were hiding at the studio."

"You *hid* my daughter?" Dad gives Jeb a look I've never seen him use with him—disappointment with an edge of scorn. It's even worse than the time we got tattoos. "I left all those calls on your cell. You had to know how worried her mom and I were. I thought you'd grown up, Jeb."

Jeb studies the floor, jaw clenched.

"So," Dad continues, "lying, evading. Then there's the vandalism. What's next, robbing a bank?"

Though he directs the question to Jeb, I shake my head. "What are you talking about? Jeb had nothing to do with school this morning."

"I'm talking about Butterfly Threads. Someone broke in through the back door. There was stuff all over the merchandise, the floor, and the ceiling. Like Silly String but more damaging. Persephone found Gizmo in the alley. What do you have to say about that?"

He's still speaking to Jeb, as if I'm too far gone to answer for myself.

I move into Dad's line of sight, forcing him to look at me. "I was too shaky to drive. I called Jeb to pick me up there. But he didn't set foot inside the shop." It's not a lie exactly. Morpheus carried him in.

Dad looks like I punched him in the gut. "Why, Allie? Persephone's been nothing but good to you. She even helped me drive your car home and offered not to call the police. Are we making it too easy for you to act out?" His left eyelid twitches, sure indication he's at the end of his rope. "You can forget about graduating with your class tomorrow. You'll get your diploma in the mail. I'm not letting you out of my sight until you talk to a psychiatrist."

Mom gasps and I clench my teeth.

"Wait, Mr. Gardner . . ." Jeb tries to intervene, but I catch his elbow and hold him back.

"I think you should go home, Jebediah," Dad says, his brown eyes cold. "This concerns my family."

My chest stings. I know Dad's just lashing out, but those words are like knives. Jeb *is* family. He's always been treated that way.

"Yes, sir," Jeb says, his voice hoarse. He starts for the front door. Mom follows to let him out, and they talk quietly on the porch while Dad and I glare at each other.

A growl of thunder shakes the room.

Dad leans against the wall, and the wrinkles around his mouth deepen, as if the artist sketching his face went too heavy on the shading. I've learned so much about him today—know him better than I ever did, better than he knows himself—yet he's looking at me as if I'm a complete stranger.

When I can't take his accusatory stare any longer, I start for my room.

"Alyssa," he says quietly, "your makeup is still a mess. And what happened to your shirt?"

I stall next to my mosaics in the hallway, my back to him. Cool air seeps through the wing slits in the shoulders. I shrug.

"Great. Nice answer." His voice is frayed, and it presses along my heartstrings like an amateur cellist's bow. "I don't even know who you are anymore."

I clasp the necklaces at my neck. "It's okay," I whisper so he can't possibly hear. "Because I finally do."

I shut my bedroom door. I don't bother to turn on the light as I change into my boxers and a lacy camisole, wishing I could shed everything that's gone wrong along with my clothes.

There's enough strained daylight coming through my curtains for me to substitute Jen's straight pins on my prom gown for safety pins and smooth the pleats in place to cover the metal clasps.

Following a knock at my door, Mom peeks inside.

I motion her in. "Where's Dad?"

"He went to get some dinner. I suggested he go to cool off. When he comes back, I'll put the sedatives in his drink."

I nod, not feeling the least bit hungry, considering what we're about to do. We're going to knock out my father for no good reason. It's the same thing my mother lived through for years at the asylum.

I can tell by her tight lips that she's as uncomfortable as I am with the idea.

We sit together on my bed with my lights off and the aquarium glowing blue. My eels swim gracefully, like angels under water—a serene counterpoint to the emotional uproar in my head. A thrum of distant thunder echoes my unease.

"I'm sorry." Mom fluffs my gown's slip to a cloud of periwinkle netting. "Your father . . . he's just out of his mind with worry. Once this is all behind us, he'll make up with Jeb. I won't let you go through what I did. He won't send you to the asylum. Okay?"

I want to believe her, but a soul-deep foreboding is starting to wind through me. "Why can't we reunite Dad with his memories? He would stop thinking we're crazy all the time. And we could use his help tonight since Morpheus isn't here." My voice falters on Morpheus's name.

Dad didn't mention any corpses found wrapped up in the Silly String—large insects or otherwise.

"Sweetie, we can't bring your dad into this. Those memories would hurt him."

"More than he's hurting now?"

Mom looks thoughtful. "I can't even describe the horrors I saw when I watched his past. Can't even conceive of what else he must've endured."

I sit quietly, not sure I agree. If he was able to survive the looking-glass world as a child, surely he's stronger than we've ever given him credit for.

I start to point that out, but Mom interrupts me. "Jeb asked to see you. He's waiting out back under your willow tree."

My jaw drops. She's known about our sanctuary all along?

Mom presses her fingertip against my dimple to coax my mouth closed. "Allie, I'm not completely oblivious. I remember what it's like to be a teenager in love." She winks, and I smile back. "I'm going to take a shower and get ready. Make sure you don't get caught in the rain and that you're inside before Dad gets home."

I pull on a pair of boots and a hoodie and trek through the garden. The plants and bugs are eerily quiet. The sky swirls overhead—a frothy gray that makes it look like six o'clock instead of four thirty. Cool wind snatches my hair and whips it around my face. The gusts are so loud I can't hear the fountain gurgling.

Jeb's already waiting for me, wearing a tight T-shirt with jeans, as if he couldn't wait to shed Morpheus's jacket.

He holds a fluttery curtain of willow leaves open, and I duck inside under the green canopy.

Crouching, I hug him. "I'm sorry. My dad didn't mean any of it."

"I know." He kisses my temple and rakes away some leaves so I can sit. "I'm not here so you can pat my head and make me feel better."

I attempt a smile. "Aw, c'mon. You'd like that."

He grins. "I'd like a kiss more." Hazy light filters through the leaves and hits his dimples and labret—making him appear boyish and playful, even though his voice is filled with tension.

We're both pretending like everything's right with the world, when it couldn't be more wrong. We're being delusional. Jeb shouldn't be involved in this at all. If Sister Two could take Morpheus down, what chance does a human have in this battle?

"I don't think you should go tonight," I blurt out. "Call Jenara and keep her from going, too."

"Are you kidding me? I'd be in more danger standing between Jen and prom than fighting resurrected toys."

"Stop joking. This isn't a game."

Jeb frowns. "Just like it wasn't a game when you hid the truth from me all those months because you were afraid it would hurt me."

Ouch. "Or hurt us," I say.

Grasping my elbows, he drags me closer. He presses our noses and foreheads together. "We're stronger than that. And we're so much better as a team, when our heads are together. It's when one of us is trying to protect the other by taking everything on ourselves, that's when we mess up. Don't you think?"

I sigh. "Yeah," I answer, reluctant.

"So I won't stand in your way tonight. You do what you have to do. But don't ask me to do any less. Deal?"

"But the things we're facing—"

"Are things I've already faced. And like you said, I did pretty good, for a human. And don't worry about Jen. I'll get her out if we can't stop Red from coming through."

I touch his lips. "This is all so messed up. It's not what prom should've been."

He kisses my fingertip. "The party might be a bust. But once we send all the creepers running, we can still have our prom night."

His optimism is contagious, even if it's a transparent ploy to buoy my spirits when he's as worried as me.

It doesn't matter if everything somehow works out and we defeat Red. I still can't be with Jeb tonight. Not with the vow I made to Morpheus. Maybe it would be easier for me if he really was gone, captured by Sister Two and trapped in her web. But I can't let myself imagine it might be true. I *want* him to survive.

The leaves rattle around us and thunder shakes the ground.

"We should hurry." Jeb pulls a plastic box from behind him. Inside is a wrist corsage made of miniature white rosebuds, the tips airbrushed the same periwinkle as the lace gloves I'll be wearing, all held together with navy blue ribbon and a bow.

I catch my breath as I look at it closer. I knew Jenara was making this. What I didn't expect was a silver ring pressed into the middle of one of the roses. A dozen tiny diamonds sparkle in the setting: a heart with wings.

My whole body feels at first heavy, then light. "Is this . . . ?"

Jeb looks down, dark lashes cloaking his eyes. "I got the idea for the wings from my paintings of you. Had no clue how spot-on they've always been till today." He swallows. "I was planning to give it to you at the studio after prom tonight. But just in case—" He stops himself, as if speaking the worst might make it materialize.

He pops open the plastic lid and plucks the silver circle free, then lifts me to my knees, so we're eye to eye. My heart is pounding in my ears. Grass tickles my knees, but I don't dare scratch the itch because Jeb's looking me in the eye, and the expression on his face is the most somber I've ever seen.

"Alyssa Victoria Gardner." Hearing him speak my full name makes my toes curl in anticipation. "You once told me on a rowboat in Wonderland that one day you wanted to have two kids and live in the country so you could hear your muse and answer when it called. I'm telling you now, here in our sanctuary, that when you're ready for that life . . . I want to be the guy to give it to you."

He waits, mouth half-open in anticipation, crooked incisor casting a shadow across his straight white teeth. All that's familiar about him spins around me: the green eyes that know me like no one else's; the paintings that bare my soul; the arms that promise power and strength each time I'm in them.

Only Jeb, with his human flaws and vulnerabilities, can fit the human side of my heart. He's been planning to ask me this since before he knew everything, and he still wants it even now.

As for me, I've known ever since our first summer years ago how deep my feelings run. Yes, I want to spend a lifetime with him. But I have two possible futures. Two lives to live. Two parts of my heart. How can I commit to either of them until I've thought everything through?

Then another doubt surfaces unexpectedly, something I haven't considered until now. "Wait. Is this how you and Dad worked things out? You caved and told him you'd marry me before we got to London. Is that what's going on here?"

Jeb's hopeful expression falls. "No. That's not—well, yes, it played a part in the timing. But you gotta know, Al. This is what I want. It's what I've always wanted. A future with you. A life with you, my fairy bride. Forever."

"Always said . . . the boy . . . was a bloody wordsmith . . ."

My heart skips as the familiar cockney accent fills my head.

A moth dives into the canopy, surrounded by blue static. It struggles against the wind, and the static spreads, reaching up to the branches, as if to hold it in place. Jeb and I scramble backward as the insect transforms into a man, slumped to his side on the dirt. His breathing is labored and his wings drape across him, hiding his body.

"Son of a—"

"Morpheus." I interrupt Jeb's outburst, lifting one of the satiny wings so I can see his face. I'm thrilled he's alive, but he doesn't look like he will be for long.

"Hello, luv," he says through a thick curtain of blue hair. "Hope I'm . . . interrupting." He draws his knees to his chest, coughing.

The leaves rattle overhead as the rain begins.

I touch his forehead, shocked at how hot he is. "He's burning up. We have to get him inside."

Jeb hesitates, mistrust shadowing his face.

I put my hand on his arm. "We need all the help we can get tonight." I can't tell Jeb that I care beyond that. Not yet. We don't have time to sort through that mess.

Gritting his teeth, Jeb takes the heart pendant from my neck and laces the ring through the chain. He holds it out for me. "Will you hang on to this? Until we can talk later?"

I nod and loop the chain around my neck.

Jeb drags Morpheus out from under the leaves and hoists him onto his shoulder. "Get those, Al." He gestures to the wings dragging on the ground behind him.

I maneuver Morpheus's wings, trying to curl them around his body so he won't get wet. Mom meets us at the back door in her robe. She looks as confused and panicked as I feel but ushers us in.

"Take him to your room. Hurry. Your dad just pulled into the driveway. I'll get the sedatives in him. Let's hope they work fast. We only have an hour till we need to go."

We trudge down the hall, leaving wet prints on the carpet. Morpheus's wings scrape the walls, knocking a few of my mosaics crooked. Mom follows and shuts the door to my room from the other side. I hear her straightening my mosaics as she heads toward the living room.

I flip on the lamp and move my dress from the bed, laying it over the chair at my desk. Jeb plops Morpheus down. His beautiful wings drape both sides of the mattress, limp. It's entirely unsettling to see someone as animated as him be so still and vulnerable.

I kneel next to the bed and push his hair back from his face. He's shivering. His eyes are closed, and his jewels blink a sickly grayish green—dull instead of glistening—like stagnant, murky water. Black veinlike strands swell and move under his pale skin, as if snakes were writing inside him. His blue magic pulses around the strands, trying to contain the poison, but the black keeps multiplying.

My stomach turns over. "Did Sister Two do this to you?"

Morpheus squints through one eye and coughs, nodding. He yelps as the black veins tangle and knot at his neck. My body aches, as if I've caught the poison. It hurts that much to see him suffering.

"Shh." I squeeze his hand. His palm feels clammy. "We have to try to keep it down, okay? We don't want my dad coming in."

He grits his teeth against more shivers. "Always knew I'd end up in your bed . . . and hear you say those words one day." He manages a smirk.

Jeb snarls. "Unbelievable. Even when he's at death's door he's a tool." He arranges a pillow beneath Morpheus's neck. "Why don't you keep your mouth shut while we help you."

Morpheus laughs weakly, his skin flashing with blue light. "What say Alyssa"—his breath rattles—"gives my mouth something else to do?"

Jeb narrows his eyes. "*What say* I give you a fist to chew on?"

Morpheus snorts, which triggers several more coughs.

I glare at them both. "Are you guys kidding me right now?" Shaking my head, I roll up Morpheus's sleeve to expose his birthmark. I cringe as the black snaky veins follow my touch. It's like they're drawn to my movements.

Sitting on my bed, I start to work off my boot.

Jeb stops me with a hand on the buckles. "What do you think you're doing?" he asks.

"I have to heal him."

"And what if this poison is contagious?" Rain pounds on the window and roof, as if punctuating Jeb's concern.

I pause.

Jeb glares down at Morpheus, who's faded out again.

"Hey." Jeb pats his face, oddly reminiscent of when Morpheus did the same to him at the studio.

Morpheus's eyes flutter open.

"She wants to heal you," Jeb says. "Is it safe?"

Morpheus grunts. "The stinger . . . my stomach . . . take it out first." Another cough. "Drown it."

I start to work the buttons open on Morpheus's black shirt, but Jeb brushes me aside and takes over.

Morpheus places his hand on Jeb's busy fingers, eyes opened to slits. "Ah, my pretty pseudo elf." He takes a labored breath. "Is it time at last to express our unrequited feelings?"

Jeb's ears flush red. He's about to retort when Morpheus groans, doubling over again. Biceps bulging, Jeb holds him flat to the bed so I can finish opening his shirt.

There's a puncture wound the size of a quarter on Morpheus's abdomen. The black, inky poison seems to stem from the site. His blue magic blinks once and grows dim, as if defeated.

I shudder.

"Careful with that thing," Jeb mutters.

I nod, using a Kleenex off my nightstand to protect my fingers as I work the stinger from the wound. It wriggles in my hand as if trying to escape. Shuddering again, I toss it into a glass of water next to the tissue box. The stinger fizzes and drifts to the bottom, disintegrating within seconds. The black veins under Morpheus's skin writhe wilder, as if they're fighting to survive without their source. Morpheus's eyes slam shut, and he grinds his teeth in agony.

Unable to bear his pain any longer, I press my ankle to his forearm. Heat surges between us. The black veins slow their movements and fade until all that's left is the puncture mark. His blue static reappears and pulses through the wound, leaving behind a silvery scar.

I ride a wave of euphoria as Morpheus's natural coloring comes back. He opens his eyes—alert and stronger by the second. He holds my gaze as I feel his forehead. His fever's gone. Jeb's watchful eye burns into my back, and I withdraw my hand.

Morpheus snags my ankle before I can slide off the bed, thumb running across my wing tattoo. The touch sends a prickly sensation through my wing buds.

"Moth," he whispers soundlessly. The Morpheus I know has returned, teasing and taunting, reminding me of my vow.

Jeb comes up behind me and pries Morpheus's fingers free. "Hands off, owl bait."

The guys exchange scowls as I climb off the mattress with Jeb's arm securely around my waist. It's nice to see some things never change.

Morpheus sits up, his wings unfurling around him. He stretches—languid and graceful—then drops his feet to the floor. Jewels sparkling green, he watches me as he rolls down his sleeve and buttons his shirt. "Thank you, Alyssa. And, Jebediah, I suppose we're even now."

"Not even close," Jeb says. "You brought Red here. And you're going to help send her back."

I put my hand on Jeb's chest. "Wait. First, tell us what happened with Sister Two."

Morpheus sighs. "It was going so well. She fell for my ruse and captured the cardboard man in my place."

Something clicks in my mind. "The Brandon Lee silhouette from the *Crow* shrine . . . of course." I smirk. "Impressive."

Morpheus shrugs, though he's obviously pleased with himself. "While she was busy reeling 'me' in, I transformed into a moth and rematerialized behind her to get the upper hand. I wrapped her in her own web and dragged her through a mirror and into the rabbit hole. She broke loose inside, turned on me." He looks down at the scar on his abdomen, then secures the last few buttons over it. "Left me for dead."

"Yet you made it all the way back here," I say.

"I had good incentive." Morpheus stands and straightens his shirt. "I was missing my car."

I bark a laugh, and Morpheus grins. Jeb watches the two of us.

My momentary lapse into giddiness is short-lived as I sort through the implications of this new development. "Does this mean Sister Two is back in Wonderland now? She's at her post?"

That could solve everything. Maybe Red didn't get to the restless souls in time.

"I would like to think so," Morpheus answers. "But we should keep our guard up. Especially you, Jebediah."

The door handle wiggles and we all freeze. Mom appears at the opening and we breathe a collective sigh of relief.

Tightening the belt on her robe, she looks Morpheus up and down and he returns her appraisal. It's obvious there's still no love lost between them.

"Allie deciphered her first mosaic," Mom says to him. "Red is on her way to the human realm to attack prom. We have a plan to stop her. I'll fill you in after I get dressed."

Morpheus glances at me and Jeb. "How deliciously dangerous."

"This isn't a game, Morpheus." Mom gives him an annoyed glare and turns her attention to Jeb. "Could you help me carry Thomas to our bedroom? He's not asleep all the way, but he's groggy enough."

"Is he going to be okay?" I ask.

Mom's expression softens. "The pills are harmless. He'll be safest this way."

I nod, though it's hard to stomach treating him like a pawn.

Jeb starts after her as she heads down the hall. He pauses at the door and gives Morpheus a meaningful glare. "Mind your manners, bug-eyes."

"Always." Morpheus tips a nonexistent hat.

Clenching his jaw, Jeb steps out.

The minute he's gone, I back up to the wall, limping unevenly with one boot on and one off.

Morpheus watches me like a predator, smiling. "Trying to put some distance between you and your feelings, little plum?"

"I don't know what you mean."

"Mmm. You lie with such finesse. Becoming more of a netherling every day." He strides toward me, as stealthy and menacing as a black panther. He props his forearm against the wall over my head and, wings curled around me, cuts off my surroundings. "I looked inside your heart after our melding. I saw how worried you were."

I clamp my mouth shut, hoping that was all he saw.

His gaze dips down to my necklaces. His features harden as he loops his pinky through the ring. "This will never do. You obviously haven't told our pseudo elf about the vow you made to me."

Now more than ever, I can't give Morpheus what he's asking. My mind searches for a way to reach his sympathetic side. I know he has one. I've seen it. "I learned something about you today."

That wins his full attention. He draws me into the fathomless depths of his eyes. "What would that be?"

"Every time you try to do the right thing, you get screwed."

My observation is met with silence. He scoops up my other necklace, closing the key, heart, and ring within his fist.

I take a shallow breath, heartbeat stumbling as I try to read him. "So it's a battle to make that choice, yeah?" I ask.

Morpheus offers a smug smile. "A battle would mean I have to care. I've ceased caring."

"Your actions say otherwise. I know what you did at Butterfly Threads. Sister Two came into the storeroom while I was getting dressed in the bathroom. You lured her out to the main floor in moth form to keep Jeb safe."

Morpheus fidgets. "I was just having a bit of fun with the wretch."

"What about what you did for my mom? Even though she betrayed you, you never once told Sister Two that my dad was her stolen dream-boy."

"I made a life-magic vow."

"No. I asked my mom about that vow. The wording never specified protecting Dad's identity."

He looks down, as if searching for some rebuttal.

I lift his chin with my fingertip. "I'm trying to tell you that if you keep following the good impulses, no matter how insignificant they might seem, I won't let you down like the others. I'll come back to you." I bite my tongue, careful not to show all of my hand. He can't know I've witnessed our future, only that I'm keeping a tally of his past.

Morpheus laughs. "Come back to me?"

"Someday."

"Perhaps I won't want you then. Perhaps I'll tire of waiting."

I swallow my pride. "Then it will be my turn to win *you*. I'm up for the challenge."

His sneer is sardonic if not impressed. "Of course you are." He pulls me closer with my necklace charms, tightening his fist around them. "But I'm not surrendering our day together after we defeat Red just because of a few pretty words and empty promises."

I bite my tongue, tempering my impulse to lash out. That would only feed his ego.

"Then you're not doing the right thing," I say evenly.

He pouts. "No? Because my good impulses are telling me that the right thing is to make you honor your vow. You're just going to have to bite the bullet and tell your mortal toy about our accord."

I slap his wings in an attempt to get out. They don't budge. "You make me crazy!"

His eyes light up, glittering onyx against a backdrop of violet jewels. "And you inflame my soul." He squeezes my necklaces, blue light pulsing from inside his fingers. "Ask yourself, Your Majesty. Are you truly angry at me, or at the fact that your little ruse to sweet-talk me backfired?"

I blink away the burning sensation under my lids. "It wasn't a ruse. Everything I said is true."

He huffs and attempts a glare. But underneath, I see the same doubt and vulnerability I heard in his voice when he sent me to the train without him. I also see something more: a damaged and enchanted fairy who pushed aside his selfishness and faced the bandersnatch for me, who looked a train dead-on, who put himself between Jeb and Sister Two, and who saved my dad from having his life sucked away.

I'm overwhelmed with compassion and gratitude and another emotion I don't dare put a name to. I have to convince him that there's a place for him in my heart, too.

Just not yet.

I glance at the wings covering me, at his body, immovable in front of me, then rise up on tiptoe and take his smooth face in both my hands. He tenses for an instant—suspicious—but relaxes slowly, each muscle surrendering bit by bit as I stroke his jaw.

"I'm just asking you to wait a little while," I whisper. "Isn't forever worth that?" Not giving him the chance to answer, I press my mouth to his cheek, a promise for someday. One pulse of my lips for my childhood friend, and one for the man I'm only starting to know.

Morpheus gentles beneath me, for once letting me take the lead. His free hand rests in the hair at the nape of my neck, the other grows hot where he holds my pendants.

It's a peck on the cheek, innocent and heartfelt, until he turns his face without warning, catching my mouth under his. His lips are warm and silky, flavored with tobacco. He groans and sinks into me, sweeping me into the current of his passion.

Before I start to drown, I push him away, my lips throbbing and speechless. His jewels are like fireworks, a prismatic array of emotions. He studies me with astonishment, so like the boy from my dreams those rare times I defeated him in a game or a challenge. His wings are lax, no longer a wall around us.

A muffled curse comes from the doorway. I jerk my head to find Jeb there, blood drained from his face. His gaze is fierce yet dejected, a deep and gut-twisting wound I haven't seen since his dad was alive and tormenting him.

My stomach falls. "Jeb."

He doesn't yell. He doesn't even attack Morpheus. What he does is so much worse.

He leaves.

"Jeb, wait!" I feel as if my insides have been gored—a pain so powerful my legs give out.

Morpheus's fist at my sternum holds me pinned to the wall, keeps me from going after him.

"There's a pity." Morpheus glides his free knuckles down my cheek. "I am sorry he had to be hurt, luv. But it's better this way. It would've driven him mad to give you up to me for a day. Things would never have been the same between you after that. And he could've been killed tonight. You probably just saved his life."

My cheeks flame. "No. This isn't how it's supposed to end. This time was supposed to belong to us!"

Morpheus releases me and steps back. "*Time*. You'll have no such constraints in Wonderland. Let that be your silver lining. Now pull yourself together. We must prepare for Red."

On the way out, he stops and strokes the pearls on my prom dress where it hangs on the chair. He smiles tenderly, and I know he's thinking of Ivory's vision—of a wedding and a child with hair like his and eyes like mine, who will bring dreams to Wonderland and make stealing human children obsolete.

With a final glance at me, Morpheus leaves.

I slide to the floor. Warmth radiates between my collarbones where my necklaces glow, bright blue and hot from Morpheus's magical grip. The key, heart, and ring are melded together—a scrap heap of metal as useless as any explanation I could offer Jeb.

I never saw it coming. It was me all along. *Me* who would betray myself in the worst possible way.

PROM-POCALYPSE

It's not so easy to pull myself together.

I make us late leaving the house, and by the time we stop off at my dad's sporting goods store for some supplies Jeb wrote down—two sets of walkie-talkies, ten soccer-ball carrying nets, four pairs of night-vision hunting goggles, and two paintball guns, along with a couple of boxes of white and yellow paintballs—Mom and I pull up in Underland's lot only thirty minutes before prom is scheduled to start. The student council and some chaperones have already arrived. There are at least a dozen cars here, and one of them is Taelor's. This night just gets better and better.

The activity center is a huge underground cave with a rock ceiling stretching as high as forty-eight feet in places. There's a ground-level entrance outside: a small structure that looks like a dome with the letters u-n-d-e-r-l-a-n-d blinking in neon orange, red, and purple above the gym-style double doors. Once through the doors, a ramp curves down to the main floor where the glow-in-the-dark activities are laid out: a skateboard bowl, a miniature-golf area, an arcade, and a raised café. There's also a place for dancing, about the size of the school gym, with wall-to-wall mirrors. It's an improvement on the gym at school, since in lieu of traditional lighting, it uses black lights illuminating fluorescent murals. The perfect setting for fairy tales and masquerades.

Underland's rear doors open to a small locker room where employees store backpacks, jackets, and personal items while working. It also has a freight elevator used for carrying down weekly shipments of food and supplies.

That's where Jeb is waiting to let us in. We're going to take the elevator so we can enter behind the café and blend in easier.

Jeb's still helping in spite of how I broke his heart. Not just because his sister could be in danger but because that's what Jeb does. He protects the vulnerable.

Just like I was supposed to protect him, and failed.

I drive Morpheus's Mercedes into the back parking lot with Mom riding shotgun and Morpheus fluttering in moth form outside my window. He's attending tonight as the British exchange student. Taelor will be ecstatic. Not only has "M" returned, but Jeb and I are on the outs.

Best prom *ever*.

Under the black lights, Morpheus's true appearance will look like part of a costume. In keeping with that, I've let my wings out again.

Mom helped me wrap periwinkle netting around their base and pinned it in front with a sparkly brooch, like a shawl, to camouflage how they protrude from my skin. If I wasn't so crushed over Jeb, I might actually get a kick out of showing off my wings and eye patches.

We park next to Jeb's motorcycle. The sight of it tears my heart a little more.

He came early like we'd originally planned and had free run of the place before anyone arrived. He messaged me with: *Nothing suspicious.* Curt, concise, and emotionless. I deleted it. It had no place among the flirty, heartfelt, and romantic texts that make up the rest of his thread on my phone.

The wrist corsage stares up at me from atop my periwinkle glove, a taunting reminder of the ring he offered along with the rest of his life. The ring that's now fused to the heart pendant and key. I clutch the metal jumble at my neck, then tuck it under my netted shawl.

I would cry, but this is so beyond tears. My eye sockets feel hot and scratchy, as if I poured desert sand into them, then shoved my eyeballs back in.

Suck it up, Alyssa. The voice in my head could easily be Morpheus's, but it's mine. I secure my air-brushed half mask with silver fringe in place, tying the band around my head.

Mom and I step out of the car. The rear parking lot is abandoned except for us. With one press of the key remote, the doors glide down. A cool gust flaps my wings and my gown's scalloped hem. I bend to adjust my blue-gray platform boots, working part of the hem free from a buckle.

The storm from earlier has passed, leaving a peachy orange

sunset. The gravel shimmers like neon sequins, but that's only on the surface. There's something dark, ancient, and menacing buried under this sleepy realm, and the humans can't see it.

The bugs are back—no longer tossing out warnings but offering support. Their white noise unites into one whisper:

We're here, Alyssa. Keep our world safe. If you need us . . . call.

Mom comes over to my side of the car to center my tiara and webbed veil. She smooths the silver wig Jenara lent me so it falls to my hips in straight, glossy strands. My real hair is tucked under an itchy wig cap.

Jeb told Jenara we were planning to attend prom incognito because he didn't want me to miss it, pretending everything is okay with us. Jen was thrilled to go along with our charade and also brought over a backless cocktail dress for Mom, at my request.

The tea-length hem flatters her, as do the feminine layers of blushed chiffon that match the wispy cap sleeves. Jen helped her braid strands of hair at her temples and clipped mauve rhinestone barrettes in place so her hair glistens like her skin. She looks stunning. I wish Dad could see her.

Before we left the duplex, I put his truck in the garage next to Gizmo so it would look like no one was home. The thought of him being there alone makes me sad all over again.

"I know, Allie." Mom's intense sky blue eyes read me through her rose-tinted mask. "I hate tricking him like that, too. But I can't see any other way."

Morpheus swoops down in moth form to hover beside me, one of his wings brushing my cheek teasingly. I wave him off and bite back the anger I've been suppressing since we kissed. He changed that moment into something it wasn't meant to be yet.

And I suspect he planned it. That he purposely let his wings fall so Jeb would see.

Morpheus transforms three feet in front of me. "Alyssa, there are no words for your beauty." He bows graciously.

"Can it, Morpheus."

He grins and straightens, wings high and regal behind him. I glare at his costume. It's so typical *him*. A mix of medieval and rock star: brown leather forearm guards with studs over a ruffle-cuffed white shirt, and a cavalier doublet in burgundy with a gold lace overlay. The hem hits above his muscled thighs, so the skintight burgundy hose taper smoothly into knee-high brown boots, leaving nothing to the imagination. Worst of all, he has a crown.

He dressed as a fairy king. The irony doesn't escape me.

I scowl.

"Problem, luv?" He looks down on me from behind a gold lace half mask while adjusting the ruby-jeweled crown over his blue hair with velvet-clad hands. Tiny moth corpses are suspended in the rubies, like stained-glass fossils.

I shake my head. "I'm pretty sure you'll be the only one wearing anything tight enough to need a codpiece. Always have to be the showstopper, don't you?"

"Oh, I assure you, what I chose to show is only the start."

Mom and I roll our eyes simultaneously, and his grin widens. Together, the three of us dig out the duffel bags filled with supplies from the trunk and trek to the back door.

Jeb's there before we knock, holding the door open. He's morbidly beautiful with the fake webs, dusty streaks, and strategic rips

Jenara incorporated into his tuxedo. The navy blue velvet-flocked jacket with frog closures makes him look even broader and taller, and his pants drape fluidly down his muscled legs. A periwinkle dress shirt and matching half mask complement his olive skin and dark wavy hair, playing off his green eyes with flecks of gray. The satin cravat at his throat combines all the colors in a paisley print.

He shaved and is wearing the brass-knuckle labret I gave him, but it's not for me. It's because he plans to kick zombie ass.

"Jeb . . ."

He looks through me. "You all need to hurry. We have plans to discuss."

To have him address us as a collective stings like a slap. The familiarity of him is so painfully close I don't want to move. Morpheus wraps an arm around me to nudge me along, and Jeb's gaze flits to the connection before he looks away again, jaw tight enough to crack.

We unload the duffel bags on a wooden bench next to some lockers. Jeb unzips them to check our supplies while laying out his strategy.

"The soccer-ball nets are for the toys, since they can't be killed. We'll have to immobilize them to get them inside." He drags out the walkie-talkies. After testing them, he tosses one to each of us. "We'll separate into teams. Bug-guts and me, and then you ladies. Stay in contact with your partner via radio."

The radio is no bigger than a cell phone, so I tuck it into my cleavage.

"The potted trees they're using are huge," Jeb continues. "Looks like an actual forest surrounds the dance floor. It's going to be hard to keep watch through them." He drags out the night-vision goggles and paintball guns, then looks up, frowning. "I said four sets of goggles."

"Thomas only had one in stock," Mom answers.

Jeb scowls. "Okay, we'll make do. There are two boxes of new donations I haven't checked yet. Our first priority is to look through those for threadbare toys. And if we don't find anything, we guard the mirrors on the dance floor."

"And if we do find something, O-Captain-my-Captain?" Morpheus asks, an acerbic edge to his voice.

Jeb loads one of the paintball guns and aims it at Morpheus's chest. "Then I shoot the creeper, so we can track it under the black lights, trap it, and send it back to the hole it crawled out of, *forever*."

Morpheus and Jeb stare each other down. The tension is palpable. I have no idea how they're going to work together to get this done. For that matter, I have no idea how I'm going to get through this, knowing how badly I've already screwed up.

Mom steps between them and guides the gun's barrel to the floor. She looks at the three of us, and I can see her putting together what's happened in her mind. "Before any shooting starts, we'll have to get the people out."

Jeb's intense gaze settles on Mom. I've never been so envious of her. "Right. We need to set off each sprinkler head so the whole place gets wet. They're triggered when their glass globes break. Do you think you and Al can bust them with your magic? Set them *all* off and send everyone running? That'll be the signal to clear and then barricade the place. Mothra can take care of the entrance while I short-circuit the elevator."

Mom nods. "We can do that, right, Allie?" She watches me with a concerned tilt to her head, and I know she sees right through me.

"Sure," I answer. Jeb's plan is so well thought out, yet I haven't managed a coherent thought since he left our house. Obviously our breakup hasn't affected his productivity like it has mine.

We take the large elevator down. Jeb is in the far corner with the duffel bags, manning the button panel, and Morpheus stands between me and my mom. When we reach our stop, Jeb holds the Door Close button. He focuses on me for the first time tonight. My heart dances.

"Be careful," he says, his voice deep and gravelly with emotion.

"You, too," I murmur.

Morpheus's wings sweep up, an obvious reminder of what happened between us earlier.

I frown as Jeb looks away and opens the doors, leading us out onto the main floor, ignoring me again. Snacks are being arranged in a corner next to a half dozen pool tables with felt surfaces so dark they're almost invisible. Neon balls, pockets, and cue sticks tempt gamers to play.

At the buffet, a glowing blue concoction fizzes inside a punch bowl, and cupcakes with neon rosettes of icing cover the rest of the table. We tuck our supplies behind the hanging tablecloth, keeping them hidden but close for easy access.

It's time to blend and search.

We fit right into the ultraviolet scene. The people milling around appear just as wild as Morpheus and me. Some of my classmates even have antennae and two sets of wings like dragonflies—made of wire, cheesecloth, and fluorescent spray paint.

The trees Jeb told us about really do look real, and they are at least three times the size of the ones we made in art class—fat trunks and long branches that stick up from the top like serpentine hair.

They've been painted white and, against the black lights, add a phantasmal element.

I shiver.

Mom pulls me aside and leans close to my ear. "I know something's going on with you and Jeb, but don't get distracted. The only way to make it through this is to remove yourself from your emotions. Be cutthroat and cunning. Think like a netherling queen. Okay?"

I nod. She kisses my temple, leaving the scent of her perfume wafting over me as she splits off from our group to sign in at the chaperone table. Her dress and mask appear to float through the darkness, radiant pink swirling around a shadowy blue silhouette. The student volunteer at the table hands her a fluorescent name tag and complimentary tiara of cardboard, paint, and tinsel. She puts them in place, then walks to a box of donations a few feet away. She turns her back, and the radio in my bodice comes alive with her voice.

"I'll check this one. Look for the other. *Over.*" Then there's static, barely noticeable under the eighties monster ballad blaring out of the speakers above.

"We're on it," Jeb tells me from behind. "Get to the dance floor. You should find a spot now, before everyone else shows up."

"Right," I mumble.

Morpheus drags a velvet fingertip from my shoulder to my elbow as he passes. "Keep your head about you, Alyssa. I won't stand for you losing it." The Wonderland implication behind his words winds a knife through my gut. Then he's off toward the miniature-golf course.

Jeb shifts his stance behind me, as if he's leaving, but pauses as a crackle bursts through the overhead speakers, shutting off the music.

"Five minutes till we open the door!" a bubbly teenage girl says over the intercom. "Chaperones, man your stations, and student council members, make your way to the entrance to welcome our fairy-tale guests and take donations!"

Jeb and I wait for the crowd to thin out. I'm concerned that we haven't found the spirit-filled toys yet. I'd hoped we could do this without Jenara and Corbin and the other students being present. I fidget, and my wing brushes Jeb's abdomen, causing my face to flush.

He leans in, breath hot on my neck. "You got this, skater girl," he whispers softly and touches my wing tip, sending warm shimmers through my whole body.

His faith in me, in the face of what I put him through, is so unexpected, I turn to thank him. But he's already walking away, his back barely visible in the darkness. My wing's membranes ache from his touch.

Jaw clenched, I head for my post, ducking around busy classmates in reflective costumes. I keep my sights on the phantasmal trees. Once I get inside the forest, my own dress, hair, and wings will blend with their glaring white trunks and branches. From a few yards away, some of the trunks look as if they're frowning—an odd anomaly formed by the wood grains. The sight triggers a distantly familiar discomfort.

Mom's voice comes through my radio. She verifies she couldn't find anything out of place in the box of toys and that Morpheus didn't find anything in the other box. People stare at my talking chest from behind beaked or glittery masks, their purplish blue silhouettes as unrecognizable to me as I am to them. I ignore them and keep moving toward the dance floor and mirrored wall.

Glancing over my shoulder, I spot Jeb in the distance, his silhouette dark against the citrusy orange skating bowl rising up behind him. A temporary metal partition has been placed on the shallow end—painted the same shade as the bowl and half as tall—to keep amorous couples from stealing inside for make-out sessions.

A shadowy princess stands beside Jeb in a red sequined dress and monarch wings that flare from her shoulders, as incandescent as flames. She places a hand on his lapel, caressing the fabric. I'd know that body language anywhere. Taelor has discovered Jeb, and she's thrilled he came without me.

Remembering Mom's words and Morpheus's warning, I shake off the jealousy and continue toward my assigned destination. As I pass the arcade—a few feet from the white forest—I hear a rustle, like plastic flapping in the wind.

I backtrack and duck my head into the arcade. The dark room's alive with bouncy music, eerie sound effects, and animated lights. The plastic crinkle continues and draws me in. I pass a line of arcade game machines. Bright colors and graphics streak in my peripheral vision as I focus on the rattle. It's coming from the Skee-Ball section, where fifty or so prizes, wrapped in cellophane bags, hang from a Peg-Board on the back wall.

Minute movement inflates and deflates the bags, as if something's breathing inside them. My pulse pummels underneath my jawbone as I creep closer, the prizes becoming visible through their plastic covering: teddy bears and stuffed animals, vinyl clowns and porcelain dolls—all moth-eaten or eyeless, with stuffing oozing from their necks, under their arms, and out of empty sockets.

The restless souls . . .

"Sneaky," I whisper and pull out my walkie-talkie with trembling hands. Backing up, I trip over my train and drop the radio. It busts apart on the stone floor.

"Crap." I bend down to pick up the pieces that are scattered beside a small potted flower I didn't notice before. It's a buttercup, strangely out of place here, yellow petals reflecting in the ultraviolet setting like a yield sign struck by headlights. There's something glowing inside the pot, too, just atop the soil. I lean down and find a half-eaten mushroom, the freckled side gone.

"My child." A husky purr erupts from the flower's center. One of the leaves grabs a strand of my silver wig before I can pull back, holding me hunched in place. Rows of eyes open and blink on every petal.

"Red," I whisper.

She starts to grow along with the pot, a slow and torturous trans-formation. The spiny teeth in her mouth snarl. "Let's get a look at you," she says, as tall as my thigh now and still growing. Her leafy arms and fingers stretch and knot through my wig, holding me close to her gruesome face. "What happened to your hair?" she scolds, obviously displeased. Her breath smells like wilted flowers. "How dare you despoil my vessel."

"I am *not* your vessel." I rip free, letting my mask, wig, and scalp cap flop off. My real hair cascades all around my shoulders—a mass of tangles. I take one step back before my crimson strand jerks against my scalp, dragging me toward Red, as if remembering she created it, as if wanting to let her inside again. I freeze, that fingerprint on my heart incapacitating.

"Ah, better." Red's spiny, slimy teeth curl into a smile as she grows tall enough to look me in the eye. "That's the welcome I expected." She catches the restless strand of hair with a leafy hand. "I'll always be part of you." My body feels the intrusion, as if she's draining all my blood and filling my veins with hers.

Gathering my wits, I shove her stalk, and she topples, losing her grip on my hair as she hits the floor, pot overturned and leaves rattling. Her mental hold is broken.

"You'll never be part of me again." I shake off the attempted possession.

Growling, she rolls on the floor, then uses her vinelike arms to drag herself toward me. Soil spills out of the overturned pot, and she pauses, staring at it. Her hundreds of eyes glare up at me. "Help me or suffer my wrath."

"Right," I mutter sarcastically, the netherling in me taking over. The memory of my confrontation with the flowers last year in Wonderland returns. "You can pick up roots, but you can't move unless you're connected to the soil. Not the smartest choice, showing up in a cement cave." I sidestep her attempt to grab at me, heartbeat hopeful. That must be why she didn't bring the flower fae . . . why she chose the toys as her army. "I say you just lie there and rot."

Seething, she lengthens her arms. The leaves protruding from her vines slap the floor next to my feet, an inch away from snagging me. I withdraw farther, watching, almost pitying her helplessness. But I know better. There's nothing helpless about her, and mercy has no place on the battlefield.

I need to dispose of her, permanently—send her back to the cemetery to stay, although I'm not sure how to get her there. Maybe Morpheus has a plan. I'll incapacitate her somehow . . . hold her here until he can help me.

Ripping an extension cord from the wall, I stand back far enough to stay out of her reach and guide the cord with my mind as if I were casting a fishing line. I catch her, then roll her up in it so she can't move. It's satisfying being on the giving end of this trick for once.

She growls, struggling in the binds. "Stubborn twit. I'm not the enemy. Do you not realize, I am the only way for you to keep the Red kingdom? Your mother wishes to steal it from you. She's lied all these years. She wants the crown. Actually tried to win it once. You didn't know that, did you?"

"I know everything about my family." *Thanks to Morpheus.*

I continue wrapping her in the electric cord. If I hadn't seen my father and mother's memory, I might actually have fallen for Red's lie. As it is, her false accusations only make me angrier. I'd electrocute her if it would have any effect.

She grumbles as I finish knotting the cord and ease back another step.

"The spider lurks in the shadows," Red grumbles. "She wants to give your fairy-tale prince a different ending this time. Release me and I'll tell you where she hides."

Sister Two?

I lift my dress hem and run out, leaving Red incapacitated.

"Catch the girl and wake the trees!" Red shouts. The toys on the wall rattle their packaging to break free.

Wake the trees. Those words are a sick validation for my earlier premonition. Those frowns I saw were more than wood grains.

Jeb sees me run from the arcade entrance and tries to maneuver through the crowd. There's no time to get Mom. I have to clear out the place before the toys escape and humans get eaten by tulgey wood.

I stare up at the purplish fluorescent black lights on the endless ceiling, envisioning the bulbs on the sprinklers, pretending that they're rosebuds in a garden, waiting to bloom. I imagine a nurturing rain, their petals opening wide in a push for life.

Popping spreads from one side of the cave to the other, followed by a fall of cold water sweeping in until my hair and clothing stick to my skin. The crowd's reaction is instantaneous. Screaming girls and cursing guys push their way to the ramps, while others race around, trying to salvage costumes and food.

The chaperones attempt to control the chaos and herd everyone to the exit. I duck behind the arcade sign, and when the last chaperone rushes out of the gym-style doors, Morpheus swoops in to wrap a chain through the push bars, barricading the entrance.

The sprinklers stop at Mom's command.

"The army's in the arcade!" I shout as she comes into sight and the four of us are reunited—skin, hair, and clothes soaking wet. "And watch out for the trees . . . they're tulgey wood."

Jeb looks completely baffled, but Mom and Morpheus exchange anxious glances through their reflective masks.

A stampede of decomposing toys scrambles out of the game room and heads for the trees by the dance floor. I can't see the extent of their hideousness in the shadows. Doesn't matter. I can still picture the way they looked in those bags—miserable doll eyes blinking, clown faces snarling in pain and rage, teddies and lambs losing their stuffing through rips in their bodies—all of them carrying souls delirious for a chance at freedom.

Their small, shadowy forms slip and slide into each other on the wet cement. They grumble in mass confusion. It would be comical if it weren't so ominous.

"Get the supplies!" Jeb shouts.

Morpheus takes to the air, his crown falling to the floor with a metallic clatter. I swoop up behind him. He's a floating mask, doublet, and ruffled shirt skimming toward the buffet; everything else, his hose and wings, are too dark to see. Jeb and Mom follow on the ground, a hovering dress and a glowing periwinkle mask. All those years of balancing on a skateboard are paying off. Jeb does an impressive job of sliding along the drenched floor while also keeping Mom from falling.

There's nothing but static coming over the intercom and speakers now. Flapping my wings, I scan the darkness below. It's broken up by fluorescent platforms in the middle, murals, and ghostly trees to the north that will soon come alive, and, just a few yards perpendicular, the arcade. I cringe. It's like looking down on a nightmarish pinball machine. As I glance at the pool tables and the glowing balls that look like marbles, an idea starts to take shape.

Morpheus interrupts my thought process, shouting over his shoulder, "Red?"

My hair blows in the gusts coming off his wings. "She's overturned on the floor, bound and coughing up dirt."

"That won't last." For once he doesn't have a joke.

And he's right to be serious. I only managed to keep the humans out of her path and bought us a little extra time. She wants my body back and Morpheus on a platter. She'll figure out a way to make those two things happen. At least for now she's incapacitated, which makes finding Sister Two top priority. I shiver, remembering Morpheus's reaction to her sting. A human, without magic to fight off the poison, doesn't stand a chance at survival.

Morpheus and I reach the buffet first. He lands expertly on the floor and slides to a stop. I alight clumsily on the table, my left boot squished inside a soggy fluorescent cupcake.

"Practice, luv. It's all in the ankles," he says as he drags out the duffel bags.

I shake off the wet cake and hop down, using my wings for balance so I don't wipe out on the slick floor.

Jeb and Mom arrive after taking a detour so Jeb could short-circuit the elevator. Now he's in full battle mode. "Al, let me have your shawl," he says upon seeing me, whipping off his jacket.

I take off the brooch. "Jeb," I mumble as he spins me around to unwrap the netting from the base of my wings while Mom and Morpheus unload stuff a few feet away, their backs to us.

"Yeah," Jeb says, concentrating.

"Those trees, they swallow things. Then they either spit them out as mutants, or the things are lost in—"

"*AnyElsewhere*. Your mom told me on the way over." His fingers keep working at the netting.

"And Sister Two is here."

He pauses.

I look over my shoulder at him, a knot forming in my throat. "Your plan is brilliant, but this isn't your war. You aren't equipped to fight these things."

His wounded gaze penetrates, even through his mask. "But *he* is, right?"

I look over his shoulder at Morpheus. His wings block him and Mom as they untangle the nets.

I turn, concentrating on Jeb. "No matter what you think happened between the two of us, I love you. We share battle scars and hearts. I don't want to lose that."

He studies my necklaces and the soldered clump of metal at my neck. "Yeah, I see how well you took care of my heart."

I wince at the honesty behind the dig.

"But you should know by now that I never give up without a fight." He catches the necklace, jerks me close, and presses his lips to mine—a counterclaim to Morpheus's kiss, marked with Jeb's flavor and passion. When he releases me, his jaw is set stubbornly. "You and me? We're far from over."

I'm too shell-shocked to respond.

Our moment is cut short as the undead toys awaken the trees. Wide mouths yawn open on the trunks, and their serpentine limbs palpitate. Like Red, they're limited to the pots and soil they're in. But I remember the snapping retractable teeth and gums I saw on the tulgey shelves in my memory. If the toys can round us up into the forest, we're all as good as eaten.

After waking the trees, the toys disappear into the shadows once more. The intermittent sounds of sloshing water and gruesome whimpers and moans are the only indications of their whereabouts. Other than a silhouette here and there, they're impossible to see, being so small and close to the floor.

Without another word, Jeb rolls the netting into a strip to make it stronger and fashions a makeshift harness around his chest and shoulders. He digs out the night-vision goggles and tears off his mask to slide them into place. Then he snags a paintball gun and shoves all the boxes of paintballs into one duffel that he hangs on his shoulder.

He steps up to Morpheus, catches his arm, and turns him around. "Think you're man-bug enough to give me a lift?"

Morpheus snorts. "Child's play. Although I can't promise a safe landing."

The threat doesn't faze Jeb. He turns so Morpheus can ease his arms through the back of the harness.

"Morpheus." I shoot him a meaningful glance, trying to get his assurance he'll play nice. But neither guy looks my way. I hope they can manage to work together without killing each other.

"We'll tag them." Jeb looks down at us as Morpheus hoists him up, his powerful wings flapping hard enough to stir up gusts. "And you two bag them."

Mom hands me a net as the guys rise toward the ceiling. Jeb's shirt is a streak of glaring purple in the shadows. The thought of Sister Two lurking gnaws at the edges of my heart, but I have to keep it together. I can't let my fear for Jeb get the best of me, or it will prove Morpheus right: that Jeb's my downfall.

I won't let that be true. He's my partner, just like he was in Wonderland. Even if I have lost his trust.

A splatting sound erupts as Jeb blasts paintballs into the darkness. Creepy toys clamber out of hiding places, growling and groaning. Spatters of paint mark them—smears of neon light scuttling to and fro.

Mom and I bob and duck, sway and slide, as gnashing teeth and angry snarls attack from all directions. With the wet floor beneath us, we can barely stay upright to fight them off, much less capture them in nets.

"If we're going to get the upper hand," I shout over the commotion, knocking a few undead toys away with a pool cue, "we'll have to go aerial." My wings itch to take flight and I climb onto the table.

Mom looks up at me, a hint of reservation behind her mask. "I'm not that great at the flying thing." She looks scared, just like I was when Jeb and I skated across the chasm in Wonderland on a sea of clams. But Jeb persisted, and we made it out. I'll be just as strong for Mom.

A half dozen neon-smeared toys tumble our way, panting and rabid.

I drag her up onto the table next to me. "Now, Mom."

Biting her lip, she nods. There's a *whoosh* as she releases her wings—almost exact replicas of mine. After tonight—seeing her Wonderland wildness set free—I don't think she'll ever have any problems with my miniskirts again.

A trance-techno dance song bursts out of the speakers, and wicked laughter echoes through the intercom. Some toys have found their way to the sound booth.

Mom and I launch into the air—nets in hand—as several restless souls scramble onto the table. A mildewed teddy bear and a pink kitten with only one eye tug at my arms and hair, trying to pull me toward the waving, yawning trees. I slap away the toys with my pool cue as I rise.

Mom's not gaining altitude fast enough. A worm-eaten vinyl doll clamps onto her ankle, biting her. She screeches and sinks a few feet. Blood trickles down her shoe to the table below.

Diving toward her, I slam the doll with the pool cue, sending it into the darkness. The toy yelps, and I follow its soaring white reflection as it hits the top of the skate bowl and slides down the orange incline, coming to a stop at the bottom. It tries to climb out but keeps slipping down again. The enclosed concave, combined with the moisture from the sprinklers, makes it impossible to escape.

The partially formed idea from earlier hits me fully now.

"Zombie pinball," I yell to Mom, both of us high enough that our wing tips nearly brush the overhead black lights.

She looks down at the layout, not quite getting it.

To demonstrate, I focus on a pool table, imagining the balls are tumbleweeds caught by the Texas wind. They begin to spin, then roll, dropping off the table's edge like rainbow-fluorescent waterfalls.

They capture some toys in their spin, and I guide the mobile mass with my mind and imagination, herding it toward the skate park, hitting the tulgey trees and other fluorescent obstacles along the way but coaxing it along. From our altitude, the glowing scene looks like a hundred pinball games playing at once.

Mom catches on and uses her magic on another pool table, until the floor is covered with glowing balls and off-balance toys. We combine our powers and send all of the balls and toys siphoning into the skate bowl. Mom's white teeth beam at me across the shadows, and I smile back. We're winning.

In the distance, Jeb and Morpheus catch the corner of my eye. They're close to the arcade. A steady buzz of paintballs rains down. They're going after Red. I push my concern out of my mind, trying to stay emotionless, and keep working with Mom until we've piled most of the toys inside the tall bowl. The few remaining ones scamper into the tulgey forest.

I fashion a giant scoop, using my net and cue. Descending close to the skate bowl, I lower it. The toys clamber dumbly inside. I'm able to snag at least fifteen on my first try. Their wiggly weight works as a counterbalance to help me cinch the top closed. I drop the net off on my way to the buffet table for another one. I grab two pool sticks, handing one off to Mom as she hovers close. She swoops away, and I reach under the tablecloth for the last duffel bag.

Something slices my wrist through my glove. I yelp and jerk my arm back, blood drizzling across the floor. Garden shears rip through the tablecloth from the other side, and Sister Two scutters out, rising to her full height and lashing at me, stingers bared.

Darkest Night & Strangest Light

Gasping, I block Sister Two's venomous hand with a pool cue.

She screeches as one of her poison-tipped fingernails gets stuck in the wood. I ditch the stick and run, heart slamming with every slippery footstep.

No one can see me through the waving white tulgey trees—Red, the guys, or Mom—but I see them. Jeb and Morpheus have landed and are rounding up the toys they marked—the ones that got by me and Mom. Morpheus uses blue magic to walk the zombies like puppets toward Jeb, who then swings a golf club, driving them into a net they've propped open. Leave it to guys to make a game out of a life-and-death situation. They're almost to the arcade's door—and Red.

Mom's in the distance, scooping up toys from the skate bowl, as oblivious as the guys. I start to lift off so I can get to her, but Sister Two's scissors hack into my right wing.

A fiery agony shoots from my shoulder blade to my spine. My knees fold under, slamming me to the wet cement. I attempt a scream . . . to warn the others . . . but the pain gores deep and sucks the air from my lungs, locking my voice box.

Sister Two scutters over, eight feet tapping in morbid synchrony across me. My wing is in tatters. Jeweled pieces fall around me like snow at midnight, reflecting brilliant white under the black lights.

"I told ye, that day ye trespassed on me hallowed ground, that I would make confetti of ye. Be glad I'm stopping at this." She stabs my wing with the cue, then drops it next to me as I curl up in agony. "Since ye gathered my runaway souls and brought Red back to my keep, I've decided to let ye live. Yer mortal dreamer and yer mother . . . that's all I need for restitution. Ye may consider yer debts paid."

I struggle to move. *No. Please don't take them.* My chest swells with the plea, voice trapped inside, banging around like a caged bird.

She sends a web into the air and lifts away, obscured and lethal in the darkness. She flashes in and out of my vision, so high she's virtually impossible to spot.

Red's wicked cackle booms through the cavelike expanse, and I wrench my neck to check out the arcade door. Her floral form is taller than Morpheus now. The toys must've helped her escape my binds. She uses her snaky arms to propel herself along, lifting her pot and swinging it, reminding me of an orangutan. One of her extra limbs slinks out to catch Jeb. Morpheus encases Red in his blue magic as if in hopes of controlling her like he did the undead toys, but she's too powerful, and she captures him, as well.

I cry out, sound finally ripping from my throat.

Resolved to help, I wrestle against the agonizing spasms in my back and wing and almost stand but drop down to my stomach again as a prickly hot rush pierces through my vertebrae. Is this how it felt for all those bugs I used to stick with pins?

I whimper—a sorry excuse for a queen, for a daughter, for a girlfriend and a friend. Icy hot spasms travel from my torn wing to every nerve center, shuddering through me in a shock wave. I shiver, my muscles jerking. Water squishes all around me, making me even colder.

My mind numbs. I'm being sucked into unconsciousness, like when the mud swallowed me days ago in my dream. I remember Morpheus's voice as I was being pulled down. How he told me to find a way out, that I wasn't alone. And when I reached out to the bugs, I was rescued.

When we arrived at Underland, the insects promised their loyalty and their aid. *Call us,* they said. So that's what I do now . . . I reach for them in my mind, beg them to reawaken the wraiths, because that's the only way to salvage the human realm.

There's a whisper of affirmation, barely audible under the loud music, as if bug scouts have been waiting inside Underland for my signal all along. Relief floods me. The ants will fix it. The wraiths will come and take everything back that belongs in Wonderland.

A bitter realization hits. They'll capture Morpheus, too. He'll be swept into Wonderland alongside Red. He'll still be in danger.

"Oh, no," I mumble and drag myself to a crawling position, shutting out the pain.

High overhead, Sister Two swings stealthily toward Mom's hovering form.

"Mom!" I yell, but the spidery gardener shoves her off balance before Mom sees her.

Mom plummets toward the pile of haunted toys in the skate bowl, her dress a beautiful cascade of luminous pink against her purplish black silhouette. The crazed toys descend on her.

"Get off of her!" I scream.

A cacophony of wretched, wailing screams drifts from the dance floor, louder than my voice, louder than the static now playing over the intercom. Through the white trees, a portal has opened in one of the mirrors on the wall, and it glows against the darkness. Black oily sludge oozes from the rabbit hole, seeping into our realm. In a blink, they split into phantoms, siphoning into the air like smoke.

They race over me and sniff, their wails splintering through my bones, shaking my wings. They leave their oily marks behind as I cry out and push forward, toward Mom piled under the undead toys. I can't let the wraiths think she's one of them. But Jeb and Morpheus need my help, too.

I make the mistake of looking toward the arcade. Red still has the guys wrapped within her leafy arms as Sister Two faces her down. Red uses her extra vines to drag herself toward the tulgey wood, and Sister Two skitters after them—a spider chasing a flower, just like in my mosaic. I gasp, realizing before it happens what Red's planning to do. Just as Sister Two casts out a net of web to catch Jeb, her prized soul, Red dives into a tulgey tree's yawning mouth, taking Jeb and Morpheus with her.

They're gone.

I drop to my stomach, propped on my elbows, slammed with disbelief. Fighting back tears, I stare and wait. "Please don't come out again . . . please don't," I mumble, unable to fathom a world where Morpheus and Jeb are twisted and mutated like the looking-glass rejects.

Seconds pass by as long as hours. I clench my eyes closed, fighting against looking. On the inside of my lids I see their faces looming, nightmarishly deformed.

I struggle to breathe.

Driven by the screeches of the wraiths, I open my eyes and exhale. The tree's mouth has stayed closed. Jeb, Morpheus, and Red are nowhere to be seen. But dread nips at the heels of my relief. Both of them have been accepted at the gate, which means they're trapped in AnyElsewhere along with thousands of Wonderland criminals.

The wraiths dip and rise overhead, the air so thick with them it's like a swarm of giant locusts. I can't undo the horror of Jeb and Mopheus's fate. I resolve to help them later, promising myself there's a way—somehow.

For now, my mom's still in danger.

Heartsick, I creep toward the skate bowl's edge, unable to see her for all the toys clambering inside. Plucking up the cue she dropped in her fall, I poke at the restless souls. They snarl and part, revealing Mom. Her dress is torn and her mask askew, but she's conscious. She shoves aside the toys clawing at her and reaches up to catch the stick. Her weight tugs my shoulder, and I grit my teeth against the ripping sensation in my back.

An instant before her hands grip the skate bowl's edge, she's caught in a funnel of wailing wraiths swirling around us, sending bloodcurdling screeches and harsh, cold wind over me.

"Stop!" I scream, arms covering my head for protection. "She belongs here!" They ignore me and touch down, funneling into the bowl. I force myself to stand against the agonizing pain.

"Take me, too!" I plead.

The twisting, wailing cloud sucks up everything but me: the glowing tulgey trees, the undead toys holding on to Mom, Sister Two and her spinnerets. I limp toward the mirrored wall as the cyclone filters through the portal, leaving only oily streaks behind.

Hoping to dive inside the glass before the portal closes, I throw myself into the mirror, but it's too late. I slam the glass just as it's closing, and the mirror cracks, slicing me, cold and unyielding. All I can do is bleed and watch the nightmare I conjured play out through the broken reflections.

The wraiths siphon down into Wonderland with their plunder, and the rabbit hole implodes upon itself, as if the impact of the entry was too violent. Nothing remains but overturned dirt and a broken sundial fountain.

No way in. Ever again.

❋··I··❋

Other than my nurse and me, the courtyard is deserted. I'm seated at one of the black cast-iron bistro tables on a cement courtyard that has been stamped to look like cobblestone.

The legs of the furniture are drilled into the ground in case an out-of-control patient should try to throw a chair in a fit of rage. A black and red polka-dotted parasol sprouts up from the center of the table like a giant mushroom and shades half of my face. Silver teacups and saucers glisten atop placements. Two settings: one for me and one for Dad.

I'm here because I've lost my head. My mind is unhinged. That's what the doctors say.

Dad believes them. Why wouldn't he? The police have proof. The vandalized state of Underland is just like what he saw at home in my room, at Butterfly Threads, and in the school gymnasium. There's blood that matches Mom's DNA on the tablecloth from the buffet table, along with my blood on Jeb's shirt that they found in my backpack in the garage.

Jeb and Mom have been missing for a month. I'm not so much a suspect as a victim. Of a cult, maybe. Or a gang. It could be sacrificial, or brainwashed violence. But I must've had help. After all, how could one small girl wreak so much havoc on her own?

They can't get me to talk about it. When they ask, I become rabid, like a wild animal—or a netherling unleashed.

When the firemen first found me among the debris at Underland, I was broken—beyond the crippled wing I'd already absorbed back into my skin, beyond the gashes in my skin from the mirror's glass. I couldn't talk at all. I could only scream and cry.

Dad refused to let the asylum workers sedate me, and I love him for that. Since I couldn't be drugged into submission, they brought me to a padded room to ensure I wouldn't hurt myself. I hunkered in the corner for a week, limp and exhausted, surrounded by nothing but endless white. White like the tulgey trees that haunted my nightmares. I tormented myself with the mosaics and how each one played out that fated night.

There were never three fighting queens. There were only two: Red and me—the two halves of myself I struggled so hard to keep separate. Red was eaten alive by some vile creature—the tulgey—leaving my netherling side standing amid a storm of magic and chaos, and my human side wrapped up in something white, like web—my nemesis, the straitjacket.

Now those darkest nights have passed. The two sides of me are united as one. I'm letting the magic out again, privately, subtly, deliberately, to soothe the hollow ache in my heart. My right wing is still damaged, but by stretching it each day, it's piecing itself back together, bit by bit.

Claustrophobia no longer has any power over me. I've learned to manipulate the straitjacket's Velcro closures. Rip them open with just a thought. Once my arms are free, I cover the surveillance camera over the door with the jacket, release my wings, and dance around the pillowed floor, half-naked, imagining I'm back in Wonderland, in Sister One's cushioned cottage, eating sugar cookies and playing chess with an egg-shaped man named Humphrey. By the time the asylum employees realize my camera isn't working, I've already absorbed my wings and am bound by the Velcro and cotton again, slumped in the corner, silent and unresponsive.

I sneak out of my room at night, when all is still and silent. And I watch the humans sleeping, study their vulnerabilities, and savor the fact that I will never be helpless like them again.

I *am* mad, and I embrace it. Madness is part of my heritage. The part that led me to Wonderland and earned me the crown. The part that will lead me to face Red one final time, until only one of us is left.

Until then, I'm a queen with no way back to my kingdom, which bleeds for me. My two faithful and beloved knights, Jeb and Morpheus, are trapped in AnyElsewhere—the looking-glass world, the land of the exiled and the gruesome. And my mom is alone in Wonderland, at the mercy of Sister Two. That's unacceptable. I didn't get her back just to lose her again.

The rabbit hole has collapsed, and my key is melded to a nugget of worthless metal. But I have another key—a *living* key—that can open the way into AnyElsewhere through the mirrors of this world. And now I have the tickets to trade for it.

Last night I crept into Mom's old room after lockdown, longing to see it while it was empty between patients.

In the shadows, a soft, strange glow radiated from behind the picture of geraniums on the wall, detectable only to someone who'd learned to find light in the darkness.

The same picture hangs in every room, but the flowers on this one glimmered—neon green, orange, and pink petals. Following a hunch, I moved the frame aside to find the painting had been rubbed to paper-thinness behind the petals. Even more mysterious, there was a fist-size hole dug into the plaster wall, filled with soil and flourishing ultraviolet fungi.

Mom was harvesting mushrooms from Wonderland while she was a prisoner here. When she told me netherlings always have an escape plan, she meant it.

I sat on the bed for some time after, mushrooms in hand, wondering how often she used them to get out when she needed an escape. It eased my mind to know she'd had that chance, and even more, that she'd passed it on to me.

"Hey, Allie." Dad's arrival shakes me back to today. I inhale the outdoor air, feeling a resurgence of energy. The half of my face in the sun is hot, so I scoot further into the umbrella's shade.

"Hi." I offer him that much, then return to my conversation with the two monarch butterflies fluttering around the flowers on the table. They tell me to hurry, because London's a long way for them to fly and daylight is preferable.

Dad watches me with the bugs, tired and defeated. "Allie,

sweetie, try to stay focused, okay? It's important. We need to find your mother and Jeb. They're in danger."

Yes, they are, Dad. More than you know.

"If you'll send away the nurse," I offer in a demented, singsong voice, "I'll tell you everything I remember." I scoop Salisbury steak from my teacup and spoon the salty, meaty bite into my mouth, letting the gravy drip down my chin. It's the only way I'll eat now, with teacups and saucers. And I dress like Alice every day. I know how to emulate crazy. I learned from the master.

It hurts my heart to see Dad's expression as he directs the nurse to leave. He's afraid to be alone with me. I don't blame him. But I shove my human empathy aside. He's going to have to be strong for the journey ahead. If he wants to rescue Mom, his own sanity will be put to the test.

It's okay, because I have faith in his strength.

He's the key to all of this, and to make him fit the lock, I will be cutthroat and cunning enough for the both of us.

Left eyelid twitching, Dad looks at me. "Okay, Allie. We're alone."

I turn my lips into a savagely sweet smile. "Before we talk about prom night, take a bite of your food. It's tasty."

Narrowing his eyes, he draws a fork out of his teacup, dripping with meat, mushroom, and sauce, then shoves it in his mouth.

I prop an elbow on the table and my chin on my hand. "While you're busy eating, may I ask you a question?" My voice sounds stilted and deranged, even to my own ears. All the better to unbalance him.

He shakes his head, swallowing. "Allie, stop playing games. We're losing time here."

I pout. "If you won't play with me, I'm sure my other guests will."

I lean forward and whisper to the flowers on the table, watching him from the corner of my eye.

He makes a choking sound, almost turning green. "Fine. What do you want to know?"

"I was just curious." I grip the glowing mushrooms wrapped in Kleenex in my apron pocket. He doesn't realize I laced both of our Salisbury steaks with the smoothest half of one, that within moments we'll be the size of beetles, riding upon the backs of butterflies. "How do you feel about trains?"

ACKNOWLEDGMENTS

I'm humbled to be acknowledging the contributors to a second novel.

First and foremost, thank you so much to every *Splintered* fan out there! Because of your enthusiasm and passion for the story and characters, I was given the green light to make it a trilogy. You're the best!

Next, my most heartfelt gratitude goes to my husband, daughter, and son, and other family members—whether related by blood or through marriage—you're each and every one an integral part of my writing dream. You've encouraged me at the low points and cheered me at the highs. And I know that no matter where this dream may lead in the future, you will continue to support me. You are a blessing and a treasure. Be assured that I'll never take you or your sacrifices for granted.

Grateful hugs to all the usual suspects: My #goatposse, my WrAHM sisters, and of course my critique partners: Jennifer Archer, Linda Castillo, April Redmon, Marcy McKay, Jessica Nelson, and Bethany Crandell. Without your writerly wisdom, online support, and faith in my work, none of this would be possible.

Thank you to my *Unhinged* beta readers: Ashlee Supinger, Kerri Maniscalco, and Kalen O'Donnell. Your input and excitement over the manuscript were priceless. You are amazing writers, and it will be an honor to share the shelves with you one day soon!

Sincere respect and gratitude to my fearless and tireless agent, Jenny Bent; to my insightful editor, Maggie Lehrman; and to my savvy publicists, Laura Mihalick and Tina Mories. Thank you also to Jason Wells for knowing all the best places to eat while on tour, and to Maria Middleton and Nathália Suellen for being the most imaginative and artful book design team.

Thank you to my GoodReads' *Splintered* Fan Page moderators: Nikki Wang, Soumi Roy, Hannah Taylor, and Nobonita Chowdhury. You've made my debut year a delight! Not a week went by when you didn't make me smile. And hugs to all of the Fan Page followers. Hanging out with you is one of my favorite pastimes!

Also, special thanks to Gabrielle Carolina for her outstanding work on my virtual book tours, to Stephanie Foster for inspiring Alyssa's ankle tattoo in *Unhinged*, and to Lewis Carroll for writing the incredible novels that light my muse on fire.

A blanket thank-you to my twitter and FaceBook followers, book bloggers, and fellow authors/writers, and to my friends—online or otherwise. Being a writer can be a solitary endeavor. Having you reminds me that I'll never be alone.

ABOUT THE AUTHOR

A. G. Howard wrote *Splintered* while working at a school library. She always wondered what would've happened if Alice had grown up and the subtle creepiness of *Alice's Adventures in Wonderland* had taken center stage in her story, and she hopes her darker and funkier tribute to Carroll will inspire readers to seek out the stories that won her heart as a child. She lives in Amarillo, Texas.

This book was designed by Maria T. Middleton. The text is set in 10.5-point Adobe Caslon, a revival of the mid-eighteenth-century classic created by the legendary engraver and type designer William Caslon. Designed in 1990 by Carol Twombly, Adobe Caslon is based on William Caslon's original type specimen drawings. The display font is Yana Swash Caps I, designed by Laura Worthington for Umbrella Type.

This book was printed and bound by R. R. Donnelley in Crawfordsville, Indiana. Its production was overseen by Alison Gervais.